A
DEADLY
ENDEAVOR

A
DEADLY
ENDEAVOR

A DEADLY TWENTIES
MYSTERY

———◆◆◆———

Jenny Adams

**CROOKED
LANE**

NEW YORK

Copyright © 2024 by Jenny Adams

Published in the United States by Crooked Lane Books, an imprint of The Quick Brown Fox & Company LLC.

Crooked Lane Books and its logo are trademarks of The Quick Brown Fox & Company LLC.

Library of Congress Catalog-in-Publication data available upon request.

ISBN (hardcover): 978-1-63910-695-0
ISBN (ebook): 978-1-63910-696-7

Cover design by Jessica Khoury

Printed in the United States.

www.crookedlanebooks.com

Crooked Lane Books
34 West 27th St., 10th Floor
New York, NY 10001

First Edition: March 2024

10 9 8 7 6 5 4 3 2 1

For my Aunt Beth, who introduced me to Nancy Drew and never said no to a trip to the bookstore.

I wish you could have read this one.

"All I want to be is very young always and very irresponsible and to feel that my life is my own–to live and be happy and die in my own way to please myself."

—Zelda Fitzgerald

CHAPTER 1

April 22, 1921
Philadelphia

Edie Shippen wanted to close her eyes and wake up a century from now, like Rip Van Winkle. Only prettier.

She rolled over and pressed her face against the pillow's downy softness as laughter drifted up through the closed door to her childhood bedroom. In the ballroom downstairs, a string quartet warmed up their instruments, readying themselves for the crush of Philadelphia's upper crust in one of the city's most extravagant mansions—a sprawling stone castle far from factories and filth to the southeast.

Edie had once loved parties, loved slipping into a new dress and holding onto the promise of a dance card filled by a bevy of handsome men, ready to spin and flirt and whisper promises they never intended to keep. She loved the way she sparkled as brightly as the diamonds at her throat, the jewel of one of Philadelphia's oldest families. But that had been before the influenza killed her mother and nearly took her too, before the three long years spent hidden away in her great-aunt's house in Los Angeles, battling the swirling despair and painful headaches that lingered, ever ready to pull her under into darkness.

Torture. This party would be torture. Faint shadows glittered at the edges of her vision, threatening a migraine before morning. It was one of the reasons she was here, hiding in her bedroom like a petulant child while everyone who was anyone in Philadelphia arrived at her family's Chestnut Hill estate to celebrate her twin sister's engagement.

A soft knock interrupted Edie's attempt to will the impending headache into non-existence. Probably someone sent to chide her into going downstairs. She ignored it and pressed her face further into the tear-damp pillow as a frustrated breath filled the air over her head.

"Miss," Lizzie said, hovering. "Your hair."

"I don't care," Edie said to the maid, her voice muffled even to her own ears through layers of linen and down. "Just leave me here to die. Please."

"Can't do that, Miss," Lizzie said, the lilt in her voice turning the words to music. "I burned myself twice for those curls."

"And I'm sorry about that," Edie replied through the pillow.

"Pardon?"

Edie lifted her head, pouting up at the red-headed maid, dressed in the ridiculous livery her grandmother insisted upon. "I said," she repeated, "That I'm deeply sorry you suffered on my account. But I cannot—will not—step foot downstairs this evening."

Lizzie didn't even bat an eyelash, just held out her hand. A small, amber brown glass bottle rested in her palm. "I'm under orders from your gran."

Edie stared at her outstretched hand and the offered medicine. "Lizzie. I'm an adult. Not a child. I don't need a nanny to boss me about."

"I know that. I also know that it's just a party, Miss Edie. Not an execution." Lizzie's hand stayed in the air between them, and finally, Edie sighed and took the bottle. She was the picture of compliance as Lizzie led her to the velvet stool in front of the vanity table and sank her toes into the plush carpets, deep enough to grow roots, as the maid pulled her brand-new party dress from the wardrobe and hung it on the valet stand.

"It may as well be an execution," Edie grumbled, as opened the bottle. The liquid swirled inside, and she grimaced as she let three bitter drops of the tincture her latest doctor prescribed hit her tongue. Just three—enough to stave off the headache, but not enough to knock her senseless. "The execution of my hopes and dreams."

Lizzie moved behind her, tsking over the state of Edie's long waves, the glossy coal-black strands snarled together. "I know it can't be easy. But—"

"But Frances is happy." The dress's delicate fabric shimmered under the glow of the electric bulb on the vanity table, pale green silk and gold lace. Aunt Mae had ordered it during Edie's recovery, desperate to give her something to celebrate. Something to live for. She'd made Edie promise to wear it when *that young man* finally returned from Europe. Well. Edie supposed she would be keeping that promise tonight, even if this wasn't what Aunt Mae had imagined.

Because Theo Pepper had proposed to Frances.

Theo. Edie's Theo. The boy who had spent long, lazy afternoons painting Edie in slanted rays of sunlight, the young man who had made a hundred different promises to Edie as he marched off to war, was marrying her twin sister.

She knew that she had no right to be upset. While she'd been bundled off to her aunt's home in Los Angeles to regain her strength, Theo had been fighting for his life—first in the trenches, and then from a hospital bed. Edie hadn't returned his letters—what was she supposed to say? *I'm so sorry you met the wrong end of a gun, darling, but can I take a moment to tell you how I dream of walking straight into the ocean and never returning?*

So she didn't write. Not then, and not when he was discharged from the hospital, or when he decided to continue his medical studies in Vienna, long after his letters to her had dwindled to silence. And when he finally came home to Philadelphia, Edie's perfect, beautiful sister was there, waiting.

Edie didn't blame him for loving her. Frances was the best person she knew.

And Edie shouldn't blame her for loving him. Theo was incredibly lovable.

The only person Edie could blame was herself.

"Do you have a sister?" Edie asked Lizzie suddenly.

Lizzie froze, her eyes going wide in the mirror, and inwardly, Edie cursed herself for being so familiar. It was Lizzie's job to learn how her mistresses took their tea, the way they liked to wear their hair. To hold her employer's secrets close. Not the other way around.

Never the other way around.

Three years away had made her forget herself. Three years with Aunt Mae's eccentricities had made her forget how things were supposed to be.

"I'm sorry," Edie said, her voice softer. "I shouldn't pry."

"No." Lizzie lifted a long lock of Edie's nearly-black hair and twirled it around a curling rod. "I don't mind." She gave a small, sad smile. "I had a sister-in-law, once. But now I'm just stuck with my brother."

"I'm sorry," Edie said again.

Lizzie shook her head and set the rod aside. "It was a long time ago, and we've all lost someone, haven't we? Do you need help getting into the dress?"

"Just the buttons." Edie stood, dropped her dressing robe, and took the dress from the hanger. It rustled as she stepped into the skirt and pulled the low-cut bodice up over her chest. Edie's grandmother would have a fit when she saw it. The square neckline showed off a daring bit of skin, and the dress hugged the curve of Edie's waist, following the flare of her hips before swirling out to hit mid-shin, leaving her legs exposed to the straps of her dainty golden pumps. A sheer golden overdress, diaphanous and as shimmering as spider's silk, gave the appearance of modesty as it kissed Edie's collarbone, draped over her bare shoulders, and swirled around her calves. It was daring, and modern, and she loved it.

"It's so strange to be back after all this time—like I stepped right back into another life." Edie rubbed at her temple. This room was a part of it: a child's room, decorated in soft yellow roses and delicate white wicker furniture. She'd loved it as a girl, but now it felt claustrophobic, like she was squeezing herself into a dress she'd outgrown. "It's like no one even noticed I was gone."

Lizzie fumbled over one of the silk-covered buttons, her hands stilling for a heartbeat. "We'd best get you downstairs, miss. Everyone is waiting for you."

Edie held out her arms as Lizzie wrapped a wide green sash around her waist, tying it in a large bow at her back. She smoothed her hands down over her hips and inspected herself in the mirror as Lizzie busied herself fixing the mess Edie had made of her hair, producing a pair of curved golden combs from somewhere and arranged it up to reveal the pale column of Edie's throat.

You chose the wrong sister, Theo Pepper, Edie thought as she clipped on her heavy emerald earrings. *And I'll prove it to you.*

"There," Lizzie said finally. She smiled at Edie in the mirror as she draped a delicate gold chain over her collarbone. The deep green emerald of the necklace rested just above the swell of Edie's breasts and the scalloped edge of the gold overdress. "May I speak freely for a moment?"

"Of course."

Their gazes met and held. "I know your heart is aching, Miss Edie. But look at you. You're beautiful."

"You're very kind, Lizzie," Edie demurred.

Her eyes dropped. "No. No, I'm not. But I'm also not wrong. You don't deserve to be anyone's second choice. Not tonight. Not ever."

Edie lifted her chin and studied her reflection as the maid slipped from the room, and realized Lizzie was right. She was Edith Shippen, after all, not some heartbroken girl to be pitied. There would be a dozen men, young and old, waiting for her downstairs. Eager to take her for a spin around the dance floor, hoping for a moonlight walk along a secluded garden path, ready to ease her sorrows in the shadows. There would be a hundred more gossips and busybodies watching to see how she carried herself, to see what sort of scene she would make, ready to tear her apart in tomorrow's papers.

Well. She wouldn't give them the satisfaction. She blinked hard, as if she could hurry along the tincture's effects, and leaned forward. With two quick strokes, she painted her lips burgundy, the color as sinful as wine.

Theo Pepper was her past.

Edie didn't know what her future held, but she wasn't going to shy away from it like a coward. She was going to grab it with both hands and make it her own.

CHAPTER 2

Gilbert Lawless bent low over his patient, taking great care to make sure that his stitches were quick and even, his hand steady as he pulled the thick, waxy thread through split skin and into the muscle beneath. Not that it mattered, not when his patient had been dead far too long to feel anything, her bloodless flesh gone stiff and cold. Corpses didn't have the vanity of the living, or care about the pain his needle inflicted.

Gilbert preferred his patients this way, preferred the already dead to the dying. The dead didn't fill the air with rattled gasps and moans, with cries for their mothers. Or worse, bargains. Gilbert had seen enough of the dying for a lifetime—death was everywhere he turned, first in the crowded slums he'd lived in as a child, where it stalked the mills and the childbed; on the battlefields in France; and then again when he returned home to a plague-stricken city, where so many succumbed to influenza. He still heard the death rattle in their throats when he closed his eyes at night, haunted by the fact that he couldn't save them.

The headless young woman on his table had been discovered along the banks of the Wissahickon Creek earlier that morning. It had been, by all accounts, a gruesome scene. Gilbert's supervisor, Dr. Knight, had conducted the autopsy in his usual detached manner, the two men working silently together as they assessed cause of death. Normally, Gilbert worked alone. But today, Dr. Knight had insisted on joining the autopsy, which Gilbert was glad for. Insisted on writing the cause of death in a clear, steady hand on the city-issued certificate: homicide. And then he lingered just a heartbeat longer than normal, reached out and gave the dead girl one last pondering look before he turned on his heel and left the examination room, leaving Gilbert to finish his work.

Gilbert finished his last stitch and snipped the thread close to the knot, closing the cadaver's chest cavity. His mouth set in a line as he pondered, again, her missing head, the charred skin striping her torso. The pinprick on her inner arm. Sometime in the last forty-eight hours, she had been drugged. And then, for reasons Gilbert couldn't begin to fathom: beheaded and electrocuted. But he had a job to do, and so, he turned away from his patient's still form and turned to the sink, where he washed his instruments, and dried them carefully. The girl's clothes had been taken by the police for evidence, so he wrapped her in a clean white sheet.

"Ar dheis Dé go raibh a hanam," Gilbert said softly, his hand resting on her forehead, his native Irish flowing easily over his tongue. *May her soul be on God's right hand.* The words were automatic, a benediction baked deep into his bones, despite Gilbert's own misgivings about a God who abandoned humanity to the ravages of war and disease. He hoped, as he returned the body to her drawer, that the police would be able to identify her soon. No one deserved to end up in the potter's field.

He washed his hands and shrugged out of his white lab coat, exchanging it for a dark blue jacket, and left the autopsy room for the day. Cecelia, the morgue's secretary, looked up at him through dark lashes as he dropped the death certificate on her desk.

"Yes, sir," she was saying into the telephone. "It looks like the official cause of death is listed as cardiac arrest. Yes, sir—his heart stopped. No, sir. I don't have any other information. Sure. I'll pass along the message."

Gilbert gave her a wave and set his hat on his head. He turned to leave, ready for a few days off, when Cecelia's voice summoned him back.

"Oh! Gil, before you leave for the weekend . . ." Cecelia spun in her chair and picked up a slip of paper. She held it out to him. "Call came in for you about an hour ago. A girl. Someone special, maybe?"

Gilbert snatched the paper from her hand, heat creeping up his neck as he scanned the message. *Off tomorrow. Meet you at the usual place. L.* "My sister," he said. The slip crumpled in his fist, and he slipped it into his pocket.

"Oh." An odd note colored Cecelia's voice. "Gil?"

Gilbert's head snapped up. "What is it?"

She hesitated, glancing quickly in either direction. Then she leaned forward, her file in her hand. "I was wondering if you had any plans tonight?"

His hand drifted to this pocket of his own accord, to the crumpled message from his sister, Lizzie. Cecelia watched him closely, her big blue eyes soft behind her spectacles. He had the dreadful suspicion that she was about to ask him to some sort of social engagement, and he wished he'd lied and told her that Lizzie was his wife. But that wouldn't work. Cecelia knew he was a widower; she had asked about the slim gold band on his finger the day they met, nearly two years earlier. She'd know he was lying.

"You're serious?" Gilbert asked, instead.

"As a heart attack," Cecelia deadpanned.

Gilbert's mouth lifted in the ghost of a smile, and she answered it with a wide, dazzling grin of her own.

"A smile? From Gilbert Lawless? I don't believe it!" Her laugh danced through the air between them. "Bette owes me a chocolate bar."

"My smile's only worth a chocolate bar?" His eyebrows rose, and he leaned closer, propping his elbows on the counter. "I would have figured on at least a soda."

"That's for a laugh," she said primly, but her blue eyes sparkled. "A chocolate for a smile, a soda for a laugh. And a ticket to the pictures for . . ."

"For what?" Gilbert prodded.

"For a date, Lawless." Marco Salvatore, one of the other coroner's assistants and Gilbert's partner, said, his voice booming through the open room. He snapped his own file on Cecelia's desk, where it landed with a sharp crack that made Gilbert's chest thump. *Steady,* he told himself.

Marco kept talking. "The girls are crazy for you, don't ask me why. They have a bet on who you'll take out first."

Gilbert flushed, and he wasn't sure if it was from Marco's jab, or the familiar tremor beginning to rock through his fingertips. "Ah, Cecelia. I—"

"Don't pay any attention to him, Gil," Cecelia said. "I'm not trying to win a bet. I'm asking because I'm keen. And—"

He clenched his fists in his pockets, forced his breathing to slow. "I'm sorry, I have to go."

"Gil, wait." Cecelia was standing now, her eyes pleading.

Gilbert straightened his spine and stepped back from the desk, forcing himself to walk slowly, even though the tremor spread up his hands, his wrists.

"I'll see you Monday, Cecelia."

"Gil . . ." Cecelia's voice floated after him, but he didn't stop. He didn't dare, not here, not where anyone could see him. He turned the corner to the corridor and broke into a run as the trembling spread up his hand, his wrist. His biceps rippled with the effort to hold his hands still, and the corridor around him rippled as well, rippled and twisted, the sterile white tiles bleeding into the dark browns and grays and bright, brilliant reds that lingered, as ever, at the edges of his consciousness.

Gilbert crashed through the door to the men's room and slammed it behind him, throwing the bolt as his knees gave out, sending him sprawling onto the floor. The far wall of the bathroom was gone, gaping open into an endless gray sky, broken only by the jagged loops of barbed wire and the solid line of thick brown mud.

His breath came in ragged gasps, as sharp and ear-shattering as the explosions he knew would follow. He closed his eyes, bracing himself for the impact again, for the way the air would go still, as if the very world was sheltering, as if the earth knew what was coming. It didn't help—even with his eyes closed, he saw the trenches sprawled out before him, felt the cold barrel of his rifle between his fingers, the weight of his metal helmet on his head.

"Brace yourself!" The voice beside him was hoarse, as if it had been shouting orders for hours, and the body it belonged to pressed close, his warmth seeping through the damp wool they both wore.

Gilbert wasn't going to look this time. He wouldn't. *Not real, not real, not real*, he repeated to himself, and forced his trembling hands into his coat pocket, where his relief waited in slim metal tubes, each capped with a sharp needle sealed in wax as red as blood.

The blast would shake him down to his soul. The blast would change everything. He had to act quickly, as he knew what was to come.

The man beside him pressed closer. "Gil," he said, his bright blue eyes filled with terror, "Gil, tell him we can't. Tell him it's suicide. Tell him—"

Gilbert squeezed his eyes shut, willing himself not to listen. His hands found the tin in his breast pocket, and he pulled it free, flipped it open. He found the syrette and pulled the wax cap off with his teeth. He spat it out, ignoring the man's desperate pleas beside him. *Not real,* he reminded himself, and jabbed the needle into the soft inner skin of his elbow, not even bothering with the tourniquet. The other man grabbed his collar and forced Gilbert to look him in the face as the world around them exploded in a deafening concussion of dirt and rock and blood, blood that ran from his hands to drip, drip, drip onto the white tile floor beneath him. His body arched backward from the blow, meeting the heavy wooden door at his back as past and present battled for dominance and the morphine's sweet heat took hold.

Gilbert sat still long after it had passed, gulping in the morgue's cool air and staring at the toilet in front of him, until his sweat-drenched shirt cooled, his skin as clammy and chilled as the poor girl he'd had on his table not an hour before. He stared down at his hands, at the pale blue tangle of veins pulsing with life beneath his skin, and he let out a deep, shuddering breath.

Shell shock, some doctors had called it, though others spoke more plainly: cowardice. It didn't matter to Gilbert what it was called. It didn't matter that he knew, intellectually, that he had returned from France two and a half years ago, that he was safe. He'd left a piece of his soul in those trenches.

He didn't know how much longer he'd be able to carry on without it.

CHAPTER 3

The party was in full swing by the time Edie's medication chased the glittering shadows in her vision to the edges, where they lingered. Beaten back, but not vanquished. Music and laughter floated through the glass doors beyond the observatory, thrown open to the sweet evening air. Spring was finally here, as evidenced by the slight curl in Edie's hair and the green growth on the trees outside. She snagged a round glass of champagne from a passing waiter and tilted back her head to drain it in one huge, unladylike gulp. *Bon courage*, she thought, and tucked it behind one of her late mother's beloved potted birds-of-paradise plants, the bubbles fizzing in her mouth like tiny stars, bursting in time with the tapping of her heels on the parquet floor of the ballroom.

A quick glance around the room was like stepping back in time; if she overlooked the shortened hemlines and faces that had gone missing since the night she and Frances had debuted into society, six years earlier. Her cousin Wyatt had perished in a desolate trench in Belgium. Scandalous Sarah Pepper, Theo's older sister, was four years dead. She lived on as a cautionary tale whispered to the girls coming out, a warning about falling in love below their station. George Shoemaker had drowned in his own blood after contracting influenza. The entire Biddle family was absent, too—all four children dead to the twin horrors of war and epidemic. And of course, the absence of Edie's mother was palpable, a gaping void in the midst of all the merriment. Edie knew she would have loved a night like this, loved to have seen Frances so happy and full of life. At least her father was still here, holding court with his colleagues from the City Council near the tall glass doors that led from the ballroom to the observatory. Her sister, too, and her cousins. Her grandmother.

Theo.

Edie had told herself she wouldn't look for him, that she'd avoid him. That she'd let him come to her, so she could stand prettily, laughing a little too loud, and show him exactly what he'd given up. Her traitorous soul, however, spotted him almost immediately, and Edie stilled.

He stood off to the side of the crush on the dance floor; his golden hair shining under the scores of electric bulbs Edie's father had spent a small fortune on. Theo looked older than the last time Edie had seen him, almost four years ago. His back was straighter, his stance wider. Even his hair was different, slicked back with pomade, the thick blond waves tamed into submission.

As if drawn by the same current that pulsed through the wires strung in the air between them, Theo lifted his head, his gaze colliding with Edie's with such force that for a moment she was rendered nearly breathless. Heat crept up, twining long fingers around her throat. She knew she'd been caught staring, but instead of dropping her eyes and playing the demure good girl, she lifted her hands and wiggled her fingers in his direction.

"Edie!" Franny's arms closed around her sister's midsection, drawing Edie's attention away from Theo. "Grandmama said you had another spell. I was worried you wouldn't make it downstairs—are you sure you're all right to be here?"

"Everything's jake, darling," Edie replied. She pressed a quick kiss to Franny's cheek, pushing down the heat that had sparked through her limbs at the sight of her sister's fiancé. "I can't miss your special night, can I?"

Franny squealed in delight; her hands clasped under her chin. The walnut-sized diamond on her left hand sparkled. "I still can't believe it."

Neither can I, Edie wanted to say, but swallowed her words. Instead, she offered a simple: "You look beautiful."

It was the truth. Franny twirled once, her sky-blue skirt spinning in a circle around her knees. Delicate seed pearl embroidery covered the bodice and spilled down over the dropped waist to the scalloped hem.

Franny preened for a moment. "Isn't it, darling? But enough about me. Look at you! Has Grandmama seen you yet?"

When Edie shook her head, her sister grinned. "Oh, Edie, she'll die when she sees that dress. And come on. I know Theo's eager to say hello. He's been asking about you." Frances tugged at Edie's arm, and Edie followed dutifully, her protests dying in her throat as Theo stepped up to meet them.

"Edie." His voice was low, filled with the jagged rumble of a thousand broken promises. "How was California?"

"I bet it wasn't half as exciting as France," Edie blurted.

Theo flinched slightly, a quick tightening of the skin around his blue eyes. "Franny and I barely knew what to do without you," he said. He slipped his arm around Franny's waist, but Edie's sister gave him an apologetic smile and slipped from his grasp.

"Oh! Ophelia Van Pelt just arrived. I should say hello."

Edie and Theo watched Franny leave. The music and laughter around them faded into the background, and Edie's entire world narrowed to Theo, the shadows shimmering at the edges of her sight, and the frantic flutter of her pulse under her skin. Theo watched her, his eyes as hungry as Edie knew her own must be.

"You seem to have managed just fine." Edie finally found her voice, the words bursting forth like a freight train, flattening any protests her brain tried to erect in its path. "When I heard you were hurt, I was so afraid, Theo. I thought . . . well. It doesn't matter, does it? Look at you! Are you sure you aren't part cat? How many lives do you have left?"

"Edie." Theo glanced around, like he was checking to see if anyone could overhear. He stepped closer, close enough that the flutter of her pulse increased to a thundering tattoo, close enough that if Edie raised herself on tiptoe, the way she'd done a million times before, their lips would meet and . . .

"I didn't know how to tell you," he said. His gaze was pained, like he knew exactly what he'd done to her. "I didn't—we didn't—"

"There you are, Edith." Edie's grandmother broke whatever spell had been cast between them, sending the light and noise crashing down to the parquet floor under Edie's high-heeled pumps. The family matriarch gave a disapproving sniff, her shrewd stare enough to cause Edie to take a step back. "I see you've found our young doctor."

"Mrs. Shippen." Theo inclined his head and took two steps backward of his own. "Miss Shippen. I'll leave you two to catch up—I think I just saw someone I've been meaning to speak to."

He melted into the crush before Edie could protest, leaving her alone with the woman she had spent her entire life disappointing. Flora Shippen looked her granddaughter up and down, her eyes lingering on the spring-green taffeta swirling around Edie's calves. "I see Mae dressed you," she said. "I'm surprised at you, Edith. I don't know what passed for proper out there, but it's a little showy for your sister's engagement party, isn't it?"

"Grandmama." Edie tried not to roll her eyes. Mae was her grandmother's youngest sister, an artist, confirmed spinster, and eternal source of gossip for the rest family. She'd saved Edie, in more ways than one, and Edie felt the need to defend her. "You should have taken Mae up on her invitations. A little California air would have served you well."

Grandmama's mouth twisted, and Edie braced herself for another cutting criticism. But before it came, Edie's older cousin Rebecca approached, taking all of Grandmama's attention. She struck a pose, one hand thrown back against her head, against a circlet of pale pink feathers—the most demure part of her outfit. The hot-pink dress, Edie realized, with a sense of both surprise and admiration, was not a dress at all, but a loose-fitting pair of trousers, gathered at the ankles in giant golden bows. Altogether, the effect was rather flamingo-esque, and Edie, along with their grandmother, was struck speechless.

"Grandmama! Edie!" Rebecca gave a wide, cheerful grin. "I thought I'd take a walk around the garden. Would one of you like to join me?"

"Happily," Edie said quickly. She slipped her arm through Rebecca's. Tossing a quick glance behind her, she added, "Ta, Grandmama."

Rebecca giggled as she tugged Edie through the open doors to the humid warmth of the iron and glass conservatory, past the bubbling fountain, and down one of the curved paths lined with exotic flowers. "You looked like you needed a bit of a rescue," Rebecca said, once they were safely out of earshot.

"You'd think Franny's engagement would keep her mind off of me," Edie said.

Rebecca shook her head, her expression grim. "She won't rest until she sees every last one of us married off," she said, the venom dripping from every word. She sounded, Edie thought, remarkably like their Grandmama. "She doesn't realize the world has changed."

Rebecca was right. Much to Flora Shippen's consternation, her three sons had produced nothing but daughters. Six of them, to be exact. She despaired greatly, knowing this branch of the storied Shippen family ended with them and was determined to see every one of her granddaughters make an advantageous match, romance be dammed. If her great-grandchildren couldn't be Shippens, Flora would see them belong to the other old families: the Pennypackers, the Van Pelts, the Cassats, the Penroses, the Rushes, the Whartons, the Gowens. The Peppers.

"Is that all we're good for? Marriage?" Edie asked. She didn't know if it was the champagne talking or the way her stomach turned sour at the thought of Franny and Theo together, but she suddenly wanted nothing to do with any of it.

"You and I know better," Rebecca said. She nudged her elbow into Edie's. "Can you keep a secret?"

I am in love with my sister's fiancé.

"Of course," Edie replied.

Rebecca pulled Edie deeper into the conservatory, to the places where shadows stood guard, the dark shapes swirling with the blurred edges of Edie's vision mixing with the humid air. Rebecca threw one last glance over her shoulder, making sure they hadn't been followed, and leaned in close. "I've decided to devote myself to my art," she whispered.

Edie blinked. "What do you mean?"

Rebecca's mouth dipped down. She trailed her fingers over the nearest orchid, something hot pink and delicate. Frances loved these things—Edie found them tiresome. They were too delicate, requiring constant maintenance and attention.

But Rebecca was speaking, drawing Edie's attention away from the flower. "I've decided to leave Bryn Mawr and enroll in art school."

"Whatever for?" Art school was for new money girls, or those of the upper middle class, looking to make themselves a career, perhaps as a cartoonist for the newspaper. Not for young ladies like the Shippen girls, destined for ballrooms and charity lunches and a slow, graceful decline into the invisibility of motherhood and middle age. Girls like Edie and Rebecca were meant for finishing schools. Not art school.

"I've been speaking with Ophelia Van Pelt—remember her from school? She's become quite the bohemian since you've been away," Rebecca explained. "She's met this incredible group of women artists. They're professionals, Edie. They're showing their art, making a difference. Changing the world. And I've decided to be a part of it."

"And your parents agree?"

Rebecca's face fell, only a little bit. But then she shook her head. "It doesn't matter. I'm grown, now, with full access to my trust. I'm a modern girl, Edie. I'm going to do it my way, or not at all."

She looked so sure of herself. So fierce, so proud. Edie had always thought of Rebecca as the strange one of her cousins, the dreamer, the artist. The bluestocking with her head in the clouds. But here she was, passionate, her dreams made tangible.

Since her illness, Edie had felt alone. And in the months since her great-aunt's sudden death, she'd felt cast adrift, totally and hopelessly. She looked up at Rebecca, desperately jealous that her cousin had found something to cling to. Something bigger than herself.

Edie wanted that. Needed it.

She looked up at Rebecca, who was watching in a way that made Edie want to squirm—like her cousin had read her mind and knew exactly what she needed to do. "I'm proud of you," Edie said.

Rebecca reached out and squeezed Edie's hand, her touch warm and surprising. It was the first time anyone had touched her—really touched her—since Mae died. "I'm meeting them—the artists—on Sunday. You should come, too."

In the ballroom, a gong sounded, signaling the end of cock-tails. Dinner's first course would be served soon, followed by hours of dancing. Rebecca's laugh choked off into a gasp, and her hand flew to her throat, leaving Edie's skin cold. Edie spun around, not knowing what to expect. An intruder, perhaps? But it was only Artie Van Pelt—Ophelia's older brother, and one of Theo's school chums—already stumbling from the champagne.

"Ladies," he slurred, raising his glass in mock salute. "Having fun?"

Rebecca laughed. "Sure am, Artie. We were just talking about your sister."

He made a face. "Why on Earth would you do that?"

"Should we go in?" Edie asked. She'd never liked Artie much—he had had a cruel streak as a child, and she doubted the years had improved his disposition.

"You go. I'll be there in a moment." Rebecca stepped closer to Artie, plucking the glass from his hand. He said something, too low for Edie to hear, and her cousin laughed, the sound reassuring. Edie relaxed, and headed inside, buoyed by a renewed sense of hope.

Rebecca had found her path, found her purpose.

Perhaps with her cousin's help, Edie would be able to do the same.

CHAPTER 4

Gilbert waited at the rail station at the corner of Broad and Callowhill, the way he did every other Saturday morning, when Lizzie had the day off. He checked the watch on his wrist, the familiar radium-painted arms displaying the time: 9:05AM. Hopefully, Lizzie would be on time, and they could take the 9:15 to Manayunk, the mill neighborhood perched on the hills between Schuylkill River and the woods surrounding the Wissahickon Creek, not far from where the poor young woman he'd autopsied yesterday had been discovered.

He ran his thumb over the ring on his left hand, the slim band almost worn thin where Sarah's name and their wedding date were engraved, and his thoughts turned to his wife, another young woman stolen from life too soon. His heart lurched beneath the weight of his grief, and he forced his hands into his pockets before it threatened to drag him down to the depths. He could hardly believe it was already April, nearly four years since her death. He'd been without her for so long.

He'd grieved her longer than he had loved her.

He'd been barely twenty-one when he'd fallen in love with Sarah Pepper, a girl high above his station. They'd met by accident, just a few weeks before her debutante ball. Their affair was

fast and furious, as only young love could be. He never stopped to think about the consequences, about what his love would do to her. He still remembered going to her father with a battered gold ring in his pocket, to tell the old man he'd be a good husband, a good father. What a fool he'd been.

She'd lost that first pregnancy. And the second. And two years later, it turned out that she would lose everything, loving him. She lost her home, her family, and in the long, brutal hours she labored to bring their sweet Penelope into the world, he thought, just foolishly, that she wouldn't lose anything else. That they'd be together, a family.

Instead, she'd died in his arms, sending him into a grief that had chased him to the blood-slicked trenches of France and back again.

The train's approach dragged him back to the present. The boards on the platform's edge vibrated, sending tremors up his legs from the soles of his shoes. "Train up to Manayunk, Norristown, and Pottstown, boarding now!"

"I'm here!" Lizzie materialized beside him as the train lurched to a stop, belching a cloud of steam as its brakes hissed and popped and screamed. She smiled wide at him. "Bet you a penny Mam's making meatloaf again."

He scowled at his sister and handed her a paper ticket. "And I would have gone on to eat it without you. What took you so long?"

"Missed the earlier trolley," she explained. "It was a late night, and Dottie quit without notice on Wednesday. Just left in the middle of the night, knowing we had this huge party to work this week. I'm hopping mad, Gil. Mrs. Smith's in a tizzy and rightfully so. Dottie didn't even tell me she was going. She just up and left, after I stuck my neck out to get her the job."

The train's sharp whistle blew once, twice, three times, saving Gilbert from having to reply. He offered his hand to his sister, and she took it to steady herself as she climbed aboard and headed down the narrow aisle. She chose seats near the back of the train car, closest to the door they'd use to disembark, and he settled himself on the wooden bench beside her.

"He's back," Lizzie said, after a moment. "I almost didn't believe it, not until I saw him myself. I know you like to pretend he doesn't exist, but I thought I should be the one to tell you."

He looked down at his shoes, letting Lizzie's words pass without comment. The brown leather was scuffed at the toe, a sign of carelessness that his father would be sure to remark upon. The elder Lawless was a serious, hardworking man who had left behind everything he knew to try to provide for his family in America. He prided himself on his punctuality, his precision . . . and his perfectly presentable appearance. Those traits had served him well in the yarn mills along the river—he'd risen from nothing to become one of the foremen, overseeing the work of the spinners on the floor.

Gilbert had long since resigned himself to being a disappointment in the eyes of his father, and doubly so since he returned from France with a coward's tremor and no desire to practice medicine. A scuff on his shoes was hardly anything by comparison.

Lizzie reached out and wrapped her hand around her older brother's. "How are you doing, Gil? Really doing, I mean? You look tired."

"I haven't been sleeping much," he admitted as up ahead the conductor shouted one last call for boarding. "Just a lot on my mind."

"Do you want to see him?"

He gave his sister a long look, one she read easily—and, judging by the roll of her eyes, one she disagreed with. "Of course not. I don't know why I even asked."

"Liz."

"Gil."

Gilbert's frustrated sigh was drowned out by the train's sharp whistle and the roar of the steam engine as the car beneath them lurched into motion. He took the disruption as an excuse to change the subject, to talk about something—anything—other than himself and the one person on the planet whom he would do anything to avoid. He dug in his pocket and pulled out a brown paper bag. He handed it over and asked, "Do you think Penny will like this?"

Lizzie pulled out the small wind-up toy—a tin monkey that clapped a pair of cymbals. "I think the tiny terror will love it," she said, her smile wide as she turned it over in her hands. "Mam's going to hate it, though."

"I don't know. She's gotten soft in her old age."

Lizzie handed the monkey back to him, and they exchanged knowing glances. Penelope, the youngest Lawless, turned four this week. Gilbert's mother, despite her protests that she was too old to raise another baby, was completely enamored with her granddaughter. They all were, to be honest, but it provided Lizzie and Gilbert endless amusement to see the strict woman who'd raised them both wind up completely wrapped around a child's little finger. Even their father doted on the girl, singing her songs and taking her on long walks up and down the neighborhood.

The city rolled past them as they chugged along, climbing up and down along the river. Luckily, they didn't have far to go—within twenty minutes, the siblings disembarked at Shurs Station, where the factories and mills belched black smoke into the clear blue sky. They took their time walking up the hill, passing the sharply pitched houses on either side of the wide street that connected the mills of Manayunk to the middle-class enclave of Roxborough.

His parents lived in a snug brick row house, two stories tall, tucked on a narrow street behind a church—Methodist, much to his Catholic mother's consternation. Mam's lavender was in full bloom in the window boxes, and Gilbert couldn't help reaching out to run his fingers over the fragrant buds as he climbed the steps to the front door. The smell carried in through the tiled vestibule, where he hung his hat and coat on the peg rail, and into the narrow front parlor, where his father sat in a wingback chair, unlit pipe clenched between his teeth. Penny played at his feet with a pile of wooden blocks. The small girl leapt to her feet and raced to Gil, throwing her tiny arms around his waist. He bent down and picked her up, even though she was getting much too big for that, reveling in the way she clung to him, like he was her hero.

God, he wished he could be.

"Aoife! Yer children are here," the elder Gilbert Lawless bellowed.

"Nice to see you too, Da," Lizzie said. She bent and kissed the top of his bald head before stealing Penny from her brother's arms. The girl squealed in delight as Lizzie spun her around, their identical red-gold curls dancing in the late-afternoon light.

"Come give your Mam a hug," Aoife bustled out of the kitchen, wiping her hands on her apron. Gilbert complied, wrapping his mother's small, round frame in his arms.

"You're too skinny, Bertie," she said, tut-tutting. She squeezed his arm and frowned before tugging him towards the kitchen. "Come, sit. Meatloaf's not ready yet, but I'll make you a snack."

"You owe me a penny," Lizzie crowed from the parlor, and Gilbert couldn't help but smile as he allowed his mother to push him into one of the ladder-backed chairs at the kitchen table.

This cramped house was the one place on earth he felt safe. The one place he felt whole. Where for a moment, he could close his eyes and remember the boy he used to be, could imagine the life he could have led.

Aoife returned from the icebox with a plate piled high with pickles and cheese and set it before her son. His stomach rumbled, and his mother patted his shoulder affectionately.

"Hello!" Penny's small form crashed into his legs. She scrambled into his lap and helped herself to a pickle. "Did you bring me a present?"

Her brown eyes, so like his—and so unlike her mother's—stared up at him owlishly, and the wave of grief he'd fought off earlier came rushing back.

"Ach, Penny, that's not polite," Aoife chided. "How do you ask?"

"Do you have a present, please?" Penny said around a mouthful of pickle.

"How do you know I've brought you a present?" Gil asked, putting on a serious face. "I only bring presents to good little girls."

"I'm good!" Penny protested.

Gilbert looked up at his mother. "What do you say, Mam? Has she been naughty?"

Aoife laughed. "My granddaughter? Naughty? Never, right Pen? Go on, tell your Da you've been a good girl."

Penny beamed up at him. "Da, I've been good, I promise!" she repeated, and Gilbert's heart swelled. He held his daughter close and pulled the tin monkey from his pocket. She squealed in delight, clapping her hands he wound up the spring on the toy's back, and practically danced in his lap as the monkey hopped around the table, cymbals clanging together.

Penny wiggled out of his lap. He watched her bounce back to the front room, tin monkey in hand. He wanted to tell his Mam about the poor dead girl on his table, about the weight he'd been carrying in the long years since he'd come home from the war. But he didn't want to trouble her; already, Aoife worried too much about him.

"Garden looks good," he said instead, looking through the open back door, where new fencing lined either side, the lumber still bright and fresh. Vining flowers climbed the stone wall at the back, almost ready to bloom. A quilt flapped on the line, drying in the warm spring sun.

"Hmm? Oh, yes," Aoife said. "Tommy came by and put the new fence up for us. He's a good boy."

Gilbert choked on a laugh. Tommy Fletcher—Gilbert's former best friend, and current leader of the Cresson Street Crew, the Irish gang that ran this part of the city, was anything but a good boy. "Mam. I've told you, stay away from Tommy."

"I've known that boy since he was in diapers, Bertie. I've known his *mother* since we were both weeuns. I'm not afraid of him."

She should be. Tommy and his boys ran rum, and Gilbert had seen more than one of the Cresson Street Crew come across his table, killed in a fight with rival gangs or a still explosion or a car crash. But his mother wouldn't listen. She never listened. In her mind, Tommy Fletcher was still the gap-toothed little boy stealing cookies from her kitchen table—not a gangster intent on making his fortune in illegal booze. Definitely not a hardened criminal, rubbing elbows with the kings of Philadelphia's underworld: Mickey Duffy, Max Hoff, Harry Rosen, and the Butcher of Broad Street himself, Leo Salvatore. It had been over a year since Gilbert had spoken with Tommy. Tommy had offered him a job, and Gilbert turned him down.

Gilbert should have known Tommy wouldn't let it go so easily; after all, Tommy had never taken no for an answer.

"He left this for you, by the way. Seems keen on talking." His mother pulled a sealed envelope from the tin where she kept the mail near the door. "He said you'd know where to find him."

Gilbert stared down at the envelope, his name scrawled across it in precise black letters. And then he picked it up and tore it into tiny little pieces.

CHAPTER 5

Edie woke with a mouth as dry as the California desert, a splitting headache, and the feeling of a tiny tongue lapping at her hand. She grumbled and rolled over, but Aphrodite, Edie's three-year-old-pug, followed, desperate for Edie's attention. And then the curtains were ripped back, flooding the room with brilliant rays of sunlight.

"Oh, jeez," Edie cried out, lurching upright. "Was that necessary?"

"Good morning to you, too." Rebecca perched herself on the edge of Edie's mattress. Her cousin was already awake and coiffed, her blonde bob curling around her chin, and looking entirely too cheerful for someone the morning after a party. "You're looking ducky this morning."

"What time is it?"

"Ten." Rebecca pointed her chin toward the tray on Edie's vanity table, where a teapot and bit of buttered toast waited. "Careful with that. It's been sitting so long you're likely to break a tooth."

Edie's stomach turned. Aphrodite wiggled into her lap, her tiny body practically shivering with anticipation as Edie worked her fingers against the dog's soft fur. "Not that I'm not happy to see you, Rebecca. But . . . to what do I owe the pleasure?"

"I was serious about you coming to meet my friends tomorrow," Rebecca said. She held a slip of paper between her fingers and waved it in Edie's direction. "I've written down the address. But Grandmama will have a cow if she finds out where you're going. I thought we need to come up with an excuse."

"I'm a grown woman, Rebecca. I can go into the city whenever I want."

"Please." Rebecca rolled her eyes. "You underestimate Grandmama's powers. But . . ." she trailed off, her gaze sweeping the room. She settled her attention on Edie's bureau. "Even she can't argue with the need to visit the millinery. On account of your hat."

Edie narrowed her eyes. The hat in question was one of her favorites for summer, with a wide white brim, a silk ribbon, and feathers. Grandmama detested it, which made Edie love it all the more. "There's nothing wrong with my hat."

Rebecca was already across the room before Edie realized what was happening. She plucked the hat from the stand and twirled it on her finger, sending ribbon and feathers dancing along the edge. "I'm sorry, Edie."

"Rebecca!" Edie scrambled out of bed, but she was too late. Rebecca dropped the hat to the floor and crushed it under her delicate patent-leather pump.

Edie crumpled, as wounded as if she'd suffered the blow herself. From behind her, Aphrodite let out a sharp bark, and Edie scooped up the bashed remains of her hat into her arms. "You didn't deserve that," she told the hat, giving its mangled feather a gentle stroke. "Miss Elaine will set you right. I promise."

Rebecca snorted. "Get a wiggle on, Edie. You know she hates it when we're late for breakfast."

Edie made a face at the door after Rebecca left, but she knew her cousin was right; Grandmama abhorred tardiness. One of the staff had left Edie a pressed day dress in a pretty blue silk hanging on the valet stand, and she dressed quickly. She left her hair down, her waves tumbling loose over her shoulders like Mary Pickford, a style she'd grown used to wearing in California. She selected a jeweled peacock brooch with a wide fan tail to fasten at the lapel over her breast, and then she dashed downstairs, hoping she wouldn't be the last one at the table. A girl could only take so many pointed sighs.

Thankfully, the table was still only half full when she arrived. The south-facing floor-to-ceiling windows let in a breathtaking view of the wooded gorge behind the house, and Edie's mother had attempted to complement it with the breakfast room's decor, all deep greens and dark wood, and filled with potted plants. It was Edie's favorite room in the entire house—the one place she felt her mother's presence, even after all these years without her.

"Good morning, Edith," Edward Shippen, Edie's father, said from behind his newspaper as she settled herself across from him. "You're looking well this morning, dear."

"Thank you, Daddy. Where's Franny?" Edie glanced around the room. Her entire extended family appeared to have spent the night, and she watched as her aunts, uncles, and cousins trickled in.

"She's probably still fast asleep. You know how much attention drains her." Edie's grandmother sipped at her tea from her seat beside Edie's father. Even though she spoke to Edie, her eyes never left her youngest granddaughters a few seats to Edie's left. The little girls, eight and six, squealed with laughter, and she frowned. "Honestly, Ned. Your brother needs a governess."

"It's his business, Mother," Edward said. "Mary made it known that she meant to raise the girls herself."

Flora sniffed. "That's what he gets for marrying his secretary."

Edie had always been fond of her Aunt Mary and leaned forward. "I think it's sweet," she said. "Could you have imagined spending that much time with your children, Grandmama?"

Flora startled, her teacup hitting the saucer with a clatter, and finally looked at Edie. "Heavens, no," she said. "Your father, perhaps. But the rest were always into some sort of mess, and dear Nanny was a *professional*. I dare say she knew best how to raise three gentlemen of good character."

Rebecca sat several seats away, which was for the best. Between the hat and the headache, Edie wasn't sure she trusted herself to be polite.

"Oh! Edie!" Rebecca called sweetly. "I've made us an appointment with Miss Elaine for tomorrow, for your hat."

Flora looked up sharply, and Edie cringed. "Your hat? What happened now, Edith?"

Edie avoided looking at her cousin, half-sure her look would strike the other young woman dead. "It's a tragedy, really. It's completely crushed. I'm bereft."

From a few seats down, Aunt Grace, Rebecca's mother, pointed at Edie with her spoon. "It's a risk you run when you travel, dear. I never bring my favorite pieces with me, just in case you can't trust the help."

"Elaine LaBelle will set it to rights," Edie said. "Perhaps I'll get a new one, too."

Edie's grandmother waved a hand. "Take the car. Straight there and back, understand?" Her tone made it clear that she was to be obeyed.

"Oh," Rebecca made an apologetic face. "I have to go back to school tonight. I'd planned on meeting Edie at the train station. You understand."

"It's supposed to be a nice day, Grandmama. I think I'd rather take the train in," Edie said quickly, before their grandmother could protest. "The doctors have said exercise is the best medicine."

Flora's lips compressed into a flat line, and for a moment, Edie thought she would argue, but Ned came to her rescue. "That sounds lovely, Edie. Take that maid with you, all right? The red-headed one."

Across the table, Rebecca winked. Before Edie could reply, the wait staff whirled into action, starting the coffee service. Franny's seat stayed vacant as the fruit course was served first, melons and grapes, quickly followed by creamed wheat and gossip about last night's activities. Edie managed a few bites of the porridge before it was replaced with a plate of sliced steak, poached eggs, peas, and potatoes.

"They make a handsome couple," Aunt Grace said to Ned. "You must be so proud."

"A perfect match," Flora added. "The Peppers are a fine family, Ned. She couldn't have done much better."

"I know Mrs. Pepper must be relieved, after all of that trouble with their girl. Running off with some paddy from the mills. What a nightmare." Grace cast a sideways glance at her own daughter. Rebecca, deep in conversation with one of the little girls, didn't seem to notice.

Flora followed Grace's gaze, her own expression grim. "She paid for her sins, as must we all."

Ned cleared his throat. "I couldn't ask for a better son-in-law," he said, deftly turning the conversation. "I know he's keen on medicine, but I hope I can persuade him to take an interest in politics. We could use some new blood on City Council."

Each word struck Edie like a fist. She poked at her food, silently fuming as the image of Frances and Theo's perfect future life played out in her mind—the wedding. Babies, of course. A career in politics, Frances gracing the top of the society pages. The life that Edie had always imagined for herself. By the time the coffee and pastry course was finished, Edie's annoyance with her sister had grown to fill the empty seat beside her.

The minute Grandmama stood, dismissing the family, Edie leapt from her seat. She pressed a kiss to her father's cheek and practically bolted from the room, which she was sure dismayed her grandmother even further. She hurried up the stairs to Frances's room, directly beside her own.

"Go away," her sister called from beyond the door. "I told you; I don't want breakfast."

Edie ignored her. "It's me," she said softly as she slipped into the room and shut the door behind her. The still-closed curtains pitched the room into darkness, and as her eyes adjusted, Edie could just make out the lump of her sister under the blankets on the bed. "You missed Grandmama's sighs during breakfast."

Frances shifted just enough to make room for her sister, and Edie kicked off her shoes to climb in beside her. As soon as she was settled, Frances came close, resting her head on Edie's shoulder. "I'm sorry I wasn't there to save you," Frances said.

"Thank you. The entire time I sat there, thinking, you know who's terrible? Franny, for getting some sleep and leaving me alone."

Frances laughed softly, like Edie had been kidding. Edie hadn't been, and she pushed down the sour feeling in her stomach and forced a smile as her sister gave a happy sigh, the picture of contentment. "Last night was amazing, wasn't it? It felt like a fairy tale."

"You looked like a princess," Edie agreed.

"And Theo looked every inch my Prince Charming." Franny closed her eyes, her smile cut through Edie like a knife, because Edie just knew her sister was imagining Theo's broad shoulders in that jacket, his eyes gleaming in the dim light, his mouth pouted just so. "I still can't believe I get to marry him," Franny added.

Edie swallowed hard. "Neither can I," she admitted, and tried to push away the envy clawing at her insides.

"Edie." Frances propped herself up on her elbow. "You're all right with this, aren't you? I know . . . I know the two of you had feelings for each other as children. Say the word and . . ."

"Stop," Edie said, hating herself. "That was ancient history. I'm happy you're happy," Edie said, as truthfully as she could. *But it should be me*, she added silently.

"I don't know what I did to deserve a sister like you," Frances said, and the knife she'd stuck in Edie's heart with her smile twisted.

"Stop that," Edie said. "You're the good one, not me. Everyone says so."

"Everyone isn't me, and I'm always right. You're the good one, Edie. You'll see."

"I don't know. Being the bad one is more fun." Edie reached out and tickled her sister, breaking through the guilt that had formed a wall between them.

Franny shrieked and jerked away. "I take it back, you're horrible," she laughed. "The worst."

"That's more like it," Edie said, but she was laughing, too. For a moment, they were little girls again, teasing each other in the nursery. Edie thought about confiding in her sister about her trip into the city with Rebecca, but she could scarcely find the words to explain where she was going, or what she was searching for.

She couldn't exactly admit that she needed a new start because of her brush with death and her hurt over Franny's engagement to Theo. So she didn't say anything at all, just kept it close, one more secret piled atop the others.

"Edie?"

"Hmm?"

"I almost forgot to tell you! Theo and I are having a small party tomorrow evening at his place with his school chums. Everyone will want to see you—it's been forever."

Edie sat up. "Everyone?"

"And then some! Artie's friend is a medium, and she's agreed to give us a séance! Please say you'll come."

"A séance." Edie was glad the dim room hid the skepticism scrawled across her face. "You can't be serious."

Franny sat up, too. She reached forward and grabbed her sister's hands. "Please, Edie? For me?"

A night with Theo was the last thing Edie should pursue. Especially when he was the only thing she wanted, and, thanks to her sister, the one thing she could never have. But Edie gave her sister's finger a squeeze, even as tendrils of dread wrapped themselves around her heart. She'd never been able to say no to Frances.

"Anything for you," she said. And she meant it.

CHAPTER 6

Gilbert settled into the chair beside his daughter's bed as Lizzie pulled the curtain closed over the window. The sky outside faded from brilliant pink to the dusky purple of the approaching twilight. It had been a good day, spent chasing Penny around the neighborhood and playing tea party with her dolls in the parlor, and ended it with cups of lemon water ice from the little shop on Ridge Avenue. But now, as Penny snuggled beneath her blankets in the room that had borne witness to Gilbert's greatest joy and most devastating tragedy, her red hair in tight plaits and her skin scrubbed pink from the bath, his heart grew heavy.

Leaving her in the care of his parents ate at him in a way nothing else did, but his Mam knew he was in no state to raise her, not on his own. Not like this. The fact that he'd had to take another dose of morphine while she was in the tub to quiet his trembling hands and racing mind cemented the knowledge that he wasn't fit to be the father Penny deserved.

"Time for a story, mo leanbh," he said, pulling the soft quilt up under her chin. "Which one do you want?"

"Tell me one about Mama," Penny said, her little face serious as she scooted to make room for him. He curled himself around her small body, his legs dangling from the edge of the bed. He shouldn't have been so surprised. His daughter had been more and more curious about her mother lately, which Gilbert supposed was natural.

"Once upon a time," he began, his voice rumbling out from his chest. Penny snuggled close. "There was a girl."

"Mama." Penny said.

"Yes. Your mama," Gilbert said, smiling at her interruption. "Her name was Sarah, and she lived in a big house on the edge of a big city, with a fancy horse and pretty clothes. Everything she could ever want. Except one thing: she was lonely."

"*I'm* not lonely," Penny said. "I have a Granny and a Grandda and an Aunt Lizzie and a Da."

"That you do, mo leanbh. You're a lucky little girl." His throat thickened with emotion. "But Sarah wasn't so lucky. She had a brother, yes, and friends, but she often found herself alone. She used to take walks on the woods near her big house, down to the creek, and pretend to make friends with the animals nearby. One day, she was skipping rocks across the creek, when she spotted a boy on the other side."

"You!" Penny knew this story. She sat right up and poked her little finger into his chest. "That's you, Da."

"That's right," he laughed. "And she was so surprised to see anyone else, that she fell right into the creek. She knew how to swim, but the boy didn't know that. So he dove right in after her and tried to save her. Only to be walloped over the head for his trouble, because she was a smart girl, and knew better than to accept help from any strange boy who appeared in the woods," he added.

"But she forgave you." Her words grew rough-edged with sleep, and she rubbed her nose against his shirt.

"She did. Eventually." Gilbert said. "And we fell in love, and got married, and then you arrived. And she loved us both so very, very much."

Penny didn't answer. He waited a few moments longer, until her breaths grew deep and even, her little body slack, before he extricated himself from her limbs and climbed from her bed. He gave her one last goodnight kiss, then slipped downstairs to bid goodbye to his family before taking the last train back to Callowhill.

A few hours later, Gilbert woke to a pounding at his door.

He scrambled out of bed, dragging his shirt on as he scurried across the room to yank open the door. His landlady stood on the landing. She yawned wide, holding a hand over her mouth. "Dr, Knight called," she said.

Nellie was no stranger to these late-night calls. And neither was Gilbert.

"Thank you," he said with a duck of his head. "Sorry to trouble you."

"No trouble at all, love. Be safe, yeah?" Nellie was barely middle-aged, made prettier by the strands of silver contrasting with her dark hair and light brown skin. The silver shimmered in the yellow torchlight, and Gilbert swallowed hard. Her husband had been Gilbert's commanding officer during the war, and he'd died right in front of Gilbert. Some nights, as Gilbert drifted off to sleep, he wondered if maybe he should marry her and take care of things the way Captain Thatcher would have wanted.

But Nellie deserved better than him, better than a grief-stricken boy who'd marched off to war and returned a broken shell of a man. So he paid his rent early and brought the children candy and trinkets whenever he had the chance and made sure none of his neighbors gave her any trouble—she'd had enough hardship in her life.

"Always," Gilbert said.

She reached out and patted his cheek, her hand warm against his skin. He clutched at the doorway, every muscle coiling to keep from leaning into her touch. "You're a good boy, Gilbert. I'll lock up behind you."

He dressed quickly in the dark and made his bed, the sheets tucked in tight beneath the mattress. Then, he descended the stairs, allowed Nellie to give him one more pat—this time on his shoulder—and hurried out into the humid night air in his Fairmount neighborhood. He lived only a few blocks from the morgue, and he walked them quickly, his steps carrying him past the tall boarding houses on Spring Garden Street and across Broad Street's aptly named expanse. By the time he arrived at the morgue at 1301 Wood Street, sweat beaded on his brow. He hoped whatever had called him from his bed was already waiting in the underground examination room, where the temperature was carefully controlled to keep the corpses fresh.

The sight of his partner waiting on the building's wide marble steps, however, proved he'd have no such luck.

"Good morning, sunshine," Marco said. He tossed a key ring at Gilbert as he jogged down to the sidewalk, the gas lamps throwing his features into shadows. "Hope you're awake enough to drive. I've got to get the camera ready."

Gilbert caught the keys easily and followed Marco around the side of the morgue building to the small car barn tucked along Carlton Street. A series of repurposed ambulance trucks waited for them. He climbed into the driver's seat and turned the key in the ignition. Marco scrambled up beside him as the engine roared to life. Gilbert looked over at him expectantly.

"Strawberry Mansion Bridge," Marco said. "Some sort of accident. Cops need us to process the scene so they can reopen the road by dawn.

Dawn. Gilbert glanced in his mirrors as he drove west down Vine Street. A hint of pink sky sat in the distance, peeking past the construction for the yet-to-be-completed parkway and the unfinished buildings on either side leading from City Hall to the river. They'd have to be quick. "What's the hurry?"

Marco shrugged. "Theirs not to reason why, Lawless."

Theirs but to do and die, Gilbert thought as he turned on to East River Drive, past the stately boathouses wrapped in early-morning mist and the entrance to the park. *And into the valley of death rode the six hundred . . .*

"Cecelia didn't mean to upset you yesterday," Marco said suddenly. "I think she may actually be sweet on you, don't ask me why."

Gilbert glanced over at the other young man, surprised. Marco stared straight ahead, his arms crossed over his chest. They'd known each other since the dark, dizzying days of the influenza epidemic, when their fellow doctors tended to the living and they were sent to the morgue to help sort through the stacks of the dead. Gilbert knew why he had stayed on for the last three years, but Marco had never given a reason as to why he had also abandoned the living—Marco, who seemed so full of *life*, always laughing, and flirting, and cracking a joke, often at Gilbert's expense.

But this gentle concern from Marco was new. Gilbert wasn't sure how he felt about it.

"It wasn't her," Gilbert said slowly, his sleep-addled brain reaching for the words to shape the lie. "My sister had telephoned. I was worried for her."

"That's why you spent an hour in the men's room?"

Shit. Gilbert's palms slipped against the wheel and the truck slammed into one of the many potholes marring the pavement along East River Road. He'd been careless. He'd almost had an episode where someone could see. He—

"I'm not going to say anything," Marco said quietly. "You were over there, weren't you? My brothers were too."

Gilbert nodded, the words stuck fast in his throat. But they'd arrived at the scene, the tall iron skeleton of the Strawberry Mansion Bridge stretched overhead. He pulled off onto the grass along the river and parked beside a gaggle of uniformed police officers carrying lanterns and flashlights. A detective leaned against the police truck in a black suit, smoking, the red tip of his cigarette glowing in the purple predawn light. Gilbert recognized the man's broad shoulders and hangdog face immediately and cursed under his breath. Finnegan Pyle, Tommy Fletcher, and Gilbert had been an inseparable trio as boys in Manayunk. Finnegan Pyle had never forgiven Gilbert for leaving the neighborhood and attending Central High School, let alone college, and the years hadn't softened Gilbert's former friend one bit. He'd built a life for himself in the Philadelphia Police Department the old-fashioned way—a steady paycheck and brute force, supplemented by healthy bribes from Tommy and his Cresson Street Crew.

Gilbert grabbed his kit and left Marco to deal with Pyle and the rest of the policemen. He didn't need to ask for details, not when his truck's headlights illuminated the body so clearly.

The woman was face-down a few yards from the river's edge, her nearly translucent white slip a bright spot against the new grass. He performed a mental cataloging of the scene, committing every detail to memory, from the heavy scent of death in the air, to the droplets of dew beaded on her skin, to the way her fingers curled in slightly toward the strange black marks on her wrists, to the small bare feet. Her ankles, too, were ringed in black. Singed, almost. Gilbert frowned.

She couldn't have been dead very long, though with the chill in the early spring night, it was hard to tell. This wasn't a popular spot for picnicking—the bank here was too narrow, and the traffic from the bridge overhead made for an unpleasant atmosphere. Cars whizzed by with predictable frequency during the daylight hours, which meant she hadn't been here when the sun set, or someone would have seen her.

Marco picked his way over the long grass, his camera clutched in his hands. "Mayor Moore's nephew wrecked his car just up around the bend. He claims he found her when he went to get help."

"I think he's telling the truth." Gilbert squatted down beside the woman, setting the lantern down in the grass beside him. There was no evidence of broken glass, or tire tracks in the soft mud. No blood. "This doesn't look like a car accident."

Marco craned his head up, his gaze sweeping the iron structure towering above them before returning to the body. "Doesn't look like she jumped, either."

Gilbert had had the same thought. If she'd jumped, there'd be some sign of the impact on the body, but the girl looked as if she had been placed gently on the grass, almost if she were sleeping.

Marco lifted his camera, and Gilbert turned quickly, closing his eyes before the camera's bulb flashed, streaking light through the darkness. He gave the other man a few minutes to work, the sound of the camera shutter whirring in the space beside him, taking great care to keep his breaths even as the flash bulb popped and Marco wound the film. He continued his survey of the bank, taking in the smallest details: the still-chilly air on his skin, the sound of the river rushing past, the way Marco's footsteps crunched on the grass as he moved around the body, and then grew quieter as he retreated to the truck.

Together, they turned over the corpse, careful not to disturb too much of the grass beneath her. Her limbs were limp as they rolled her over, one arm flopping back on the grass; she hadn't been gone long enough to go stiff. Marco sucked in a breath and Gilbert braced himself for the first look.

She was much younger than Gilbert had assumed. Early twenties, maybe, still more girl than woman. He thought of Sarah, and swallowed down bile. From the neck up, she looked almost alive, her features soft. The girl's open eyes stared up at them, blue and cloudy, her slack lips parted and still painted red, her blonde hair cut into a fashionable bob.

But from the neck down . . .

Shit, Gilbert thought.

"Shit," Marco echoed aloud.

The front of the girl's gossamer slip was cut open, revealing a gaping wound from clavicle to navel, the white bones of her ribcage cracked open and jutting forward into the humid night air. Dark, dried blood stained the front of her dress, smeared up her neck and down her arms, her legs, though, mysteriously, the grass beneath her was dry. Gilbert leaned closer, even though the hair rose on the back of his neck and every instinct he had told him to look away, to turn, to run, as he peered into the gaping cavity of the girl's torso. Her internal organs should have been visible, but they were gone. Removed, as if she'd been gutted and cleaned, leaving only a deep black void behind.

This wasn't a car accident. It wasn't an accident at all. Truth be told, even *murder* seemed too soft a word for the savage violence the poor girl had suffered.

This was the work of a butcher.

CHAPTER 7

Rebecca was late.

Edie checked her slim platinum wristwatch again, the diamonds glittering in the morning sun. Half past ten. Lizzie bounced on her toes beside her. Edie couldn't tell if Lizzie was excited or anxious—and to tell the truth, she wasn't sure about herself, either. She considered pulling the address from her pocket again—perhaps they'd gone to the wrong place. Perhaps Rebecca had been mistaken.

Perhaps they should just go home and forget all about this.

"I think those might be the artists, Miss Edie," Lizzie said. "Look."

A small number of women gathered in front of a stately red brick townhouse at the corner, some carrying easels, other boxes of paints and palettes.

"Do you see Rebecca?" Edie asked.

Lizzie shook her head, her curls bobbing. "No. But . . . wait. Is that . . . ?"

Before Edie could stop her, Lizzie darted across the street to where a young blonde woman wrestled with an easel. Clearly, she was someone Lizzie knew. They hugged, and then spoke animatedly, the blonde's hands dancing in the air between them. Lizzie turned and waved to Edie, beckoning her to join them.

Beckoned. She'd been beckoned by her maid. Maybe she'd have to have a word with Lizzie about boundaries.

"Miss Edie, I think we're in the right place! This is my friend, Athena Kostos. She works in the Pepper House."

Athena, who was short and cherub-faced, bobbed a quick curtsy. "Pleasure to meet you, Miss Shippen."

Another woman, this one dressed in a vibrant orange coat stopped on the stoop, clearly overhearing. "Shippen? Gracious, Edie, is that you?"

"In the flesh," Edie said. The woman looked vaguely familiar, with a glamorous blond bob, a long straight nose, and glittering brown eyes. It took Edie a moment to reconcile the elegant woman before her with the gangly, awkward girl she'd remembered Ophelia Van Pelt to be. "It's swell to see you, Ophelia. We're looking for my cousin—we were supposed to meet her here. Have you seen her?"

Ophelia frowned. "I've been looking for her too. We'd planned to paint in the back garden today. She had volunteered to model for us."

"Perhaps she's running behind," Athena said. "The train from Bryn Mawr could be late."

"That's not like her." Ophelia said. She looked ready to say more, when a short brunette with thick spectacles barreled down the stairs.

"Ophelia," the brunette barked. "Are we getting started, or what? Who's this?" The woman's gaze swept over Edie from the toes of her shoes to the tip of the feather on her second-favorite hat.

"Miss Edith Shippen. Becca's cousin, actually," Ophelia said. "Edie, this is—"

"Colleen Spencer." The girl held out her hand to shake. "Did you bring Rebecca with you?"

Edie felt rather dizzy. "No. I was supposed to meet her here."

"Well that puts us in a pickle." Colleen chewed on the corner of her lip. "It was her turn to model."

"Can't someone else do it?" Lizzie asked.

Everyone swung their attention to Edie's maid. She flushed as red as her hair but continued anyway. "I just mean. If you need a model . . ."

"Who's this?" Collen asked.

"My maid. Lizzie Lawless," Edie said.

Lizzie straightened her shoulders and held out her own hand, mimicking Colleen. "It's a pleasure, ma'am."

Colleen's face brightened, and she took Lizzie's hand in hers, shaking enthusiastically. "That's more like it! How did a nice girl like you wind up working for the oppressing class?"

"Cols is a communist," Athena explained. Her words held only the barest trace of an accent. "She's very concerned about the plight of working people."

Colleen pushed up her spectacles and continued as if Athena hadn't spoken. She leaned in close to Lizzie, and said in a conspiratorial whisper, "You don't have to put up with any abuse, you know. There are plenty of other jobs out there for smart girls like yourself."

Lizzie flushed, her skin going as red as her hair. "I'm quite happy," she stammered. "Miss Edie and I are fast friends."

"Hmph." Colleen scowled. "Friends."

"Yes," Edie said, grateful for Lizzie's defense, though she wasn't exactly sure why. "Friends."

"Now, Cols," Ophelia said, "There will be plenty of time to convince her to embrace the proletariat later. But we need to get started. Perhaps . . . Edie? Would you mind sitting for us, until Becca arrives?"

"Me?" Edie fluttered her hand against her chest, feigning surprise. Deep down, Edie thought she'd make a fine model, but she hadn't wanted to volunteer. She didn't want to look *eager*. "Well. I suppose I could."

Relief washed over Ophelia's face. "Splendid. Colleen, get her situated? I'll get set up."

"Fine. But stay close," Colleen said. She stalked up the stoop and inside, leaving Edie and Lizzie to hurry at her heels. She spoke as quickly as she hurried them down a well-appointed corridor. "Is this your house? It's lovely."

Colleen shook her head as she led them back outside again to a small, walled garden. "It belongs to one of Ophelia's friends. She lets us use it when she's out of town." Colleen pointed to where someone had spread a blanket on the grass. "We'll have you here. Are you comfortable taking your clothes off here, or do you want some privacy?"

Beside Edie, Lizzie let out a strangled choking noise. "I beg your pardon?" Edie asked.

"We're painting nudes today," Colleen said slowly. "That's what Rebecca was volunteering for. Unless that's a problem?"

Nude. Well. It had been a few years since the last time anyone had painted Edie unclothed—not that anyone but Theo knew that, of course. And she'd never posed outdoors. Let alone in front of so many people.

She could back out. She could refuse, collect her things, and head home. She almost did just that, until she remembered why she'd agreed to meet Rebecca here in the first place.

She was a new woman. A modern girl, embarking on a new life. So she dropped her handbag on the grass, shrugged out of her coat, and said, "No problem at all."

As the morning stretched on, Edie realized two things: first, that modeling was hard work, and second, the spring air was cold, despite the sunshine. Especially unclothed. Every muscle ached from holding her pose. She reclined on a blanket on the grass, one hand beneath her head, while the other held a bright bouquet of flowers over her breasts. A shimmering cloth draped over her hips completed the effect. The women sat in a close circle their eyes studying Edie's every curve and dimple with hawkish attention while their brushes moved carefully across canvas. Even Lizzie was hard at work, sitting cross-legged in front of Athena's easel. She borrowed supplies from the others, and, to Edie's surprise, worked with a quiet, capable confidence. Edie found herself wondering at what other talents her maid—or any of the help—might have, if only they had the time and resources to pursue them.

Perhaps Colleen was rubbing off on her already. Edie contemplated this as she tried to ignore the throbbing behind her eyes. The sun moved out from behind a cloud, and Edie squinted against the sharp pain brought on by the light. An older woman *tsked*, but Ophelia came to her rescue.

"That's time," Ophelia said, clapping her hands under her chin. "Let's pack it up." To Edie, she said, "You were a great sport, darling."

"Done already?" Edie asked, though she was secretly glad of it. Sitting for too long had turned her limbs to jelly. She wobbled a bit as she stood, her stomach swooping. Thankfully, Lizzie was already there to steady her. With her maid's help, Edie dressed quickly.

"You were a natural," Ophelia said, as Edie and Lizzie approached. Already, the easels were packed up and the paints stowed. "You'll have to come to our next show."

"That would be lovely," Edie said, and meant it. She might never be an artist like her cousin or any of these women, but she'd done something for herself.

It was a first step.

She hummed to herself as she and Lizzie made their way back toward the train station. The side street they were on was quieter now, almost deserted. Edie was so lost in her thoughts that she didn't notice the pair of young, rough-looking men approaching until it was almost too late. They crowded close, putting them-selves directly in Edie's path.

"Pardon me," Edie began to say. She stepped to the side, out of their way.

One man nodded, as if in apology. Then, quick as a snake, his hand darted out and grabbed her handbags with a vicious yank.

"Hey!" Edie cried. She tugged her handbag back, startled. Behind her, Lizzie screamed. The second man swung his fist. Pain exploded in her shoulder, and she went sprawling to the sidewalk, her grip loosening. Her face smashed against something hard—a brick? Light exploded across her vision as the world slowed. Stopped. She pushed herself up, heat spreading down her face. The men were already gone, and her bag with them.

"Miss Edie!" Lizzie's voice trembled as she helped Edie up. "Are you all right?"

"Did they . . . did they just rob me?" Edie asked. She clung to Lizzie's arm. "Is that what happened?"

"You're bleeding," Lizzie said quickly. She stepped back and fished a handkerchief out of her own handbag and pressed it to the wound on Edie's forehead. "Hold that there, Miss Edie. We need to take you home. Then we can call the police."

Edie wobbled a bit, but her hand held the handkerchief tight against the cut despite the throbbing pain. "I can't go home, not like this," she said. "My grandmother will never let me out again."

Lizzie pursed her lips, clearly thinking. Finally, she blew out a frustrated breath. "Come on. It's only a few blocks."

"To where?" Edie asked.

"To my brother," Lizzie answered. "He'll be able to help us."

CHAPTER 8

Gilbert allowed himself a moment to slump against the cool tiled wall of the autopsy room, exhaustion washing over him in waves. As soon as he and Marco had returned from the early morning scene, two dead gangsters had arrived, each bearing tattoos proclaiming their allegiance to The Butcher of Broad Street: matching snakes curled around their biceps. Gilbert spent the rest of the morning among the dead, carefully taking notes to complete the homicide reports as the vice detectives hovered, talking in low voices. The men had been ambushed, probably by a rival gang. Leo Salvatore was known for his ruthlessness, and only time would tell which of the other gangs in the city claimed responsibility. Gilbert had wondered as they left if Tommy or his boys from Manayunk were involved but didn't voice his thoughts; it wasn't part of his job.

A commotion from the main room outside interrupted his calm. Shouts and a crash echoed through the building. Gil poked his head into the corridor, not knowing what sort of madness he'd encounter. He certainly didn't expect to see his sister charging toward him like Gráinne Mhaol, the pirate queen, with her red hair streaming loose from beneath her straw hat. The front of her yellow dress was stained with blood, and Marco and another assistant were fast on her heels.

Blood. Gilbert blinked, sure he was seeing things again. But when he opened her eyes, she was nearly on top of him. "Liz?"

"Gilbert!" she shouted and threw herself into his arms. "Tell these oafs I'm your bleeding *sister!*"

"She's my sister," Gilbert repeated.

"She nearly gave poor Cecelia a heart attack, charging in here like that," Marco said. "Why didn't you knock like a normal person?"

"It's an emergency," Lizzie said, her words leaving her in a desperate torrent. "It's bad, Gil. We were robbed, and Miss Edie is hurt, and we were only a few blocks away. I didn't know where else to go. *Hurry.*"

Gilbert held up a hand when Marco opened his mouth to interject, silencing the other assistant.

"Slow down, Liz. Who's hurt? Are you all right?" He could have sworn she'd said *robbed*, but . . . that couldn't be right. He was still trying to piece everything together when his sister let out a frustrated scream and grabbed his tie.

"She's outside," Lizzie whispered. She pulled his face close to hers. "She won't let me take her home, and she didn't want to come in, either. Please, Gil." Her tone turned pleading. "Please."

"I'll do what I can," he said finally. "But I say the word, and this woman goes to the hospital. Understood?"

Lizzie led them around to the courtyard at the back of the morgue. A small figure sat on the filthy ground wrapped in a peacock blue coat, her back against the brick wall, her long dark hair a frizzy halo around her face. Blood seeped through the sodden handkerchief she held over her eye.

Gilbert hesitated, his heart pounding the way it did before he received orders to charge over the top of the trenches, the blood rushing in his ears, every sense on high alert. He patted his vest pocket, as if to reassure himself his vials were still there and took a deep breath. Then another.

She's just a girl, he told himself. *She's hurt. She needs help. You can help her.*

Lizzie, as if she sensed his hesitation, turned and looked back over her shoulder and gave him a look he knew all too well. He nodded once, more to himself than to her, and followed his sister.

"Miss Edie," Lizzie said gently, "I've brought help. This is my brother, Gilbert."

Miss Shippen squinted up at him, her stormy gray gaze alert. That was good, considering the head wound.

"You don't look anything alike," she said.

"Same eyes," Lizzie said, waving her hand in front of her face. "But don't worry, miss. Gil's a doctor. He was a medic in France too. Has medals and everything. He'll fix you."

"I'm not that kind of doctor," Gilbert protested. He knelt beside the woman. His pulse thundered. He needed to breathe. Needed to calm down. "I mean, I am a doctor, but I never formally practiced. May I?"

He waited for Miss Shippen's nod before proceeding. He moved slowly, like he was tending to a wounded animal and not a society girl, explaining every action. "I'm going to just take a look, all right?"

Another nod.

He covered her hand with his own. It was small and soft, and slick with blood. He moved it gently back, pulling the cloth away from her skin.

Miss Shippen whimpered, and Gilbert swore. A wave of fresh blood poured forth from the gash above her brow, spilling down over her eye. With his free hand, he pulled some of the gauze from his pocket free and pressed it to the wound. It needed cleaning, badly, but it didn't look deep enough for stitches.

"You were robbed?" He looked over at his sister, who hovered like a worried mother hen.

"Aye," Liz said softly. "We were walking down the street, minding our own business. These two fellows came out of nowhere and grabbed her bag. One of them hit her when she wouldn't let go."

He pinched the bridge of his nose. "Miss Shippen. Can you walk, or should I carry you inside?"

"I am perfectly capable of moving under my own power," Miss Shippen said. She pushed to her feet, eager to prove her mettle, as tough as any soldier he'd served with. She only swayed slightly, and he grasped her elbow, giving her some support.

"Thank you, Dr.—"

"Lawless. Gilbert Lawless," he said.

"Pleased to make your acquaintance, Dr. Lawless," Miss Shippen said, her voice soft. "Unfortunately, I think I'm going to be sick."

She lurched forward, and Gilbert managed to step back just as she retched, hot bile and vomit hitting the cobbles at her toes. He wasn't surprised. Head wounds were a nasty business. But he was surprised by the anger surging through him. Anger at this silly woman, who tried to stop a robbery. And anger at the brutes who did this to her.

"I'm going to carry you," Gilbert said, his voice brokering no argument, but he needn't have been so stern—Miss Shippen looked up at him and gave him a weak nod. He scooped her up carefully, one arm beneath her shoulders and the other beneath her knees. She nestled into him immediately, resting her head against his shoulder, like she had been born to fit in his arms like this, pressed against his chest. Probably getting blood everywhere. Nellie wouldn't be happy with him.

Lizzie hurried along behind him. "Thank you, Gil."

He glared at her. "We will talk about this later, Liz," he said.

They burst through the back door of the morgue. Cecelia and Marco stood from their desks, eyes wide, as Gilbert shoved past. Miss Shippen raised a hand in a weak wave, and Lizzie trailed them, her brown eyes blazing. "I'll be in the autopsy room," he snapped at them, but he didn't wait for an answer as they hurried down the corridor, their footsteps ringing along the tile floor.

"Did you say autopsy room?" Miss Shippen lifted her head from his shoulder and craned her neck to peer up at him. Her breath danced over the skin of his throat, and he gritted his teeth as he pushed through the swinging door. He set her on the stainless steel table in the center of the room as gently as he could and pivoted, putting as much distance between them as possible. He bent low, pulling supplies from the cabinet as he found them— gauze and stitching—and took in a deep breath, trying to forget the way she'd felt in his arms, alive and whole.

She's not for you, Gilbert reminded himself. His fingers brushed the first-aid kit shoved way in the back, reserved for accidents. He pulled it out and flipped it open, happy to see plasters and iodine inside—supplies the dead didn't need.

"I'm a coroner, Miss Shippen," he said shortly. "I don't usually have living patients."

"I'm sure I'm not worth all this trouble. I'll be fine."

"I'd like to see to it myself, Miss Shippen. If we're lucky, it won't scar." He washed his hands, then wet a cloth to clean her forehead.

"Scar?" her voice cracked. "Oh dear. Oh dear. A scar would mean . . ." Miss Shippen trailed off, and he turned in time to see her sway. "Bangs. *Forever*. I imagine I would look dreadful in bangs. Do what you must."

His sister hopped up on the autopsy table beside Miss Shippen to steady her. Their shoulders pressed together, their hands entwined, and Miss Shippen stared at him with a sort of horrified stupor across her face. The blood made it easier to look at her, he decided. Easier to ignore the pink bow of her lips, the dusting of freckles across her nose.

Easier to pretend he didn't notice how beautiful she was, or the way his sister clung to her like a lifeline.

"Did you fall, Miss Shippen?" he asked, as he took her hand and lowered the handkerchief.

"Excuse me?" She blinked up at him. The bleeding had slowed, thankfully.

"When the man hit you. Did you fall?" He wanted to distract her while he worked, to have her focus on him and not the movements of his hands.

"I did," she said slowly. "He hit my shoulder, and I think I hit my head on something on the sidewalk. The curb, perhaps?"

Christ. He pressed the cool cloth to her forehead, working quickly to clean the broken skin. She hissed and jerked away, into the palm he'd already placed behind her head to hold her still.

"Sorry," he said softly. "I have to make sure it's clean. The street is filthy."

"I know," she whispered. "Just hurry, please."

He did. He worked quickly and efficiently to clean the wound with iodine. Thankfully, he'd been wrong in his earlier assessment. It wasn't deep enough to need stitches—just a shallow gash, easily closed with a pair of plasters. "There," he said finally. He leaned back and wiped his hands on his already bloodstained white coat. "You're lucky, it wasn't worse, Miss Shippen. A few inches to the left and that curb could have killed you."

Miss Shippen looked up at him and gave a watery smile. "I supposed I would have ended up on this table either way, then," she said. She reached up and traced the edges of the surgical tape across her brow. Her lips quivered, then, like his words had settled in. "Thank you, Dr. Lawless."

"It's going to leave a nasty bruise, but that's all," he said. He shrugged out of his bloody coat and washed his hands again. "You'll be fine, Miss Shippen. I expect it'll be a long time before I see you on this table again."

At least, he hoped it would be.

CHAPTER 9

Edie sat in a daze, her head pounding, as Lizzie argued with her brother about what to do next. They didn't look very much alike. Lizzie was small and full of soft curves under a cascade of unruly red curls. Her brother, by contrast, was tall and angular, from the sharp line of his nose to his broad shoulders. His hair was a deep chestnut brown; not as dark as Edie's own, but definitely not red. Though she didn't exactly trust her vision at the moment—already, a glittering cascade of stars floated everywhere, like the entire room had been coated in a fine sugar. Usually, her migraines were predictable things—triggered by a black mood, or her existential dread over the future. Too much sunshine or too little water or an approaching thunderstorm. Now, she could add "head wound" to the list of things that made her vision blur around the edges and her stomach clench.

Edie didn't remember her first migraine spell, only that it happened sometime soon after her fever broke, when she woke to the news that she had survived and her mother had not. At first, she wanted to believe the ever-present shadows and glimmering shapes in the corners of her gaze were her mother's ghost, but years of doctors and various treatments had dispelled her of those romantic ideas. Science said there was a problem with her brain, a lingering after-effect from the high fever. It left her prone to hysteria, to melancholy. Maybe even madness.

Lizzie's brother, the doctor who insisted he wasn't *that kind of* doctor, put a gentle hand on Edie's shoulder. Something about him—maybe the sharp angle of his jaw, so at odds with the soft line of his mouth, tugged down in the corners—intrigued her. Or maybe it was the oncoming headache, blurring her sight.

He was speaking to her, she realized, his deep voice rumbling from deep in his chest. "Pardon?" she asked.

His frown deepened. He had very nice eyes, Edie decided, even if they were sad. Like two big brown pools of chocolate. Sad chocolate. Was there such a thing?

"Liz," he said, "give me your purse."

"I'm not paying you, you dolt," Lizzie said, but handed over the bag. He rummaged through it for a second before producing a mirrored compact. It wasn't engraved silver like Edie's, but a cheap celluloid decorated with jade green swirls.

She should buy Lizzie a nicer compact. Was that an appropriate gift for saving someone's life?

Lizzie's brother stepped close, close enough that Edie could see he hadn't shaved this morning. He smelled like coffee and peppermint. Edie probably smelled like regret and broken promises, if those things carried a scent. Did they, on some deep, primal level? Edie figured they must. Perhaps that's why Theo chose Frances. Edie smelled too sad.

"Miss Shippen," Lizzie's brother said, "Look up for me?"

Edie complied, staring up at the ceiling. A crack traced through the plaster. It looked suspiciously like a rabbit—two ears, one bent. A tiny little nose. And then Lizzie's brother cupped her face with a big, warm hand, and any thoughts that Edie had about the hare-like nature of ceiling cracks evaporated. He did something with the mirror, tilted it in a way that sent stars dancing again, and she winced, leaning into his palm.

He made a small noise in the back of his throat and pulled his hand away. Concern creased his face, tugging his lips into an even deeper frown. "That hurt? The light?"

Edie nodded. "Yes, but . . ." She meant to tell him about her migraines, about how at certain periods even a thin slant of light felt like shards of glass slicing directly into her brain. But before she could, he turned to his sister.

"I'm going to have Cecelia call you a ride. Keep a close eye on her. Don't let her sleep for the next few hours, no matter how tired she says she is. Is that clear?"

"Crystal." Lizzie wrapped her arm around Edie's shoulders and helped her stand. Edie wanted to say a million things—to ask a million questions. But he was gone before she could even thank him, gone so quickly that if it wasn't for the plaster stretching across her forehead, she would have wondered if she imagined the entire thing.

"Come along, Miss Edie," Lizzie said. "Let's get you home."

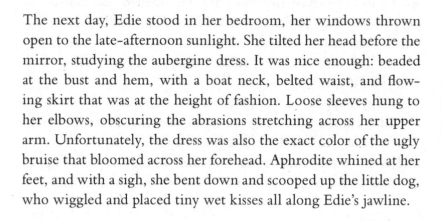

The next day, Edie stood in her bedroom, her windows thrown open to the late-afternoon sunlight. She tilted her head before the mirror, studying the aubergine dress. It was nice enough: beaded at the bust and hem, with a boat neck, belted waist, and flowing skirt that was at the height of fashion. Loose sleeves hung to her elbows, obscuring the abrasions stretching across her upper arm. Unfortunately, the dress was also the exact color of the ugly bruise that bloomed across her forehead. Aphrodite whined at her feet, and with a sigh, she bent down and scooped up the little dog, who wiggled and placed tiny wet kisses all along Edie's jawline.

"It's the dress, isn't it?" Edie asked.

Behind her, Lizzie winced and shook her head. "It's not the dress, miss. It's your face."

Edie blew out her breath and leaned in close. The wound on her forehead had bruised quickly, turning from an angry red to a deep, dusky purple overnight. Thankfully, the staff was discreet, and she'd been able to stay out of her family's sight for now. Somehow, she had also managed to talk Lizzie out of calling the police to report the incident. The last thing Edie needed was her grandmother catching a whiff of this—mugged on the street, the first time she left the house on her own! She'd never be allowed out again.

"I can't go to the party like this," she said, finally. "It'll cause all sorts of gossip. Isn't there anything we can do? Pressed powder? Or some rouge on my cheeks, to draw the eye away?"

Lizzie hesitated. "There's something we can do." She crossed to the wardrobe in strong, determined steps, and rustled about in the bottom for a moment. When she stood, she bore a pair of sharp sewing scissors in one hand and a white towel in the other. "It's the only thing I can think of."

Edie stared at the scissors, a mounting horror clawing through her gut. Lizzie was right. There was only one thing to be done. Otherwise, there would be a number of questions she wouldn't be prepared to answer. She crossed to her vanity and sat. Long, dark waves cascaded nearly to her waist. The last time . . . well. She still had nightmares about it. But she was out of options. Aphrodite settled into Edie's lap, tail wagging.

"Do it," Edie said simply.

Lizzie clutched the scissors to her chest. "Miss Edie."

"Do it," Edie repeated, and closed her eyes and braced herself for the first cut of the blade. Lizzie parted her mistress's hair with gentle fingers, careful to avoid the bandage on Edie's brow.

"Ready?" Lizzie asked.

"No," Edie said, "But go on."

"Do you want me to see if I can find another dress? There might be something of your sister's you can borrow," Lizzie said. Edie's eyes snapped open in time to see the scissors snip just over her nose, cutting the hair with a sharp *snick*. A long black strand drifted to the floor.

'What's wrong with the dress?" Edie asked. It had cost a fortune, its deep purple silk an extravagance she'd been denied during the war years. And once the war had ended, she'd been too ill to wear pretty clothes.

Something she was making up for now.

"It just seems a bit dark for a springtime party, doesn't it?" Another snip. "I know Miss Frances has a yellow one put away for the summer. I could press it for you."

"I can't wear yellow to a séance, Lizzie. It just isn't done."

Lizzie froze, the cool metal of the scissors pressed against Edie's eyebrow. "You don't have to go," she said suddenly. "You know that, right?"

Edie peered up at her maid through half-trimmed bangs and decided to let the familiarity pass without comment. "Don't be ridiculous, Lizzie. I must. My sister is the future Mrs. Pepper. She'd be crushed if I didn't go, and people would talk. They'd think I oppose the match. They'd call me jealous." *And the worst part is, they'd be right.* Edie didn't have a choice. She had to attend.

Lizzie's hands trembled as she finished cutting Edie's hair, snipping the strands around her chin, and she didn't say a word as she brushed off the cut bits and picked up the curling rod.

Edie smiled at the girl in the mirror, trying her best to be reassuring. "I know we've had an exciting few days," she said softly. "And I'm sorry about it, Lizzie. But we've come out of it in one piece, haven't we? And I was able to meet your brother. You didn't tell me he was so handsome."

Lizzie made a soft sound as she wound Edie's hair around the hot metal rod. "He's not handsome, Miss Edie. He's my brother."

"Well, believe me. He's handsome, and a doctor to boot. What's he doing hiding away in the city morgue? You'd think he'd have patients lining up to see him."

"It's . . . complicated." Lizzie set the curling rod aside. "He'd be cross if he knew you were planning a night out. You should stay in and rest."

"Well it's a good thing he doesn't know," Edie countered. "I'm fine. You're fine. All's well that ends well, right?"

"We still haven't heard from Miss Rebecca," Lizzie pointed out. "Do you think something's wrong?"

"I'm sure she's fine, too," Edie said. "I'm sure I'll even see her tonight. And then she'll owe us for the rest of her life for abandoning us down there."

Lizzie quirked a smile. She tucked one last pin into Edie's hair and stepped back. "There," she said. "Have a look."

"Must I?" Edie tried to keep her voice light. But she leaned close, turning her head this way and that. She'd expected the worst, but Lizzie had worked some sort of miracle: Edie's newly cropped bangs framed her face, completely hiding the plaster and bruise on her forehead. She had even cut the rest of it into a fashionable bob, the ends curling under her chin. "I look famous. Like Irene Castle," Edie said. She brushed her fingers over the fringe in awe, shocked to find it wasn't anywhere as terrible as she had imagined. "You're a wonder, Lizzie. You mustn't ever leave me, not until the end of time."

Lizzie smiled widely, pink tinging her cheeks, her eyes brightening for the first time since Edie had mentioned the seance.

"You'd be a beauty even without hair at all," she said softly. "But I'm glad you like it."

"Like it? Theo's going to die when he sees me—" Edie cut off abruptly, realizing her words. She forced a laugh instead, light and cheerful. "Well. Maybe I'll catch someone's eye tonight? Wouldn't that be a story?"

"That's the spirit, Miss Edie," Lizzie said. "Onto bigger and better things."

Yes, Edie thought, looking in the mirror as Lizzie held out her long black gloves. In just one weekend, she'd made new friends, became an art model, survived a mugging, and gotten a sharp new haircut.

Bigger and better things were coming. Edie just knew it.

CHAPTER 10

The girl looked even younger under the harsh electric lights of the morgue. Gilbert tried to put aside his personal feelings, but he couldn't stop staring at the small, pale body of the young woman, ready for her autopsy. His anger simmered just under the surface as he washed his hands. Gilbert had seen terrible things in his time as a coroner's assistant. Things that would haunt a normal man, things that should keep him up at night, if his dreams weren't already occupied by the terrors he'd witnessed during war. But he had a suspicion that this girl, and the casual cruelty of her death, would follow him to the grave.

Based on the evidence, the girl was already dead when the killer made his first cut. A small blessing.

Marco finished washing the instruments and laid them out in a neat row on the porcelain counter beside the autopsy table. He sighed, and shook his head, sending a pomade-stiff lock of hair flopping over his forehead. "Do you think they'll find him? Whoever did this?" he asked.

Gilbert paused, his pen blotting on the paper. "I think hell has a better chance of freezing over," he said. "Especially if Mayor Moore wants to keep this quiet."

"Her family might take issue with that," Marco pointed out.

"If she even has a family." Gilbert looked down at the girl. With her eyes closed, she looked so young. Sarah's face, pale and still, swam through his mind, and he shook his head, banishing the memory. "You know that as well as I do. Girls die all the time."

"Girls like her, though?" Marco shook his head. "This isn't some immigrant girl hustling to make a living, Lawless. Look at her nails, her hair. That face. She had money."

And money talked.

Gilbert set aside the paperwork and checked his watch. It was just past noon. Dr. Knight was scheduled to introduce a speaker at the medical college in less than an hour. If they left now, they would be able to speak with him about the girl, convince him to return as soon as the lecture was over. And with any luck, Finnegan Pyle would be able to match her with someone reported missing. Because Marco was right—a girl like her would be missed.

It was a quick walk from the morgue at Thirteenth and Wood Street to Hahnemann Medical College, where Dr. Knight still taught several classes per term. Knight was the rare coroner with a medical degree, and unlike his predecessors, he didn't see the office as a stepping stone to further political glory, but as his calling. Gilbert was proud to work beneath him and would forever be grateful to his former professor who had offered him a lifeline during his darkest days.

Still, Gilbert hesitated on the red-brick steps before the building, his hands shoved far into his coat pockets to hide his trembling fingers. This place . . . these halls. They would always be a reminder of his failures as a doctor. As a man.

"That's where we're going, yeah?" Marco asked, utterly unaware of Gilbert's nerves. He pointed his chin at a large poster behind a glass screen at the front door.

Community Lecture: Dr. Arthur Van Pelt on the European Advances on the Use of Galvanism on Limb Paralysis in Wounded Veterans. Hahnemann Medical College, Main Lecture Hall. Sunday, April 24, 1:00 PM.

"Galvanism." Gilbert's jaw clenched tight. "They can't be serious."

"Electric shock therapy has proven useful in several areas, especially in asylums," Marco replied. He tugged the door open. "Why not limb paralysis?"

"Duchenne tried it, and all it did was maim the patient," Gilbert said. "As it stands now, it's barbaric. *Especially* in asylums," he added, parroting Marco's words back at him. And then he felt bad about the tone of his voice—it wasn't Marco's fault. Marco didn't know. Marco . . .

Marco laid a hand on Gilbert's shoulder. "I'm sorry," he said. "You're right. Sometimes . . . sometimes it's easy to forget that their patients aren't like ours."

Gilbert accepted the apology with a duck of his head as they headed inside, their shoes ringing on the black and white marble floor. Straight ahead, the doors to the main lecture hall were closed, muffling the sound of voices behind thick, polished wood. The last time Gilbert had stood here, this foyer had been full, the bodies of the dead stacked like cords of firewood as Gilbert and Marco and the others had worked to save the sick before they succumbed themselves.

Gilbert had been home barely a month the first time Dr. Knight came to see him. Despite his combat decorations from over a year of service as a medical officer in the AEF, Gilbert had been wounded and discharged after the second battle of the Marne, when the Army doctors had tried everything to treat him and failed. His fits came more often back then—his limbs convulsed and his brain went black—and he spent most days locked in his dark childhood bedroom, unable to get out of bed. Dr. Knight, who had been Gilbert's professor, visited often. He had just been named coroner, and within a few weeks, had convinced Gilbert to join him as an assistant. Knight had understood that Gilbert's fits and shakes would render him unable to ever practice medicine, and despite this, the older man had offered him a lifeline, one Gilbert gladly grabbed.

And then the influenza struck, spreading through Philadelphia like wildfire. The hospitals were quickly overwhelmed, and those with any medical training—like Gilbert—were needed more for the living than the dead as doctors and nurses fell victim by the dozens, infected by the people they were trying to save. The flu was an enemy as deadly as mustard gas, as relentless as mortar shells. There was no rest, no quarter given.

The influenza had spared so very few.

But the foyer was still now, the polished marble floors shined and gleaming.

He gripped the handle of the door harder than necessary in order to calm his tremor and slipped inside the auditorium. The lecture would begin shortly, but until then, the men from Hahnemann Medical College and a handful of women from the nearby Female Medical College of Pennsylvania were standing, chatting, milling about from their seats in the warm air.

"Do you see Knight?" Marco asked.

Gilbert scanned the crowd, searching for their mentor. His gaze caught the tall, white-haired man near the front. He was speaking to three others: a Black man in a neat blue suit, and two young white men, one short and slim with a shock of brown hair, and the other a tall, broad-shouldered blond.

Dr. Knight waved as they approached. "Ah, good. You're here."

Knight's companions turned to get a look at them. The Black doctor gave Gilbert a friendly nod. The smaller white man looked familiar, in a way Gilbert couldn't place. But the blond . . .

"Gil, Marco, I'm sure you remember Artie Van Pelt and Theo Pepper, don't you?"

Gilbert felt his heart drop to his shoes. *Stay here*, he told himself. His finger tapped furiously against his thigh. *Stay here. Stay here.*

Marco launched into small talk. Gilbert barely heard him. He couldn't spare the attention, not when Theo was standing before him, healthy and whole. His eyes, so like his sister's, stared directly into Gilbert's own.

Gilbert took a half step backwards. He'd known Theo was back. Lizzie had told him just the other day. But seeing him now—*here*—was a different story.

Theo's mouth lifted in a grin, even as his eyes stayed distant. He'd grown a mustache, Gilbert noticed. It looked terrible. "Hello, Gilbert."

"Theo."

"Ah." Dr. Knight's face flushed scarlet beneath the auditorium lights as the puzzle pieces clicked together. "Of course. I forgot you were acquainted."

Gilbert gave a tight nod. He stepped in close, angling his body away from Theo and toward Dr. Knight's.

"Actually, sir," Gilbert said, voice pitched low. "I was wondering if I could speak with you privately. About this morning's case."

Knight nodded, and the two stepped a few feet away, leaving Theo behind with the others. "The car accident. I assume you and Marco have everything in hand?"

"It wasn't a car accident," Gilbert said. He leaned in, dropping his voice even further. "You need to see it. As soon as you can."

Knight's mouth compressed into a thin line. "The Mayor won't be happy about this." He looked to the big clock at the rear of the auditorium—five minutes to one—and sighed. "Your timing could be better."

"We can wait," Gilbert said, but the other man shook his head.

"Moore will have my head if we don't get this settled quickly." He picked his jacket and hat up from his seat in the front row. To the others, he said, "Gentlemen. I'm afraid I'm going to have to return to the morgue at once. Duty calls."

"You're missing the lecture, William?" Van Pelt's face dropped in disappointment. "I was hoping you'd be here."

"I know, Artie," Knight said, apologetically. "I'm so sorry, and please know that we are all so excited to have you join the faculty. Perhaps Dr. Pepper could introduce you?"

Color rose in Theo's cheeks, and his terrible mustache twitched. "Of course. Of course. I'd be honored."

"May I come?" The Black doctor detached himself from his conversation with Marco. "Not to interrupt, but I find your work fascinating, Dr. Knight. I'd love to learn more."

Knight didn't miss a beat. "Of course, Dr. Harrison. We can always use more good doctors in our department.".

"Gilbert Lawless." Theo stepped up beside him, his voice pitched low, despite the hum of the auditorium, as Knight and the others started for the aisle. "Should have figured we'd run into each other, sooner or later."

Gilbert had hoped he'd never see Theo or any other Pepper ever again. "Stay away from my family," he said, instead.

Theo didn't even blink. "I'm not the one with a history of forgetting my place," he said.

Gilbert fisted his hand at his side, but he turned on his heel and left. Theo's low voice echoed in his head long after he rejoined the others, chasing him all the way back to the morgue.

"This should have been simple," Knight said, his well-heeled shoes ringing on the tile floor when they arrived in the autopsy room. He picked up the notebook near the door, his eyes scanning Gilbert's notes from the scene. His face paled. He handed the notebook to Dr. Harrison and hurried to the autopsy table. Gilbert had drawn a sheet over the girl before they left; it hadn't seemed right to leave her so exposed.

Knight lifted the sheet and swore. He swiveled, fixing his assistants with a penetrating stare. "Do you know who this is?"

"No sir," Gilbert said. "There was no identification at the scene."

The coroner pinched the bridge of his nose. He knew the girl, Gilbert realized. Marco had been right. Whoever she was, she had moved in the same society circles as their boss.

Before he could ask for her name, Knight said, "She was found like this?"

"Yes, sir," Marco answered. "The photos are developing now, but as you'll see, there was no evidence of an accident. Most likely, she was dead by the time she was dumped along East River Drive."

"Definitely dead. And drained of blood shortly postmortem," Gilbert added. "There's no bruising or pooling on the body. And there's another thing, sir—whoever did this removed her organs."

Knight had returned his attention to the girl. He lifted her arm and inspected her hands, the insides of her arm. But Gilbert's words made him look up sharply. "What?"

"Heart, lungs, digestive system—all gone. Even her reproductive organs." Gilbert tried not to look at her as he spoke. He kept his eyes focused on the coroner, who had gone even paler behind his spectacles and thick white mustache. "The killer knew what he was doing."

Knight's frown deepened. He rolled his sleeves and held out his hand expectantly. Gilbert was ready with the magnifying glass, though Knight wouldn't have to look too closely to see that the girl had been gutted like a deer. The killer had sliced her down the middle, peeling her open like a piece of fruit.

Dr. Knight muttered a string of profanities under his breath as he inspected the body, dictating to Gilbert in short, sharp sentences.

"Look in her eyes. Tell me what you notice." Knight beckoned his assistants close and pulled the overhead light to focus on the corpse's face.

Gilbert set his notebook on the table beside him and approached the body, taking the magnifying glass from Dr. Knight's outstretched hand. He bent low and peered into her eyes, the blue irises clouded over and surrounded by small reddish spots in the whites of her eyes. Broken capillaries, caused by a lack of oxygen. He frowned and stood, taking care to close her eyelids. "Petechial hemorrhaging is present," he said.

"Very good, Dr. Lawless. Dr. Salvatore? Dr. Harrison? Anything to add?"

"We noted a needle mark on her upper arm," Marco said, pointing to the small red dot. "We assume she was drugged, but without blood or any organs, we can't be sure."

"Good." Knight turned to Harrison. "What else?"

Harrison leaned low on the other side of the table and ran his fingers along the girl's throat. "Her windpipe is concave, and there's faint bruising on this side." He fit his own hand over her neck and winced. "It's about the size of my hand—too large for a woman's. The killer is most likely a man?"

Marco and Gilbert had been so focused on her chest wound, that they both failed to notice the obvious: the girl, whoever she was, had been strangled before she was mutilated.

"But why?" There was a dark fury behind Marco's gaze, his mouth set in a hard line. "Why would anyone go through all this trouble?"

"That's not our job," Knight reminded his assistants, though his voice had lost some of its certainty. He crossed the room to the sink and washed his hands as he spoke. "Our job is to record how she died. We'll leave it to Detective Pyle to figure out who did this and why."

Gilbert and Marco exchanged glances. "Yes, sir," Marco muttered.

"Get the report typed and close her up. I need . . . I need to call her father. Be gentle with her, make sure she's presentable. They don't need to see her like this."

He didn't wait for them to acknowledge him before he was gone, taking Dr. Harrison with him. Gilbert picked up the needle and thread from the tray beside the table. He looked up at Marco. "I'll stitch if you write?"

"Deal," Marco said, but his eyes never left the body. "Who do you think she is?" he asked, after a moment. "Knight recognized her immediately."

"It's not our concern." Gilbert's stomach twisted as he parroted Dr. Knight's words at his partner, but the other young man only scowled at him before turning his back, the furious scratch of his pen against paper the only sound in the room.

Gilbert pulled the sheet up over the girl, giving her as much dignity as he could. He understood Marco's anger, his drive to right the world's wrongs. The Gilbert Lawless he'd been before the war would have burned with the same fire, the same righteousness. But that was before Gilbert learned that there was no such thing as right or wrong. No such thing as justice.

CHAPTER 11

Edie decided to take advantage of the pleasantly cool evening air and walk to Theo's. Franny had gone over early to oversee party preparations, and Lizzie had been given the evening off—and, based on her reaction to the mere suggestion of a séance, she wouldn't have been keen to accompany Edie, anyway. She could have asked for their driver, but all of that would have taken longer than the walk itself did. The Peppers' home was only a short distance from her family's summer estate, closer to the hustle and bustle of Germantown Avenue, just on the other side of the station where Lizzie and Edie had boarded the train to Center City the day before. Edie trailed her fingers on the sturdy stone railings as she crossed the bridge over the tracks, willing her nerves to steady.

She had nothing to fear. She would make a splash tonight as a new woman with the hair to match. *Watch out, world.*

The Peppers' butler answered the door as soon as she knocked. He gave her a pitying smile, which she answered with her most dazzling grin. She'd be damned before she accepted his pity. Or anyone else's.

"Your sister and Dr. Pepper are in the library, Miss Edith."

"Thank you, Hampton." She handed him the wrap she'd worn, as the spring night had a bite about it, and breezed into the foyer. "I know the way."

And she did. She knew every inch of the Pepper family's house and grounds as well as she knew her own. She had spent countless hours beside Theo and Franny there as children, terrorizing the staff and getting into all sorts of mischief. Before the war, Theo and Edie had spent long, languid afternoons hidden in one room or another as he painted, drew, sketched. Her knees weakened as she remembered the way his fingers stroked her skin and his mouth whispered promises they'd both believed he'd keep. She'd been so certain that all of this would one day be hers. Theirs, together. Her chin wobbled only a little as she shoved those memories into the past where they belonged and pushed open the door to the library.

Only to find Franny and Theo locked in a passionate embrace on the leather chesterfield sofa. Her stomach felt as if it would hit the floor as Frances gave Theo a shove and flushed scarlet, her hands scrambling to the front of her dress, and Theo turned quickly, adjusting his own clothing.

"Oh, thank goodness," Franny said, realizing it was her sister. She let out a breathless giggle. "It's just Edie."

Edie's smile felt as pasted on as the bandage covering her forehead. "Just me!" she said, a touch too brightly. "But perhaps a bit more discretion in the future, dear?" She crossed the room quickly and helped Frances straighten her hair, trying her best to ignore the red streaking across Franny's neck and jaw.

"What time is it?" Theo asked. He was looking everywhere but at Edie. Her heart dropped down to her toes.

"Oh, silly me, I forgot a watch." Edie's voice came out sharper than she intended. She couldn't look at them without feeling as if her own heart was breaking in the process.

"Half past seven," Frances said brightly. "Edie, what on earth have you done to your hair?"

"Oh, this?" Edie patted one of the curls framing her chin. "I thought it was time for a change. I don't want anyone mistaking me for the future Mrs. Pepper, after all."

Frances stared at her sister as if she'd grown a second head. *Maybe I have*, Edie thought. Maybe her fall had addled her brains, because in that moment, she'd wanted Frances to feel bad about stealing every single one of her dreams for the future.

But then the moment passed, and Edie was left feeling terrible all over again. Thankfully, the others arrived, and she was spared from having to think too deeply about it.

Artie Van Pelt was the first to step into the room. More interesting than Artie was the woman on his arm, who towered over him by about four inches. A modern Amazon constructed of power and grace and swathed in shimmering black taffeta. Even her lipstick was dark enough to be considered black.

She didn't say much as Artie made the rounds, introducing her to his school friends. Edie watched as she inclined her head, lowered her chin, and fluttered her lashes as she moved from person to person, her quiet demeanor at odds with her statuesque appearance. She didn't seem the type of person who could swindle an entire room full of people, but then again, who would believe anyone who *did* seem the type? Edie took a canapé and a gin cocktail from one of the footmen and perched on the edge of the nearest table, eager to observe as they drew closer. What on earth was such a woman doing with someone as dreadful as Artie?

"Hello, stranger," Ophelia said, clinking her glass against Edie's, her voice pitched low. "Thank you again for yesterday."

"I'm glad I could help," Edie replied. "If you ever need another model . . ."

Ophelia laughed. "How about something a little less formal? We all meet up on Wednesday evenings, at my apartment in Rittenhouse. I'll ask Rebecca to send over the address."

"You've seen her, then?" Edie looked up. "I'd like to have a few words with her. I can't believe she stood me up yesterday."

Ophelia frowned, then craned her neck to survey the room, the emeralds in her ears glittering in the library's low light. "No. I thought she'd be here—she isn't? Oh—baloney. My brother. I can't stand to talk to him right now."

"Edie Shippen, in the flesh." Artie appeared as Ophelia darted off. He took Edie's hand and bent low over it. "I had hoped to speak with you the other night, but you really made yourself scarce."

"Well, I'm here now," Edie said, trying to keep the annoyance out of her voice. Ophelia scurried to the veranda, shutting the door behind her.

"That you are. I want to introduce you to my friend, Miss Celeste DuPont."

"Please, call me Celeste," the medium said. Her voice was surprisingly deep, and her eyes, wide and black, fixed on Edie's with a startling intensity. Edie swallowed, then gave the medium a gracious nod.

"Celeste, this is Miss Edith Shippen," Artie said. "We've known each other for ages."

"Since our school days," Edie confirmed, her smile tight. "Frances said you gave quite the lecture yesterday, Artie. She said you and Theo have been working together?"

He nodded. "Yes, yes—we're working on using electromagnetic currents to help restore limb mobility to paralyzed war veterans. My research suggests—oh, say, is that Nick? He owes me on a bet. Excuse me." He darted off, waving his hand to get the other man's attention.

Celeste sipped her drink. "Shippen, you say? Are you related to Rebecca?"

"My cousin," Edie replied, then gasped as Celeste reached forward and grasped Edie's arm. Her nails dug furrows into Edie's skin, forcing Edie to focus on her.

"Is she here tonight?" she asked, voice low. "She missed an appointment yesterday. I'm concerned about her."

"I haven't seen her," Edie answered.

Celeste frowned. "Tell Rebecca to call me, as soon as you can. I must speak with her. She'll know what it's about."

"I—I promise," Edie stuttered. She stared after the medium, struck speechless, as she moved on to the next set of guests. Edie took a quick glance around the room, curious to see if anyone else had noticed, but no one seemed to be paying any mind.

Edie straightened her spine, grasping desperately for her composure even as her fingers still felt Celeste's desperate grip, the intensity of her stare. She wished, suddenly, that she had asked Lizzie to accompany her. She dismissed the feeling as immediately as it came on—she was a new, independent woman. She didn't need to hide in the shadows, whispering with her ladies' maid. Even if that maid had saved her life.

She's not my friend, Edie reminded herself. Lizzie was her servant. Her actions weren't out of kindness or heroism: she was simply doing her job.

Edie looked around the library, at the small groups clustered around the room, waiting for the evening to get underway, at the people she had known for her entire life, her school chums and the boys they'd chased together, as they gossiped and flirted. Edie realized that she wanted nothing to do with any of them except for Ophelia, who was laughing at a joke Edie hadn't heard.

She lifted a hand to her forehead and brushed the bandage under her bangs as the ache behind her eyes intensified.

Maybe she had addled her brains, after all.

After an excruciatingly long dinner full of idle chit-chat, Edie's head felt like it would explode at any moment. She sipped at her drink in a shadowed corner of the library and contemplated slipping away into the night. Surely, no one would miss her. Ophelia was busy flirting with half the room. Even Frances had barely spoken two words to her; her sister had been thoroughly monopolized all through dinner and dessert, as their schoolmates *oohed* and *ahhed* over the carats on Frances' left hand. Edie had found herself feeling very much like an afterthought.

Edie had never before been an afterthought.

She stepped backwards, slipping through the door leading to the long veranda. Maybe Celeste would be outside, and Edie could ask her more about how the medium knew Rebecca. But the veranda was nearly deserted; only a solitary figure leaned against the rail, lit only by the glowing ember at the tip of his cigarette. *Theo.* When had he left the party?

She hesitated for a half-heartbeat. She shouldn't approach him. Shouldn't be alone out here with him, not where people could see.

They'd talk.

Another peal of laughter carried through the open window, and suddenly, Edie didn't care. *Let them talk,* she decided. She straightened her shoulders and joined her former beau at the railing.

He passed her the cigarette without comment, the way he'd done a million times before, the brush of his fingers against hers throwing an electric thrill up her arm. He smiled down at her, the gentle tilt of his mouth sending her insides into a tizzy.

"Edie." Her name was a statement, not a question.

"I needed some air," she said. She took a quick drag, holding the smoke in her lungs for a moment before exhaling, imagining she was releasing the pressure in her skull.

"So did I," he said. For a moment, he sounded just like the boy she remembered, baring his heart to her. "Sometimes, since I've been home . . . well. Sometimes it's hard."

Edie passed the cigarette back to him and propped her elbows on the banister. "I know exactly what you mean," she said honestly, like they'd never been apart, like he wasn't marrying her sister.

"Do you?" His eyebrows rose and Edie felt instantly foolish. Of course she didn't know what he meant. She'd never know what horrors he'd seen, or what it must have felt like to have been hurt the way he was. *Wounded in no-man's land,* Frances' letter had said. Edie shuddered, thinking again about how close she'd been to losing him.

"Frances says you suffer from migraines," he said, drawing her out of her thoughts. "How long has that been going on?"

Frances again. Edie waved her hand dismissively, despite the pain wrapping her head. "Oh, don't worry about that. It's nothing but a leftover from the flu. A little souvenir."

"I'm sorry I wasn't here." He frowned in the evening air. "It was bad over there, too. Bad everywhere, I suppose. But it was hard, being so far from home, knowing that the people I loved here were suffering."

Loved. He had loved her, once—past tense. Edie's heart broke a little more. She'd never stopped loving him, even in the long years they'd been apart. He had been so sweet, so gentle as a boy. Always playing her knight in shining armor.

"You had enough to worry about," she said, before she could stop herself. "When I heard you'd been shot, I—I feared the worst. And then when you headed back to the trenches, I worried you'd used up your luck, but you made it through the war. And then medical school! A doctor. It makes sense that you were too busy to write. I don't blame you for not thinking about me."

"I never said I didn't think about you." He handed her back the cigarette, which she accepted without comment. Her face burned as she smoked—she'd said too much, hadn't she? Revealed too much. She couldn't even look at him as she passed the cigarette back.

"I've been thinking about your headaches," he said, changing the subject. "You know, there's been some research suggesting electric therapy—"

"Theo?" Frances' voice called from the doorway, interrupting whatever Theo was going to say next. "Are you out—oh. Edie. I didn't even notice you weren't inside." Her gaze bounced between them, her face unreadable in the darkness. "We're waiting on you, dears. Are you feeling better?"

Theo stubbed out the cigarette and tossed the butt into the garden below. "I feel wonderful now that you're here," he said, tucking his arm around Frances' shoulders. He kissed her cheek, his entire body curving toward hers. She leaned into him with a happy sigh.

Edie's nails bit into her palms as she followed them back into the library, where the entire party waited around an octagonal table, the kind gentlemen usually played cards around after dinner. But the cards and cigars were absent; instead, a dozen of Philadelphia's richest and brightest young things pressed together, knees and thighs and elbows close enough to fill the scandal sheets. Ophelia rolled her eyes toward Celeste Dupont, who sat at the head of the table, her back as regal and ramrod straight as a warrior queen of old.

Edie slid into the last open seat, smashed between Frances and Ophelia, and looked up, catching Celeste's eye. The medium gave her a small, secretive smile . . . and then the lights switched off, plunging the room into darkness. Matches whispered as flames danced to life on candlesticks, a slight of hand produced by the Pepper's veritable army of black-clad household staff.

Celeste leaned back slightly as a single candle—a fat onyx pillar—was placed on the table in front of her, its flame flickering in the slight breeze from the open windows.

"Welcome to all—both the living and the dead," Celeste purred. "To the living: please join your hands, open your hearts and your minds to the great beyond. To the dead: we welcome you."

A chill worked its fingers down Edie's spine, and against her will, she shivered. On her left, Frances pressed her knee to her sister's and twined their fingers together. "All right?" Frances whispered.

"Just a chill," Edie whispered back. "I—"

"We must have silence." Celeste's voice, stern as a governess, cut through Edie's excuses. The medium stared at her from across the table, her dark eyes like liquid pools of blackness. She paused for a moment, allowing her words to linger, before she continued. "Now. As I said. Join hands."

Edie reached her right hand out and found Ophelia's cool, small palm.

"Close your eyes," Celeste continued in the same slow, measured tone. "Tonight, we gather and bid welcome to the spirit world. If there are good spirits here, please make yourself known."

All around the table, everyone's eyes snapped shut. Edie's were slower to close, her skepticism rising as silence was the only response to Celeste's plea.

"Spirits," Celeste said again. "Please. Make yourselves known."

A sharp rapping noise came from the center of the table, startling them all. Edie's eyes flew open as Frances nearly leapt from the seat beside her, her fingers clamped so hard that Edie could swear she felt their bones grind together.

"That's not funny." Edie looked around the table until her gaze collided with Theo's—the only other person disobeying Celeste's instructions.

"It wasn't me," he said, but he smirked, the way he had when they were children and he and his sister were up to mischief.

"It was a communication from the beyond." Celeste's tone brokered no argument. "Spirit, we welcome you."

Edie settled back in her chair, forcing herself to take a deep, calming breath and closed her eyes. She wouldn't let Celeste, or anyone else, scare her silly.

"Do you wish us harm?"

Edie's eyes opened, but the table was silent. A presumable *no*. Frances' fingers loosened ever so slightly,

"Are you a good spirit?" Celeste pressed.

Another knock.

"In life, were you known to anyone assembled here?"

Another knock.

Gasps filled the room, but Celeste continued her line of questions. "Can you show yourself?"

The knock this time came after a pause. Like it was less sure. Or maybe because it was all a great act.

"Show yourself," Celeste whispered.

The full weight of her migraine settled over Edie—a sharp, cold pain radiating from up from the back of her neck and over the top of her head. From there, it inched down over her scalp, her ears, her face. Her open eyes.

Across the table, Celeste sat still, her head thrown back, her eyes open and rolled until all Edie could see was a sliver of white peeking out from between dark lashes.

"I see . . ." she said, her voice breaking, limbs twitching. "I see . . ."

Edie leaned forward, squinting into nothingness. Goosebumps raced over her flesh, and her teeth chattered, her jaw quivering. Her head hurt so badly—she needed to find somewhere to hide until it was over. She needed to go home.

"A young woman." Celeste gasped out. "A woman with child, taken too soon."

The table erupted in whispers. Theo lurched forward, pain lancing his words. "Sarah?"

Edie's chest seized tight. Theo had felt his sister's loss so keenly—she remembered holding him as he wept when they learned the news. Her death had broken something in Theo, had ripped something wide open. To bring it up now, like this? Scandal or not, this was too much.

This was cruelty.

Her chair hit the floor as she scrambled backwards from the table, her ice-cold fingers pressed against her temples. She tripped over something in the darkness and fell with a shriek. She had to get outside. Had to breathe.

"Edie?" Frances was beside her in an instant. "Are you all right?"

"My head," Edie said. "I need—"

"I'm here," Frances's hands found Edie's in the darkness, and she pulled Edie to her feet.

"You don't think—?" Someone else asked.

"Will someone turn on the damn lights?" Theo growled.

Overhead, the lights blazed on, sending stars dancing across Edie's vision. She moaned in pain and rolled, covering her eyes with her palms.

"Edie, darling." Frances' hands were warm on Edie's upper arms, gentle as she helped Edie to a nearby sofa. "Let's take a moment. We'll call for your medicine."

She couldn't see. She couldn't breathe. She couldn't think, couldn't move, not when the iron bands around her clamped down, holding her still.

Hands, she realized, belatedly. Then, a pinprick, sharp and fierce, a moment before heat surged through her veins.

"There." Theo's voice was velvet in her ear. "Don't be scared, Edie. Everything is all right"

"Was that necessary?" Frances asked from far away. Everything was far away, Edie realized, and sagged back against Theo's warm, solid chest. Her vision dimmed.

"It won't hurt her," Artie said. "It's just to sedate her until her spell passes. She'll be as right as rain in the morning."

"She hasn't been the same since the flu. She's very delicate," Frances was saying. Edie tried to focus on her words, on the firm grip of Theo's arms, as comfortable and familiar as her favorite blanket as she drifted off into the darkness.

CHAPTER 12

On Monday morning, Cecelia stopped by Gilbert's desk a few minutes after eight o'clock with a hot cup of coffee and a fat file folder. He took the mug and the paperwork with a nod of thanks. She lingered, resting her hip on the scarred wooden desk corner, arms crossed over her chest. She swept a critical gaze over him, frowning at the dark circles he knew rested beneath his eyes.

"Morning, Gil," she said. "You look like you needed this."

"Thanks." The coffee was black and bracing—exactly the way he preferred it. "Have a nice weekend?"

She smiled widely. "Yes, actually. Bette and I went to the pictures, and then afterwards we went dancing at Club Rouge. I think I may have even met someone."

Gilbert sipped his coffee and made an agreeable noise. He wasn't sure why Cecelia felt the need to tell him this, or what the proper response was. *Congratulations* felt premature, and maybe a little rude. Best not to say anything at all.

"Have you been there? Club Rouge, I mean," she asked. At his blank look, she gave a little laugh and adjusted her glasses. "No. Of course not. You don't seem like the dancing type, Gil. No offense."

"None taken," he said.

"It's the bee's knees, really. Everything's red. And the band is to die for." She gave a happy little sigh and pushed off the desk. "Maybe we can go sometime. If you change your mind about the dancing."

He took a big gulp of coffee, scalding his mouth, the hot liquid burning down his throat. He sputtered.

She laughed. "Enjoy the java, Gilbert. Knight has scheduled a meeting with the family at ten, and a press conference with the police at eleven. He wants you and Marco both there. Look sharp, okay?"

And then she was gone, leaving Gilbert with a burnt tongue and an uncomfortable swirling in his stomach. He wasn't sure if it was from the idea of standing in the front of a room full of reporters with their flash-bang cameras, or at the prospect of being in proximity to Finnegan Pyle for any prolonged amount of time.

He finished his coffee and opened the folder Cecelia had pulled together. Inside was the neatly typed incident report for the girl they'd found by the river. Marco's photos of the scene followed. More notes were inside—pathology had returned their analysis. Despite the missing organs and lack of blood, they'd found traces of morphine in the girl's iliac arteries. She'd been drugged, then strangled. Then mutilated, both with a sharp blade and whatever had left those strange scorch marks on her wrists and ankles. The killer, as deranged as they clearly were, had been very precise.

Marco arrived a little after nine. He collapsed into his chair, sending a pile of papers cascading to the floor. His desk, pressed opposite of Gilbert's, was a health hazard; stacked high with unfinished reports, candy wrappers, forgotten cups of coffee. Gilbert reached forward and pushed some of Marco's mess back over from where it encroached onto Gilbert's own workspace.

"All right?" Gilbert asked.

Marco groaned. He pressed his hands over his eyes and leaned back in his chair, far enough that Gilbert was amazed he didn't topple over. "No. Not even a little."

Gilbert didn't give him a chance to elaborate. He held out the file. "Look at this."

Marco sat up at that and took the papers. He flipped through them carefully, his frown deepening as he read. "There's something . . ." he muttered, his voice trailing off. Then he stopped, his face paling. He raked a hand against his scalp, mussing his carefully pomaded hair. "Wait. Wait." He dropped the file on his desk. Gilbert grabbed it as Marco shuffled through one of his piles, clearly searching for something. "I know it's here."

Gilbert leaned forward. "What?"

"There was another—here." He tugged a file from the middle of the pile, sending the others sliding across his desk. He flipped it open to a crime scene photo. "The headless girl you autopsied on Friday, the one from the creek. The lab work came back the same. Large amounts of morphine in her system. And those burn marks on the wrists. It can't be a coincidence."

Gilbert studied the crime scene photo—he hadn't seen it before the autopsy. It was even more gruesome than the body on its own had been, somehow. The headless body wore a dark dress and white apron, that, while intact, was stained dark and torn in several places. From the photos, it wasn't clear if the staining was mud or blood. But still—something about the woman's apron caught Gilbert's attention—black embroidery at the center of the sash. He opened his drawer and retrieved his magnifying glass from its designated place without taking his gaze from the picture. "Did anyone ever get any identification?"

Marco shook his head. "Pyle said it was a dead end when I sent him the report, and we had her buried in the potter's field yesterday. Why?"

Gilbert leaned close, even though he knew exactly what he'd find stitched at the waistband of the woman's apron. The magnifying glass focused, bringing the blurred, bloodstained sash into focus, where a black, swirling S rested, surrounded by a delicately embroidered oval. Most young women in this city hired on as maids wore similar garb—dark dress, white apron, and sturdy shoes. But there was one house in particular who enforced a strict dress code for the help. One household who branded their employees with an S, from the housekeeper to the footmen to the maids in the scullery. Gilbert knew this, because he'd seen it a million times on his own sister.

He set the magnifying glass down, mindful of the tremor in his hand. He had a sudden, desperate need to call Lizzie, to make sure she was all right, even though he'd seen her the day before, and this poor girl—someone she *knew*—had been dead on his table last week. How had Pyle overlooked this evidence? Gilbert had his personal reservations about the man, but even he was forced to admit that Pyle was, generally, good at his job. A sour feeling spread through his middle.

"Marco," he said, "What time is it?"

Marco frowned and checked his watch. "9:30. Why?"

"I need to call my sister," Gilbert said. "This girl worked for Councilman Shippen, and Lizzie can tell us who she was."

The row of phones on the other side of the bullpen was blessedly deserted. Gilbert slipped into one of the booths, pulling the glass door closed behind him.

"How can I connect your call?" The operator at the other end of the line asked.

"Shippen House, Chestnut Hill," Gilbert said.

"One moment."

As Gilbert waited, he read through the carefully typed report in the file. Cecelia had combined his notes from the autopsy with Dr. Knight's observations. And stapled to the end, just as Marco had remembered, the report from the lab upstairs. Morphine.

Drugged and electrocuted.

"Shippen House," a man on the other side of the telephone line answered, interrupting Gilbert's thoughts. "How may I help you?"

"This is Dr. Lawless from the city coroner's office. I'm looking for Lizzie."

The voice on the other side was silent for a moment. "What's this about? I can assure you—"

"Official business," Gilbert said quickly. "Please. It'll only take a moment."

"Hold, please." The line clicked, and Gilbert hoped Lizzie wasn't in the middle of something important. Christ, Lizzie would kill him with her bare hands if this cost his sister her position.

A moment later, the line clicked again. Lizzie, sounding breathless, spoke first. "This is Lizzie."

"Liz." Gilbert clutched the receiver with both hands. "It's me."

Her voice dropped to a hiss. "What are you doing, calling me at work? You know how Mrs. Smith is."

"Last weekend, on the way out to Mam's. You said a girl had quit with no notice."

"Yeah. Right before the party. The whole staff was in a tizzy."

"Who was she?"

"What?" A familiar note of irritation crept into her voice. "What's this about, Gil? Why are you suddenly curious?"

"A name, Liz. I need a name."

"Dottie Montgomery," Lizzie said. "Why?"

"Dottie Montgomery." The name sounded so familiar. "Do I know her?"

"She used to run with me and Molly Fletcher, when we were in school. I got her the job here, remember?"

Gilbert had a vague memory of a gap-toothed, dark-haired girl in braids. She'd barely been in high school when he went to France But Pyle would have known her, known where she worked—the detective still lived in Manayunk, next door to his parents on Terrace Street, just a block away from the Montgomery family. Across the street from Tommy Fletcher. The sour feeling in his stomach spread.

"When was the last time anyone saw Dottie?"

Lizzie was silent a moment. "Wednesday evening, after dinner service. Her room was empty the next morning—she didn't come down for breakfast, and Mrs. Smith sent me to check on her. You don't . . . she isn't . . ."

"Yeah. I'm sorry, Lizzie." Gilbert swallowed, hard. The headless young woman he'd autopsied had been killed twenty-four to forty-eight hours before she was found on Friday morning. The timeline matched. "Did she take anything with her?"

"That was the strange thing," Lizzie said. "She left all of her things behind—her purse, her clothes. Even her rosary. It was like she'd just vanished."

Not vanished. Murdered.

He had to talk to Dr. Knight immediately. The girl Finnegan Pyle had sent to the potter's field had a name. An identity.

Dottie Montgomery. A girl who'd grown up in his neighborhood. Maid to one of the most powerful men in the whole city. And Finnegan Pyle had sent her to rot without even investigating it.

CHAPTER 13

Edie knew that word of her episode would sweep through the family like a sudden storm on the Schuylkill River—swift and devastating. She wanted to take breakfast in her room to avoid it all, but Lizzie hadn't appeared to wake her. Instead, Annette, her grandmother's stern-faced maid, had shaken Edie awake at half-past nine. Annette muttered to herself the entire time as she pulled and tugged at Edie's hair, intensifying the ache behind Edie's eyes and sending glittering arcs of light dancing across the room. When Edie requested a tray sent up, Annette replied with a curt, "Everyone's expected at breakfast, Miss Edith. Even you."

Still, Edie lingered as long as she could. She settled on the perfect jewelry for the day: hammered gold bracelets that circled her wrists like gauntlets and a dangling pair of earrings. She pressed a hand to the plaster on her forehead, trying to soothe the dull ache, as she stepped into the hall. Raised voices from behind Frances' door stopped Edie short. Her sister didn't yell—she was too ladylike for such outbursts of emotion—but she was close to it now. Lizzie barreled out into the corridor, face red. The door slammed behind her, hard enough that a framed sketch on the small table beside the door fell over, toppling onto the carpet at Edie's feet.

"Lizzie, are you all right?"

"Fine, miss," Lizzie said, though her chin wobbled. She hurried by. "I'm sorry. I'm needed downstairs."

Edie watched her go, frowning. She bent down and picked up the frame that had fallen, and immediately wished she hadn't. She recognized the delicate black strokes at once—it was one of Theo's from before the war. He'd sketched on a sunny day on a bluff high above the creek, capturing the entrance to Hermit's Cave as the light hit it just so. When she'd brought it home, she'd made up an elaborate story about buying it in a gallery on Society Hill. Her mother had called it beautiful, and had it framed.

She put it back on the table gently, her heart aching.

When she arrived at breakfast, her grandmother fixed her with a pointed glare. Edie knew that look. She'd seen it a million times before—when she'd trimmed Franny's hair at age seven and again at ten when Edie, Theo, and their sisters had all stripped down to nothing and painted themselves with the mud from the banks of the Wissahickon, pretending to be the infamous hermit who had spent his days searching for the secret to eternal life. Theo had been obsessed with the legend that the Philosopher's Stone had been thrown into the convergence of the Wissahickon Creek and Schuylkill River, and it was forever getting them into trouble. By now, she had considered herself immune to her grandmother's disappointment.

She was wrong.

"Edith." Flora Shippen sounded pained to even speak her granddaughter's name. "Every time I think you're past your childish impulses, you surprise me yet again."

"Grandmama—" Edie tried to protest, but Flora steamrolled right over her.

"You are the most selfish, spoiled, attention-seeking young woman I've ever encountered. When your sister's fiancé carried you into this house last night, I nearly fainted. I thought you'd died, Edith. Died! How could you?"

"I'm . . . I'm sorry?" Edie had expected a lecture, not worries over her death.

Frances, as always, swooped in to save the day. She appeared in the doorway, her face flushed red, the skin around her eyes puffy, like she'd been crying. "It wasn't Edie's fault, Grandmama. She can't help her headaches." Frances turned to her sister. "Are you sure you're all right?"

The pain behind Edie's eyes intensified. She rubbed at her temple. "Everything's jake," she said.

"Edie." Frances exchanged a long look with their grand-mother, then took a deep breath. "Actually, I'm not sure it is, darling. Theo agrees. He'd like for you to come into his office so he can give you a full exam. That's what I was coming downstairs to tell you—we're leaving at once."

"That's an excellent idea," Flora said. She looked pleased for the first time all morning. "He's a good boy."

"Do I get a say in this?" Edie asked, but Frances was already heading for the front door, where a pair of footmen waited with coats. She hurried after her sister, shrugging into her freshly cleaned blue coat and taking her black musketeer hat and handbag when it was offered. "Franny. Franny, wait!"

Frances kept walking. "We don't have time for this, Edie. We're running late as it is."

"What if I say no?" Edie stopped on the front steps. "I've seen a million doctors, Franny. I don't know what Theo will tell me that I don't already know."

Frances' face softened and her shoulders drooped. Her sister looked defeated. "Theo cares deeply about you, Edie. He just wants to help."

If he cared so deeply, he wouldn't be marrying you, Edie wanted to say. But instead she stepped closer to Frances and put her hand on her sister's arm. Frances leaned close, resting her forehead against Edie's, the way they did when they were girls, and Edie felt herself softening. She needed to stop this. She'd missed Frances terribly when she was away—she needed to stop acting like the spoiled child her grandmother accused her of being and do whatever it took to make her sister happy. Frances deserved that.

"Fine," Edie said. "Let's go."

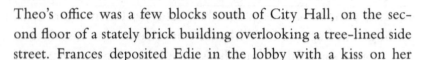

Theo's office was a few blocks south of City Hall, on the second floor of a stately brick building overlooking a tree-lined side street. Frances deposited Edie in the lobby with a kiss on her cheek. "Wait," Edie said. "Aren't you coming up?"

Frances shook her head. Her mood had improved significantly since they'd left Chestnut Hill, the redness around her eyes nearly vanished. "Nonsense, dear," she said. "If I'm going to be a doctor's wife, I need to respect his patients' privacy, don't I? And besides, I thought I'd surprise Daddy at work."

If their situations had been reversed, Edie would have insisted on staying. But that was Frances, wasn't it? Trusting to a fault. Edie had given her sister her blessing, and Frances accepted it. "All right," Edie said. "Tell Daddy I said hello."

"I'll be back in an hour. Don't let Theo get you into trouble," Frances said. And then she was gone, and Edie was left alone in the lobby, staring at the letterboard by the stairs proclaiming *Doc. Th. Pepper: 205.*

Fine. She'd go up and she'd see Theo. She'd play the perfect sister-in-law. Because she and Theo would have to learn how to exist around each other without being together, two planets orbiting Frances' bright, shining star.

Theo didn't have a secretary. Instead, he answered the door when she knocked, pulling it open before she could even lower her hand. "Edie."

"Dr. Pepper." Edie blinked up at the sight of him, tall and golden, his hands on his hips. She had always thought him beautiful, with a face like some sort of ancient hero. Back before the war, he had been a boy who exuded a warmth, a vibrancy, that made him impossible to ignore. She wondered, again, what sort of man had been made in the trenches.

"I didn't think you'd actually come," he said, and Edie had to push down the surge of heat that shot through her at the timbre of his voice. His eyes swept down her, like he was cataloguing every feature. Her eyes, her mouth. The slope of her shoulders, the curve of her waist. He cleared his throat and looked down at his feet.

Edie lifted one shoulder in a shrug. "I take my health very seriously."

Theo stepped backwards, lips twitching. "As do I," he said. It was only then he glanced behind her, finding the hallway empty in either direction. "You're alone?"

"Frances thought she'd visit our father." Edie's hand brushed against Theo's as she entered the office, entirely by accident. As if their hands were magnets, drawn together by nature's unstoppable force.

"Ah." His fingers curled against hers for one single, tantalizing moment.

The interior of Theo's office was comfortable. A small exam table sat off to one side, behind a privacy screen. A black metal box fitted with tubes and wires sat on a table beside it. He had a desk in front of the large windows, where a pile of books was stacked haphazardly, flagged with torn scraps of paper. Two dark paneled-walls were lined with books on anatomy, medicine, and science, in English and French and German. The third, the one directly ahead of Edie, was dominated by a large, framed oil painting. She recognized it immediately as Theo's own work—he'd always loved color and the juxtaposition of dark and light. But she'd never seen Theo's art like this. Short, angry brush strokes of brown and red muddied together in the middle of the canvas, bleeding into the black edges like fingers reaching, grasping.

It looked like one of her migraines brought to life.

"So." Theo touched a hand to the small of her back, his palm hot even through the fabric of her coat. Edie leaned back into him. She'd missed his hands. His touch. "Your headaches."

Edie tore her gaze away from the painting. She turned quickly to face him. His eyes widened in surprise for a moment before they shuttered, his gaze darkening.

There, beneath the man, was the boy she knew. The boy with the curious mind and warm heart. So much had changed in the last four years. She had thought, on the day that she stood on a train platform and embraced him as he marched off to war, that their separation would be temporary. That their love would conquer the miles between them. Even as the years rolled on, Edie believed it was only a matter of time until they'd be together again, twin halves of a whole.

"I like the haircut," he said softly. Pink colored his cheeks as he reached out and twirled a cropped wave around his finger.

They were seventeen again, before the war, before the influenza, and suddenly, nothing mattered. The years vanished in an instant, along with everything standing in their way: the war, California. Frances. With every ounce of her being, Edie wished she could erase the obstacles between them and turn everything back to how it used to be.

"Theo," she whispered. She wasn't sure if it was a plea, an apology, or a command, but that didn't matter. Because he was stepping closer, both hands cupping her face.

Their mouths crashed together, furious and wanting, his tongue slipping between her lips for a single, tantalizing moment before he kissed a hot trail down her neck.

"Theo," she said again, tilting her head back. Somehow, her thighs hit the desk behind her and he pulled at her skirt, hiking it high over her knees. Their mouths met again, hands roaming.

"Edie," His breath shivered down her skin, his touch searing her skin. She turned her head, her gaze settling on the swirling red and brown paint strokes, each one filled with rage—a reminder of everything that had changed.

"Stop." Shame and horror washed over her as she remembered where she was. And when. She pushed him away, even as every inch of her body cried out for his. Frances. He belonged to Frances. She had to remember that. "Stop. Theo. What are we *thinking?*"

He gripped the edge of the desk and leaned over her, his perfect hair mussed, his chest rising and falling as rapidly as her own. "I wasn't."

Of course he wasn't. She shoved at his chest, needing to find her feet. Needing to get away from him, to put space between them. He was engaged to Frances. He'd *chosen* Frances.

"You picked her." She couldn't look at him, not when he was standing so close. She'd lose her nerve and kiss him again. "You should be thinking about her, not me—"

He caught her hand as she pushed at him again, his fingers clamping around her wrist. "I'm sorry," he said, as if that could fix everything.

Edie yanked her arm free and cradled it against her chest. "We can't," she said. "We can't, not ever again. Not while you're going to marry her."

"Edie." He stepped close to her, some of the steel melting away from his frame. He tilted his head, the hard line of his mouth softening, and with it, Edie felt her resolve crumble. "I know things have been difficult. Frances said last night—"

Last night. Frances. His words were sandbags, reinforcing her defenses. "You drugged me," she whispered. "You and Artie."

"You were hurting." He stepped closer and tugged her back into his arms. "We were trying to help you. I know how it feels, how it . . ." he trailed off and shook his head as she rested her head against his chest, his heartbeat warm and solid under her ear. "We're the same, you and me," he said, like it explained everything. "We always have been."

She allowed herself one final moment of weakness. He was right. They were the same—selfish. Impulsive. Two pieces of tinder, just waiting for a spark so they could burn everything around them to ashes.

"You chose her," Edie said again. She pushed away from him, the tears already welling behind her eyes. She crossed to the window. A small figure in a camel coat hurried across the square, holding her hat with one hand. *Frances.* God, she was a terrible sister. At least . . . at least she'd put a stop for it. She turned back to Theo, her voice firm. "I won't be anyone's second choice. Not even yours."

"Edie." He scrubbed his hand through his hair and turned away. "You don't understand. We didn't mean for it to happen. We didn't mean to hurt you."

"It doesn't matter," she said. "This—whatever this was, it's over. It can't ever happen again. You promised Frances you could help me. So do your job. Help me."

A muscle in his jaw twitched, but he didn't argue. He picked up his pen and scribbled something down on a pad of paper. He ripped it free and held it out. "Here. There's been research that a compound of chloral and ergot can help with migraines. This should work better than whatever laudanum you've been taking. But be careful—it's potent stuff. Take only that exact amount, and only in an emergency."

She took the prescription and tucked it into her pocket. She wanted to cry, but she couldn't, not when Frances burst through the door a moment later, a low keening sound bursting from her lips as she slumped to her knees on the floor.

Edie's heart tore. Somehow, Frances knew. She *knew*.

She looked up into Theo's grim face, hysteria rising in her blood.

"Franny," Edie said quickly, falling to her knees beside her sister. "What is it? What's wrong?"

"Oh Edie," Frances wailed. "It's terrible. Rebecca is dead."

CHAPTER 14

Gilbert didn't get a chance to address Dottie Montgomery with Dr. Knight. The press descended upon 1307 Wood Street in a frenzy, shouts and the sound of flashbulbs popping on the street outside carrying through the closed windows. A police escort cleared the way for the family of the girl they'd found on the riverbank. It turned out that Marco had been right: Rebecca Shippen was the daughter of one of the most powerful families in the city.

The same family that had employed Dottie Montgomery.

Gilbert still clutched the folder as Councilman Ned Shippen stepped into the building, his gray-faced brother, Charles, on his arm. The younger Mr. Shippen's eyes were vacant, his steps uneven. He wore the look of a soldier ordered into no-man's land, a grim-faced certainty that he could not imagine the horrors about to befall him.

Gilbert drummed his index finger against his thigh, the gentle cadence grounding him in the moment. *Stay here*, he told himself. *It's Monday morning. Eleven o'clock. Stay here.*

"Bill." The Councilman stopped in front of Dr. Knight, hand outstretched.

"I'm sorry to be seeing you under these circumstances." Dr. Knight said, in his practiced, sympathetic voice.

"It might not be her," Charles said from beside his brother. "She's a strange bird, my Becca. She's probably tucked away somewhere, painting and forgetting the time. Not . . ." His words trailed off, and Gilbert and Marco exchanged a look.

"This way," Dr. Knight said gently. "These are two of my assistants, Doctors Salvatore and Lawless. They were the first on the scene."

Both young men nodded at the Councilman and his brother. Knight led them down the hallway to the viewing room, where Rebecca's body would be displayed beneath one of the glass-topped compartments set into the floor. Cecelia had helped arrange her hair; the girl looked peaceful, almost like she was asleep, but Gilbert knew it would make no difference. Charles Shippen was about to step into a scene that would haunt him for the rest of his life.

Penny's face appeared in Gilbert's mind, and he squashed down the terror that threatened to overwhelm him at the thought of one day encountering her like this, of the life drained from her sweet, cherubic form. Death always won, in the end, and all Gilbert could hope was that he'd be lucky enough to go before his daughter. It was the natural order of things.

He didn't follow the Shippen brothers into the viewing room. He waited outside, his back pressed against the brightly tiled walls as a sharp moan filled the air. Beside him, Marco let out a shaky breath.

"Told you she'd be missed," he said softly.

Councilman Shippen stepped out into the hall, his eyes shining with tears. He looked over at the two assistants, and said, "Do either of you have a light?"

Marco pushed away from the wall, but Gilbert spoke before he had a chance. "I do, sir."

The Councilman tilted his head toward the door at the end of the hall, which led to the private courtyard that led to the alley off of Carlton Street. "Join me for a smoke, son? I could use a bit of company."

Gilbert ignored the confused look that Marco gave him as he stepped around the other man and led the Councilman outside to the small landing and the stairs that led down to the driveway. He tucked the folder under his arm and pulled out his lighter—one he'd carried with him since France, despite the fact he didn't smoke. His commanding officer, Nellie's late husband, had fashioned trench lighters for his squadron of medics from spent machine gun shells. He passed it to Councilman Shippen, who only raised an eyebrow at it before lighting his cigarette. Shippen took a long drag, blew out a ring of smoke, and looked over at Gilbert, his eyes sad.

"You look familiar," the older man said. "I'll be damned if I know why. You ever work in politics?"

"No, sir." Gilbert tucked the trench lighter into his pocket. He rested his arms on the rusting metal railing. The last time they'd seen each other, Gilbert had been thrown out of the Peppers' household with an infant Penny in his arms. He had thought that Sarah's parents would want a relationship with their granddaughter after Sarah's death, but he'd been wrong. Shippen had been there, stone-faced, as Sarah's mother wept and her father raged. Gilbert wasn't fool enough to remind the Councilman of that evening.

"I'll think of it." Shippen took another puff of his cigarette. He, too, leaned against the rail, mirroring Gilbert's pose, his golden cuff-links glittering in the morning sun. "Knight said you were at the scene. There wasn't—there wasn't anything you could do to help her?"

"No, sir," Gilbert said again. "There wasn't."

Shippen nodded and blew out a long, long breath. "I had to ask."

Gilbert understood.

After a few more minutes, Shippen reached into his pocket. He passed Gilbert an embossed ivory card, his name and contact details pressed in deep blue ink. "Thank you for taking care of my niece. And for the company. If there's ever anything I can do for you . . ."

Gilbert ran his fingers over the letters, then slipped the card into his jacket. "Actually, sir," he said, leaping at the chance. "There's something you might be able to help me with right now."

Shippen looked startled. Of course, he hadn't expected Gilbert to ask right away—if ever. "Of course," he finally said.

Gilbert pulled the file from under his arm and flipped it open on the railing in front of them. "I'm hoping you can help me with a case. We found a body at the mouth of the Wissahickon late last week. Friday morning, to be exact. She was wearing this."

He turned to the crime scene photo and pushed it over toward the Councilman. He tapped the area over the maid's apron. Shippen breathed in sharply. "She worked for me?"

Gilbert wasn't given a chance to answer. The door behind them banged open, steel clanging against the building's brick surface.

"That's enough, Gilbert." Dr. Knight strode forward, his face purpling. Beside him, Finnegan Pyle stood, cross-armed. From the doorway, Marco mouthed *I'm sorry.*

"I apologize for my assistant, Ned," Dr. Knight said, though his eyes never left Gilbert's face. "I'll make sure this is addressed."

"Dr. Knight," Gilbert protested, but Shippen was already moving. He dropped the cigarette on the concrete below them and stamped it out with a quick twist of his heel.

"I'll see you out, Councilman Shippen," Pyle said. "I already told your brother, but I promise you, the department is committing every resource to making sure we find the person responsible for your niece's death."

Dr. Knight waited until the door was firmly closed behind them, cutting off their conversation sharply, leaving the two men alone in the alley. Somewhere in the distance, a car horn blared.

Knight held out his hand. "Let me see it."

Gilbert handed over the file. The coroner read it quickly, the line between his eyebrows deepening as he flipped through the pages. He held up the note Gilbert had scrawled in the phone booth—*Dottie Montgomery*.

"You think this is the headless girl?"

"My sister is a maid in the same household," Gilbert said. "She said Dottie disappeared on Wednesday. No one has seen or heard from her since."

"The Councilman's household." Knight didn't wait for Gilbert to reply. He snapped the folder shut. "You should have come to me first. You know that."

"I know, sir. I'm sorry." And Gilbert was sorry—sorry for the embarrassment he'd caused his mentor. Sorry for taking advantage of a terrible moment in Ned Shippen's life. But he also hadn't been wrong. "But I—"

"The man was grieving, Gilbert. Your actions were inappropriate. Impulsive. Unlike you. You overstepped."

"Finnegan Pyle didn't even try to identify her," Gilbert said. He tried to keep the disdain for the detective from flooding his voice, but from the way Knight looked at him, he'd failed at that.

"That's not our job," Knight said, echoing his words from earlier in the week. "We stick to the science and leave the investigating to the police. Is that going to be a problem for you?"

Gilbert swallowed. He needed this—this job, this relationship with Dr. Knight. He'd already lost so much—who would he be if he lost this, too?

"No, sir," Gilbert said. "It won't be a problem at all."

CHAPTER 15

"Miss Shippen, you have a phone call." Lizzie stood in the doorway, her voice low, like she was afraid to shatter the strained silence that had wrapped around the Shippen House like a shroud.

Edie looked up, surprised. "Me?" she asked, setting aside *Flappers and Philosophers*. Truth be told, she'd had to skip the entirety of *Bernice Bobs Her Hair*. She couldn't bear to read a story about cousins, even one as dreadful as Marjorie. "You're sure it isn't for Frances?"

"It's Miss Van Pelt," Lizzie said. "She asked for you."

Poor Ophelia. She had to be as cut up about Rebecca's murder as the rest of them.

Murder. Edie shuddered.

Rebecca was murdered. No one would tell Edie how it happened, or why. Her father refused to divulge the lurid details and had banned the local newspapers from the house since he and Uncle Charles had returned from the morgue, eyes red-rimmed and downcast. She had overheard snippets and pieced together a bare understanding of the events: some monster had snatched Rebecca sometime between the time she left for the train station on Saturday and the gathering with Ophelia and the other artists on Sunday. According to what she'd sussed out, Rebecca had been in the morgue at the same time Lizzie's brother had tended to Edie's head wound.

She struggled against a wave of emotion as she followed Lizzie down the hall to where the upstairs phone waited, tucked in an alcove between two potted palms. Edie settled herself on the delicately curved telephone bench and picked up the receiver. "Hello?"

"Edie, it's Ophelia." The other woman's voice sounded subdued. "I'm dreadfully sorry about Rebecca. I can't believe . . . I can't . . ." Her voice trailed off.

"Thank you," Edie said, and she meant it. "We're all devastated. Are you all right, dear?"

There was a sniff at the other end of the line. "Truthfully, no. But I'll be all right. I wanted to tell you that our salon is still happening tonight. It won't be the way it normally is, of course, but the girls thought we should carry on. It's what Rebecca would want, isn't it? Anyway, I understand if you aren't up for coming, but we wanted to make sure we extended the invitation."

Right. Edie remembered that Ophelia had mentioned something about Wednesday evenings the last time they'd spoken, but she'd completely forgotten in the blur of the last few days. She was touched that Rebecca's friends had remembered her. Wanted her there.

"Edie?" Ophelia asked, and Edie blinked, realizing she was still waiting for an answer.

"I'd love to," she said, finding her voice. "I think—I think that sounds really swell."

"I wish it were under happier circumstances," Ophelia said. "See you at seven?"

"I'll be there," Edie said, and scrawled down the address Ophelia rattled off—a swanky apartment building only a block or so from the Shippen's city house in Rittenhouse Square. As children, Edie and Frances had split time almost equally between the two properties. Edie's mother had preferred the serene, bucolic Chestnut Hill Estate, while Ned preferred to stay close to the hustle and bustle of City Hall. Edie assumed that his mother's permanent presence at the Chestnut Hill house also had something to do with his preference for the other house—after barely more than a fortnight at home with her grandmother, she was longing for some space.

Her grandmother, however, had other ideas. "Absolutely not," she said, when Edie shared her evening plans over the noon luncheon. "Edith, I'm about to bury one granddaughter, or have you forgotten?"

"That's exactly why I need to go, Grandmama," Edie replied, idly stirring her soup. "Ophelia was a dear friend of Rebecca's. She's hurting, too. I promise I won't go anywhere else," she added, to assuage her grandmother's fears. "I'll be driven straight there, and I'll call Daddy when it's time to go home. I'll be just as safe in the city house as I would be here."

Or safer, Edie thought, but didn't dare speak the words aloud. It was entirely possible, Edie reasoned, that Rebecca had been abducted out here in Chestnut Hill, or somewhere along her trip back to the tiny dorm room she shared with another girl at Bryn Mawr. She'd left shortly after breakfast Saturday afternoon, claiming she had to study for exams. Edie had still been cross about her hat, and refused to say goodbye. She hadn't known that would be her last chance.

Edie blinked furiously, willing her tears to evaporate. But the sight of them appeared to soften Flora Shippen. She reached a

gnarled hand across the table and patted Edie's hand with unchar-
acteristic affection. "Take that maid with you, and go straight
there," Flora said sternly. "Are we clear?"

"Crystal," Edie said.

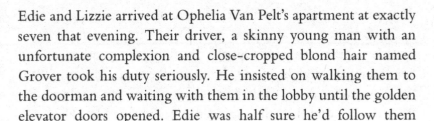

Edie and Lizzie arrived at Ophelia Van Pelt's apartment at exactly
seven that evening. Their driver, a skinny young man with an
unfortunate complexion and close-cropped blond hair named
Grover took his duty seriously. He insisted on walking them to
the doorman and waiting with them in the lobby until the golden
elevator doors opened. Edie was half sure he'd follow them
upstairs, but she held up a black-gloved hand.

"Grover, please. We'll be perfectly safe from this point onwards."

Grover puffed up his chest, trying and failing to make himself
larger. "I was told to see you to the door, Miss Edie."

"And you have," Edie assured him. She pointed to the doorman across the lobby, who was watching them with something
like amusement on his face. The man was huge, well over six feet
tall and heavily built, his muscles straining at the fabric on his red
uniform jacket. "I don't think anyone's getting past him."

"Miss, I must insist—"

"Grover," Lizzie said. "Don't you have a girl who lives around
here? We're going to be awhile. I'm sure she'd love for you to
surprise her."

Grover flushed red. "I guess I could," he said. He glanced
again at the doorman. "If you're sure."

"Go sweep her off of her feet," Edie said. She dug in her
handbag and handed him a dollar. "Buy her a drink on me."

He blinked down at the bill, and before he could change his
mind, the elevator door behind them creaked open. Edie rushed

inside, pulling Lizzie along behind her. "Eighteenth floor," she told the attendant.

He nodded, pulling closed the exterior door, then the brass gate. He pushed the lever forward slowly, and the elevator glided upwards, the exposed walls of the elevator shaft flickering past. Another pull of the lever aligned the elevator perfectly with the doorway, and after a flourish, they were upstairs.

Edie tipped the attendant and stepped into the small foyer outside of the elevator. Ophelia lived in the penthouse, and her door was straight ahead, brass numbers proclaiming 1801. Another pair of doors flanked the elevator: one had a gold plaque labeled *stairs*, and the other, *roof*. Edie straightened her black silk dress and adjusted her hat and elbow-length gloves, swallowing hard. Formal mourning wear had gone out of fashion during the war, but it didn't feel right to wear anything else, not when . . . not when . . .

She stopped and grabbed Lizzie's hand as a sudden wave of grief washed over her. Rebecca should be here, too. It wasn't fair that she was dead. Killed. What had Edie been thinking, coming to this?

"Miss," Lizzie whispered. "Is it another spell? Do you need your tincture?"

Edie shook her head, steeling herself. She gave Lizzie's hand a squeeze, then lifted her head. "I'm fine," she said. "Let's get on with it."

A young, vaguely familiar woman opened the door. Edie, assuming she was a maid, handed over her gloves and hat. The woman nearly dropped them, and stared up at Edie, cheeks darkening. "Oh. I—"

"I'll take them, Athena, don't worry." Lizzie stepped forward.

Athena. Lizzie's friend, who worked in the Pepper house. She was a maid, but . . . Edie blinked at her, then noticed the woman's dazzling blue dress and carefully rouged lips. Not a maid tonight.

"Edie!" Ophelia's voice cut through whatever apology Edie had been about to give. Artfully, she plucked the gloves and hat out of Lizzie's hands, tucking them under her arm. "You remember Athena Kostos, don't you? She's one of us. Athena, this is Edie Shippen. Our dear Rebecca's cousin."

Athena gave a warm smile, though the flush remained in her cheeks. "Nice to see you again, Edie."

Embarrassment filled Edie from top to bottom. She pasted on a smile, hoping it was genuine. "You, too, Miss Kostos. I'm so sorry about the mix-up."

Athena turned her attention to Lizzie. "I'm so glad you came, Lizzie!"

"I am too." Ophelia ushered Lizzie inside, one arm around her shoulders. "It's a delightful surprise."

Lizzie's face turned as red as her hair. "I'm just here to help, Miss Van Pelt. I'm happy to take Miss Edie's hat and . . ."

"Nonsense." Ophelia was already depositing Edie's hat on a sleek black coat tree and set the gloves on the table beside the door. She led them down a small corridor lined with bright oil paintings, and into a large room where nearly a dozen other young women were arranged in clusters of twos and threes, voices subdued. "We're all equals here tonight, Miss Lawless. I hope you'll enjoy yourself as such." Though she said this to Lizzie, she turned and fixed her gaze on Edie's face. "Come along. I'll introduce you to the rest of the Twelve. Well. Eleven now, I suppose."

Edie finally found her voice. "Sorry, Ophelia—who are the Twelve?"

"We are."

Colleen, the small, bespectacled communist, detached herself from the group near the black marble fireplace, her footsteps padding soundlessly over the plush oriental-style rug. Without a word, she threw her arms around Edie, hugging her tight.

"I'm so sorry about Becca," she whispered. "I'm glad you're here."

Edie, taken aback by the sudden display of affection, froze. No one had touched her like this all week. Frances, despite her red-rimmed eyes, tried to carry on as usual. Her father had been absent from the house in Chestnut Hill, claiming he was needed at work. And her grandmother . . . well. Slowly, Edie's heart constricted, and she wrapped her arms around Colleen, too.

"Thank you," Edie said softly. "I'm so sorry for you, too."

Colleen finally stepped back, her glasses askew as she wiped at her cheeks. "Now then," she said, sniffing. "Let's meet the rest of the girls, yeah?"

Beside Edie, Ophelia reached down and snagged her hand, wrapping their fingers together. It was something she never would have done in school; the girls had been friendly, but never *friends*. Edie had never needed real friends, not when she had Frances and Theo, each caught in her orbit, and then her cousins, to a lesser extent. But in that moment, as her chest ached and hot tears gathered behind her eyes, Edie was grateful.

"Dear ones, we have two new friends joining us tonight—and I hope, from now on," Ophelia announced. "Miss Edie Shippen and Miss Lizzie Lawless. Edie, Lizzie, here's everyone."

She introduced the women with dizzying efficiency. Dark-skinned Augusta Brown, who wore a stunning green dress and matching headband, gave a wide, welcoming smile. Hannah Friedman, a short, curvy woman with hair as red as Lizzie's, waved from beside the fireplace. Edie waved back, and completely missed the next set of introductions. Edie's smile wavered, and Lizzie leaned in.

"They should be wearing badges," Lizzie whispered. "Did you get any of that?"

Edie shook her head, but it barely mattered. The women had turned their attentions back to each other, resuming their quiet conversations. Athena tugged on Lizzie's elbow, drawing her over to Hannah and Augusta in the corner. Edie took a step as if to follow, then hesitated. She'd acted like such a fool earlier, handing her things to Athena without a second thought. The other woman probably wanted nothing to do with her.

"Drink?" Ophelia's voice was gentle.

"Please," Edie said, not missing a beat. "Immediately."

Ophelia laughed, and Edie followed her to the far side of the room, where a bar was arranged atop an elegant, black-lacquered sideboard. An open doorway directly beside it led to a small, modern galley kitchen, with a spotless white porcelain sink and white gas range atop a black and white tile floor. There was another door on the opposite end of the kitchen, presumably for whatever servants Ophelia employed to enter and exit discreetly. And despite their absence tonight, Ophelia had to have servants, Edie reasoned. Flapper or not, Ophelia had been raised in the same upper echelons of society that the Shippens inhabited. Servants were a fact of life.

Edie turned her attention back to Ophelia as her hostess plunked two ice cubes from a covered bucket into a cocktail shaker. "Gin and tonic, or a Clover Club?"

"Clover Club," Edie said quickly. The quinine in tonic water always made her stomach queasy—it reminded her too much of the various medicines that had been forced on her during her recovery. "If it's not too much trouble."

"I wouldn't have offered if it was," Ophelia said. She was already pouring gin into the shaker. Ruby-red raspberry syrup was next, followed by a healthy splash of lemon juice.

"So this happens every Wednesday?" Edie asked. "I don't mean to be rude, but what exactly do you all do?"

"Well, we normally don't sit around looking so glum." Ophelia busied herself placing an egg separator over the top of the shaker. She fetched an egg from the icebox, and cracked it over the separator, adding the white to the drink below. She tossed the yolk into the sink, then added, "Sometimes we paint. Tonight, we were supposed to be planning our upcoming show—Isabelle Bateson, in the purple, with the blonde hair? She's dating a fellow who owns a gallery on Walnut, and she has persuaded him that our art is *exactly* what he needs to get some attention."

Edie leaned against the sideboard as Ophelia shook up the drink and poured. The resulting cocktail was the color of pink lemonade, topped with a swirl of foamy egg white. Edie accepted hers with a smile, then asked, "Do you only paint nudes?"

This time, Ophelia giggled. "Heavens, no. I mean, I won't say no," she added, waggling her eyebrows, "But we all are varied in our mediums. Augusta is a very talented sculptor, and Colleen prefers landscapes. Rebecca is—was," Ophelia caught herself, then seemed to think better of the sentence. She pressed her lips together and gave Edie a watery smile as she picked up her glass. "Cheers."

They clinked, each lost in their own grief for a moment. Edie was glad she wasn't alone, that she was here, in this penthouse, with people who had known and loved Rebecca. That feeling followed as Edie turned and located Lizzie across the living room. Her maid looked up from her conversation with

Athena, Colleen, and their friends Hannah and Augusta. Lizzie waved Edie over.

Edie, who had spent her entire life moving amongst the highest of Philadelphia society with ease, sipped at the bright, lemony cocktail as she joined the others, unsure of what to say. She'd never been in such mixed company before; the young women in front of her were Black and white, Jewish, and Catholic, and Protestant, immigrant and native born, and poor, middle class, and extravagantly wealthy, all drawn together by their love of art. Rebecca had been a part of this, and Edie, not for the first time, thought of how brave her cousin had been. How brave each of these women were. She listened carefully, then, when the conversation seemed to hit a natural lull, finally spoke.

"Are you all professional artists?" she asked.

"Oh, no," Athena said with a laugh. "You know I'm in service, like Lizzie." She met Edie's eyes directly, as if she was daring Edie to make a comment, but when Edie only nodded, she continued, pointing to each of her friends in turn. "Hannah clerks at City Hall, Augusta is a teacher, and Colleen studies Art History at Bryn Mawr."

The pieces clicked together. "Which is how she met Becca, I suppose?"

Augusta was the one who nodded. "Right. And Colleen, Hannah, and I went to Girls' High together. And Hannah's brother used to date Athena."

"A momentary lapse in judgment," Athena interjected dryly.

"And Becca brought us to Ophelia, and the rest is history," Hannah finished.

Edie was amazed. She'd known of Girls' High, of course—everyone knew the Philadelphia High School for Girls—but it had been snobbery on her part, she realized, to assume that every woman who attended college was a product of a private academy like the one she, Becca, and Ophelia had attended. "I'm afraid you all must think me a bore by comparison," she said.

"Oh no," Hannah said quickly. "We just . . . well. It's not every day you meet a lady."

Edie flushed. What on earth had Rebecca told her friends? "I'm not titled," she protested. "My mother was a lady, not me."

"Still," Athena said. "Rebecca said you and your sister met the King of England?"

Edie gave a small nod. Heat crept up her cheeks, and she tried to quickly change the subject. "Are you all communists, like Colleen? I don't know what they taught at Girl's High, but they didn't cover much about Marx at the Springside School for Young Ladies, did they, Ophelia?"

Ophelia clapped a hand over her mouth. "Oh, Edie, can you *imagine?*"

Augusta laughed too, the sound deep and rich. "Don't worry, Miss Shippen. Cols is the only Marxist here. No one else will be calling for the guillotine."

The rest of the evening stretched on in amiable companionship—Edie didn't know what sort of things usually happened when the Twelve gathered, but she was grateful to Ophelia for allowing her this. The women who lived close by left in groups of twos and threes. After what happened to Rebecca, no one wanted to brave the night alone. For those who lived farther afield, like Colleen, Athena, and Augusta, Ophelia arranged for cars, and saw them to the doorman downstairs herself. Edie and Lizzie lingered as the group dispersed; Edie knew she should call her father to see her the two blocks to their city house, but she didn't want to return to the grief-stricken silence she knew awaited her at home.

After seeing the last of the women out, Ophelia arrived back upstairs with two young men in tow: her brother, Artie, and Theo Pepper.

Edie stood as Artie stumbled through the room, an apologetic Theo under his arm. "I didn't know where else to take him, Phee," Theo was saying, "He needs to sober up."

"I'm not drunk, I'm *depressed*," Artie howled. He pulled off his cufflinks and threw them at the coffee table. One bounced from the surface, burying itself in the carpet at their feet. "The love of my life is a crook. A criminal. As good as a murderess." He descended into a barrage of sobs.

"Pull yourself together, Artie, we've got company." Ophelia gave her brother a little shake, and it was only then that Artie and Theo seemed to notice Lizzie and Edie were in the room. Artie blew his nose into his sleeve, but Theo straightened.

"What are you doing here?" He lobbed it like an accusation, and Edie took a half step back, surprised at the anger in his voice. "You shouldn't be here."

"Hello to you too," Edie replied.

"I'm serious." Theo stepped closer, then seemed to think better of it. He stopped, a heartbeat away, his fingers flexing against the dark fabric of his trousers. "You're supposed to be at home."

Ophelia rocked back on her heels. "Oh, this is interesting," she said, more to herself than to anyone else.

"I don't care who's here," Artie whined. "I want to talk about *me*. And that woman. She did this, you know. I'm sure of it."

"Celeste," Ophelia explained. "I think she might have dumped him."

"No, I dumped *her*," Artie said. "Tell them, Theo. Tell them what she did."

"Celeste Dupont?" Edie ventured. She rubbed at her wrists, as if Celeste's nails were biting into her tender flesh all over again. *Tell Rebecca to call me, immediately. She'll know what it's about.*

Edie had thought the woman intense, and a fraud. She had never thought . . .

Had *Celeste* killed Rebecca? "You called her a murderess, Artie. That's a serious accusation," Edie added, her voice shaking. "You can't just say things like that without proof."

Theo winced. He retrieved the cufflink Artie had flung before he answered, carefully setting it with its mate on the coffee table. "Artie thinks—Artie remembered something. He'd given a note to Rebecca, the night of our . . . my . . . *the* engagement party." Theo wouldn't look at Edie.

"Celeste was insistent I give it to Becca. You saw me, didn't you, Edie? I knew . . . I knew she helped girls in trouble," Artie said. He had thrown himself back on the sofa. "I thought it was noble, actually—especially after all of that business with your sister, Theo. Anything to spare a scandal like that, right? I figured Rebecca was passing along some information to a friend. A coed who found herself in a bad situation and needed help getting out of it. But now she's dead, and Celeste won't tell me who she sent Rebecca to, even though it's obvious that Celeste led her straight to the slaughter."

Edie didn't understand. She looked at Theo, then Ophelia, puzzled. Ophelia looked as startled as Edie felt. Surely, Artie wasn't saying . . .

Finally, Lizzie cleared her throat. In all of the chaos, Edie had nearly forgotten her maid was there, standing as still as a statue beside her. "Miss Edie," Lizzie said carefully, "Was it possible?"

"Was what possible?" Edie wouldn't let herself even think it. It wasn't possible. Rebecca had had a front-row seat to Sarah's scandal. She'd known better. Hadn't she?

"Was Rebecca pregnant?"

Chapter 16

Gilbert couldn't understand a word his sister was saying. She'd appeared at the front door to the boarding house shortly after midnight, long after it was safe for a woman alone to be on the streets. Lizzie was shivering and babbling, her mind moving faster than her mouth.

"Slow down," he told her, for the third time. "Start over."

Lizzie sat across the kitchen table. She was even paler than usual as she sipped from a steaming porcelain teacup. Her freckles stood out in stark relief across her nose.

"Rebecca Shippen is dead," Lizzie said. "You know that, right?"

Gilbert nodded. He hadn't told Lizzie he'd been the one to process the crime scene or autopsy Rebecca's body, but by now, the entire city knew that Rebecca Shippen had been brutally murdered. The Philadelphia Inquirer had broken the news in the Monday evening edition of the paper, proclaiming *SHIPPEN HEIRESS DISCOVERED SLAIN ON SCHUYLKILL BANKS* in bold letters above the fold. Despite scant updates, the murder had remained front-page fodder all week long. "Did you know her?" Gilbert asked, gently.

Lizzie stared down into her tea. She nodded. "There's something going on at that house, Gil. Miss Rebecca's dead, and you had all of those questions about Dottie . . . it doesn't sit right with me."

"It could be a coincidence," he said, trying to soothe her, but the words rang false even to his own ears.

Both women had been drugged. Mutilated. Electrocuted. But Knight had brushed off his concerns. Pyle wouldn't listen.

"Are you listening?" Lizzie asked, her sharp voice cutting through Gilbert's thoughts.

"Sorry. I'm exhausted," he apologized. This seemed to soften her. She reached her hand out and linked their fingers together. "What were you saying?"

"I was wondering if there was a way to find out if Rebecca Shippen was pregnant when she died," Lizzie said.

This did catch Gilbert's attention. "What? Why?"

"Miss Edie is distraught, you know. And if I could tell her not to worry, that Miss Rebecca wasn't in trouble . . . that might help. It might put her at ease."

Gilbert knew he shouldn't divulge details from an active investigation to anyone. But Lizzie wasn't anyone—she was the one person he'd always been able to count on. His rock.

"We can't know if she was pregnant, Liz," he said, weighing how much to tell her. "Whoever killed her didn't leave enough evidence for us to know for sure."

"So it's possible," Lizzie said, her voice thick with tears. "It's possible that she was pregnant, and she died because of it."

"It's possible," Gilbert allowed. The missing organs could point to a botched abortion. He'd seen it, more often than he could ever let Lizzie know. It was a dangerous thing, being a woman. And it almost made sense, when added with the mor-phine, except for one thing: if Rebecca had died during an illegal abortion, why the strangulation? Or the electrocution? Some-thing wasn't adding up.

Lizzie sipped at her tea. Gilbert sensed, more than knew, that his sister wasn't telling him the entire truth.

"Liz," he said, "You know you can tell me anything, aye?"

She rolled her eyes, the way sisters did. "Of course."

"If you know something, you can tell me. I know people who can help." He didn't want to scare her, but he had to make sure she knew. That she understood there was a killer out there, and that she shouldn't put herself at risk. "I can keep you safe, Liz."

"I know you think you can," she told him.

It was only later, as Lizzie snored in his bed and he tried to sleep on the cold, hard floor in his room, that Gilbert realized that he should have asked his sister what she meant.

CHAPTER 17

The interior of the Church of Saint Martin-In-The-Fields was stifling. It was only the last day of April, but the weather was already unseasonably warm after a week of raging storms. Edie fluttered a paper fan in the air, making the black lace veil from her smart little hat dance over her face. It didn't help, but it at least gave her something to focus on other than the way her aunt's gulping sobs echoed beneath the vaulted ceilings.

Edie hated funerals. She hated the stiff black dresses that were *always* itchy, no matter the type of fabric. She hated the tears, the way the living carried on and on. She especially hated how God-damned guilty they made her feel for being alive when by all accounts, she should be dead too.

She didn't remember much about her bout with influenza. Even the days before were hazy—it was like the entire episode had been plucked from her brain and replaced with shadows. There were black-shrouded memories of weeping and cool, sure hands, and of Frances' prayers.

To her left, Frances let out a deep, gulping sob and clasped her gloved hands around Edie's upper arm. The organ blared, leading the congregation through a somber rendition of *Amazing Grace*. Rebecca's casket stood in the center aisle, a few short pews up from where they sat. As the song shifted into the second verse, Edie stared at the polished chestnut, at the spray of white flowers draped over its mound top, as if she could force herself to wake up from this nightmare.

She drifted behind the others as they climbed into their motorcars, ready to process behind the hearse and its gleaming black horses all the way to Laurel Hill Cemetery, where Rebecca would rest inside the Shippen Mausoleum. The white stone structure sat high on a bluff, just around the bend in the river from where her body had been found. Once they arrived, Edie couldn't stop staring down at the muddy brown water as it rushed far below them. Dimly, she registered the scrape of wood against wood as her father and her uncles lifted the casket from the hearse and processed inside, but Edie's mind spun with questions. Had Rebecca been pregnant? Had she died due to the negligence of an abortionist? Or had it been random, the way that Edie's mugging had been?

Had she died afraid?

The door to the mausoleum swung shut, the click of the lock slamming through Edie's body like a gunshot. She jerked, her gaze swinging wildly to the stone letters spelling out their family name. She knew, then, *knew* that there had been a mistake. Rebecca couldn't be dead; her cousin couldn't be mourned. This was all so terribly wrong.

An unladylike sob ripped through her chest as she stepped backwards, treading on Frances' feet, but she didn't care, not about Franny's yelp of pain or their grandmother's irritated sigh. She spun, right into Theo, who caught her by the upper arms. His mother-of-pearl cufflinks shimmered in the sunlight.

"Edie?"

She wrenched herself away from him and fled down the cemetery's stone path, unable to even look him in the face after what they'd done, shame and grief mixing in her veins. She'd kissed him, so selfish and *alive,* and all the while her cousin had been dead, slowly decaying on a lonely shelf, unclaimed and alone. She ran until the path turned to a carpet of grass and small, neat headstones, until her chest burned and her legs ached, until her mourning family was out of sight.

She fell to her knees in the grass, wrapped her arms around her middle, and keened, wailing like one of the widows in the Bible, ready to rend her clothes and beat her breast. She didn't even care that she was in public, making a spectacle of herself. She didn't care.

She didn't care.

"Miss Shippen?" The voice was gentle, soft. She opened her eyes to find the kind doctor staring at her. The coroner. Lizzie's brother. The one who had patched her up in the morgue, probably mere feet away from Rebecca's corpse. He squatted down beside her and produced a handkerchief from somewhere and held it out between them, wavering like a white flag of surrender.

"Thank you," she said softly. She took the cloth and dabbed at her eyes, realizing only then that they were completely alone, out of sight of her family and the rest of society who had gathered to mourn Rebecca. A chill worked its way down her spine. *How far had she run?*

"Did you follow me?" Edie demanded.

He stared at her. "Excuse me?"

She gathered herself to her feet. "From the funeral. You . . . you followed me, didn't you? Is it you? Are you the one who—?"

"Da?" A tiny voice asked. It was only then that Edie noticed the small girl peeking out from behind his legs, all solemn brown eyes and fiery curls.

"Shh, Pen, it's all right. Miss Shippen here is just sad." He lifted the girl into his arms, where she burrowed against his chest. His daughter, she realized.

Edie cast her gaze around and noticed that she was in a different part of the cemetery all together, far from her family's row of stone mausoleums. The monuments were different here—an obelisk to their left, a weeping angel to their right. And behind Lizzie's brother, a strange glass and iron structure, about six feet long and two feet tall, surrounded by a tangle of flowers. Beneath the glass, a void of darkness waited.

"Forgive me," she said softly. "I—I've had a shock."

"I'm very sorry for your loss," he replied. He glanced down at the child in his arms, his jaw relaxing just a fraction into a softness Edie doubted very few people were allowed to see.

"I—thank you," she said. "I'm sorry to interrupt your time. Who—?"

He flinched, and Edie instantly regretted the question. But it was the little girl who answered, lifting her head. "Mama," she said simply.

"I'm sorry," she said softly as the girl wiggled in his arms. "How terribly sad."

He set the girl back down in the grass, lifting one shoulder in a shrug. He kept his eyes on his daughter as she ran off into the grass. "The childbed is dangerous for any woman," he said. "But she believed in heaven, so that's where she must be."

He was gentle, she realized. She tilted her head, studying his face. Someone like him, who spent his days the way he did, should be ghoulish. But he was handsome. Vibrantly alive, from the plane of his jaw, the generous slope of his mouth, the dark hair curled around his ears, just the slightest bit too long to be fashionable.

"You seem to have recovered," he said, breaking into her thoughts, motioning his hand in front of his forehead.

"All better, thanks to you," she replied, the bright tone of her voice sounding false even to her own ears.

"Edie!" Frances' voice came from uphill, catching Edie's attention. Her sister stood on the path between two tall pines, her black fringed shawl pulled tightly over her shoulders. "Edie, we're waiting for you!"

Edie didn't move right away. But Lizzie's brother smiled, inclining his head toward the spot where Frances waited. "Sounds like you're missed," he said.

"It appears so." Edie sighed and tucked her hair behind her ear. His eyes followed the movement, then dropped to her lips, and suddenly, Edie felt hot all over. First Theo, now this—was she thinking of flirting with a man at the foot of his wife's grave? Had she no shame? She cleared her throat and took a step backwards. "Well. Have a nice afternoon, Mr. Lawless."

"I'm sorry for your loss, Miss Shippen," he said.

Edie spared him a smile and hurried up the hill after her sister, leaving Lizzie's brother alone with his daughter to mourn his wife in peace.

CHAPTER 18

Gilbert watched Edith Shippen stalk up the gravel path in her chic black pumps, a black handbag dangling from her gloved wrist, a line of smooth pearl buttons marching up her spine. She looked like a panther, swathed in night, moving with a smooth, feline grace—the scent of vanilla lingering long after she disappeared behind the pine trees.

Christ. He shouldn't be paying attention to her like this. Not here.

Penny crashed into his legs, her arms circling his knees. She pressed her face against his thigh, and he looked down at his daughter. "Where's that girl going, Da?" she asked. "She's so pretty."

"She had her own plans today, Pen," he said. He scooped her up, her little body weighing hardly anything. "And so do we. Should we say goodbye to your mother?"

Penny pressed her lips together and gave a solemn nod. Together, father and daughter approached the glass-topped mausoleum where Sarah rested far below. He hated the iron-and-glass structure her parents had built in her memory, and he knew Sarah would have hated it, as well. It had cost a small fortune, money that would have been better spent providing for Penny's future.

But that would have meant the Peppers had to acknowledge their granddaughter's existence. It was easier for them to bury Sarah, and her choices, than to spend a moment with the child they blamed for her death.

"Goodbye, Mam," Penny said. She reached out and rested one hand on the glass roof; Gilbert reached his own hand forward and did the same, though his own throat closed, choking of his goodbye. All these years later, and he still couldn't say the words.

She's a good girl, Sarah, he thought instead, *You'd be proud of her. She's sweet, and clever, and going to bring trouble down on my head, I can feel it.*

Penelope kept up a constant stream of narration as they drove home, playing on the seat beside him in her new blue dress and shiny black shoes. It was her fourth birthday, and now that they'd paid their respects to her mother, he should focus on her. But as he turned up the hill to his parent's house in Manayunk, his thoughts kept drifting to Dottie Montgomery and Rebecca Shippen.

"We're home!" Penny crowed in her little girl voice, as Gilbert parked in front of the house. She threw her arms around his bicep, squeezing tight. "I love cars, Da."

"And I love *you*," he told her. He pressed a kiss to her head and helped her climb over the gearshift. He settled Penny on his hip as his mother met them at the door, her smile wide.

"Ah, there's the birthday girl," she said. She put her hand on Gilbert's shoulder, eyes soft. "How was your visit, dear?"

Gilbert leaned into her touch for just a moment, allowing himself—and his mother—one fleeting moment of peace. "Strange," he said, finally, as he stepped into the snug little house. This place had been his refuge since he was ten years old, a welcome escape after the long voyage from Ireland and the crowded Pennsport alleys he'd played in when the first arrived in Philadelphia. "I didn't realize they were burying Rebecca Shippen today."

His mother crossed herself. "Poor lass. It's been all over the papers. Are they any closer to catching the monster who killed her?"

Gilbert shook his head as Penny ran toward the back of the house, where her grandfather was no doubt already sneaking bits of frosting from the birthday cake. "Has Lizzie said anything?"

Aoife followed her granddaughter's path with her gaze. "No. I'd wager they're working her so hard we won't even get a phone call today."

"She should be here." She hadn't returned any of his calls, and he was desperate to speak with her. He couldn't shake the feeling that there was something he was missing. Something Lizzie knew and wasn't telling him. "I'm worried for her, with a killer on the loose."

"Aye. Well." Aoife patted his arm again. "Lizzie's a big girl. Penny is not. Let's be here for her, yeah? A child only turns four once."

"Sure, Mam." He knew his mother was right. But even as he trailed both his mother and daughter into the kitchen, he couldn't help but feel that something was terribly, terribly wrong.

"Shippen House, Chestnut Hill, please." Gilbert leaned against the wall in the boarding house in the rapidly approaching twilight, the solid oak the only thing keeping him upright as the operator connected the call. The unsettled feeling had chased him all the way home from his family's house, sinking deep claws into his gut, too sharp to ignore.

"Shippen House," the voice on the other side of the line said. "Mrs. Smith speaking."

"Mrs. Smith, I'm looking for my sister, Lizzie Lawless." He stared down at the checked black and white tiles, where the late evening shadows crept across the floor.

"You and the entire household, Mr. Lawless." The house-keeper let out an irritated snort. "But I'll leave a message."

The line clicked off in his ear. He frowned, thinking, long enough that the operator came back onto the line. "Would you like to place a call, sir?"

"What? No, no. Sorry." He hung up the receiver on the cra-dle, panic slithering over his shoulders. Ahead of him, the shad-ows stretched and twisted, dark shapes morphing into hands, grasping and plucking. And reaching; always reaching.

"Gil, honey. Marco's at the door for you." Nellie stood in the doorway to the common room, wiping flour-dusted hands on an equally floury apron. Instead of the baking biscuits he'd smelled just a moment before, the scent of gunpowder filled the small foyer, acrid and sharp enough to burn as he inhaled.

Gilbert tried to answer her, but his voice refused to come out. He just stared as the shadows crept closer, wrapping themselves around Nellie's legs, twining up around her skirts, her arms. A low moan escaped his throat as his own limbs turned to jelly. He hit the floor with a thud.

"Gil!" Nellie was beside him in an instant. The shadows warped her body, transforming her from the feet upwards, her black skirts morphing into muddy brown boots and olive drab wool. He fum-bled for his chest pocket, remembering too late that the morphine was upstairs in his jacket. Nellie's torso slid into the wide, solid chest draped in a doughboy's filthy jacket, the flour shifting from stark white to dark brown and red as the world twisted into memory.

"Gilbert!" The man was pressed against him from hip to shoulder, his voice hoarse. His blue eyes were wild. Gil had seen that look in almost identical eyes before—the man was going to die.

They were all going to die.

"Gil, tell him. We can't go. We'll die."

"It's orders," Gilbert's mouth moved of its own accord. Around them, the air was still, paused, like the earth itself was holding its breath. A deep ringing sounded in his head, a persistent pitch that he'd hear until the moment he died. "We have to."

"Over the top!" Another voice shouted from behind them. In the distance, machine gun fire blasted, ripping over no-man's land, hot lead tearing through the wooden and barbed-wire defenses mounted on the top of the trench. The black and white tile floor had disappeared, the hard-packed dirt below him already muddying with rainwater and blood.

So much blood.

Not real, Gilbert tried to tell himself, but it was no use. Fingers that were his—but not his—gripped the cool metal of the rifle, clenching hard enough that he worried he would bend the barrel. To his left, another young man scaled the wooden ladder as the gun let out another brutal round. The man seemed to hang suspended in the air for a moment that stretched to an eternity. His arms outstretched, his body convulsing under the barrage of bullets ripping through cloth and flesh, pinging from his metal helmet, showering Gilbert and the man beside him in a torrent of hot red blood.

He didn't even have time to scream.

"Please!" the man beside him screamed again. "Please, Gil—"

Hands grasped his jaw. He clenched his teeth, thrashing against the unseen opponent, but a solid weight pressed against his chest, pulling him farther away from the man beside him. Something sharp bit into his neck as his head knocked against the cold floor.

"LAWLESS!" a voice shouted from the distance. "Snap out of it. You're here. You're home."

"Gil, honey, it's all right," the woman said. "You're safe. You're safe."

That wasn't right. Women weren't at the front, not down here in the trenches. The girls were a few miles away in the Red Cross camp. Gilbert blinked, his vision doubling, blurring between the past and the present. The blue-eyed man beside him shimmered as the drugs took hold, the pitched sounds of battle fading away. His limbs and eyes grew heavy, and everything around him dulled from the brilliant reds and browns of the trenches to the shadow-wrapped foyer of his boarding house, where his landlady and red-faced partner stared down at him, each wearing mirrored expressions of concern.

"I'm all right," Gilbert said, but his words slurred together, one on top of the other, and it came out more like "iaaallight."

Nellie winced.

"Lawless." Marco squatted beside him and pressed warm fingers against Gilbert's racing pulse, frowning. "Where'd you go?"

Everything was heavy. His arms, his eyes. He cleared his throat, finding his words again. "Doesn't matter. I'm here now."

"Come on, buddy," Marco said with a sigh. "Let's get you a cup of coffee. We've got a scene to process."

◆————————◆◆◆————————◆

The mud along West River Drive reminded Gilbert of France. It sucked at his shoes, poised to devour him whole, like it was hungry from the scent of death that hung in the rancid air. He ran his teeth along the peppermint candy Marco had handed him when they parked the truck—it was one of those kinds of scenes—and followed Finnegan Pyle to the body.

It had stormed on and off over the last few days, and judging by the thick black clouds curling overhead, they wouldn't have long to process this scene before the sky opened up on them again. One of the police officers escorting Gilbert leaned over the retaining wall and retched into the river. "I'm sorry," he gasped. "It's just . . ."

He didn't need to explain.

The body, or what remained of it, was in an undignified heap near the road. At first glance, Gilbert assumed it was a fox or a deer or a dog that had veered too closely to oncoming traffic. But then his eye snagged on the unmistakable shape of a human hand along the rushes at the river's edge. The curve of a calf, the long, smooth line of torso. And beside it, a head.

"It looks like something out of an anatomy textbook." Marco's camera whirred and flashed. "Jesus."

He wasn't wrong. Whoever had left the body here had also carefully, precisely, removed every inch of skin from the body, exposing purple muscle to rot quickly in the humid spring air.

Gilbert squatted beside the corpse, trying to ignore the weak, shaky feeling left over in his limbs in the wake of his fit. Whoever they'd been, they'd been dumped on West River Drive, close to the zoo, and almost directly across the river from where they'd discovered Rebecca Shippen. In his three years working in the coroner's office, Gilbert could count on one hand the number of times he'd been called to a crime scene along River Drive. And now—two in as many weeks.

A raindrop splattered against the notebook Gilbert held, smearing the ink on the page. He cursed and flipped it shut, tucking it into his pocket and standing. The sun still shone stubbornly through the dark clouds overhead, but they didn't have much time left to work before the storm would be on them.

"No burn marks," Pyle said, the first words he'd spoken to Gilbert since he arrived. "Are we looking at the same guy?"

"The skin's been removed, so we can't tell like this," Gilbert said. "We might be able to tell once we get some tissue under a microscope."

"You ever stop and think that you do some creepy shit, Lawless?" Pyle asked. "Like, when we were kids at Saint John's, did you think this is where we'd be standing today?"

"It never crossed my mind," Gilbert said, keeping his voice cool.

"'Course not. You always thought you were better than the rest of us. Goin' off to Central. Marrying Sarah instead of one of the girls from the block. *Doctor* Lawless." Pyle spat on the mud at their feet. "You always wanted to leave me and Tommy behind."

"I wanted to make a difference," Gilbert said. He gripped the pen in hand so hard he thought it might snap in half. Finn had no right to speak to him like this. No right to speak of Sarah. "I wanted to be a good man, Finn. I wanted you and Tommy to want that too. More fool me."

"What's that supposed to mean?" Genuine confusion across Pyle's face. "Tommy is a good man."

"Ah, yes, Tommy Fletcher. On the way to sainthood, right beside The Butcher of Broad Street."

"Tommy's better than you give him credit for. He takes care of the neighborhood. Didn't turn his back on it, unlike someone else I know."

"Is that why you let Dottie Montgomery go to the potter's field? She was from the neighborhood, wasn't she? You both took real good care of her, in the end."

Pyle snapped his jaw shut and jabbed a finger in Gilbert's direction. "You have no proof that that headless broad was Dottie Montgomery."

"She's missing, Pyle. A headless body wearing Shippen livery is discovered not even a mile from their house. A maid—a girl from the neighborhood—vanishes without a trace. But maybe you're right. I'm not the detective here."

A few feet away, a dark sedan pulled off onto the shoulder. Gilbert nearly breathed a sigh of relief as Dr. Knight stepped out from the backseat, pulling his bowler hat low over his gray hair. He still wore his funeral clothes, a somber black suit beneath a black coat. Dr. Harrison, whom they had met at the lecture, followed. To their credit, neither of the men blanched at the sight of the corpse.

"The press is on their way," Knight said to Pyle, instead of a greeting. "You might want to round up your fellows. To Gilbert, he said, "You remember Dr. Harrison, don't you? He'll be joining us from now on."

Gilbert acknowledged them both with a nod, but his heart picked up. Of course the press would be interested in this: a mutilated corpse, skin removed. They would run rampant with speculations about a monster capable of such gruesomeness striking twice in such a short period of time. The police had yet to reveal the information about the burn marks to the public. But if Pyle was correct, and this victim also bore evidence of electrocution, it would only be a matter of time before news leaked to the press.

It would be pandemonium.

Knight and Harrison quickly got to work. Marco, done with his photographs, had returned his camera to the car and the men moved carefully, retrieving each of the scattered body parts.

"The body was dumped on the edge of the water. Probably on this side, since the cops were patrolling East River Drive," Marco said. "Like Rebecca Shippen, there's no sign of struggle or violence here. Just a lot of mud, and . . . well." He waved his hand in the direction of the corpse. "Based on the smell, and the state of the body, whoever this is has been out here a while."

"Any evidence?" Knight asked. Harrison looked up sharply, but Gilbert shook his head.

"There's been too much rain, and the scavengers have been here, to boot. We're lucky we're able to retrieve as much as we did."

Knight let out a frustrated sigh and stepped back so Gilbert and Marco could lift the remains and gently place them in a waxed canvas shroud.

As they did, Dr. Harrison stepped forward. "Wait," he said. He squatted down into the muck; pointing at the deep impressions the body had left on the ground. "Something's here."

Half-buried in the thick black mud glittered a single, golden cufflink.

CHAPTER 19

The funeral reception lingered well into the evening. Edie found herself tucked into a corner, as far as she could get from her aunt's tears and her grandmother's pointed conversation. She'd looked for Lizzie among the crush of black-and-white uniformed servants milling helpfully about, but Edie hadn't seen her maid's fiery curls all day.

She gained a small respite when Colleen arrived. The young woman marched through the room as if daring anyone to turn her away. She was dressed somberly, head bent, eyes red. Grandmama focused on her immediately, head swiveling, like she could sense the cheap viscose fabric of her dress. Edie, in order to stave off the brewing storm, inserted herself between the family matriarch and Rebecca's grieving friend.

"I have every right to be here, same as anyone else," Colleen said, a little louder than was strictly polite, at Edie's raised brows. "Maybe more. Becca was mine."

"No one is questioning that," Edie said smoothly. She linked her arm through Colleen's and pulled her through the doorway from the library to the glass-walled conservatory. "I only supposed you might want to be spared my grandmother's wrath."

Colleen made a small snort. The air around them blurred, thick around the edges with artificial humidity and glittering shadows, and Edie winced, pressing a hand to her forehead. She needed her medicine, but now wasn't the time to dash upstairs to find it.

"Did you come alone?" Edie asked.

Colleen rubbed her hands over her arms, her black gloves sliding over her sleeves. "Hannah had synagogue services today, and Augusta and Athena weren't sure how welcome they would be," she said.

"Everyone is welcome," Edie said, but the words rang false, even as she said them. Grandmama had stared daggers at Colleen, who was white and wearing a crucifix; how would she have handled Augusta's brown skin? Or Athena, who had waited on her at the Pepper's home? What must it be like, to navigate the world, knowing so many doors were closed to you?

Colleen watched Edie as if she could read the thoughts churning through Edie's brain. "Is Ophelia here? She said she'd meet me at the church, but I didn't see her."

"I'm not sure," Edie said. But it occurred to her that she hadn't seen Ophelia at all during the funeral—not at the church, or the cemetery, or at the reception, either. "I'm not sure I've seen her at all today."

"You haven't?" Colleen's bespectacled gaze was sharp. "That's strange, isn't it?"

Edie opened her mouth, then closed it again. Yes. Yes, it was strange—the Van Pelts usually sat in the pew directly opposite the Shippens and had for every Sunday of Edie's entire life. Artie and his parents had been there. It honestly felt like *everyone* had been there, everyone desperate to get a look at the poor murdered girl in her coffin. Everyone ready to whisper theories about what Rebecca Shippen might have done to tempt such a gruesome end.

Everyone but Ophelia.

Before her thoughts could spiral farther, Theo and Artie stumbled into the conservatory, flanked by a few of their friends. Theo stopped short, amber liquid sloshing over the lip of the bottle in his hand. His eyes flashed with something dark, a hint of mischief that reminded Edie of teenaged troublemaking. She fought the wave of nausea that followed, bile and grief and shame warring in her middle until she wasn't quite sure how she was left standing.

"Edie, who is your friend?" Frances asked.

Edie had been so focused on Theo that she hadn't even noticed her sister appear. She flushed. "This is Colleen," she explained, introducing them one by one. "She's Rebecca's roommate at college."

"I came to pay my respects," Colleen explained. "She is . . . she was very dear to me."

"It's very kind of you," Frances said. "It's so terrible, isn't it?"

Artie leaned forward, waving his bottle. "That's enough sad talk. Want a drink, dolls?"

"God, are you *drunk*?" Edie said, anger sharpening her voice. Even Frances noticed, giving Edie a wide-eyed look as Edie reached out and snatched the bottle from his grasp. She sniffed at the liquid, the smell sharp and smokey. Scotch whisky. The expensive kind her father had stocked before Prohibition. She tilted the bottle back, letting the smokey alcohol warm her up from the inside out, filling the deep, gaping chasm in her soul. "Where did you get this?"

"Hypocrite." Theo took the bottle back and draped his arm over Frances' shoulder. "This bottle came straight from the Highlands—I smuggled it in a false bottom of my trunk. Everything's on the level, ladies." He offered it first to Colleen.

She stared at the bottle for a moment, then shrugged and said, "Rebecca would want this."

Maybe Colleen was right. She probably knew Rebecca—the real Rebecca—better than anyone else. The alcohol softened Edie, turning the steel in her limbs languid and malleable. Before long, the five young people were tucked in the back of the conservatory on the slate tiles where Rebecca had extended Edie her lifeline. It seemed a fitting way to celebrate her cousin, trading stories over sips of illegal scotch. To say goodbye, one last time.

The booze seemed to soften Edie's sister, too. Frances snuggled back into Theo's broad chest, her eyes closed. Edie couldn't help but watch as Theo's long fingers stroked up and down Franny's side. Franny shivered and pressed closer.

"I heard Rebecca was quite the artist," Theo said suddenly. Edie looked up and found his ice blue eyes staring directly at her. Something she couldn't place burned in his gaze, and she shifted in her seat. The air in the conservatory was suddenly oppressive.

"She was brilliant," Colleen said. "The most talented of us."

"That's how I know you." Artie spoke up suddenly. "You're one of them, aren't you? Those bluestockings my sister slums around with?"

Red splotches appeared on Collen's cheeks. "Excuse me?"

Artie wasn't paying attention to her. Instead, he turned to Theo, hands flapping in the air between them. "From the other night, remember? Phee and her friends, playing at being artists."

"And every one of them has more talent than you have in your little finger, Artie," Edie snapped. "Don't be cruel."

He spread his hands wide. "Come on, doll. I was just asking."

"Theo is a brilliant artist," Frances said. "He kept a sketchbook during the war. You two should talk sometime."

"Oh?" Colleen's attention fastened on Theo. "I thought you were a doctor."

"I am. I paint as a hobby," Theo explained.

"He's always been talented," Edie said. She didn't know why she said it—the booze must have loosened her tongue. Theo smiled at her. Frances did, too, though her smile didn't reach her eyes.

"I intend for it to be my career." Colleen was sitting up straight now and appeared as sober as a judge. "Ophelia does too."

Artie bit back a laugh. "Oh, that's rich. My sister doesn't need a career. She's too busy with her pretty dresses and dancing all night long. It'd be like Edie here declaring herself an artist."

Theo and Frances actually laughed, and Edie reared back, as if the words had struck her. "What's that supposed to mean, Artie?"

Frances sat up, and Theo moved with her, wrapping one arm around her waist and resting his chin on her head. "Oh, Edie. It's nothing personal," she said. "You know as well as the rest of us that you're too . . . too *you* to take anything like that seriously."

"You're a butterfly," Theo added. "Bright and pretty and flitting from one bright thing to the next. You're not the serious sort."

Maybe before, Edie would have agreed with them. Before the influenza, before the war, before the years with Aunt Mae. Before her glimpse at the life her cousin had wanted so desperately to live. She wasn't the girl she had been. And no one here could accept that.

She pushed to standing. "I'm going to bed," she snapped. She looked down at Colleen, who was staring at Artie as if he were a bug to be crushed beneath her shoe. "Come on, Colleen. I'll have someone make you up a room."

"Oh, don't be such a wet blanket. We were just having a little fun. Edie!" Frances called after her. She actually sounded wounded. "Don't be mad. Please"

Edie kept walking.

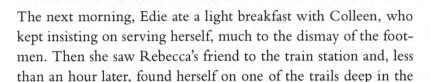

The next morning, Edie ate a light breakfast with Colleen, who kept insisting on serving herself, much to the dismay of the footmen. Then she saw Rebecca's friend to the train station and, less than an hour later, found herself on one of the trails deep in the Wissahickon, her little dog panting beside her.

The day was pleasant. The rain of the previous week had cleared, leaving clear skies and plenty of mud. She'd dressed smartly for the occasion, in a tog set consisting of serge knickers, tall brown boots, and a long, cream-colored cardigan. She topped everything with a cream beret over her cropped black waves and followed her round little dog as she bounded up and down the paths worn from generations of wandering. She had spent hours in these woods as a child, chasing after Theo, but it was the first time she'd ventured out on her own since she'd returned from California.

Aphrodite ran from tree to tree, sniffing delightedly, while Edie followed, her mind still stuck on the information that Artie had revealed about Rebecca and Celeste on Wednesday evening. She'd meant to ask Ophelia for Celeste's contact information, so she could call on the medium. She needed answers, some sense of closure. But Ophelia hadn't come to the funeral, and no one had answered her phone this morning, either. Colleen had reminded Edie that she was welcome at the Twelve's weekly salon, but Wednesday was three long days away. Edie didn't know how she could possibly make it that long.

She followed Aphrodite over the red-painted covered bridge, her footsteps echoing over the sound of the rushing water below. The noise was so loud, the creek so swollen from the week's storms, that she could barely hear herself think. She stood on the center of the bridge and closed her eyes, imagining, for a moment, that she really was the butterfly Theo had accused her of being. Beautiful and light, free from the worries, the headaches, and the pain.

"Edie? Are you all right?"

Edie opened her eyes. Frances knelt on the bridge before her, rubbing Aphrodite's wiggling stomach. "I saw you come down here alone," Frances continued. "You shouldn't be out by yourself."

Look what happened to Rebecca, her eyes seemed to say.

"I'm fine," Edie said. "I can take care of myself."

Her sister stood. She wiped her hands on her pleated skirt. Franny had grown startlingly thin, her bones as fine as bird's beneath her nearly-translucent skin. "Yes. You've made that abundantly clear."

Edie didn't know what to say to that, so instead, she said nothing. She leaned against the bridge's wide railing and watched the churning water beneath them.

Frances tried again. "You've changed," she said. "I suppose it's natural—you were gone for so long. You and Theo both were. I went from never having a second alone, to being the only one left. Just like that." She snapped her fingers. "I managed, of course. I spent a lot of time with Rebecca. With my school friends. But even so, the whole time you both were gone, all I wanted was for the two of you to come back. To come home."

"Franny." Edie felt herself softening, the way she always did. "I had to go."

"I'm not blaming you," Frances said quickly. "And I know—I know it has to be hard for you. To see me with Theo." She sent her twin a rueful smile. "It happened so fast, Edie. He came home, and you weren't here. And it felt like he saw me, you know? Like for the first time, he looked at me and saw me. Frances. Not you. And . . ."

"How long have you loved him?" Edie asked, as the pieces clicked into place. It had never occurred to her that Frances, too, might have had feelings for Theo, even then. How much had Edie hurt her, telling her all of the details of their trysts? Again, shame burned through her. She was a terrible sister.

"Always," Frances answered, swift and sure. "Even when he only saw you, I loved him. Even after . . ." her voice trailed off. "You both have changed, you know," she said, instead of whatever she was going to say. "We all have, I suppose. We all have our secrets."

What a curious thing to say. Edie knew her sister was referring to Edie's feelings for Theo, but something else clicked into place. She'd grown close with Rebecca.

Rebecca had secrets.

"Was Rebecca in trouble?"

"What?" Frances asked, but the truth of it was splashed across her face. Frances had never been able to lie. Not even a little bit. Her eyes went wide, her mouth fell open, and her cheeks pinked.

"You knew." Edie didn't mean for it to sound like an accusation. But still, Frances flinched. Then slowly, reluctantly, she nodded.

"She told me a few days before you came home. She was so upset, Edie. So ashamed. She kept saying she hadn't meant for it to happen, that she didn't want . . . didn't want . . ." Frances choked of her words and scrubbed at her face. "I told her I'd help her however I could. I reached out to Phee, who said she knew of someone. It was all to be taken care of."

It was Edie's turn to look surprised. Frances barked out a laugh.

"Don't look at me like that," Frances said. "You've been gone a long time, Edie. Girls talk. Not like it matters now, does it?"

No, Edie supposed, it didn't.

CHAPTER 20

Two days later, Gilbert's worry threatened to gnaw through his stomach. News of another mutilated body, discovered on the very day of Rebecca Shippen's funeral, had rocked the city. The front page of the Philadelphia Inquirer read: *SHIPPEN'S SLAYER STILL AT LARGE! POLICE ASKING FOR PUBLIC'S HELP IDENTIFYING ANOTHER BODY DISCOVERED ON WEST RIVER DRIVE.* As the phone lines at the morgue and police station rang with what seemed like countless tips about missing sisters and friends, Dr. Knight had taken a gamble encouraged by his newest assistant, Dr. Harrison. Harrison, like Gilbert, had served in France, and had stayed to complete his medical training in Paris. He had recalled a situation where, after a terrible fire, the police had employed dentists to put names to the scores of bodies. At Harrison's urging, Knight found a dentist, who had completed a thorough recording of the deceased's teeth. Now, it was up to Finnegan Pyle and his team of detectives to match the teeth and description the coroners had provided with one of Philadelphia's missing women.

And Gilbert's sister still hadn't returned his calls.

He hadn't mentioned it to his mother, beyond a series of probing questions about the last time she had heard from Lizzie.

It wasn't worth worrying her. Not until he knew for sure that Lizzie was missing, and it wasn't just a case of a surly housekeeper not relaying his messages.

Which is why, on a rainy Tuesday afternoon, Gilbert found himself sitting in his car at the empty gatehouse outside of the Shippens' Chestnut Hill estate, turning over the slim ivory calling card in his fingers. He had no idea if the Councilman would know a thing about his sister's whereabouts, but the fanged dread in his middle wouldn't relent until he knew Lizzie was safe.

Gilbert carefully maneuvered down the long, manicured drive, one hand on the wheel, and the other slowly pulling the lever to wipe the windshield clear of raindrops. Thunder cracked overhead, and Gilbert no longer wondered why no one had stepped out of the gatehouse to stop him; he wouldn't want to be outside in this weather, either.

The house was a monstrosity, the kind of thing built by people with more money than taste. That was the only way Gilbert could think to describe it; the fieldstone building sprawled in either direction, four stories high. A wide terrace wrapped around the first floor; a slate-topped turret dominated the western edge. Twin lions as tall as Gilbert and twice as wide flanked the wide front steps. Someone had draped black crepe around their necks, and black mourning bunting hung from every window. He parked on the driveway between the lions and turned off the car, flexing his fingers against the metal steering wheel. The last time he'd been in a house like this, it had ended so badly he'd sworn he'd never step foot in another. But he had no choice.

He dashed from the car before he could change his mind and hurried up the stairs, slick from the rain, as a bolt of lightning struck the woods on the other side of the house, near enough that his hair stood on end as the sky split with a sizzling *pop* that sent his nerves on edge. He jumped, his feet sliding, and he barely caught himself from falling right as the door ahead of him opened. The roar of the thunder drowned out the butler's greeting—or at least, what Gilbert assumed was a greeting. It very well could have been *"Who the hell are you and what are you doing here?"* but the portly man in front of him seemed too composed for that. Even the man's mustache had been waxed into polite submission.

"Hello," he said slowly, trying to remember the man's name. Lizzie had said it once or twice, he was sure.

The man cleared his throat and looked pointedly down at the marble floor, where a rapidly growing puddle had accumulated beneath Gilbert's brown boots.

At least he'd polished out the scuff.

"Welcome to Shippen House," the man said. "As you can see, the family is in mourning. Please leave your calling card in the basket, and they will be sure to respond to you as they are able."

He inclined his head to his left, to where a black-draped mahogany table sat beneath an enormous mirror in a gilded frame. A large black basket sat atop the table, filled with small ivory envelopes.

"Ah, no, sir, you misunderstand," Gilbert said, and at the sound of his accented voice, the man's thick eyebrows lowered. Gilbert had seen that look before; he pushed down the surge of anger that pulsed through him at the memory. "I'm here to speak with the Councilman."

The man's attitude shifted at once. He puffed out his chest and glowered at Gilbert. "If you're here for a job, son, you should know better than to walk in the front door." The butler walked back to the heavy front door and pulled it open. "Good day."

"Now, wait just a moment," Gilbert said. He planted his feet and straightened his back. "Would you just let me speak?."

At this, the butler laughed, a low mirthless sound. "Come now, boy. If you had legitimate business here, I'd have known you were coming. Now hurry up and go before I'm forced to remove you myself."

This was all going wrong. All of it. Gilbert scowled and ran his hand through his soaking wet hair; he'd been so out of sorts that he had left his hat on the front seat of the car. "Sir. Please. Let me explain, I'm just—"

"Looking for me?" another voice cut in. Edie stood at the top of the stairs, one hand on the banister, her mourning dress cut fashionably, dipping in at the waist and stopping just above her ankle. "Are you giving my date a hard time, Smith? Dr. Lawless is a dear friend of mine."

"Date? Doctor?" The butler's surprise was quickly covered, and he added, "We were just about to call you downstairs, Miss Edith."

"I'm sure you were, Smith." Edie fixed a warm, genuine smile on her wine-colored lips, and made her way to them. She placed one hand on Gilbert's arm, the heat of her palm searing through his jacket and shirt. And then she stood on tiptoe and pressed that perfectly painted mouth against his cheek, and said, "Shall we, darling?"

Her eyes were as gray as the storm clouds outside as their gazes collided. Gilbert swallowed hard, knowing he was about to do the one thing he'd sworn he'd never do again. *Please*, Edie mouthed up at him, and before he could think twice, Gilbert held out his arm, and whisked away another daughter of Philadelphia's high society.

"Wait!" Smith cried out as they approached the door. "Miss Edith. Let me get you an umbrella. Your young gentleman friend appears to have forgotten his in the car." The butler said *gentleman* the way another man might have said *cockroach* or *rat*.

Gilbert stared at him. "Thank you, sir," he said. "I forget that Miss Shippen isn't one of those Irish gals, used to a little drizzle."

Thunder clapped so hard overhead the windows rattled in their panes, and Edie laughed in delight. "Don't bother, Smith," she said. "I'll have to prove to him the old-fashioned way that Irish girls aren't the only ones who can get nice and wet."

Jesus, Mary, and Joseph. Gilbert nearly choked. *She didn't mean it like that.*

Edie's cat-like smile; however, indicated she knew exactly what she said. He didn't know if he was prepared to deal with Edith Shippen, but the girl didn't give him any choice—she grabbed his hand and darted outside into the rain, shrieking with laughter, her free hand covering her hair.

"You're mad," he said, chasing her down the slick stairs, leaving the bewildered butler standing in the foyer. "You're utterly and completely screwy."

Her only response was a laugh. He rushed around her, opening the door to the Model-T before she could get it herself, and helped her inside before darting to the driver's side and throwing himself on the seat. "Christ," he muttered. "It's really coming down."

Edie watched him, those stormy eyes focused on his face with an intensity that sent a curious warmth down his skin, despite his soaked clothes and dripping hair. She looked like a selkie, her wet dark hair tangled around her chin, the sodden black lace and silk of her dress molding to her body in a way that turned the warmth to hot fire, one that he was quick to dampen.

She's one of them. He forced his face into his familiar scowl and said, "What was *that?*"

"You're welcome," she said. "I don't know what you were trying to do, but nothing gets by Smith. He's probably watching us now. Quick, start the car before I have to kiss you."

Gilbert swore and dashed outside to start the car, quite simply because he didn't know what else to do. He cranked the lever outside, then threw himself back into the seat to spark the ignition. He looked over at Edie and growled, "You're in charge of the wipers."

"How do I . . . oh!" Her delighted gasp filled the car. "Like this?" She grabbed the knob and pulled the lever, sending the rubberized blades across the glass so he could see the driveway in front of them.

"You're a natural, Miss Shippen." He didn't look at her. Couldn't look at her. But her satisfaction was contagious, and almost enough to make him forget why he had driven to Shippen House to begin with.

"Edie, please. By the time I get back, the entire staff will know I made a scandalous departure with a dashingly handsome Irishman, which means my family will also know. If I'm to earn a lecture from my grandmother on your account, we can certainly be on a first-name basis."

Dashingly handsome. "You think I'm handsome?" That was not what he had meant to say. He had meant to say, *it's nice to see you again* or *my name is Gilbert* or *have you seen my sister?*, but something about her proximity had the words sticking in his mouth.

"I have eyes, Dr. Lawless," she said primly. She tugged at the wipers.

"Gil. My name is Gilbert."

"Gil." She turned the syllable over in her mouth, like she was trying it on for size. "Well, Gil. What brings you to Shippen House?"

The heat between them vanished, and any lightness Gil had felt at the way she said his name flattened out as he sighed. "I'm going to need your help. It's about Lizzie. Your housekeeper won't tell me where she's gone, and I'm worried she's missing."

Edie's eyes went wide for a moment, and then her face scrunched up in thought, her dark lips screwed to the side. "Missing? Dr. Lawless. Gil. She isn't missing. She's at home, taking care of your grandmother."

It was Gilbert's turn to blink in surprise. "What?"

Edie nodded, like she was reassuring herself. "I believe it was your grandmother? Or perhaps your aunt. No one would give me a straight answer. Some elderly relation. She took ill suddenly, and Lizzie departed as soon as she heard."

That made no sense. They had no aunt in this country, and their Nan had been dead ten years. "You must be thinking of someone else."

"No." Edie's voice was certain. "Frances—my sister—was annoyed with the entire situation. She'd defended having an Irish maid to Grandmama, you see, and then this happened. I think they're both being unfair. You have to show up for family, don't you? It's not like you or Lizzie want your aunt to be ill."

Gilbert took one hand from the steering wheel and pinched the bridge of his nose. "There's no elderly relation, Edie. No one is ill. Wherever Lizzie is . . . it's not with family. No one has seen or spoken to her since . . . when?"

"The last time I saw her was the morning of Rebecca's funeral," she said softly, cold horror dawning in her voice. "Saturday."

Gilbert swore. That tracked—that had been the last time his mother had spoken with Lizzie, too. "Do you know anyone who might be able to help? A friend, anyone?"

"There's someone." Edie pulled the wipers again. "Another maid. Athena Kostos. She works at the Pepper House."

A cold, cold stone settled in Gilbert's middle. The Pepper House. The one place he couldn't—wouldn't—be able to go. But Edie . . .

Edie could.

CHAPTER 21

Edie listened carefully as Gilbert explained what he needed from her. He steered the car down the driveway, his words punctuated by the torrent of rain overhead, sealing them in their own little world. It was easy enough—find Athena, and see if she knew where Lizzie was, or if she knew anyone who might be able to help.

"I'm happy to help, truly. But . . . Gil. Why can't you ask her yourself? Why do you need me?"

He was silent for a moment, his generous mouth set in a thin line. He looked carved of stone, all hard angles and melancholy. Only the raindrop on his nose ruined the effect, and Edie had the strangest urge to reach forward and brush it off. She yanked at the wiper's handle, instead.

"Gil?"

"Did you know Sarah Pepper?" he asked suddenly. A muscle in his jaw twitched, and Edie frowned.

"Of course I did. Everyone knew her. And we all knew what happened to her and . . ." And the name on the grave came to mind, the way Gilbert and his daughter had stared down at it with solemn faces. The girl's familiar blue eyes and heart-shaped face. *The childbed is dangerous for any woman.* The pieces clicked together, and her hand stilled.

"I happened to her," he said. He still didn't look at her.

"Well, that's dramatic," she said, after a moment. "I knew Sarah. She didn't do anything she didn't want to do."

"Wipe." The command was curt, and Edie found herself obeying without thinking twice, pulling the rubber blades against the glass.

"I'm serious, Gil. You can't blame yourself, you don't—"

"You don't know anything about me," he snapped. He slammed on the brakes, and Edie had to throw her hand against the dashboard to keep from hitting the windshield. The car sputtered beneath them, the engine stalling. "You don't know anything about *anything*, Miss Shippen. You don't know who I am or the things I've done."

"And yet I'm helping you." Her own anger surged, and she turned to him, one finger in the air. "So please, *Dr. Lawless*, tell me how big and bad and terrible you are. Shock me, if you can. Scandalize me. I dare you."

They stared at each other in angered silence. Edie's chest rose and fell rapidly, her heart threatening to tear itself from her body. Neither spoke, neither moved. The rain thundered on the fabric roof above them. Edie narrowed her eyes. She'd be damned if she backed down first.

Finally, Gilbert's shoulders slumped. "Edie." Her name sounded like an apology; one she was ready to accept. "I can't go into that house. I can't ask after Lizzie. But you can."

"I don't know how welcome I am, either. Not after what happened the last time." Edie wiped the blades again, because otherwise she'd have to look at Gilbert.

"The last time?"

"I had an episode a few weeks ago," she said softly. "A migraine. I've gotten them for years. Sometimes they're so bad that I can't even see." The flat line of his mouth grew increasingly flatter as she prattled on, explaining everything, until she reached the part where Celeste Dupont began to summon the spirits of the dead.

"That's enough," he said, crossing himself.

"I haven't even gotten to the good part yet," she protested.

"You don't need to." The look he gave Edie was withering. "That sort of thing is dangerous."

"Not you, too," Edie snapped. "It wasn't dangerous, because it wasn't real. Which would be clear if you'd just let me finish."

He folded his arms over his chest. The interior of the car suddenly felt too small, too tight, taken up entirely by his hulking disapproval. "Go ahead."

"Thank you." Out of habit, Edie reached to adjust her hat, but felt only the damp strands of her hair. They'd left so quickly she must have forgotten to grab it, and something about being so close to him in this closed space left her feeling off-kilter. Exposed. "Anyway, that night, one came on."

Tension coiled tighter around him. "Keep going."

"Well. I couldn't even see. It was dreadful," Edie gave the wipers another tug, her knuckles white against the smooth chrome knob. "Theo's a doctor too, he just finished his studies in Vienna, and he gave me something to help me sleep it off."

"He drugged you." It wasn't a question, but a statement filled with low-lying fury.

"Believe me, I've had words with him over it. It was beyond rude."

Gilbert stared at Edie for a second longer, an unreadable expression on his face. "Rude. He drugs you, and you call him rude? That could have killed you, Edie. Especially after a head wound like yours."

"I'm fine," Edie said, her hand going automatically to the scab behind her bangs, now a faded pink. "Don't trouble yourself on my account."

But Gilbert wasn't done. "I will never understand rich people," he practically snarled. "I told Liz to stay away from all of you. That it would bring her nothing but pain, but she didn't listen, not even after—" His mouth snapped shut, cutting his words off abruptly, and irritation worked its way down Edie's spine. She stiffened.

"There's nothing wrong with earning an honest living."

"There are plenty of other ways to do it that don't involve servitude. We had enough of that back home, scraping, starving, and fighting for scraps. She shouldn't have to bow to anyone, least of all some family who thinks they're above the rest of us just because they have more money than God Almighty himself."

"You'd rather her break her body in the mills, then?"

"Better than breaking her spirit amongst you lot," he spat. "But she didn't listen to me. She never listens to me."

"I find her to be quite agreeable."

He let out a noise between a snort and a grunt and Edie crossed her arms, heat creeping up her limbs. Gilbert's anger unsettled her, even more than the version of him that had patched her up with a worried frown and tender fingers. He was scared, she realized. Her cousin was dead, his sister was missing, and he was scared.

And so was she.

Edie cleared her throat. "Well. Shall we get on with it?

Edie insisted Gilbert drive to the back of the house to the servant's entrance. He didn't have to ask her for directions, and Edie wondered how often he'd come here to sneak Sarah away. It was romantic, she decided. Romantic and exciting, even if she knew the way their story ended. She knocked on the kitchen door, and wondered about the boy Gilbert must have been, and how in love they were. In love enough that Sarah abandoned everything for him.

No one had ever loved Edie like that.

The door swung open. Hampton frowned at her. "Miss Shippen? What's going on? Why didn't you come to the front door?"

Edie put on her most dazzling smile and hoped the rain hadn't made a mess of her face. "I didn't want to make a fuss, Hampton. May I please speak with Athena Kostos?"

Hampton looked puzzled but stepped aside. "Don't keep her too long, Miss Shippen. She has work to do."

A few minutes later, Athena appeared in the room beside the kitchen, where Edie was left to wait beside a long, scarred wooden table. It was so strange to see the other woman in her scullery uniform—gone was the vibrant artist Edie had met in the park, or the beauty Edie had laughed with in Ophelia's apartment, replaced with someone small and invisible. An uncomfortable awareness needled at Edie's sense of self—if Athena condensed herself to serve the Peppers, what of the household staff who had taken care of Edie her entire life? They must have hopes and dreams and worries beyond pressing Edie's gowns, and never once had Edie stopped to consider this.

Athena, for her part, looked surprised to see Edie in the scullery. "E—Miss Shippen," she said, dipping into a small curtsy, her gaze darting to Hampton. "How can I help you?"

Edie looked to the butler as well. "Thank you, Hampton," she said, forcing boredom into her voice. "I know you're busy. Don't let us keep you from your work."

The older man cleared his throat. "Yes, Miss Shippen. Athena, see me when you're finished."

Athena turned pink to the roots of her hair. But then they were alone, and her shoulders, which had climbed nearly to her ears, relaxed a fraction.

"Edie?"

"Have you heard from Lizzie?" Edie decided a direct approach was best. "I know you two are friends. She hasn't been at work, and her brother hasn't heard from her. We're worried."

Athena chewed on her lip. "I shouldn't."

So she did know something. Edie's whole body exhaled in relief. "Please, Athena. We need to know if she's safe."

"She doesn't want to be found, and for good reason. I think— I think she knows something about what happened to Rebecca."

Fear gripped Edie tightly. "What? Where is she?"

Athena twisted her apron in her hands, her knuckles as white as the starched fabric. "She'll be so cross if she knows I said anything," she said, her words tumbling out like a waterfall. "But I'm worried. She tried to get me to go with her. She said I wasn't safe here. That she would stay with a friend until she figured things out. She said she knew of someone who had helped Rebecca, and could help us, too. But I said no. My mother is sick, and I can't lose my wages, and . . ."

She covered her face with her hands, her words choking off in a sob. *Someone who had helped Rebecca.* Lizzie had been with Edie when Artie and Theo showed up at Ophelia's apartment. She'd been the one to ask if Rebecca was pregnant after hearing Artie's suspicions about Celeste Dupont. Edie touched her arm. "Please,

Athena," she said again. "Where was she going? Who was her friend? Was it Celeste Dupont?"

"She didn't say," Athena said. "I should have asked, but I didn't. She seemed to know what she was doing, and I wager, wherever she is, she doesn't want to be found."

She shifted out of Edie's grasp and fled back to the kitchen, leaving Edie standing alone, left with more questions than before.

Deflated, Edie headed back out to the car. Gilbert ran out and started the engine as she climbed into her seat. She filled him in as they drove, and instead of returning her to her house, he took a right and headed down toward Germantown Avenue.

"Who's this woman? Celeste Dupont?" he asked.

"She's a medium. A fraud, more like. I met her at the party where Theo drugged me."

Gilbert practically growled. "What does she have to do with my sister?"

"I don't know," Edie admitted. "But she certainly had something to do with my cousin. Apparently, Celeste was trying to help her."

"Help her how?"

Edie hesitated, unsure of how much to tell Gilbert. "My cousin had gotten herself into some trouble."

"That's why Lizzie asked me if I'd found proof that Rebecca had been pregnant during her autopsy."

It was Edie's turn to flinch. "When was this?"

"Wednesday." Gilbert clutched at the steering wheel. "She came to see me in the middle of the night."

She pursed her lips, as if she could stop the questions swirling in her brain from tumbling forth. Lizzie had gone to her brother right after they'd returned home from Ophelia's salon. Less than twenty-four hours later, she'd vanished. "That still doesn't explain what Lizzie knows, or where she's gone. Or why she lied about why she was leaving. Why not tell me? I could have helped her."

"I can answer that," Gilbert said. "No offense, Miss Shippen. You aren't her friend. You're her employer. But why wouldn't she come to me? She knows I'd do anything to help her."

The fear in his voice was plain, a sharp current sparking over the surface. She felt it, too. Fear, and a deep, desperate need to *act*. So she straightened her spine, the way she'd learned at the Springside School for Young Ladies, and said, "What do we do now?"

"We? We do nothing, Edie."

"Then where are *we* going?"

"You told everyone I was taking you on a date," Gilbert practically growled. "I can't bring you home after only half an hour. Everyone will think I've jilted you. We'll drive around for a bit while I think about how I'm going to find my sister and rescue her from whatever mess she's involved herself in, and then I'll return you home, and you never have to see me again."

Edie lifted her eyebrows behind her bangs. "Oh no. Not a chance. You can't be rid of me that easily."

"Miss Shippen—"

"*Edie*," she corrected. She reached out and laid her hand on his wrist as he drove, forcing herself to pay no attention to the way her heart leapt as her fingers met his skin. "We're in this together now, Gilbert. You and me. We're going to find Lizzie. Together."

Together. The word filled the air between them, bound them. Gilbert nodded, finally, after what felt like an eternity.

"Fine," he said. He turned the car abruptly, rubber squealing over the wet pavement. "I think I know where to start."

Edie should have been wary, heading off into places unknown beside a strange man. Especially in a time like this, when there was a killer on the loose. But Gilbert, with his sad eyes and steady presence, was no killer. She didn't know much about him, but she knew that instinctively. She sat beside him as they crossed the Walnut Lane Bridge, craning her neck, as always, to see if she could catch a glimpse of the Wissahickon Creek far below. Manayunk's long hill stretched down before them, and she tried not to stare at the close-packed houses as they passed. She'd spent most of her life just a few miles northwest, and despite her family's investments in the mills along the canal, had never stepped foot in the immigrant neighborhood. *Rough*, was how her father had described it. *Filthy and riddled with sin* had been her grandmother's less pleasant description, but the houses they drove by looked neat and well-kept; window boxes blooming with flowers and narrow sidewalks swept clean. The driving rain meant the streets were deserted, but as they crossed the train tracks at the bottom of the hill and Gilbert pulled the car to a stop, Edie had the sense that her grandmother's judgments were based more on fear than fact.

But still, a thrill shot through her as he cut the engine, raising his voice to be heard over the storm. "I'll be right back," he said. "Just stay here."

Hell would freeze over before she waited in the car. "Hang on. I'm coming."

He shook his head. "It's dangerous, Edie. I can't bring you with me."

She glanced through the rain-blurred windshield. The small shop they were parked in front of had a wide window filled with heaps of shoes in various shades of black. "Yes, very dangerous," she said. "Whoever designed that window display is a criminal."

Gilbert stared at her for a moment, like he was sizing her up. Edie knew she must look a fright—her hair tended to frizz in weather like this, her dress was wrinkled, and she was hatless. She decided she wasn't going to wait for him to give her permission. Lizzie was her friend. She wanted to make sure she was safe.

She pushed open her door and stepped out into the rain.

CHAPTER 22

She's incredible. It was the first thing Gilbert thought as Edie plunged into the storm without hesitation. The second, following closely on its heels as he scrambled out of the car behind her: *she's unpredictable.*

But he didn't have time to think about it. Not when Edie was barreling like a freight train into one of the most notorious speakeasies in the neighborhood, owned by one of the cities' most ruthless gangs. He hurried to catch up to her, his long legs closing the distance between them in a few quick steps. He only had a few seconds to bring her up to speed.

"Lizzie is close with the sister of the fellow who owns this place. She's not my biggest fan, but if anyone knows where Lizzie is, it'd be Molly," he said. "It's complicated. It's best if you let me do the talking."

"It's a shoe store," Edie's steel-gray eyes twinkled. "I think I can handle myself in a shoe store, Gilbert."

He didn't get the chance to correct her before she pulled open the door, bells twinkling merrily overhead. There was a boy in a news cap sitting on the counter, his heels thudding against the wooden base as he flipped through the book in his lap. He looked up, saw Gilbert, and leapt to attention.

"Dr. Lawless!" The boy nearly shouted. "I'm supposed to fetch Mr. Fletcher at once when I see you. No dawdling."

Gilbert felt Edie's curiosity pique. She stood close enough to him that he could feel the heat from her body as her arm brushed against his. Annoyance surged at his awareness of her—he had bigger things to worry about. Bigger problems. But still, he couldn't help but watch as she pushed a sopping curl from her cheek.

Christ. Why would Tommy do this? It had been almost a year since Gilbert had severed ties. Back when this had been a bar, not a shoe store fronting an illegal speakeasy. Back before Tommy ran rum and earned his ruthless reputation. Tommy had tried, since—fixing his mother's fence, sending those notes he'd destroyed without reading. Gilbert hadn't changed his mind—he didn't want back in Tommy's social circle. But he needed help, and he didn't know what else to do.

"Tell Mr. Fletcher I'm here to talk. Nothing else," he added. "Tell him it's about my sister."

The boy looked skeptical. He hopped from the counter and hurried through the curtained opening behind him, the stairs creaking as he hurried to the basement where Tommy kept his office.

Edie left his side and ran her fingers over the accumulated dust on the top of the nearest row of shoe boxes. She wrinkled her nose, then wiped her hand on her dress. "I've never been in a store like this," she said. "Their merchandiser seems . . . uninspired, to say the least. Do they do a lot of business?"

"We do well enough." Tommy Fletcher's voice held a note of laughter as he stepped into the store. His sister, Molly, followed on his heels. Gilbert hadn't known what to expect from his former best friend, but Tommy looked the same as ever: tall and solid beneath a well-cut suit, but with hair a touch too long and knuckles a bit too bruised to pass as respectable. "Who's this, Bertie?"

"Edie Shippen," Edie said, before he could introduce her. She walked right up to him and held out her hand. "Pleased to meet you, Mr.—"

"Thomas Fletcher. And this is my sister, Molly." Tommy pointed to his sister, who stood just behind him, an unlit cigarette dangling between her fingers. Gilbert didn't miss the way Tommy's gaze lingered on the curve of Edie's waist. He suddenly wanted his hand there, slipping into the soft, small place between rib and hips, to pull her close and stake his claim.

Ridiculous. He'd gone too long without affection—his attraction to Edie was misplaced at best, and a bad idea at the worst. Maybe he'd take Cecelia up on her flirting. She'd be a better match for him. She was smart and kind and pretty. And . . .

Christ. Tommy placed a kiss on the back of Edie's hand. He could at least be subtle about it.

Edie looked up at Tommy through thick lashes. "Mr. Fletcher," she said. "We're looking for Lizzie Lawless. Can you help us find her?"

Tommy straightened. His flirtatious smile vanished in an instant. Gone was the hardened man who had fought beside Gilbert in France, replaced at once by the kind-hearted boy Gilbert had grown up alongside of. "Bertie, what's going on?"

If Tommy was anyone else, Gilbert would have corrected him—only his mother could call him Bertie and get away with it. His mother and Tommy. "No one has seen her in days. She told a friend she had information that could put her in danger, and said she knew someone who'd be able to help her. Know who that might be, Tommy?" *Do you have her?* Was what he wanted to ask.

Lizzie and Tommy's relationship had always been complicated. Gilbert had given up trying to understand it.

"I haven't seen her since last week, I swear it," Tommy said, and Gilbert believed him. "I can ask some of the boys if they know anything. They all keep an eye on her, Bertie. For your sake."

That didn't ease the knot in Gilbert's throat. He should thank Tommy. He should ask . . . anything. But instead, he said, "I never asked you to do that."

"You didn't have to."

"Mr. Fletcher," Edie said, stepping carefully into the conversation. "Does the name Celeste Dupont mean anything to you?"

"Can't say that it does. Ever heard of her, Moll?"

Molly's kohl-rimmed eyes watched him carefully. She tapped the cigarette on the countertop, and said, "I might have."

"Molly, please." Gilbert was ready to drop to his knees in front of the girl and beg. He settled for clasping his hands in front of himself. "Do you know anything?"

"I don't know where Lizzie is. But it's Tuesday, right? Tuesday's the night we usually meet at Club Rouge to go dancing."

"You do *what*?" Tommy barked at his sister. His face flushed, and Molly blushed furiously, but she didn't back down.

"We're big girls, Tommy. We can go dancing if we want to. Anyway, there's a singer there—she calls herself Madame Midnight. I've heard some of the other girls talking about her—she's the one you want to see if you're in a jam. I think her real name might be Celeste, but I'm not sure."

It was something, at least. He looked at Edie, who shook her head, as if to say, *I didn't know this, either.* "Where's this Club Rouge?" he asked Molly.

Molly was already digging behind the counter for a pen and paper. She scribbled down an address and handed it to Gilbert. "You didn't get this from me, all right?" she said, then frowned. "I don't know the password tonight. Lizzie's the one who usually gets it from the fellow who delivers the milk."

Gilbert glanced down at the paper, then tucked it into his pocket. He still had one more question, one he didn't want to ask. He gathered his courage. "One last thing, Tommy," he said. "Why did Finn stop investigating Dottie Montgomery's murder?"

"What?" Molly's eyes nearly bugged out of her head. She turned on her brother, smacking him hard against the chest. "What's he talking about, Tommy? Is Dottie dead? You said—"

"I have no idea what you're talking about." All the warmth fled from Tommy's voice.

"I find it curious that he would rather see a girl from the neighborhood sent to the potter's field instead of trying to find the person responsible."

"Are you accusing me of something, Bertie?"

"I'd never do that," Gilbert said. "I just wondered if he'd mentioned anything. I know you two are still close."

He practically dragged Edie back outside into the rain. She followed, throwing a quick, "Goodbye, Mr. Fletcher!" over her shoulder as the shop door slammed shut behind them.

"Who's Dottie Montgomery?" Edie asked, tugging him to a stop on the sidewalk. From inside, Tommy still stared at them.

"A friend of Lizzie's. She worked in your house. Did you know her?"

"There was a maid who quit right around the time I arrived home. I never met her, but everyone was upset about it." Edie said it quietly, but Gilbert could almost see the wheels in her brain turning. "She's dead?"

Gilbert gave a terse nod. "Not officially. The detective on the case won't exhume her so she can be positively identified."

"Why not? Isn't that his job?" She frowned. "But that's strange, right? A girl who used to work for us is most likely dead. Murdered, you said. And then my cousin . . ."

"It's just a hunch."

The rain beat down on them, but Edie didn't seem to notice. "And now Lizzie . . ." her voice trailed off. "You think this detective is hiding something?"

"I think we need to find my sister." He shrugged off her hand and walked to the car. "Get in."

Once he got the car started, and slid behind the driver's seat, Gilbert took the paper out of his pocket and smoothed it over the steering wheel. The address was on Vine Street, not terribly far from Gilbert's boarding house, in a part of the city known for its drug dens and nightclubs.

Not exactly the type of place he'd expect his sister to frequent.

"Club Rouge," Edie said. "Sounds like a fun place."

"You think she'll be there?" He hated the catch in his voice. Hated the hope that flooded his chest, that buoyed his heart, despite his best efforts to temper his expectations.

But then Edie smiled up at him, the sparkle in her eye mirroring every emotion right back at him. "I think," she said, sweeping her gaze over his sensible trousers and sturdy work shoes. He shifted, suddenly self-conscious about the frayed edges of shirtsleeves, the cheap brass cufflinks, and knew what she was going to say next before the words left her mouth. "We need to go shopping."

◆ ◆◆ ◆

Edie Shippen shopped the way Gilbert's commanding officers had waged war: with a singular focus on the mission at hand and the desire to crush any obstacle in the path of victory. Instead of staring down no-man's land and the promise of German machine guns, Gilbert stood on the wide, clean-swept sidewalk and braced himself for the onslaught.

Edie marched into the tailor's shop on Walnut Street with her head held high. It was the third store they'd visited already; a series of boxes and paper bags filled the back seat of the car, filled with trappings Edie deemed necessary for tonight's trip to Club Rouge. A new dress for her, in black silk that apparently called for a matching feathered headband and new patent leather pumps. Her outfit alone cost more than Gilbert's monthly rent. And yet no amount of protest could dissuade her from insisting that he, too, needed a sharp suit to match.

"Good afternoon, monsieur." The round, bespectacled man behind the counter looked up as he pushed through the door, his words barely audible over the blood rushing through Gilbert's ears.

"My friend, Mr. Lawless," Edie explained. "He's in dire straits, Jacques. Do whatever it takes and charge it to Daddy's account."

The hell she would. Irritation sparked down Gilbert's spine, and he stiffened. "Edie—"

"Of course, Mademoiselle Shippen," Jacques murmured.

"Hey, now," Gilbert said, "I can pay for my own suit. How much, Jacques?"

The man blinked, owlish, behind thick lenses. "Oh, monsieur. A tuxedo, pour vous? On such short notice? I imagine— shirt and hat, as well, Mademoiselle? And shoes," he added, when Edie gave a vigorous nod. He squeezed his eyes shut as he tallied the sum. "Deux cent cinquante. At the very least."

He was going to throw up, right here in this fancy shop. "Two hundred and fifty dollars?" He took a quick step backwards.

"Two hundred and fifty bucks, for a *suit*? You're out of your minds, both of you. That car out there—" he jabbed his finger toward the street, where the Model-T sat parked on the curb, "—cost me one hundred, and I bought it used."

"Mademoiselle." Jacques sighed and tilted his shoulders, in a gesture Gilbert had learned all too well in France. That gallic shrug that meant *pas mon problème*.

The French, Gilbert decided, were a bunch of assholes.

"Gilbert." Edie pursed her lips. "Consider it a gift. For a friend."

"Don't kid yourself, Edie. We aren't friends."

He turned to the tailor and said, in perfectly accented French, "Écoutez moi, Monsieur Jacques. Je ne paierai pas $250 pour un costume, même si vous étiez le tailleur du roi d'Angleterre. Merci beaucoup. Edie." He jerked his chin at the startled socialite perched on the counter, her jaw hanging. Then he placed his hat back on his head and left, the bells on the door dancing merrily as he passed beneath and into the rain outside.

"Gilbert!" Edie joined him on the sidewalk a moment later, her face flushed. Drops fell from the brim of her new hat and speckled the bridge of her nose; she swiped them away with an impatient hand. "I didn't know you spoke French."

"You didn't know I . . ." He shook his head, raindrops flying in every direction. "You're a real piece of work, Miss Shippen, you know that?"

"What's the matter with you?"

"What's the matter with me?" He barked out a laugh and yanked open the car door. "No. I'm not doing this. Not with you."

"I was trying to be kind, and you were rude to Monsieur Jacques. He's my friend."

"That man isn't your friend, Edie, and neither am I. And please, spare me your kindness. Your *charity*."

Clarity raced across her pretty features—her stormy eyes went wide and her wine-colored lips formed a perfect circle. "That's what this is about, then. Money."

"What else would it be about?" He stared at her, incredulous. What else *could* it be about? "You just wanted me to spend two hundred and fifty dollars on a goddamn outfit."

She didn't even bat an eye at his language. "Gilbert," she said, her voice as calm and soothing as if she were speaking to a wounded animal. "I wanted to spend two hundred and fifty of my father's dollars on a goddamn outfit. Not yours."

"And that's even worse!" The words left him in a rush. "Why can't you see that?"

"It's just *money*, Gilbert. It's just going to . . . I don't know. Sit in a bank somewhere! Or be spent on a bad hand of cards. That amount . . . it's nothing. He won't even know it's gone."

For half a moment, Gilbert had imagined that Edie was another version of Sarah—Sarah, with her serious ideas and feet firmly on the ground. Sarah, who had walked away from her father's money without a second thought, who was as indifferent to her wealth as Gilbert was sickened by it.

But Edie Shippen wasn't Sarah. She was a creature of her class, of her wealth. Spoiled and selfish and so damn gorgeous, the rain plastering her black dress to the curve of her breasts, her hips. She shivered in the cool air, and gooseflesh raced down his arms in response.

She raised her chin, the challenge in her eye.

He should think her as nothing more than a silly little girl.

And yet.

"I'm wearing my own suit, Edie." He crossed to the front of the car and grasped the crank. "And that's final."

Edie sent one last, mournful look over her shoulder, to where Monsieur Jacques waited in the window, his arms crossed over his chest. And then she slid into the seat, her heavy, wet skirts squelching across the leather and turned the key. He cranked the car, the roar of the engine drowning out whatever reply she might have had. And he didn't look at her, not even once, all the way back to his boarding house, even though he wanted to.

He signaled for the turn onto Broad Street, and as Edie yanked the wipers back and forth over the glass. Once they found Lizzie, he'd deposit Edie back in her fancy mansion and leave the detective work to Finnegan Pyle and the rest of the Philadelphia Police Department, exactly as Dr. Knight had instructed.

He parked the car in the alley behind the boarding house. Edie didn't speak as Gilbert fetched the parcels from the back seat, or as he pushed open the back door with his foot. She trailed behind him like a phantom, her skirts dripping all over Nellie's freshly-washed floors, and up the narrow back stairs to the third floor.

He handed her the boxes and opened the door to his room. It was exactly as he had left it—the bed neatly made with regulation corners, the papers on his desk in a tidy stack. Nellie had left his laundry in a basket in the center of the room; he slid it under his bed with his foot. Edie didn't need to see his twice-darned socks, worn out from years of use. She probably never wore anything more than once, let alone gave anything enough use to cause a hole in the fabric.

He realized, then, that she still hadn't said a word. Short as their acquaintance may be, he knew the silence to be unlike her. Mentally, he crossed himself for strength, then turned to face her.

She stood in the middle of his room, damp and clutching the pile of boxes to her chest. The rain had washed away much of her makeup—she looked younger like this. Softer. Dark curls escaped from beneath her waterlogged brand-new felt hat, which, to Gilbert's untrained eye, looked to be beyond saving. He didn't know what he expected to find in her face—pity, maybe, for living such a simple existence. Or scorn. Anger, maybe, from the way he'd treated her at the shop.

He didn't expect curiosity.

Her lips parted, and her eyes were sharp as they met his. "It suits you," she said, finally. "The room. I've never . . ." she trailed off, like she was thinking. "I don't think I've ever been in a room and knew so instantly who it belonged to."

She set the boxes on the corner of his desk. She trailed her fingers over a framed photo of his family—Mam, Da, Lizzie, and a wee baby Penny. The photo itself was creased and water-stained, worn from being carried in his breast pocket for an entire year during the war. She glanced up at him, a small smile on her mouth, and continued her exploration.

Gilbert watched her, feeling as if his soul was being stripped bare. She ran her fingers over the thick wool blanket pulled tautly across his mattress, over the polished wood of his bureau and stopped at the only other framed photo in his room.

Sarah.

Edie picked up the frame gingerly, then sent him a curious look. "This is her debutante photo," she said. "I was there, you know. My cousin Miranda came out that night as well. There was a huge party at the Bellevue to celebrate. But you knew that already."

He nodded, not trusting himself to speak. He *had* known that because he had been there. The night of Sarah's debut was the night he stole her away, the night they'd run into the darkness of the city and hopped on a train to Elkton, Maryland. They had eloped by dawn.

"I thought she was brave. So brave. To defy her father, her family, all of society like that? I envied her." Edie stared down at the photo, then let out a short laugh. "I've never said that out loud before today. Not to anyone."

"We were kids, Edie. Dumb kids. Look where it got her."

"She wasn't dumb. She chose herself over everything else, Gil. Chose you."

"And now she's dead." He pulled the frame from Edie's hands and set it back on the dresser. "You should change. I'll see if Nellie has any dry clothes you can borrow. Stay here. And . . . and don't touch anything."

CHAPTER 23

Edie couldn't wait to touch everything.

The minute the door closed behind Gilbert, she sprang into action. Her fingers itched in anticipation as she snooped through his drawers, glanced under his bed, shuffled through the neat stack of papers on his desk. Everything about Gilbert was neat. Tidy. Perfectly in order, perfectly in control.

It was infuriating. Even his underwear was folded into squares and perfectly lined up in the drawer. He was like an automaton, not a man. If he hadn't lost his temper with her earlier, she never would have suspected that his metallic exterior concealed a human heart, hot with blood.

Losing the love of your life would do that to a person. Change them. She wondered about the boy he'd been, the boy who had a history with Tommy Fletcher—*the Tommy Fletcher*, notorious gangster!—and whose love had rocked the Philadelphia scandal sheets. What a funny twist of fate that they'd both loved and lost Peppers—Sarah, dead, and Theo . . . well.

Theo.

A small looking glass sat on the top of the bureau, beside a bowl (wiped dry, of course), a clean white towel, and a shaving kit. She leaned forward, grimacing at the frightful reflection in the mirror. Her eye makeup had run down her cheeks in twin dusky currents. She licked a finger and rubbed at it, which only served to smear it further across her cheek bones.

"For heaven's sake," she muttered. Her dress was already soaked through, and black to boot, and there was no one here to see. So she lifted her skirt and used the soft fabric to scrub at her face, clearing away the makeup, exposing her thighs to the cool spring air.

"I hope this will—Jesus, Mary, and Joseph, Edie!"

Edie whirled around at his shout; her skirt still clutched in her hands. Gilbert had flushed as red as a newborn babe, but much to her surprise, he didn't do the gentlemanly thing. He didn't turn around, or even close his eyes. Just a lingering gaze on the skin above her knees, enough to send a shiver of awareness over her.

Quickly, she dropped her skirt and reached for the dress in his hands. It was plain, but serviceable. And just as black as the rest of her current wardrobe.

"My landlady is about your size, I think. At any rate, it's dry." He thrust it toward her, his face still red. But he met her eyes. "We have a few hours before the club opens. Might as well be comfortable."

"I assume you don't have a maid?"

Gilbert let out a sharp laugh. "No, Edie. No maid."

"Is your landlady at home, then?"

"Nellie? She's gone to collect the children from school. Why all the questions? You can't suddenly be worried about being alone with me."

Edie gathered her hair in one hand and turned her back to him. "No, Dr. Lawless. I'm worried about the buttons."

"Ah." His voice was faint, and for a moment, Edie didn't think he'd do it. Didn't think he'd have the nerve to step up to her, to put his hands on her. But then he let out a sound that sounded between a sigh and a curse and his fingers were like brands against the skin at the nape of her neck. His hands trembled, ever so slightly, and Edie closed her eyes, refusing to let herself get too carried away.

He made quick work of the buttons, and left quickly, closing the door behind him, leaving nothing but an aching absence in his wake.

⸻ ◆ ⸻

They had a plan.

Edie went over the steps in her head one last time as she changed—yet again—into the black silk number she'd purchased earlier. Her underthings were still damp, despite a few hours of hanging near the fire, and Gilbert's sweet landlady had offered to lend her a pair, which Edie politely declined. She had her limits. She'd just go without.

She leaned forward and painted her lips a deep crimson, then fixed her new headband—a black Swiss-dot band, with a large feather, over her hair and across her forehead. It smoothed down the worst of the frizz, and the rest she'd tamed into submission around her chin with a few swipes of Gilbert's pomade. New, modern woman or not, she missed her maid desperately. Not just for Lizzie's skills with a curling rod—she missed the easy conversation, the teasing. The gentle concern. No one, not even Frances, had seemed to know Edie half as well, despite their short acquaintance.

Edie hoped they'd find her tonight. Hoped they'd all have a drink and laugh and put this behind them. Hoped that Lizzie didn't end up like Rebecca or poor Dottie Montgomery: cold and alone on the slab in Gilbert's morgue.

Panic seized at her middle, and she leaned forward, gripping the edges of the bureau to keep upright. It wasn't fair, was it, that Rebecca was dead and now Lizzie was missing and Frances was marrying Theo and Edie was . . . what? Playing sleuth? Inventing an attraction between herself and Lizzie's brother, who had kept up his smooth, polite mask all afternoon, while they sketched out their strategy for tonight. He didn't want Edie; he wanted to find his sister, and to wash his hands of Edie and everything she represented.

And Edie . . . Edie didn't know what she wanted, other than to feel like she deserved the life she had. To feel like she'd earned a second chance. To feel . . . anything. Anything other than anger and guilt and so much damn sadness, the kind that threatened to drown her every time she closed her eyes.

"You're horrible, Edith Shippen," she whispered.

"I'd say you're a lot of things, Miss Shippen. But horrible isn't one of them." Gilbert's amused voice came from the doorway. Edie whirled around, her hand going to her throat. "I'm sorry. I didn't mean to frighten you."

"I didn't hear you come up the stairs," Edie said. "I was just . . ." she trailed off, unsure of what to say. She was just . . . what? Hating herself? Feeling guilty for being alive? Wishing she had been the one on the slab instead of Rebecca?

"It's time to go," Gilbert said. "It's not really far enough to drive, if you're up for the walk. It looks like the rain's let up." He rubbed his hand against the back of his neck. "You look nice," he said, after a moment.

"So do you." And he did, much to her surprise. He wasn't in a coat and tails—just a simple black suit with a black vest and bow tie, his shoes shined to gleaming and dark hair slicked back. None of the boys she'd flirted with over the years would be caught dead going out in anything less than white tie. Maybe she'd been wrong, earlier, to try to force him into the same mold.

"I told you I had a suit," he said, like he could read her mind.

"Small miracles," Edie said. She picked up her new hand-bag—which was empty of anything but a small lipstick and a roll of cash she'd withdrawn from the bank earlier in the day and hurried down the stairs after him. Club Rouge waited . . . and with any luck, so did Lizzie.

Club Rouge was disappointingly nondescript from the outside. Edie didn't know what she expected from an address scrawled on the back of receipt paper, but even so, the red-brick building's windowless facade didn't match up to the anticipation that thrummed through her as she and Gilbert approached from across the street. He offered her his arm, helping her to navigate the curb. Full dark had descended since they left the house; the shadows grew closer as they made their way south through warrens of cramped boarding houses. Men and women alike sat on the stoops, glass-eyed and staring. Edie was thankful that Gilbert stayed close, his hand a steady presence on the small of her back. It was so easy to imagine a killer here, watching her from the shadows. Easier than to imagine one stalking the wide, carefully tended drives of Chestnut Hill. She shivered.

"Hold on a minute," he said. "I probably don't have to tell you this, but, ah, a lot of places like this can be pretty rough inside. You know?"

Edie fixed him with a wry stare. "It may surprise you to learn that I've never visited a gin joint before."

He raised his eyebrows. "Never?"

"I spent the last three years as the companion to my elderly aunt. And before that, I was a child. So no, please. Enlighten me as to what we're about to walk into."

A pained look crossed his face. "People . . . people come to places like this to let loose. Even if that means doing things that aren't exactly legal, per se."

"Alcohol," Edie said. "Everyone still drinks, Gilbert. My father's on the city council and you should see our wine cellar."

"Not just alcohol, Edie. Drugs, sex. And the people involved . . . there are a lot of unwritten rules, and you don't want to offend anyone. So, stick close, and let me do the talking."

He was worried about her. It was almost sweet. Edie raised a brow. "Come here often, Dr. Lawless?"

Gilbert didn't laugh. "I'm serious. A smart word to the wrong person, and we could be in hot water."

"How are we supposed to find Lizzie if I can't ask questions?"

"She'll be here. I can feel it." But he didn't look convinced, and Edie's heart dropped the tiniest bit.

"We have a plan, Gilbert. Go in, take a spin on the dance floor. See if we can see her or Celeste or anyone else I recognize. And I'll let you do the talking." She wrapped her arm around his and dragged him toward the stairs.

Her pumps clanked against the metal as she descended below street level, where a heavy iron door sat closed. She raised her hand to knock, but before she could, the peephole slid open. A slim-faced man with piercing blue eyes peered out at them, a cigarette clamped between his teeth.

"Password?"

Edie's heart kicked into gear. This was part of the plan. "Open sesame?"

The man snickered. "Good night, folks," he said.

"Wait!" Edie plunged her hand into her purse and came up holding the wad of cash she'd withdrawn from the bank. "I can do you better than a password, sir. How about . . . a hundred bucks?"

Gilbert tightened his fingers, his hand hot against her arm. They both tensed, waiting to see if it would work. After what felt like an eternity, the mechanical *click* of the door's lock opening snapped through the night like a gunshot.

Edie couldn't stop the grin from spreading over her face. She laced her fingers through Gilbert's and tugged him along, tossing the bills at the man behind the door as they passed.

The corridor was long and dark, bare bulbs overhead casting them in yellow light and they splashed through the shallow puddles on the floor. A door on the far end opened as they approached, and before Edie could even blink, they were ushered into Club Rouge.

Red was everywhere—crimson velvet swathed the ceiling, and red and gold wallpaper adorned every wall. Even the floor was red lacquer, shiny and deep as fresh-spilled blood. A jazz band played on stage; the singer crooned into a silver microphone with her face obscured beneath a red veil. The room was positively packed with people—drinking, dancing, and necking in the corners, in every sort of configuration Edie could imagine, and then some besides.

"You're staring," Gilbert hissed into her ear. "Come on. Let's dance."

He tugged her into his arms and they were on the dance floor, spinning and shaking amongst the other couples. This wasn't the ballroom dancing of the upper-class parties Edie had attended—no waltz or fox trot. Instead, the couples stood close to each other, shoulders shaking, chests swaying, hips swinging. Beads on dresses clacked, feet stomped. Gilbert pulled her close against him, the fabric of his jacket brushing her cheek. "Like this," he murmured. "Just . . . loosen up. Follow my lead."

And then they were dancing. Gilbert stepped back, his broad shoulders shimmying, feet kicking, their hands linked together. The music floated over the room, carrying their bodies to the beat in a wild, unconstrained dance that felt like nothing Edie had ever experienced. It felt like joy.

Like freedom.

He tugged her again, and she spun, skirt flying around her knees. She let her body go to the music, let the drums and the horns and the singer's smoky voice take control.

"See anything?" Gilbert asked as the song ended, drawing her attention to the fact that they were, in fact, supposed to be looking for Lizzie. She sagged against him, her heart beating wildly, and struggled to catch her breath. He rested his warm hand on the small of her back, and the rush of attraction that washed over her left her feeling weak. Breathless.

Just a show, she reminded herself. And she shook her head. No. She hadn't seen Lizzie, because she was too big of a fool to remember to look.

The crowd was a blur. So many faces swam by with wide, wild grins, their teeth flashing like pearls in the lamplight.

"Thank you, thank you. Next up on the stage is our very own Madame Midnight. Put your hands together, folks, and show her how much you love her!"

All around them, a cheer went up. A new singer emerged from behind the red velvet curtain—a black cloud against a crimson sky. She took the stage with confidence, her heels clicking across the stage.

"Good evening," she purred into the microphone, and her voice struck Edie like lightning. Celeste Dupont stood tall, her long, elegant limbs as elegant as a ballerina's. Edie stood still, her feet stuck fast to the floor, as the tall woman signaled, and the band burst to life. Her voice, deep and husky, commanded everyone's attention as she sprang into a slow, mournful rendition of *After You're Gone.* Her eyes closed; she swayed in time with the music. All across the floor, couples came together, swaying close, trading touches and whispers as they danced.

They locked eyes across the dance floor. Celeste's lips, painted black as night, curled into a smug smile. Like she knew why she was here.

Like she knew *everything.*

Edie took a step forward. She didn't know what she would do. She didn't know what she wanted to do—wanted to dance, wanted to scream, wanted to raise her voice in the same haunting chorus Celeste now sang, both hands raised high above her head.

"Gil!" Edie said, but just then, Celeste brought both hands down, and the band kicked up, horns blaring, drums thundering. All around, the crowd went wild. A young woman, probably around the same age as Edie, raised her hands above her head with a shriek, her champagne sloshing out of the glass and right down the front of Edie's dress.

Edie sputtered, but before she could protest, the girl was gone, replaced by another. And another. Gilbert grabbed Edie's arms and they spun toward the end of the dance floor. His eyes, hard as flint, were everywhere but on Edie—scanning the crowd, the band.

"I think it's a bust," he shouted over the music. "We shouldn't have come."

"Gil," Edie clutched at his arms. "The singer. It's her."

Gilbert froze. He turned toward the music, but the band was wrapping up, and the backup singers swarmed, their huge crimson fans flapping. Celeste disappeared behind the feathers, despite the disappointed groans of her fans.

"Backstage," Gilbert said. "Now."

They pushed their way through the crowd toward the edges of the stage, but there was no way to get backstage, no way to find Celeste. The platform ended abruptly, with no side entrance.

"There has to be a corridor," Edie shouted, as the band struck up another tune. A cymbal crashed, drowning out Gilbert's reply. Behind them, someone laughed, and a man stumbled backward, his shoulder catching against Gilbert's.

"Watch it," Gilbert said, but before he could get a reply, a large, black-suited man stepped in front of them. He glared down, his dark eyes hard.

"Miss Shippen," the man said, leaning close so she could hear. His breath stank of cigar and whisky and rot. "Madame Midnight would like a word."

CHAPTER 24

The crowd around them parted as the man led them back out to the corridor, like he was Moses parting the Red Sea. Gilbert kept his hand wrapped firmly around Edie's, willing his heart to calm, his fingers to steady.

Boom. The bass drum thundered, and Gilbert dropped to his knees without thinking, pulling Edie to his chest and covering their heads with his free arm.

Boom. The room around him shook, and he froze, his heart echoing in time.

This couldn't be happening.

Not now.

"Gil," Edie gasped out, picking herself up from the floor. The large man stopped, irritation crossing his features.

"What's the matter with youse?" He barked. "Don't keep her waiting."

"Come on," Edie said. She tugged on his hand, helped him to his feet. He shook free of her grip and plunged his hand into his vest pocket. The vial waited there, cool glass under his shaking fingers.

Just the band, he told himself. He was here, in Philadelphia, on a cool spring night. He was looking for his sister.

"Sorry," he lied. He didn't look at Edie. "I tripped."

The man stared at him for a long second, but he didn't say anything else. He didn't have to, not when Gilbert's lie was so hollow.

"This way," he said. He turned, his hand going to his pocket. The bulge of a gun was just visible at his waistband, and Gilbert's mouth went dry.

He hadn't been kidding before. This part of town was run by criminals and gangs as ruthless as Tommy Fletcher's crew, hard men used to using money and violence to get their way. Part of him wanted to wrap Edie up and return her safely to her wooded estate, to keep her away from all of this trouble.

But if Celeste Dupont knew something about Lizzie, he had to know.

He had to find his sister.

The corridor was blessedly quiet, the music muted by a layer of steel and concrete. He kept his fingers wrapped around Edie's and pulled her close, making sure to put his body between her and the man.

"He has a gun," Edie whispered.

Gilbert grunted, not trusting himself to speak. He didn't like this, not one bit. Another door opened. The man ushered them backstage, right as a swarm of dancers ran by, giggling behind sequined fans. Cigarette smoke hung heavy in the air. A dark-skinned man eyed them warily as they passed, his arms crossed over his chest. Something about his face nibbled at the back of Gilbert's brain, the slope of his nose, maybe, or the sharp line of his jaw.

"Wait."

The man stood suddenly, his eyes narrowing. "I know you. You work down at the morgue."

Gilbert's spine stiffened. "Have we met?"

"Not me—wait. Hey, Marco! Your friend is here." The man waved to someone behind Gil and Edie, and when Gilbert turned, he was stunned to see Marco standing there in his shirtsleeves and suspenders. A ruddy flush spread across his cheeks, and the smile he'd been wearing dropped as he stepped quickly away from the man he'd been leaning in toward just a moment earlier.

"Lawless," Marco said, his voice flat. "What the hell are you doing here? Who's this?"

"Miss Edith Shippen," Edie said, holding out her hand primly.

Marco looked down at her outstretched fingers, then back to Gilbert. "Were you . . . did you follow me?"

"We're looking for my sister," Gilbert said. "I had no idea . . . no idea." He looked from Marco's flushed face to the man beside him, who watched the scene unfold with a guarded expression. He'd seen that look before.

He'd given that look before.

He swallowed, hard. He'd met men like them, of course. Men who . . . well. Men did a lot of things in war, out on the front. He didn't blame them.

He didn't blame Marco, either. It's not like a man could choose whom he loved. He knew that better than most.

"Madam Midnight will see you now." The heavy-set man returned, breaking the awkwardness that had fallen backstage. "This way."

Marco gave Gilbert one last, desperate look as he and Edie followed the man around the corner, to a dressing room behind a heavy door. A tall, raven-haired woman sat at a dressing table with her back to them. As they entered, her black-rimmed eyes flicked to the mirror. She set her black turban on the table beside her, and said, "Leave us, Martin. I'll speak to Miss Shippen and her guest privately, if you don't mind."

"Of course, Madam," the man demurred. He left quietly, the door closing behind him with a resounding click.

At first, Celeste Dupont didn't speak. She continued whatever it was she was doing—wiping her face with some sort of cream and a damp rag, removing the cakey white makeup she'd worn on stage. Finally, when her face was bare, she set the cloth down on the table. Her gaze danced between them, a calculating expression on her face. "You're in trouble, I take it? I can't help you here, but—"

"That's not why we're here." The venom in Edie's voice surprised Gilbert—even in their short acquaintance, it seemed unlike her. He sent her a quick, searching look, but Edie kept her attention focused on the woman in front of them.

Celeste turned over the back of the chair. "I'm sorry to hear about your cousin, Miss Shippen. Have you come to make contact with her?"

"Spare me the theatrics," Edie nearly spat. Gilbert put a hand on her arm, trying to placate her. He had the feeling he'd walked into something he didn't quite understand, but he would do his best to try. For his sister's sake.

Celeste seemed unperturbed. "Did you come here to be rude, or is there another reason?"

"What do you know about what happened to Rebecca?" Edie asked, as Gilbert asked, "We're looking for my sister."

"One at a time, children," Celeste said, as prim as a school marm. She pointed at Gilbert. "You first."

"My sister," Gilbert repeated. He reached into his pocket and pulled out the creased family photo he'd carried in France. "Have you seen her?"

Celeste took the photo gingerly in her gloved hands. She traced a finger over Lizzie's face. "It depends. She's your sister?"

Hope lit in Gilbert's chest, as fierce and bright as a flare over no-man's land. "When did you last see her?" He demanded.

Celeste shook her head and handed him back the photo. "That's the wrong question, Mr. Lawless. And at any rate, it's not one I can answer. Not here. These walls . . . they have ears." She turned back to her vanity table and plucked a photograph from the top drawer. Turning it over, she scrawled an address on the back in thick black letters.

"Go to this address tomorrow and tell her I said it's all right. As for your cousin, Miss Shippen—I'm so very sorry. I never got the chance to help her."

The door opened again, and the large man beckoned. Gilbert took the photo and slipped it into her handbag.

It was better than nothing.

"She knows more than she's saying," Edie said, once they were back in the club's main room. She leaned against the bar, yanking on her long necklace with short, vicious tugs, clearly as frustrated as Gilbert felt. "What's next? Split up, ask around? See if Lizzie shows?"

"I need a drink before we do anything." Gilbert flagged down the bartender. He didn't want to do any of that. He wanted to march backstage and demand that woman tell him everything she knew about his sister and Rebecca Shippen.

The bartender took his time finishing up with the woman at the other end of the long, red-lacquered bar. "What can I get youse?"

"Your best wine?" Edie had to yell over the music. She leaned her elbows on the bar, her face serious.

The young man looked amused. "I have red. Or white."

"Anything French?" Edie asked. "Or maybe a cocktail?"

"We'll have two seltzers," Gil said, putting a stop to this, before the man charged her a fortune for a glass of wine more likely to rot her guts than anything else. They were luckier here in Philadelphia than in other places—raids were rare, and the liquor flowed freely, despite Prohibition. But a place like this or like Tommy's bar, forced underground, had to do with what they could get their hands on. And Gilbert had seen too many corpses poisoned by cheap alcohol to want to mess with any of it. When the bartender returned with their glasses, Gilbert pulled Lizzie's photo from his pocket and held it out.

"Do you know her?" he asked, tapping his finger over Lizzie.

"Elizabeth. Yeah." The young man rubbed a hand on the back of his neck. "I know her. Everyone here does."

Hope lit in Gilbert's chest. He pulled two dollars from his pocket and slid them across the bar—more than enough to cover the drinks, and a very generous tip. Not something he could easily spare, but desperate times. "She's my sister. I'm trying to find her."

The young man's brown skin turned ashen. He pocketed the money quickly, before Gilbert could change his mind, and shook his head. "Sorry, man. I don't mess with his girls. Sister or not."

"Who is he?" Gilbert asked, but the bartender had already moved on. He banged his fist on the bar, frustrated. "Damn it."

Edie took a sip of her seltzer. She gave him a long look, then set the glass on the bar.

"What?" Gilbert asked, suddenly exhausted. He didn't have time to hear whatever complaint she had about the drink, about this place, about his failure as a brother, as a man. "What's wrong?"

"I'll be right back," she said. She slipped away before he could stop her. If she didn't want to tell him, fine. That was her business. He should never have even brought her along. Edie didn't belong in his world—not in the boarding house, or this night-club, or rubbing elbows with Tommy Fletcher. She belonged in the world she was born into, the world he'd fought like hell to take Sarah from: ballrooms and expensive dresses and fast cars and too much money.

He'd let her have her fun slumming with him tonight. And tomorrow, he'd keep looking for Lizzie. On his own.

Cut the dramatics, Lizzie would tell him. She'd probably punch his arm, just to get her message across.

He missed her.

He hoped, wherever she was, she was safe. Hoped that she was happy. Hoped that, no matter what, he wouldn't be called to a scene and find her lifeless body waiting for him.

He sipped at his seltzer. By the time he set the empty glass down on the bar, Edie reappeared at his side, her face flushed a pretty shade of pink. The feather in her hair bobbed as she bounced on her toes. She grabbed his arm.

"Gil," she said. "I think I have a lead. That's what it's called, right? A lead?"

"I think detectives call it that," he said slowly, just to aggravate her. "So Edie Shippen, Lady Detective. What's your lead?"

She crossed her arms over her chest. "I don't think I'll tell you now," she said, in a prim little voice that made him lean forward, just to catch her words over the music. "I'll just have to investigate on my own. Since you won't take me seriously."

He reached out and caught her hand. Their fingers tangled together. Heat spread up his arm. But he ignored it as he tugged her close, so she could hear him clearly. She fit against him like she was made to be there, free hand splayed against his chest. He leaned down, lips brushing the soft seashell curve of her ear. "Edie, I'm joking. Please. What is it?"

She turned her head to look at him. Their eyes locked, and he couldn't help but dart a glance to her mouth. Her teeth flashed white as she chewed on her dark-painted bottom lip, and for half a heartbeat, he wanted to damn it all and see what she tasted like.

Instead, he took a half step backward, putting cool air between them. She blinked, her gaze dropping to his chest, while she, too, seemed to come to her senses. To remember who he was. Where they were.

"I found out who the bartender was talking about." Her hand patted right over his heart, racing under her fingertips. Until she spoke again, when he swore it stopped dead in his chest. "It's Leo Salvatore, Gil. I think Lizzie's gotten herself involved with the Butcher of Broad Street."

CHAPTER 25

As a child, Edie had often been accused of all manner of unacceptable behavior. She was called precocious, impetuous, boisterous. And, of course, there was the one Grandmama leveled at her most often: unbecoming of a lady.

Her time in California had taught her that there was more to life than Grandmama's rules. Mae, for all her faults, had carved out a life for herself on her own terms. She'd had a career, an apartment. Friends. As Edie stood in the front parlor before her furious grandmother, she understood why Mae had left, why she had cast off the weight of the family's crushing expectation of perfection.

Gilbert had returned Edie to Shippen House sometime after two, with a promise to fetch her again at nine. She'd risen at seven and taken her meal alone in the breakfast room. The rain from the previous night had cleared, leaving a cloudless blue sky stretching over the Wissahickon, and a crisp cool breeze fluttered through the windows. Edie had sipped her tea and closed her eyes—the day felt new. Hopeful. Today, they would visit the address Celeste had given to Gilbert last night, and find Lizzie safe.

Her bright mood lasted until eight-thirty, when her grand-mother descended the stairs, a small, silk-wrapped beacon of fury.

"Are you even listening to me?" Flora Shippen asked, her voice clipped. She didn't raise it—yelling was unbecoming. As were tears. But the old woman seemed close to both those forbidden options, now, as she gripped the mother-of-pearl handle of her cane. "I just buried one granddaughter, Edith, and now this? Out until dawn with some unknown *scoundrel?* Where were you? What do you know of this man? If you want to ruin yourself, my dear girl, be my guest. But this family will have no choice but to cast you out."

Edie, for half a moment, wanted to tell her grandmother the truth about Rebecca. That Flora's rules, her expectations, had driven her to desperation. Perhaps even into the hands of her killer.

"I did nothing wrong," Edie said instead. "I'm a grown woman. I should be allowed to have a night out with a friend. Grandmama. Frances—"

"Is engaged to a young man of the highest caliber. She is not who we are discussing at this moment. Typical, trying to cast blame on anyone but yourself. And to think! Your behavior could endanger your sister's future happiness, and then what? What would happen then?"

Edie pressed her lips together. Her behavior *could* endanger Franny's happiness—but not in the way Grandmama predicted. What would her grandmother say, if she knew the way Theo had touched Edie, just moments before learning Rebecca was dead? What would Grandmama do, if she knew the extent of their long-extinct affair? She was half tempted to admit to all of it, but that would only hurt one person: Frances. So instead, Edie rolled her shoulders back, adjusting her already perfect posture, and said simply, "You're right, Grandmama."

The older woman froze. Suspicion deepened the lines around her mouth, but Edie had, momentarily, seemed to stun the other woman into silence.

Edie barreled on. "I became used to a certain amount of freedom in California. I suppose it's shocking, really, since I left here a girl and returned a woman. I've thought about it, and in order to spare us all discomfort while we adjust to our new realities, I will be joining Daddy at the city house at once."

Edie kept her back straight as she set her tea on the side table, stood, and marched out of the room, her pumps ringing on the marble floor of the foyer. She didn't pause. She didn't look back. Somehow, she managed to take the steps at an even pace, even though every inch of her body wanted nothing more than to break into a run and slam the door shut behind her.

A housemaid—a new girl, small and dark-skinned and barely more than a teenager—dipped into an awkward curtsy as Edie passed Frances' room, her arms full of linens. Edie stopped.

"You're new?" she asked. "What's your name?"

"K-Kate, miss." Her voice was as timid as a mouse's. "Do you need something?"

"Kate, I need my things packed at once, and sent to the city house by this evening."

"Yes, miss." The girl bobbed another curtsy and hurried away. Satisfied, Edie returned to her room and packed a quick satchel—a change of clothes, some jewelry. The cash she'd withdrawn from the bank the day before. The new tincture Theo had prescribed for her migraines, which had proven surprisingly effective, despite the awful taste. And of course, Aphrodite.

The little dog watched her mistress stalk around the room from her spot on the divan. She wagged her tail excitedly—she knew something was happening and, much like her owner, she would demand to be a part of it. Edie picked up her straw cloche—the one with the peacock feather—and fixed it over her hair. Then she clipped an ivory leather leash to the jeweled collar around Aphrodite's neck, allowing herself one last look over the room she'd had since childhood: pale yellow walls and white wicker furniture. A frilled duvet and matching dust ruffle beneath the bed had been a gift from her parents on her tenth birthday. On the wall above the bed, a collection of immaculate porcelain dolls sat on a narrow shelf, their hair arranged in perfect ringlets. It was a girl's room, not a woman's.

It no longer fit.

"Where are you going?"

Edie whirled around. Frances stood in the doorway, still in her dressing gown, her hair rumpled from sleep. Dark circles bruised the delicate skin beneath her eyes and her face—which had been always thin—held a new gauntness that all together made her look even more exhausted than Edie felt. Edie had half a mind to demand where Frances had been all night. With Theo, probably, and if *that* was the case, Edie didn't want to know.

Still. Her sister should get some rest before she made herself ill.

"The city house," Edie said. She pulled on her gloves—peacock blue cotton, perfect for daytime, and a near-perfect complement to her drop-waisted green silk dress, slashed with the same brilliant blue, and matching fringed wrap. "I think it's best for everyone if I get some space."

Frances nodded absently as she picked at the skin of her bottom lip—a nervous habit she'd had from the time they were little girls. Edie wanted to reach out and grab her sister's hand, to stop her before she started bleeding all over the place, but she didn't. Frances was a grown woman now. They both were.

"That's . . . that's good," Frances said, almost more to herself than to Edie. "Yes. You should go. Today."

"I wasn't asking your permission," Edie said. She picked up Aphrodite and held the dog close to her chest. Aphrodite, always one for cuddles, wiggled her little body into the crook of Edie's arm and rested her head on Edie's shoulder with a sigh.

Frances seemed to come back to herself, her gray eyes snapping to Edie's face. She lowered her hand to her side. "Of course not," Frances replied. "But I still think it's a good idea. You're used to being independent. It's no wonder you're struggling." She reached out and gave Aphrodite a scratch between her ears. "All that stress isn't good for your health. We came so close to losing you . . ."

Edie shrugged. "I'm doing better. The medicine Theo gave me is helping. You worry too much."

"I'll always worry about you. And I'll miss you too."

"I won't be too far away," Edie said, awkwardly. She'd miss her sister too. But Frances was always busy with something—Theo, volunteering, wedding planning, attending to Grandmama's whims. She'd barely miss Edie. "It's not like last time."

Frances gave Edie a sunny smile, one that didn't quite reach her eyes. "Far enough," she said.

The unmistakable sound of tires crunching on gravel came through the open window. Edie glanced down—Gilbert's black Ford approached. A hurricane danced in her stomach, emotions she couldn't quite place swirling through her.

Frances followed Edie's gaze. "That's not one of our cars," she said, idly.

"A friend of mine offered to drive," Edie said quickly. She reached down to pick up her satchel, but Frances laid a hand on her arm, stopping her.

"Don't be silly," Frances said. "I'll call for a maid."

"I met the new one. Kate? She seems nice."

Frances crossed the room and pressed the buzzer, signaling downstairs. "She's very young. But I think she'll do nicely," she said.

"At least until Lizzie's back. Did she say how long she'd be looking after her mother?"

Frances' face was carefully schooled, but her finger returned to her mouth. "What's that?"

"Lizzie. Did she say when she's returning?" Edie watched her sister carefully, her heart growing heavier. "It's just so hard to find good help. I was hoping to bring her with me to the city house."

"Oh." Frances tugged on her lip, bright red blood welling against her soft pink skin. Edie stared at it, transfixed. Frances didn't seem to notice. "No. Her mother is very ill. I don't think she'll be returning. Mrs. Smith seems to think she was stealing, to boot. All sorts of things have gone missing lately. Daddy's cufflinks, a pair of grandmama's pearls."

Edie waved her hand. She didn't give two shakes about her father's cufflinks—the man had dozens. "Did she leave a forwarding address?" she asked. "If her mother's that ill, I'd like to send her something."

"Heavens, Edie, how should I know? She's a maid. We'll find you a new one."

"Two maids leaving in such a short time," Edie said. "Is everything all right below stairs?"

"Two?" Frances's hand returned to her mouth, swiping away the blood gathering at the corner of her lips.

"Dottie, wasn't it? The girl who was supposed to be seeing to me."

"Oh." Frances was quiet for a moment, then said, "You know how those girls are, Edie. They're always looking for a way to get out of work, and honestly, it's none of our business, what happens down there. I'm sure Mrs. Smith has it under control."

Too much. Edie had pushed too far. "You're right," she said. "I should be going."

"Safe trip," Frances replied. Some of the tension seemed to have left her shoulders. She smiled at Edie, though her eyes stayed distant. "Maybe I'll come down for lunch at Wanamaker's tomorrow?"

"It's a date." She leaned forward and pressed a swift kiss to Frances' cheek. "Ta, darling."

Frances waved her off. Edie hurried down the stairs. By the time she made it to the front hall, Kate, the new maid, was already standing by the front door, satchel in hand, and Grandmama was nowhere to be seen. The girl trailed after Edie outside to the front drive, where Gilbert waited, engine off. He hurried out of the car when he saw her, passing around the front to open the passenger door.

"Miss Shippen," he said, his hand on the brim of his hat. He looked down at Aphrodite, then back to Kate, who clutched Edie's satchel like it contained the crown jewels. "We have company today?"

"Just Aphrodite. Kate, can you put the bag in the car, please?"

"I'll take it." Gilbert reached out and plucked the bag from the girl's grip. She let out a tiny squeak, bobbed a curtsy, and ran back inside without a word. "What on earth did you do to that poor girl?"

"She's new," Edie explained. "Can we hurry, please? I don't want to make a scene."

His mouth dipped. But he helped Edie and Aphrodite into the front seat and deposited the satchel in the backseat before cranking the engine. He slid into the front seat and put the car into gear. Edie found herself paying attention to the way his fingers flexed as he gripped the gearshift.

Goodness, she was ridiculous.

It wasn't until they were halfway down the drive that he spoke. "Everything all right? You look . . ." he paused, like he was searching for the right word. Finally, he settled on, "Tired."

"You really know how to flatter a girl," Edie said dryly, though she pulled the compact out from her handbag and inspected her face. Sure, her eyes were shadowed. And a little color on her cheeks wouldn't kill her. She uncapped her tube of lipstick and patted the top with her fingertips, gently smoothing the creamy rose in the hollow of her cheekbones to add some dimension to her features. "I had a disagreement with my grandmother. I decided it'd be for the best if I spent some time at the city house. Perhaps we could stop there first, if it's not too much trouble? I can give you the address."

"I know where it is."

"What?" Edie looked over at him sharply. His gaze was fixed on the road, never wavering, but his cheeks turned ruddy.

"I dropped Lizzie off a time or two," he explained. "She's worked for your family for years."

"Of course." She felt silly. The stress of the last few days had set her on edge; Gilbert hadn't given her any reason to doubt him. She scratched Aphrodite behind the ears. "I asked Frances again about Lizzie, about when she'd be back. I asked her about Dottie Montgomery, too."

"And?" This time he did look at her. His dark eyes lit with hope, and Edie hated herself, just a little, for knowing that her next words would see that hope extinguished.

The car jolted over a pothole, and Edie winced as her very bones seemed to jostle together. "And for some reason, my sister is lying."

CHAPTER 26

"Why would she lie to you?" Gilbert forced his fingers to relax on the steering wheel. Nothing about the information they'd gathered over the last day made any sense. None of it seemed to fit together.

"I have no idea." Edie patted her little dog and stared out the window as the wooded streets gave way to big houses, then gradually smaller ones, tucked closer together. "She's a terrible liar."

"What did she say?"

This time, Edie did look at him. "She said Lizzie's mother was very, desperately ill, and Lizzie wouldn't be returning."

"So she's covering for Lizzie, or . . ." He didn't even want to say it.

"Or she has something to do with why she's left. Either way, she's making an excuse. She wouldn't even talk about Dottie." Edie's voice was sad, and it tugged at some long-forgotten chamber of his heart. He shut the feeling down quickly, but for once, a stubborn warmth remained.

Get over it. She doesn't need you to rescue her. Focus on Lizzie. So instead of pressing, he pulled the signed photo Celeste had given him from his pocket and passed it to Edie. "Do you know that address?"

Edie took it from his hand. She frowned at the singer for a moment, her brows creasing, then flipped it open to where Celeste had scrawled her address. "It's the new building at Nineteenth street, right on Rittenhouse Square. But that can't be right."

"It's an expensive address for a club singer," Gilbert agreed. "I didn't realize she was so famous."

"Oh it's not that. She's a DuPont," Edie reminded him. "Of the Delaware DuPonts, I imagine. But I know the apartment she's sending us to at this address, and it doesn't belong to Celeste. It belongs to Ophelia Van Pelt."

The name meant nothing to him. Another bloody rich family with more money than sense, most likely.

He returned his attention to Edie.

"Do they know each other?" He eased onto River Drive, and for another long moment, Edie didn't speak, just stared out at the expanse of the Schuylkill River to their right. Gilbert hated this road; he'd attended to the corpses of too many reckless drivers who had sped through the sharp curves. Drivers who now rested in the cemetery high above them. The road ribboned between the cliffs above and the steep banks of the river to the right, and Gilbert drove carefully.

"They do," Edie replied. "Celeste is—was—Artie Van Pelt's girlfriend. Ophelia's older brother. But I had the impression they didn't get along. And last I heard, Artie and Celeste had broken up. I told you about how I was with Ophelia last week, and he and Theo showed up, right? Artie was in a real state about the break-up. He blamed her for Rebecca's death."

"Could Ophelia be the one helping Lizzie?"

Edie nodded slowly. "I suppose so. It can't be a coincidence that Celeste is sending us there, can it?"

Gilbert didn't believe in coincidences. Neither, it seemed, did Edie. Her knee bounced, causing the little dog to grumble a complaint as its seat was disturbed.

"What can you tell me about Ophelia?" Gilbert asked.

"Oh, she's swell. I've known her for ages," Edie said. "If she knows anything about Lizzie, she'll tell us."

Gradually, they made their way from River Drive and onto the grid of streets leading to the Shippen's posh Rittenhouse Square address. Construction was happening on every block, from the grand buildings meant to line the future Parkway to the demolition of once-grand houses in the residential neighborhoods as expensive high-rise apartments, rich with amenities, rose to take their place. The Shippen's block seemed to be one of the last holdouts, manicured and well-kept, protected in its own bubble from the ever-encroaching development. Edie directed Gilbert to park his car in the car barn behind her family's town house, right beside a sleek silver Rolls-Royce. Edie eyed the expensive car warily as Gilbert opened her door for her and held out a hand to help her up. She hesitated.

"I didn't think Daddy would be here today. Maybe he wanted to surprise me."

"Is that a problem?" As much as he wanted to ask Ned Shippen for help finding his sister, he dreaded appearing at the man's house on Edie's arm. The last thing he wanted to do was to invite history to repeat itself.

And yet. Here he was.

"No." Edie shook her head and slipped the dog's leash over her wrist. Then she wrapped her warm fingers around his and let him help her out of the car. Her stockinged legs brushed his trousers as she stood, and he had to stop himself from leaning in close to catch a whiff of that maddening scent of vanilla.

She dropped his hand and stepped away quickly. The dog hopped out before she could help it down, landing on the pavement with a small grunt. "I'll just drop my bag and we'll head to Celeste's. I'll say hello to my father later."

"And the dog?"

Both Edie and her little dog turned to look at him, both wearing equally innocent expressions. "Oh don't be silly," Edie said. "Aphrodite goes where I go."

Gilbert sighed.

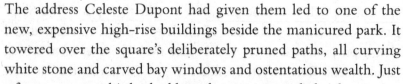

The address Celeste Dupont had given them led to one of the new, expensive high-rise buildings beside the manicured park. It towered over the square's deliberately pruned paths, all curving white stone and carved bay windows and ostentatious wealth. Just a few years ago, this lot had been home to a stately brick mansion once owned by the president of the Pennsylvania Railroad. The city was changing in every direction by the day, and sometimes, it felt hard to keep up.

Edie didn't linger. She crossed the street and smiled at the doorman beneath the ornate cast-iron awning, who greeted her by name.

Gilbert raised an eyebrow. "Do you know everyone, Miss Shippen?"

"Baird used to work for my Aunt Ida," Edie explained with a laugh. "He was a footman, before the war."

"And you were a troublemaker," the middle-aged man flashed her a bright smile. Everyone seemed to love Edie.

"Say, Baird," Edie continued, "We're visiting a school chum, Miss Van Pelt. You wouldn't mind letting us up to see her?"

Baird's smile dimmed a bit, as if the thought of disappointing Edie physically pained him. "I can't leave the door, Miss Edie, and the fellow who runs the elevator just went for a smoke break. Can you wait a minute?"

"She's expecting us," Gilbert cut in. "We don't want to be late."

"And you know how she is," Edie added, leaning close. "I don't suppose we could go up on our own?"

The man considered this, then gave a slow nod. "If you're sure. It's quite the walk."

Edie leaned forward and pressed a kiss to the man's cheek. He turned pink, then waved them toward the red-carpeted marble stairs in the lobby just beyond the doors.

"All right," she said to Gilbert. "Let's go to the penthouse."

"The penthouse?" Gilbert eyed the stairs dubiously. The pug sat down in protest. Edie tried to tug her along, but the dog refused to move.

"Baird," she sighed, "Can I leave Aphrodite here with you? She's feeling lazy today."

Gilbert doubted that today was any different for Aphrodite; the dog was low and round and looked more suited to being carried around than any sort of strenuous activity.

"How many floors?" Gilbert asked.

Baird winced. "Eighteen, sir."

Edie was already heading toward the stairs. "Oh come on, Gilbert. It's just a few flights of stairs. How hard could it be?"

◆————— ◆❖◆ —————◆

Gilbert's thighs ached. Sweat beaded his brow, and he slowed, glancing back to where Edie limped along behind him. A lock of his hair escaped his pomade and flopped down over his brow. He pushed it back impatiently.

Edie winced, shuffling her feet awkwardly. Her heels must be killing her. "I'm wondering who on earth decides they need to live on the eighteenth floor," she said. "The second floor is a perfectly respectable address. Or even the . . . tenth," she added, glancing up at the landing, where a gold placard displayed the number *10* in an elegantly carved script.

"Rich people," Gilbert said, but he left his usual malice out of the equation. He descended a few steps until he was frustratingly close to her. He offered her his arm. "You all have more money than sense."

"Not all of us." Edie eased off her shoes and gave a tiny little moan as the ball of her foot hit the cool marble step, and Gilbert suddenly wanted to do anything to coax that sound from her again.

Instead, he reached out and plucked the pumps from her hand. "Come on. A few more flights."

She gave him a coy look, fluttering her lashes over her stormy eyes, as she ran her fingers slowly over his bicep and linked their elbows together.

He could barely think as they climbed higher, as her maddening vanilla scent filled the air and her warm body pressed snug against his side. He kept his eyes firmly fixed ahead as they moved as one. He shouldn't be thinking about her like this. It wasn't . . . proper. She was a friend. An ally. A partner in finding Lizzie, and nothing more.

Until they reached the landing that read floor *18*, and he gathered his courage to glance down at her profile.

And caught her staring back.

Surprised, she stumbled, her toe catching on the lip of the step. His heart plunged, and he dropped her shoes, sending the pumps clattering down to the landing below, and caught her as she teetered backward, toward the rail and the gaping space that led to the ground, hundreds of feet below. In one smooth motion, he spun, pulling her to safety, caging her against the wall.

They blinked at each other, pressed together from toe to hip to chest, close enough that he worried she could feel his heart pounding through his shirt. He searched her eyes for moment that stretched on forever, then looked down, to her full lips—bright red today—and he was lost. He couldn't remember the last time he was this close to a woman, couldn't remember what came next. *Kiss her*, his hindbrain screamed. His breath left his lungs in a woosh as his gaze fastened on her mouth. He needed to do something. *Anything*. But he stayed rigid, barely even able to breathe.

Edie stepped back abruptly, bumping against the wall. She pressed a hand to her mouth and flushed as red as her lipstick. "Clumsy me," she whispered.

Jesus. He'd misread the entire situation. He dropped his arms, putting a safe amount of distance between them. "Be more careful next time." His voice was practically a growl, low and feral.

Edie Shippen was going to be the death of him.

CHAPTER 27

The tall, arched door to apartment 1801 waited just across the corridor. The warm wood glistened in the sunlight streaming through the corridor's tall windows, and its brass hardware gleamed. Edie's footsteps seemed to echo across the polished black and white marble floor as she stepped through the door from the stairs, her pumps back on her feet. She paused for a moment to fix her hair before the mirror beside the elevator doors, her hands shaking. She had very nearly kissed Gilbert, like the foolish girl he very clearly thought she was. For a moment, he'd looked at her like he wanted to kiss her, too, but . . . no. It didn't matter what he looked like, as she'd clearly misread the situation, and there were more important things at hand. Nerves settled, she stepped back and joined him in front of Ophelia's apartment.

Gilbert raised his fist and rapped against the door. It swung open on soundless hinges under his touch, and they exchanged a wordless, worried glance. Edie had assumed it was his nearness that left her feeling so off-balance. Unsteady. But she wasn't so sure.

"Maybe she doesn't like locks," Edie said.

Gilbert said nothing for a spell, his frown deepening. "Wait here," he said firmly. Then he pushed the door open the rest of the way and stepped inside. "Miss Van Pelt?"

"Like hell I will," Edie muttered, and followed on his heels. He turned over his shoulder and gave her a disapproving look, his mouth tilted and his eyebrows drawn down low, and Edie answered with the brightest grin she could muster.

"Ophelia!" Edie trilled. "Darling, are you home?"

No answer.

Ophelia's apartment was even brighter during the day than it had been last Wednesday evening. Sunshine poured through the tall arched windows spanning the far wall. A crystal decanter, open and half-filled with brown liquid, sat on the coffee table, an empty glass beside it. A pair of women's black pumps were askew on the floor in front of the velvet sofa, as if Ophelia had kicked off her shoes, poured herself a drink, and then . . . what? Stepped out?

"I don't think she's here," Edie said. "Should we come back later?"

"Something's not right," Gilbert said. "No one leaves their door open like that."

"I'm sure I have," Edie said. "Usually one of the staff closes it behind me."

Gilbert rolled his eyes and poked his head into the small kitchen. "Does she have servants?" he asked. "The service door is bolted."

"There weren't any here the other night," Edie said. "It'd be unusual, but it's possible she lives alone."

They both looked to the corridor at the same time. "Should we check the bedrooms?" Gilbert asked.

"Wait here," Edie said. "Maybe she's still asleep. Better I wake her up than a strange man in her room."

He didn't look happy with that idea but didn't move to stop her. Not that she would have listened, anyway; worry and annoyance battled within her as she hurriedly peeked in the empty rooms along the blue and gold papered corridor. A marble bathroom with a big tub. A bright studio, with large windows, an easel, and blank canvases stored against the wall. A guest bedroom, the bed neatly made.

"You'd better be asleep in there," Edie whispered as she reached the room at the end of the hall. The door creaked open, and Edie stepped into darkness, broken only by a single beam of daylight pushing its way through the crack of the curtains. She fumbled on the wall for the switch plate and pushed the button.

The light clicked on.

The low, modern bed was empty, the blue blankets rumpled, but that wasn't what caught Edie's attention. A chair near the closet was overturned, its legs standing straight up into the air. The contents of the vanity table scattered over the floor, the broken cosmetic palettes mixing in a dusty clump on the carpet, and an odd, coppery tang hung heavy in the air. The hair on Edie's arm rose as she stepped into the room. The carpet crunched beneath her feet.

Crunched. Her stomach lurched, and she looked down.

The rug leading from the corridor was a pure, white ivory, spotlessly clean. But the bile in her stomach rose as she stared down at her feet, at the dark stain splattered across the floor.

Blood.

She fought down the wave of nausea that rolled through her. "Gil," she said, but her voice came out in a strangled rasp. She inched forward, the dried blood crunching with every step, and cleared her throat. "Gilbert!"

She didn't wait for him to answer. She pushed open the door to the adjoining bathroom, where another smear of blood had congealed on the floor. She followed its trail as it swirled over the slick black and white marble tiles. Up the side of the white porcelain tub.

"Ophelia?" Edie asked. She was almost afraid to approach it. What if Ophelia was inside? How long had she been there? Edie pressed her hand to her mouth, and forced herself to look.

The tub was empty.

"What is it? What—*shit*." Gilbert slid to a stop behind Edie, his words dying as he stepped into the tiny space. "Shit."

"She's dead," Edie said, which felt like a stupid thing to say. Hysteria shimmered at the edge of her voice. "She's dead, isn't she?"

Gilbert didn't reply. Not for a long while. "It's a lot of blood," he admitted, finally. "I don't know who could—how anyone—" he cleared his throat. "It's unlikely anyone could survive this amount of blood loss."

A thin moan escaped Edie's lips, and she swayed. Gilbert's steady arms came around her, and he turned her face into his broad chest, shielding her from the sight of her friend's lifeblood splattered across the bathroom like paint. He led her back to the living room, where he gently helped her sit on the sofa. He disappeared into the kitchen for only a moment, reappearing with two glasses. He poured them each a stiff shot from the decanter and passed one to Edie. His hand, she noticed, was trembling as badly as her own. He reached up and brushed shaking fingers across her damp cheeks, catching her tears as they fell.

She hadn't even realized she was crying.

"Drink," he said. "It'll help. Not much, but some."

She drank the contents in one swallow, then coughed and sputtered as the whisky burned a fiery path down her throat. He poured her another. And another. And then he stood, fists gripped tight at his sides.

"Stay here," he said. "I have to make a phone call."

CHAPTER 28

Gilbert escaped down the hallway, away from Edie and her tear-stained face. The blood . . . it wasn't Lizzie's. It couldn't be Lizzie's. He wouldn't allow it to be Lizzie's.

He lifted the telephone.

"How can I connect your call?" The operator chirped on the other end. "Hello?" the voice asked, again, after a few heartbeats of silence.

"Municipal Five, City Morgue." Gilbert gripped the receiver like a lifeline. "Thank you."

"One moment please."

The call clicked through. On the other end, Cecelia's familiar voice answered. "Philadelphia City Morgue, how may I help you?"

"Cecelia." Gilbert's own voice sounded far away, even to his own ears. He slammed his eyes shut, but even so, all he saw was blood.

"Gil? Is that you?" Something clattered on the other end. "What's wrong, sweetheart?"

"I need . . . I need help," he said. "Tell Marco to track down dental records belonging to Ophelia Van Pelt."

"Sure thing. Are you all right?"

Gilbert didn't answer. He hung up. Sweat beaded at his brow. His pulse thundered as he lifted the receiver again. "Municipal Three, Police Headquarters." When the call connected, he nearly shouted Finnegan Pyle's name. Finally, Finn himself answered the phone.

"Pyle."

"I'm in the penthouse of 1830 Rittenhouse. You need to get here. Fast."

"Lawless? What's going on?"

"Hurry," Gilbert said. He slammed the phone down and flung himself in the hall bathroom, clutching at the jade green sink. There had been so much blood.

Breathe.

He needed his medicine. He couldn't lose himself now—not with Edie a few feet away and Pyle arriving at any moment. He closed his eyes, but all he could see was the blood. He sucked in a breath and reached for the tin in his pocket. The metal rattled against the porcelain as he set it down, his hands shaking so badly he didn't know if he'd be able to open it.

Breathe. The air was wrong. Thick with smoke, hot and acrid and choking. No. There wasn't any smoke. Because he wasn't in France. He was in Philadelphia. In a swanky apartment filled with blood.

Or was he?

"Get up!" His friend—closer than friend, his *brother*—reached down and grabbed his arm, his blue eyes wild. Gil tried to shove him off, to open the tin in front of him. "Move, Gil, or—"

"INCOMING!"

Another explosion landed, rocking the trench—no, bathroom. Bathroom. His tin skittered across the floor, and he crawled after it, his fingers feeling smooth tile, even as the smell of blood and shit and mud swirled threatened to drag him under. He picked up the tin and looked up into his friend's face. "Get up," he cried. "We have to. We have to."

His friend didn't seem to hear his pleas. The blue-eyed man looked up sharply as a plane soared overhead, bullets pinging over the wood and wire defenses just ahead of them. He said something, and shoved at Gilbert's arm, and Gilbert nearly dropped the tin again, but his hands found the syrette, even as the blue-eyed man turned back to yell something else. He forced himself back against the wall of the trench, ignoring the gun at his feet. He was a medic. A healer. Not a warrior. The man in front of him picked up his gun and gave him one last, desperate look.

And he couldn't do this. Not now. He plunged the needle into his arm and squeezed the syrette's bladder, sending the morphine straight to his veins. The relief was almost instantaneous—sweet darkness sweeping through his body, his muscles uncoiling, his breath evening out, the browns and reds bleeding from his vision. He closed his eyes and let his head fall to his chest, let his hands fall limp at his sides.

"Coward," he muttered to himself as he returned to the present. As the drug took hold, steadying his hands, his heart. He wanted to stay there, on the floor of the bathroom, for as long as he could, but Edie was on the sofa, just a few yards away from him, and when he thought of her alone in this apartment, he felt dangerously close to spiraling out of control all over again.

If the blood wasn't Lizzie's, it reasoned that it belonged to the apartment's owner, Ophelia Van Pelt. He thought back over the description of the flayed victim he and Marco had assembled during the autopsy: a childless woman between the ages of eighteen and twenty-five, who stood about five foot four with a slim build.

The description could fit half the young women Gilbert knew—Cecelia, Edie. Lizzie.

And perhaps Ophelia Van Pelt.

Edie rose to her feet when he stepped back into the living room. The alcohol seemed to have steadied her nerves. "Are you all right?"

"Fine." He didn't mean to sound so . . . curt. "Detective Pyle is on his way."

"Pyle." Edie was pacing now, her hands twisting in the green silk of her dress. "The same Pyle you accused of covering up a murder? The same Pyle who's on a first-name basis with Tommy Fletcher?"

"Yes." Gilbert didn't elaborate. The morphine coursed through him, sending waves of calm cascading over his consciousness. "Can you describe Ophelia?"

Edie stopped. "Why?"

"This tall, about?" Gilbert asked, holding his hand about to his shoulder. "Slim?"

Edie nodded.

"Did she have any children?" He continued.

"No, of course not. Why do you ask?" The answer seemed to come to her suddenly, and she whirled. "You know something."

"Any information will be able to help the detective," Gilbert said.

"Gilbert."

"Edie."

They stared at each other, neither side folding. And Gilbert didn't know who would have folded first if Finnegan Pyle hadn't burst through the front door.

"Lawless," Pyle barked. "Who's the broad?"

Edie stepped forward, holding out her hand. "Miss Edith Shippen," she said, and Gilbert was proud to see her arm was steady. He was beginning to realize that she was stronger than anyone seemed to give her credit for, himself included. "Perhaps you know my father? Councilman Edward Shippen?"

Pyle's face paled. "Ah. Miss Shippen. Apologies. You have a lovely home." He stared at her hand for a moment, as if he was considering whether to bend low and kiss it. He settled on a handshake, a quick bob up and down before tucking his hand into his pocket.

"It's not mine," Edie said quickly. "It belongs to a friend of mine. Ophelia Van Pelt. As far as I can tell, no one has seen or heard from her since late last week.

Pyle whipped his head to look at Gilbert for affirmation. When Gilbert nodded, he asked, "Think it's her?"

"Take a look in the bedroom. Last door on the left," Gilbert clarified. "And the bathroom."

Pyle headed down the hall without a second to waste. A barrage of swears followed. When he reappeared, his face was pale. He mopped at his forehead with a white, lace-edged handkerchief, a delicate square at odds with his heavy jaw and hangdog eyes. "No body," he said.

"Miss Van Pelt was about the same size as Miss Shippen," Gilbert said. Edie had moved to stare out of the window, her small figure silhouetted in the morning light. She looked even smaller now, in her grief—her shoulders were rounded, head bowed. Gilbert remembered the way she felt in his arms and wanted to go and comfort her, to offer her the shelter of his arms, the strength of his shoulders.

He stayed rooted to the floor.

"I'll send some of the boys to talk to her folks," Pyle said. He pulled a cigarette from his pocket and stuck it in his mouth, but didn't light it. "I'll get the rest to see if our guy left any evidence behind."

"How would the killer get in here?" Edie said suddenly, turning back to the men.

"Pardon?" Pyle dropped his cigarette.

"If Ophelia's dead, someone killed her in her bedroom," Edie said. "And, presumably, removed her body. How? This building has a twenty-four hour doorman. We're on the eighteenth floor. It's not like a prowler can climb in through the window."

"Service door?"

"Bolted from the inside," Edie said. "So the killer must have walked right through the front door."

Pyle shot a surprised look at Gilbert. A flicker of pride, however misplaced, lit in Gilbert's chest.

"What are you saying, Miss Shippen?" Pyle asked.

Edie came to stand in front of them, her hands on her hips. "What I'm saying, Detective Pyle, is that it is very likely Ophelia Van Pelt knew her killer. Knew him well enough that he was able to get past the doorman and ride upstairs on the elevator. And back out again, with her body, without raising an ounce of suspicion."

Gilbert saw where Edie was going with this. "Did she have a beau?"

"Not that I know of," Edie said. She took a deep breath. "But she did have a brother. His name is Arthur. Arthur Van Pelt."

———◆◈◆———

The dental records were a match for Ophelia Van Pelt.

Dr. Knight brought the files to Gilbert himself early the next morning, and Gilbert couldn't help the relief that coursed through him, as much as he hated himself for it.

The body wasn't Lizzie's.

If Knight noticed the way Gilbert's body relaxed at the news, he didn't comment on it. He spoke quickly, updating Gilbert on Pyle's investigation.

"Pyle questioned the brother. Artie Van Pelt—do you remember him? He was a year or two behind you, in the same class as Theo Pepper. He's a new member of the faculty—absolutely brilliant. He insists he saw his sister last Wednesday evening, alive and well. As far as we can tell, no one has been in that apartment since." Knight leaned against the desk, his hands spread wide. "Which is why I'm curious as to how you and Miss Edith Shippen found yourselves there?"

"I was looking for my sister," Gilbert answered honestly. "Someone—a friend of hers—told us that we could find Lizzie there. Lizzie works for Miss Shippen as a maid, but no one has seen her in several days. Given that two young women connected to that family are dead, Miss Shippen and I are both worried."

"Two young women?"

"Rebecca Shippen and Dottie Montgomery. The headless young women Pyle sent to the potter's field."

"The girl you ambushed the councilman about." The doctor sighed. He removed his spectacles and rubbed them on his shirt. Deep circles painted the skin beneath his eyes, and the grooves around his mouth seemed deeper than ever. "Gilbert. Son. I think you may need a few days off. The last few weeks have been difficult, even without this trouble with your sister. It's not good, for someone in your condition. You need to rest."

Two quick raps on the door stopped Gilbert from protesting. Ceclia poked her head in, her eyes sad. "Sorry to interrupt, sir," she said, though she sounded anything but. "The superintendent's office called. Some coeds found another girl down by the boathouses. Gutted like a fish. He's demanding you get there immediately."

Every muscle in Gilbert's body tensed, and he swung his head to stare at his mentor, who let out another sigh. "Never mind," Knight said. "Fetch Marco."

An eerie sense of deja-vu settled over Gilbert as he and Marco processed the scene. Much like Rebecca Shippen, this corpse was a woman, pretty and young—and even worse, Gilbert recognized her. Athena Kostos had been a friend of Lizzie's. His sister had tried to set them up on a date earlier last year, which had been a disaster. Athena had pointed Edie toward Celeste Dupont just a few days ago.

And now she was dead.

The day's heat lingered, and Marco swatted flies away as he and Gilbert gently wrapped her in a clean canvas sheet and climbed into the truck.

Gilbert was sure the autopsy would reveal that she had been drugged, strangled, and burned like the others before her. This time, the murderer had taken her tongue and her eyes with surgical precision. With the precision of a doctor.

Ophelia's brother was a doctor.

Gilbert paused at the door to the truck. "Hold on a minute," he said to Marco, who gave a nod. Gilbert turned and hurried back to the boat house, where the police superintendent, James Robinson, conferred quietly with Pyle and Dr. Knight on the long porch. The three men looked up at his approach.

"Sorry to interrupt," Gilbert said. "Doctor Salvatore and I wanted to let you know that the evidence is consistent with the other victims. Our killer is a doctor. Maybe even a surgeon."

Pyle leaned forward. "It's Van Pelt. We'll bring him back in."

Both Robinson and Knight exchanged glances. "Not so fast, Detective," Robinson said. "You can't just bring a man like Arthur Van Pelt in for questioning. His lawyers will eat you for breakfast. Make sure your evidence is iron-clad before you make a move."

"Sir—" Pyle began to protest, but a raised hand from Robinson made him swallow his words.

"One more thing." Gilbert had to try now—now, in front of the police superintendent. He didn't look at either Dr. Knight or Pyle as he spoke. "There was a Jane Doe we autopsied a few weeks ago who displayed a similar profile. Drugged, mutilated, electrocuted. It might be worth reopening her case."

Pyle narrowed his eyes at Gilbert. But before he could reply, Robinson nodded. "I like your initiative, son. Pull her records, Pyle. Let's see if there's anything in there that can connect her to Van Pelt. Every shred of evidence helps."

"Yes, sir," Pyle said. "Right away."

Dr. Knight stood with his arms crossed, his expression unreadable. For the first time, Gilbert wasn't sure where he stood with his mentor.

"Thank you, Dr. Lawless," Knight said, his voice tight. Gilbert knew when he was dismissed, and ducked his head, unease settling over his shoulders as he climbed back to the truck where Marco was waiting.

He'd taken a gamble. If he was right, he'd help to catch a killer. If he was wrong . . .

The engine roared to life. Marco glanced over at Gilbert as he pulled onto East River Drive, beneath the looming construction of the future art museum above the Water Works, where an army of masons and builders swarmed like ants over the palatial skeleton. "The other night. At the club. I didn't expect to see you there."

"I was looking for my sister," Gilbert said. "We thought . . . we thought she might be there." A thought occurred to him, and he turned to face the other man. "Do you . . . I mean. Have you seen her there before?"

Marco lifted a slim shoulder in a shrug. "I don't pay much attention to the girls," he said, and gave Gilbert a pointed look. "I'm usually occupied."

Gilbert knew Marco was trusting him with damning information. Information that would destroy his career, his credibility, if anyone were to find out about it, much the same as Gilbert's shell shock.

They sat in silence for a moment, two men bound together by secrets. Finally, Gilbert said, "I won't tell anyone."

"I know," Marco said. "And . . . neither will I. For what it's worth."

"It's worth a lot," Gilbert answered quickly. "Do you go there often?"

Marco let out a short laugh. "You could say that. My brother runs that joint."

"Leo Salvatore is your brother?" Gil stared at his friend, trying to piece together the mild-mannered man beside him with the lurid newspaper stories about the ruthless Salvatore Brothers, four of the most brutal mobsters in South Philadelphia. "You're . . . ?"

"The fifth brother," Marco said. "The baby. Too soft for the family business."

"I need to speak with him." The bartender's words, *I don't mess around with his girls*, rang in his ears. "Please."

Marco let out a sigh as he pulled onto Carlton Street and cut the engine in the alley behind the morgue. "He's no fan of the

Irish—no offense," Marco added quickly. "He's working on some sort of truce with Tommy Fletcher's boys, but he's suspicious of everyone these days. He probably won't talk to you. But maybe your friend, what's her name? Edie?"

"Miss Shippen," Gilbert corrected, but his heart was racing, the blood pounding in his ears. This seemed dangerous. Meeting with Tommy was one thing; Gilbert had grown up alongside the man, and he knew, when it came down to it, that Tommy wouldn't hurt her. But Leo Salvatore . . . Jesus, Mary, and all the saints.

What had Lizzie gotten herself into?

"You want me to send Edie Shippen to meet with a gangster? The man known as the Butcher of Broad Street? By *herself*?"

"Do you want to see what Leo knows or not?" Marco cut the engine and pushed open his door. "I'll work out the details—just be there with Miss Shippen. I promise, if he knows anything about your sister, he'll tell her. Leo can never resist a pretty face."

Gilbert tried to picture Edie holding court, on her own, with a murderer and criminal overlord, and rubbed his forehead. He had no idea if she would even be interested in continuing to help him—perhaps the last few days had just been a lark, an adventure. But even as he tried to convince himself that she'd never agree to this plan, he knew the truth of the matter.

It was a terrible idea. She was going to love it.

CHAPTER 29

Two days after Edie and Gilbert had discovered Ophelia's empty, blood-stained apartment and one day after Athena Kostos' slaying hit the newspapers, Edie sat in the front room of the modiste's shop, sipping a glass of lemonade in the midmorning light, and doing her damnedest to ignore her grandmother's pointed sighs. Of which there were many. She decided to concentrate, instead, on Aphrodite, who was currently splayed belly-up in her lap, wiggling beneath Edie's gentle fingers. She'd put a white bow around Aphrodite's neck, in honor of the occasion. It was very large and silly and made Edie forget, just a little bit, about the fact that Athena had died shortly after Edie insisted on asking her about Lizzie.

The papers were running rampant with wild speculations. *SCHULKYILL SLASHER STILL AT LARGE*, the Inquirer had proclaimed that very morning. *POLICE REOPEN INVESTIGATION OF HEADLESS BODY AS SLAYINGS SHAKE HIGH SOCIETY.* They'd gone into lurid detail, describing the way each of the four women—two glittering bright young things and two girls in service to some of the richest families in the city—had been mutilated after their death. Beheaded, disemboweled, skinned. Parts missing.

Dottie. Rebecca. Ophelia. Athena.

Each of them dead at the hands of a monster.

Each one of them a thread connected to Edie. And not just to Edie. To Lizzie, too. Lizzie, who was still missing.

Flora Shippen snapped her fan shut and fixed her granddaughter with a disapproving look. "Honestly, Edith. Did you have to bring that dog?"

"She's part of the family, Grandmama. You did say this would be a girls day." She gave Aphrodite another pat, and the dog snorted.

So did Flora, but in a more ladylike fashion. Irritation sparked in Edie's chest. "Grandmama," she began, but the rest of the words died in her throat as Frances stepped out of the dressing room, flanked by a small army of seamstresses. The dress was stunning, of course, made up of yards of white satin as blindingly pure as the season's first snow. But Edie looked past the fashionable dropped waist and the long, glittering train, up over the sleek boat neck, to her sister's face, where happiness radiated like a halo, the picture of beatific grace.

At least now, Edie could pretend the tears welling in her eyes came from happiness, not from the ugly emotions that had been swirling in her middle since she left Ophelia's apartment.

"Oh, my dear." Flora pushed to her feet and dabbed at her cheek with a lace-trimmed handkerchief. "You're stunning."

"No one will be able to take their eyes off of you," Edie agreed. She held Aphrodite against her chest as she stepped closer. "Grandmama, you're going to let her wear the tiara, aren't you?"

Their mother had worn the tiara on her wedding day to Edie's father. Family lore said it had once belonged to Queen Victoria, their late mother's great-aunt by marriage, and the girls had never, in their entire lives, been allowed to touch it. It currently sat in a dusty bank vault somewhere on Market Street, a dangling carrot meant to entice them into doing their grandmother's bidding. Flora gave her a sharp look.

Edie pretended not to notice.

"Oh, I don't know," Frances demurred. "I wouldn't want anyone to think I was bragging."

"You must! That dress is practicality screaming for it, Franny." And it was. The tiara's platinum and diamond swirls would complement the sparkling stardust embroidered at the dress's hem and cuffs. "Tell her, Grandmama."

"I had hoped it to be a surprise." Only her granddaughters would notice Flora's carefully clipped tone, which meant Edie's jab had found its mark. "But . . . your sister is right, Frances. I want you to wear it. It's what your mother would have wanted."

Had Frances not been carefully pinned into the dress from neck to ankle, she probably would have fainted from joy. Edie's own chest felt tight, as it was; she sucked in a breath, then another. Aphrodite placed a tiny kiss on her jaw.

"Aphrodite needs a walk. I'll be right back," she blurted, and before her grandmother could say boo, she adjusted her hat and escaped out the front door to the manicured park across the street. She set Aphrodite on the grass and let the little dog tug her toward the fountain in the center, where a gaggle of other dogs waited, each at least twice the pug's size. Aphrodite sniffed the other dogs politely and waited her turn when it was time to be the sniffee. It was broad daylight, and still, unease wrapped around her, heavy as a fur coat.

Her thoughts turned, again, to Gilbert Lawless. He'd very nearly kissed her—she'd seen it in his eyes—and then left her alone, traumatized, in that apartment while he called for the police. He'd barely looked at her once Detective Pyle arrived and hadn't bothered to reach out to her since. There was a murderer on the loose, Lizzie was still missing, and Gilbert hadn't even called to make sure Edie was alive and well. And it's not like she could even reach him if she tried—she didn't know the phone number for his boarding house. He'd taken one look at how she reacted to stumbling upon the scene of her friend's *murder* and decided that he no longer required her assistance. She had thought, foolishly, that unlike everyone else in her life, Gilbert Lawless had seen her for who she really was: smart. Clever. Capable. But she'd been wrong.

"Goddamned *bastard*."

The man across from her, who was holding the leash of the beefy bulldog Aphrodite was tongue kissing, coughed in surprise, and Edie realized she had spoken aloud. "I . . . I beg your pardon," he said quickly. He tugged his dog away, and hurried to the opposite side of the park, throwing a worried glance over his shoulder.

Edie scowled at him, then knelt to fix Aphrodite's bow. "Don't worry, darling. We don't need them. We're modern girls, after all."

Aphrodite whined and rolled her big brown eyes at her mistress. Edie scooped her up and snuggled her close. The last thing she wanted was to head back to that dress shop, but something— whether that be the lingering guilt about kissing Theo or some sort of twinly duty—carried her inside Thankfully, Flora was discussing payment with the modiste, and Franny had changed back into her street clothes, a lightweight summer dress in a delicate dove gray. She fixed Edie with a giant smile.

"It doesn't feel real, does it?" she asked.

"Not at all," Edie agreed. "Not at all."

◆———————◆◆◆———————◆

Later that evening, long after Edie's grandmother and sister had fled for the safety of the Chestnut Hill estate, Edie clipped Aphrodite's leash onto the dog's collar. She was going mad in the city house, under the watchful eyes of O'Meara, the butler. She could feel him watching her even now from the window, as if she'd be snatched from where she stood on the front steps.

Twilight had stretched around the city, painting the wide square in gray and blue and violet. The streets, which would normally be bustling on an evening like this, were empty, still. It felt as if the entire city was shut up behind closed doors, waiting for the newspapers to share word of another slaying.

Edie, too, felt unsettled. *Dottie. Rebecca. Ophelia. Athena.* Would Lizzie be the next name added to the list? Or someone else? Frances? Or perhaps another one of the Twelve. She should write to Colleen and the others, beg them to be safe. She shivered, allowing Aphrodite to sniff for a few moments at the grass separating the sidewalk from the street.

Suddenly, the dog froze, her little head swiveling to the right. The hair on the back of Edie's neck prickled, and she looked up in time to see a dark figure melt from the shadows, faintly outlined by the gas lamps overhead. Her heart leapt into her throat. There wasn't time to run, time to scream, even, before Lizzie was right beside her.

"Miss Edie."

Lizzie looked terrible. Her face was pale, her eyes ringed with dark circles. She'd scraped her red curls back into a tight bun and wore a black hat with a veil pulled down over her face.

"What are you doing here?" Edie blurted.

Lizzie flinched. "I—I must be quick." Her gaze bounced around the nearly-deserted block like a butterfly dancing over a garden—flitting and indecisive, barely landing before taking off again.

"Where have you *been*?" Edie's voice rose. "Do you know what you've put me through? Your *family*? Gilbert—"

"I didn't mean to upset anyone," Lizzie said, stepping close. She grabbed Edie's arm, her fingers digging into skin, warm and solid and reassuringly *alive*.

"You should tell him that yourself."

Lizzie barreled on, ignoring her. "It doesn't matter. It's too dangerous for him. For both of you. You need to stop before he realizes what you're up to."

"Before who realizes? Leo Salvatore?"

Lizzie flinched. "How did you . . . ? Just stop looking, all right? I promised her I'd lie low. That I'd let her handle it. But your meddling is putting you in danger. You have to stop."

"Who is she? Is she Celeste DuPont? Does she know something about the killer?"

"Celeste has nothing to do with any this. She was only trying to help us."

"Why did she send us to Ophelia's apartment?"

"Ophelia . . ." Lizzie's face crumpled, but she pulled herself together. "Please, Miss Edie. Leave it all alone. You don't know what you're walking into."

"I know that four women are dead, and your brother has been worrying himself sick that it'll be you to come into the morgue next. Don't you care?"

Panic flashed across Lizzie's face, chased by clear resolve. "I know. It's why I'm here. Tell him to meet me tomorrow at one, in front of the polar bears. He can see I'm fine, and then leave things alone until she tells me it's safe."

"Lizzie," Edie reached her own hand out, but Lizzie was already gone, melting back into the shadows, her footsteps ringing on the brick sidewalk as she disappeared into the night. "I don't even know how to call him!" she shouted into the night.

Lizzie kept walking.

Edie stood, staring in the direction where Lizzie had gone, for longer than she was proud of, trying to wrap her mind around what had just happened.

Lizzie was here. Lizzie was *alive*. Lizzie was . . . Lizzie was . . . Lizzie knew something about the murders.

"Oh God," Edie said. She sat down on her front steps, hard, and rubbed her forehead. Aphrodite hopped up beside her and placed a single, snuffling kiss on Edie's ear, warm and reassuring. Edie patted at the dog absently as she tried to figure out what she was to do. Obviously, she'd go to the zoo the following day, with or without Gilbert.

The poor girl looked terrible. Fearful. But of what? *Before he realizes what you're up to.* Who was he—the Butcher of Broad Street? Was the mobster the Schuylkill Slasher? Or was it someone else? And why would she and Gilbert be in danger? Why wouldn't Lizzie go to the police? The questions swirled around, and a shiver worked down Edie's spine as she made up her mind as to what she would do. She stood and hurried inside, past O'Meara, who greeted her with a gentle, "Good evening, Miss."

"Hello," she said shortly, trying her best not to take her frustrations out on the poor man. She handed the dog's leash off to him and picked up the telephone. The operator clicked on before Edie could change her mind. He worked at the morgue—she'd try there first.

"Operator."

"City Morgue, please. I'm afraid don't know the exchange number."

"Municipal Five. One moment please, I'll connect you." The line clicked in her ear as the operator connected the call.

One ring later, a woman's bored voice answered the phone. "City Morgue. How may I direct your call?"

"Dr. Lawless, please," Edie said.

The voice on the other end paused for a heartbeat. "He's not here. Can I take a message?"

Edie's heart sank, and she clutched at the phone receiver as if she could keep the woman on the other end there by sheer force of will. "No. Yes. Wait! Do you have his home number? It's important I reach him."

"I can take a message, ma'am. But I cannot give out city employees' personal information." The woman said this calmly, as if she'd had this exact conversation dozens of times before. Did people really try to do that? Besides her, of course. She had a good reason.

"Fine. I'll—I'll leave a message."

Another heartbeat. "What's the message, ma'am?"

"Oh! Oh. Right. Well. Tell him that Miss Shippen called, and I would appreciate he telephone back immediately. And tell him that I don't care if he's cross with me, it's urgent." She stressed the last word, but the woman didn't seem to care.

A note of amusement colored the response. "I'll pass it along. Have a good evening."

The line went dead in her ear.

Edie stared down at the receiver and gnawed at her bottom lip. *Damn it all.* She pressed down on the hook and lifted the phone to her ear again. What was the address of his boarding house? Somewhere on Spring Garden, wasn't it? Would it have a private phone, or a party line?

"Operator."

A knock on the door interrupted her. She jumped and shrieked, sending the entire phone crashing to the ground. O'Meara appeared beside her in a flash.

"Miss Shippen, are you all right? You look as if you've seen a ghost." He righted the phone table and gave her a serious look. "Perhaps you should lie down. Or I can fetch your tincture?"

"I'm all right, O'Meara. I promise." Another knock, three sharp raps. "Why don't you answer the door?"

The butler gave her a final once-over, and, apparently deciding she wasn't going to melt into a puddle on the floor of the foyer, acquiesced. He stepped into the vestibule. The door creaked open, and a low murmur of voices carried through the wide double doors, where Edie waited. After a moment, he reappeared. "A visitor for you, Miss."

Gilbert stepped out from behind him, as if she had summoned him by sheer force of will. Edie's heart leapt at the sight of him. His hat was in his hands, and his dark hair was mussed, a thick strand falling across his forehead. A day's worth of stubble climbed his jaw, and Edie forced herself to ignore how rakish it made him look.

"Dr. Lawless," she said.

"Edie." He stepped forward, ignoring O'Meara's sniff of disdain at his familiar use of her name. "I tried calling, earlier. They said you were out."

"I just tried calling you," she said. "I have news."

They both looked at O'Meara, who gave a nod and backed into the adjacent parlor and closed the door.

"I'm sorry I haven't called." His voice was low, and mournful, his hat gripped tightly in his hands. "Work has been busy."

"Yes. Well. I saw the papers." She looked anywhere but at him; if she looked at him, she felt like she'd burst into tears. "What are you doing here?"

"I need your help," he said. "If you're still willing."

A strange sort of satisfaction rooted in Edie. "My help?" She cast another glance at the parlor door. Edie knew, without a doubt, that the butler would be pressed to the other side, eager to hear what they had to say. She let out a short, flirtatious laugh. "Why, Dr. Lawless. It's so kind of you to escort me out this evening. You're right. A girl can't be too careful these days."

Gilbert looked puzzled. "Are you all right?"

Edie pointed to the door and interrupted him. "Everything's jake, darling. Let me fetch my things, and then you can sweep me right off my feet. Still not going to tell me where we're going on *our date?*"

Finally, understanding dawned in his gaze. He glanced toward the closed door. "If I told you, I'd spoil the fun," he said, his accent thickening. Edie knew he was putting on a show for O'Meara, but still, her foolish heart flipped over.

Edie tilted her head and scanned him one more time. He wasn't wearing his suit, again, so the club was out. In fact, he was dressed rather roughly in brown trousers and a white shirt unbuttoned at the neck, no vest or tie, just a linen jacket over top. "Where?" she whispered.

His mouth lifted into the ghost of a smile. "A boxing match."

CHAPTER 30

Marco had given him an address—a warehouse along the Delaware waterfront—and a time—nine o'clock. He stood anxiously in Edie's front hall as he waited for her to descend. He had worried that she'd grown bored with playing detective, that she wouldn't want to help him after discovering the blood in Ophelia's apartment, yet he'd been wrong. Something strange curled through his middle, spreading through his insides like slow, low hanging fog.

Hope.

After what seemed like an eternity, she appeared at the top of the stairs. She had clearly made an effort to tone herself down. Her navy dress was almost plain, with minimal black beading along the neckline, and she had shed most of her jewelry, save a strand of black beads around her neck. She wore a simple black cocoon wrap and black pumps. She looked almost demure if he ignored the hat. The hat—a black and blue beaded three-cornered cavalier hat affixed with a large, dangling, plume of black feathers on the left side—was another thing entirely.

She noticed him staring, and patted it, smiling wide. "Isn't it darling? Madame LaBelle made it specifically for me."

Gilbert made a small noise in the back of his throat, which Edie, thankfully, took as a compliment. He offered her his arm and they hurried out to the car. She was an old hand at helping him start the thing by now, and in a few moments, the engine was running smoothly. The doors slammed, shutting them inside.

"I need you to meet with Leo Salvatore," he blurted, at the same moment she said, "I saw Lizzie."

It felt as if he'd been punched in the stomach, and he was glad that he hadn't shifted the car into gear, as he likely would have run off the road.

"You saw Lizzie?"

"Leo Salvatore. The mobster?" Edie's eyes were round in the evening light.

"Edie." Gilbert's heart was slowly returning to normal. "Tell me about Lizzie."

She wasn't listening. "Tommy Fletcher is one thing, but Leo Salvatore is *famous*. The Butcher of Broad Street! I heard he once dated the actress Ruth Roland, and got into a fistfight with her ex-husband at a party at the 21 Club. That can't be true, can it?"

"Edie. Lizzie."

"Right." Embarrassment creased her face for a moment, like she couldn't believe she'd forgotten to explain herself. But then she explained everything. And the longer she spoke, the heavier his heart sank.

"Who is *he*? Leo?" he asked. "And who is *she*? Is she talking about Ophelia Van Pelt? Celeste DuPont? And why didn't Celeste just tell us she was helping Lizzie in the first place? Why send us to Ophelia's apartment?"

"Maybe that's where she thought Lizzie was staying? Lizzie specifically said that Celeste was helping 'us.'" Edie rubbed her forehead.

"I don't understand. Why wouldn't she come to me? Why you?" He didn't want to admit how much that hurt—that Lizzie had gone to Edie over him. He was Lizzie's brother—Edie was only her employer. Not even her friend.

"Perhaps," Edie said gently, "Because she knew I couldn't stop her from leaving again."

Gilbert didn't know what to say to that. "What if she doesn't show tomorrow?"

"Then at least we know she was alive today," Edie answered. "And maybe Leo Salvatore will be able to give us some more answers. If she's one of his girls, like that bartender said, he'll probably have an interest in making sure she's safe."

Edie was right. He shifted the car into first gear, gliding under the streetlamps. "Marco doesn't think Leo will talk to me. But he apparently can't resist a pretty face, so he's offered to introduce you."

"And you let me wear *this*?" She slugged his arm, a little harder than necessary. "Gilbert Lawless, I can't believe you want me to seduce a notorious gangster while wearing this! This is unequivocally the least seductive dress I own."

"No one said anything about seduction," Gilbert practically growled, pushing any images of Edie's other dresses from his mind. He practically stomped on the clutch and leveled a serious look at her. "He's dangerous, Edie. You're just going to talk with him. And maybe use some of your feminine wiles."

"You think I have wiles?"

Gilbert was suddenly glad they were sitting in the dark because he could feel the flush rise in his cheeks, hot and unwelcome. "No comment."

She made a little humming noise that had him thinking about the way she'd felt pressed against him. He gripped the steering wheel tighter and refused to look at her. He needed to stop thinking about her like that. Edie had made it clear, in that stairwell, that she wasn't interested. And he didn't blame her—what did a man like him have to offer a woman like her? He wasn't interested in repeating his past mistakes.

"He's dangerous," he said again. "Don't underestimate him."

"Did you bring me a gun?"

"What?" This time, he *did* look at her, and much to his horror, she gave no indication that she was pulling his leg. In fact, she looked more serious than he'd ever seen her. "No."

"Afraid I'll shoot you?"

"More like I'm afraid you'll hurt yourself."

"You just told me how dangerous the man is, Gilbert. I should have a gun."

"You're not going to shoot the Butcher of Broad Street," he said. A vein pulsed in his temple, and he spoke slowly and carefully, so she would not misunderstand him. "You're going to see what he knows about Lizzie, and then you're going to get out of there. Without shooting him or taking your clothes off."

She crossed her arms. "I never get to have any fun," she said. "And what about you? What will you be doing while I speak with Mr. Salvatore from a respectable distance that befits a young lady of my station?"

The fifth Salvatore brother met them around the corner from the warehouse, a hat pulled down low over his eyes. He held out a satchel as they approached. "Gil. Miss Shippen."

Gilbert took the bag. It was heavier than he expected.

Marco was all business. "We'll go in the side door, I'll take Edie to the floor. We'll watch the fight while we wait for Leo to call for us. He knows we're coming," he said to Edie. "He has some other business to attend to first."

"I'm so glad you invited us along, Mr. Salvatore," Edie said, and Gilbert could practically *see* the wheels spinning in her head. She took Marco's arm and tucked it through her own, then tugged him along like she knew where she was heading. "I've never been to a boxing match before, but I've heard there's often gambling involved."

Marco said something in reply, quietly enough that Gilbert couldn't overhear, but whatever it was must have been absolutely hilarious, since Edie threw back her head and cackled.

Gilbert had the sudden urge to hit something. Which was probably for the best, he thought, as he followed Marco and Edie into a side entrance to the warehouse. "Get changed down there," Marco said. "I'll make sure she's safe."

Edie stopped, pulling her hand from Marco's arm. "Wait. Gil. Why are you getting changed?"

Marco grinned down at her, and Gilbert flushed, hands gripping the handle of the bag so hard he feared he'd break it in half. "He didn't tell you? He's fighting."

"Oh!" Edie's eyes lit up with glee. Marco pulled her down toward the warehouse floor, which had been cleared of materials and was now packed with people on makeshift bleachers, all surrounding an honest-to-goodness boxing ring, with ropes and all. And Gilbert headed down the narrow corridor, to a dimly lit room that smelled like sweat and blood and booze. A few fighters lounged about on the low wooden benches, some nursing black eyes and split lips. The man nearest to him grunted a greeting, which Gilbert returned with a nod.

Gilbert changed quickly into the clothes Marcus had provided for him: a pair of tight-fitting shorts that tied at the waist, a black terry cloth robe, and at the bottom of the bag, a set of heavy leather boxing gloves, which accounted for the heft of the bag. He picked up the gloves, turned them over and imagined what it was going to feel like when one of them hit him square in the face.

It'll help us find Lizzie. Resigned to his fate, he tied up the thin leather shoes that Marco had packed for him. One of the other fighters, a young man with a badly broken nose that was still dribbling blood down onto his chin, looked up at him.

"First time?"

"Yeah," Gilbert said. "Any advice?"

The man smirked. "Hit him harder than he hits you, pal."

Marco had told him to make his way down to the floor, and someone would meet him there. The blood rose in his veins as he walked, every inch of him primed and ready for battle. The tremor in his hands was gone, shockingly replaced by a sure, capable feeling.

He didn't want to think about why that was.

A dark-haired man, wearing a blue suit and cap, waited with his back to the door. He was as tall as Gilbert, but broader. As he approached, the man turned, and Gilbert stopped short.

This had to be a joke.

"Hello, Bertie," Tommy Fletcher said. "Let's take a walk."

"I'm supposed to be meeting someone," Gilbert said.

"Yeah," Tommy said. "Me. You're fighting under my colors this evening."

"This doesn't make sense. Marco—"

"The Salvatore Brothers and the Cresson Street Crew have recently come to an agreement," Tommy said, as if Gilbert hadn't said anything. He slung his arms around Gilbert's shoulders. "Instead of fighting each other for scraps, we should set our sights higher. Work together in a way that benefits us both."

"What does that have to do with me?"

"Nothing. Or everything. I'm not sure yet," Tommy said. "Finn said you've been working on this Slasher business with him. He said you've found some interesting similarities."

"Finn shouldn't be telling you anything," Gilbert said.

"Ah, Bertie, you know how it is with us. Bosom buddies." Tommy waggled his eyebrows. "I know everything."

"Then where's Lizzie?"

Tommy frowned. "Everything except that," he admitted. "You think Leo knows something, though?"

"He hasn't said anything?"

"We're not exactly pals, Bertie. More like . . . associates. Allies." The crowd around them pushed close. This wasn't the time or place for this conversation, and Tommy also seemed to sense it. He changed topics. "Your Miss Shippen seems to be quite the girl," he said.

Gilbert followed Tommy's gaze, searching for Edie and her distinctive black and blue feathered hat. It was easy to spot her; the number of women in the crowd was sparse. The specter of the Slasher had struck fear in the heart of Philadelphia's young women. He found her near the sign that read *Bookie*. He shouldn't have been surprised. She had sounded entirely too excited at the prospect of gambling, and Gilbert just hoped she wouldn't lose too much money on him. He'd already done enough damage.

"She's not *my* Miss Shippen," he said. "She's only helping me find Lizzie."

"Well. If she's not spoken for . . ."

Gilbert went still. "Leave her alone."

Tommy laughed, his smile splitting wide across his face. "Oh, pal. Keep lying to yourself."

Strong hands clapped him on the shoulder. Another man, short and thick-waisted, tugged Gilbert toward the ring. "You're up, Bertie!" Tommy said. "Let's go win some money."

A booming voice broke through the noise of the crowd. "Ladies and gentlemen," it roared. "Next up in the ring: Bloody Bertie versus Philadelphia's own Whistlin' Jack McConnell!"

Bloody Bertie. Gilbert added the name onto his mental list of grievances with his childhood best friend. But he didn't have time to think about what Tommy's presence meant, as a slim muscled man at least half a head shorter than Gilbert ducked through the ropes on the opposite side of the ring.

Well, Gilbert thought, *this won't be too hard.*

He mimicked the other man's movements, slipping between the stretchy ropes, and gave a test bounce on the floor. It was springy—surprisingly so, especially for an underground operation like this. Still, he didn't want to be the first one to hit it. He had some pride, after all.

He slipped off his robe, donned his gloves. The stout man leaned forward; his red face serious. "All right, Bertie. This guy is . . ." The man paused, searching for the words. "No. Better not to say anything. Just don't underestimate him," he said.

Gilbert gave a nod, the weight of the boxing gloves unfamiliar on his hands. He slammed his fist together—he'd seen boxers do that, hadn't he?—and took a deep breath.

This was it.

He stepped to the center of the ring where the referee, dressed all in black, was already waiting with Whistling Jack McConnell, who scowled up at Gilbert through a shock of black hair. He had slim, fine-boned features and a determined set to his jaw. If he wasn't standing across the ring, Gilbert might have even called his opponent pretty, the kind of young man Lizzie would have fallen in love with at first sight.

"All right," the referee said. "I'm supposed to tell you we want a good, clean fight—but let's give them a hell of a show, eh boys?"

Gilbert barely had time to nod before the referee raised his arm in the air. A bell rang sharply, drilling all the way to Gilbert's marrow, and the fight began.

Jack's first punch, a quick, savage blow to Gilbert's ribs, stole the breath from Gilbert's lungs. He flinched back, keeping his gloves high as they circled each other warily, like two dogs fighting for dominance. Gilbert sent out a test punch, the weight of the gloves making his arms awkward. Jack dodged it easily and returned with a punch of his own—a quick strike to Gilbert's head. His vision flashed red, chased by a hot, searing pain. Gilbert shook his head. He had to focus. Had to keep his attention on the task at hand: giving a good enough show that Edie would have time to speak with Leo Salvatore.

So he swung again and this time unexpectedly his glove connected with Jack's head. The smaller man went cross-eyed for a moment and stumbled to the side. Behind them the crowd erupted in roars and hoots and jeers. Gilbert barely had time to celebrate when Jack was on him once again, fists flying with rapid fury. All Gilbert could do was raise his own arms to protect his face from the onslaught. The smaller man chased him around the ring, landing punch after punch.

Gilbert hadn't fought since his days in the schoolyard; he hadn't been one for it, even as a boy. He wasn't like Finn and Tommy, always quick to blows. He had usually been the one trying to talk them out of using their fists, with little success. One of Jack's punches broke through his arms, hitting him square in the mouth. His lip burst, his mouth filling with hot copper, and he danced out of Jack's reach. The other man retreated as well, both circling warily. Gilbert's breath left him in hot pants as he looked for an opening . . . there. He drew himself to his full height and attacked, landing one punch then another and then probably even a third. The crowd roared around them, but all Gilbert could focus on was the meaty *thwack* of his glove against Jack's flesh. He stumbled, his arms protecting his face, and Gilbert thought that this was it, this was going to be the moment of triumph; he was going to win. He straightened his back and almost smiled, even as Jack's glove connected with his jaw, and the world went dark.

Chapter 31

Edie lurched forward as the small man hit Gilbert with a vicious blow. It had been satisfying, at first, to see Gilbert fighting—some deep, primal part of her wanted to roar in triumph. But quickly, her interest turned to unease, and she flinched with every hit the smaller man landed on Gilbert. And when Gilbert collapsed on the floor of the ring, Edie's stomach heaved.

"Holy smokes," Marco breathed. He was staring at Edie with something like awe, and it took her a half second to remember the bet she'd placed.

The bet she just . . . *won.* She raised her arms and let out a triumphant scream, even as the arena around them went silent in shock.

The bookie had told Edie that the odds on "Bloody Bertie" winning were ten-to-one; Marco, apparently, had talked a good game when he booked Gilbert on the schedule, giving Gilbert a reputation Edie wasn't sure he had earned. But Edie had taken one look at the man Gilbert was fighting—a small, wiry fellow with lean muscles and a mean little smile—and handed the bookie a crisp $100 bill. "Put my money on Monsieur Bonaparte down there," she'd said.

The bookie raised an eyebrow. He looked at Marco, who shrugged indifferently.

"You heard the lady," he had said.

Now, Marco was cheering alongside her. "Miss Shippen. You just won a thousand bucks!"

"A thousand dollars!" Edie threw her arms around Marco's neck and hugged him, her blood buzzing. "Serves him right. I wonder if he's hurt?"

Marco grabbed her arm. "We'll find out later. Leo's ready for you." He tilted his head toward the windows overlooking the warehouse floor. A moment ago, the curtains had been drawn tight, blocking out the light. Now they were thrown wide, tall rectangles lit between the steel skeleton holding up the roof.

Edie's mouth went dry. But she didn't have time to be nervous, not when Marco's hand was clamped so tightly around her upper arm, and they wove through the crowd. A large man in red suspenders was helping Gilbert up—he was clearly dazed but standing. Her traitorous heart resumed beating.

Marco led her up a set of narrow metal stairs, and she was thankful for him, as her pumps disagreed with the grated stair treads. By the time they'd made it to the office, nearly twenty feet above the floor, her legs were shaking, and she knew she'd be going down those stairs barefoot—propriety be damned.

She took a moment on the landing. She straightened her hat, adjusted her gloves, and smoothed out a wrinkle in her skirt. Then she raised her head and looked Marco in the eye. "All right, Mr. Salvatore," she said.

"He's not likely to hurt a pretty thing like you," Marco said, and Edie realized, with a start, that he was trying to reassure her. "Still, though. He commands respect, Miss Shippen. So . . ."

"Don't bite?" Edie supplied. She grinned at him, ignoring the way her hands were clammy against the black lace of her gloves. Goodness, she hoped mobsters didn't expect to shake hands. That would be embarrassing.

Marco gave her a sharp look as the door opened but didn't reply.

A short, swarthy man holding, of all things, a machine gun, stood at the door. Yet another reason to be annoyed with Gilbert—he'd caused her to be under-accessorized.

"Good evening, Mr. Salvatore." She glanced back and forth between Marco and the machine gun man, trying to puzzle together the family resemblance.

There was none.

"Not *him*," Marco said. "Leo's inside."

"Little brother." The voice from the dimly lit booth was silky smooth and deep. The kind of voice that could croon a love song. Or make a girl believe any sort of nonsense he was likely to whisper in her ear. Edie's skin prickled as the owner of that voice stepped into a pool of light. Leo Salvatore didn't look like an infamous mobster. He was tall and lithe, like his brother, and shared the same mane of silky black hair—his slicked straight back—and elegant roman nose. His eyes were dark, glittering pools of obsidian, black and sharp. "Are you going to introduce me to your gorgeous friend?"

Edie sniffed. Tommy Fletcher had tried the same smooth talk on her—apparently gangsters used the same playbook, no matter what neighborhood they hailed from.

"Miss Edith Shippen, private investigator," Edie said, before Marco had the chance to introduce her. The title was an improvisation, but Leo looked suitably impressed. Or amused. Edie couldn't tell which. "I'm looking for a girl."

"You're direct, Miss Shippen. I'll give you that." Leo motioned them into his office. As Edie's eyes adjusted to the dim light, she realized that the room wouldn't have looked out of place in any number of posh houses Edie had been in, whether here, in California, or visiting her mother's people in England—papered in a dark, expensive pattern and filled with the type of heavy furniture men favored, all dark wood and bold carvings. So. Leo Salvatore was a mobster who fancied himself a gentleman. This *would* be interesting. "I didn't know the Councilman's prodigal daughter was a bona-fide sleuth."

Ah. So maybe she wasn't as convincing as she could be. "A girl needs to have some mystery about her, doesn't she? It adds a little je ne sais quois, don't you think?"

"I think, Miss Shippen, that you're wasting my time."

"Wait." This was going badly. She had to course-correct. "I don't know if your brother has told you, Mr. Salvatore, but there's a lot of chatter about this slasher stalking the streets of Philadelphia. Women are dead. I knew all of them. My cousin. A school friend. A brilliant artist. Now another friend is missing. And word in your club is that she's one of your girls."

Leo's face darkened. "People at my club say a lot of things, doll."

Edie didn't even blink. "She told me herself." Lizzie hadn't, not exactly, but the look on her face when Edie had mentioned the gangster had said enough. "Just tell me if you know she's safe."

His obsidian eyes stayed hard. "In my line of work, Miss Shippen, no one is safe. Ever."

"Leo." Marco stepped up beside Edie. "Help her. For me."

This seemed to soften the mobster. His shoulders dropped almost imperceptibly, but to Edie, it might as well have been a white flag of surrender. She stepped forward, sensing weakness.

Leo Salvatore might be a murderer, a criminal, a thug—but underneath it, he was a man.

And Gilbert *had* told her to use her feminine wiles.

"Mr. Salvatore." Edie dropped her voice, softening it. She reached forward and rested her hand on his forearm, tilted her face up to his, so he could see the tears pooling in her eyes beneath her veil. "I'm desperate. My friend is in danger, and I believe you're the only one who can help me." Edie produced Lizzie's photo with a flourish that would make a magician proud. "You know Lizzie, don't you?"

"Elizabeth. Yeah." The mobster set his jaw. "I know her."

"She's a close friend," Edie said. "I just need to know she's safe. You understand, don't you? I've lost so much already. My cousin. Two friends."

Leo locked eyes with her. "I don't even know where to start. She came to me a few weeks ago. I'd seen her before, of course, at the club. She shows up with Tommy Fletcher's little sister sometimes."

This wasn't news to Edie. But she didn't dare interrupt him.

"The Fletcher girl has got a thing for our brother Ignatius. They think they're being slick, sneaking around. They think no one knows. I let it go on, because Tommy and I have been working things out, like the gentlemen we are. But he's Irish, see? So I let this little romance go on between my brother and his sister. And in case he thinks to double cross me—I'll be able to hit him where it hurts."

He'd kill Molly Fletcher just to hurt Tommy, despite whatever feelings his own brother had for the girl. He didn't come right out and say it, but he may as well have. There was something dark brewing in the mobster's gaze, and Edie shifted, uncomfortable.

Leo cleared his throat. "Anyway, I know the girl. She's a pretty thing, so I've bought her a drink, here and there. Nothing serious. And then about a week and a half ago, Elizabeth showed up at the club, looking pale as a ghost, and trying to find our jazz singer, Madam Midnight. Another woman was with her—richer than God, that one. I can always tell."

"Ophelia Van Pelt?"

Leo shrugged. "I never got the broad's name."

"Did she tell you what was going on?" Edie leaned forward.

"She didn't tell me anything. But they talked to Celeste, and they all left together. That was that, until . . . I don't know. A few days ago—maybe three? Four?—Elizabeth showed up here again. This time, she was alone. And she was real scared. She came right to me, and asked me to help her lie low for a little while. I agreed to hide her in a place no one would think to look for her until things cooled off."

"Leo." Marco's voice was stern. "You didn't."

"I did. Ma loved her." The gangster gave his youngest brother a bashful look. To Edie, he explained, "She stayed with us for the last few days. It was the only way I could make sure she was safe, you know? And she was. Until this morning, when I woke up and she was gone without a trace. Not even a note."

"I can't believe you brought her home," Marco said. He scrubbed his face with his hands. "You're a lunatic. Ma's gonna be planning your wedding. You know that, don't you?"

"Shut up, Marco," Leo said. "I know what I'm doing."

Edie didn't have time for sibling squabbles. "Why help her at all? No offense, Mr. Salvatore. But you don't seem like a man who would do something out of the goodness of your heart."

"I think you know the answer to that, Miss Shippen."

Her thoughts were still spinning when Leo let out a deep sigh. "She seemed real spooked after the third girl showed up in the papers yesterday. Do you think that's why she left? To go after that slasher on her own?"

Edie didn't know what to think. The thought of Lizzie tracking down the killer on her own . . . . it was enough to make her sick. "Is that what you think, Mr. Salvatore? Did she tell you anything?"

"Miss Shippen," he said. "I told you. She didn't tell me anything."

It had been worth a try. Edie tried to hide her disappointment. "Right. Well. Thank you, Mr. Salvatore. I think we're done here."

He slammed his glass down on the sideboard, the loud *crack* splitting through the confined air of his office. Edie nearly jumped out of her skin. Marco put a calming hand on her shoulder, steadying her, as his brother sucked in one deep breath. Then another.

When he turned back to face them, his eyes were hard again. "Wait."

Edie's heart hammered in her chest, but she forced a look of bored indifference on her face—one she'd worn a thousand times before, in ballrooms and society lunches. "Yes, Mr. Salvatore?"

"When you find her, you'll tell her I helped you. Understood?"

She held out her hand. "You have yourself a deal, Mr. Salvatore." She gave him a firm handshake. "Now. Who do I see about the thousand bucks you owe me?"

Her traitorous heart stutter-stepped when they reached Gilbert. He sat in a small room off a dark corridor while another fight raged on the warehouse floor. His bowed back faced the door, and he didn't look up until they were nearly on top of him, the dark shadow of a bruise already haunting the angle of his jaw. Edie's chest constricted, and she had to remind herself that she was still angry with him.

Marco asked, "Are you hurt?"

"Not terribly," he said, but he winced as he spoke. Blood trickled from a small cut beneath his eye. "Did he give you anything useful?"

"I'll go get some arnica," Marco said quickly. "Good fight, Gil."

Edie knelt in front of Gilbert, forcing her breaths to even out. This wasn't the time to be bothered by the confusing tangle of emotions rising within her, not when he was here, in front of her, half dressed, bloody, and bruised. He was *sweating*, for heaven's sake . . . and yet, as she reached forward and took both of his hands in her own, hot sparks swirled from the places where their skin met.

"What did he say?"

Edie recounted the conversation with the mob boss, and with every word, tension coiled through Gilbert's body.

"She must know who the killer is," he said, finally. His grip tightened almost painfully on Edie's fingers. "Edie."

"We'll find her." She gently ran her fingers across his bruised knuckles. "Leo Salvatore promised to call if he hears anything."

He leaned forward. "You convinced him to help us?"

"I don't think it was my wiles that did the convincing," Edie said carefully. "He's the one who's been hiding Lizzie. In his house. With his mother. Who seems to be planning their wedding?"

"What?" He blinked at her. "Lizzie and Leo Salvatore?"

"The good news is, he seems very protective of her." She smiled weakly. "Even if he was immune to my charms."

Gil huffed a laugh. He turned his palm, catching her fingers in his own, and raised the back of her hand for a kiss. The sparks swirled faster, igniting an inferno. She bit her bottom lip, to stop from leaning forward.

She didn't know what she was doing. What he was doing.

But she didn't want him to stop.

"If he's involved, it could be dangerous." His mouth brushed over her skin with every word, but his eyes were deadly serious, fixed on her own. "You could get hurt."

"And if I do nothing, I could be the one the killer takes next," Edie said, and it was the truth. Each of the victims so far had some connection to her: Dottie, a maid in her house. Her cousin. Her friends. His lips stilled on the back of her hand. "I could die tomorrow," she repeated, her voice shaking. "I could die without ever really having the chance to live."

Before she could say anything, Marco returned, stomping loudly into the space. Gilbert dropped her hand and sat up, quickly putting space between them.

"This is for him," Marco said, without ceremony. He thrust a bottle of arnica into Edie's outstretched palm. Gil's grunt of thanks was nearly lost behind his intake of breath as Edie gingerly dabbed the salve on the swelling beside his eye.

"Sorry," she whispered.

"And this, Miss Shippen," Marco continued, reaching into his pocket, "Is for you."

Edie set the bottle aside and took the wad of cash carefully. Her smile grew as she counted each crisp hundred-dollar bill— ten in total. She made a show of fanning herself with the money, meeting Gilbert's stunned gaze. One thousand dollars—of her own money. Not her father's or grandfather's. Not some husband's, either.

Her own.

"See, boys? You needn't worry about me," Edie said, as she tucked the money into her handbag. "I can take care of myself."

CHAPTER 32

Neither of them spoke until Gilbert pulled to the curb in front of the Shippen's city house. An awkwardness filled the car between them, thick as molasses. Edie made a small noise of surprise as he idled the engine, like she'd forgotten where they were headed. Gilbert knew he should turn off the car and open her door, but for some reason, he couldn't bring himself to move.

She'd bet against him.

He shouldn't have been surprised. Not with her. Of course she'd bet against him. Nothing this woman did should surprise him, and yet . . .

He glanced over at her, silhouetted in the passenger seat, a strange sort of warmth rooting in his chest.

He wanted more of her surprises.

He squashed that thought down as quickly as it came on. *She's not for you*, he reminded himself, but this constant refrain sounded tired, even to himself. He couldn't force her to stay out of danger. If he knew nothing else about Edie Shippen, he knew that she would make her own choices.

And Mother Mary help anyone who tried to choose *for* her.

"Gil?" She reached across the seat between them, her touch reassuring. "We'll see her tomorrow. She'll let us help her."

It took him a moment to respond. He'd been so focused on her that, at first, he didn't know what she was talking about. But then everything—the murdered girls, the Salvatore Brothers, Lizzie—came rushing back in. And he hated himself for forgetting.

He pulled his hand free, and gripped the steering wheel, hiding the way his hands trembled, as the horrible weight of reality settled back over his shoulders.

That was the problem with girls like Sarah. With women like Edie.

For better or worse, they drove men to distraction.

He closed his eyes. But he could still feel her staring at him, feel the weight of her gaze on his bruised jaw, the breadth of his shoulders. His trembling hands.

She scooted closer, the seat between them dipping beneath her weight. "I meant what I said earlier," she said, suddenly serious. "I've only just started living the life I want, Gilbert. And that all could be taken away in a moment."

"Edie, I won't—"

"I don't want to be alone." Her words burst forth, filling the space between them. "Not right now. Please."

Another surprise.

"Edie." He should say no. Should put a stop to this, right here and right now, before he broke her heart.

Because he would. Break her heart. And his own, in the process. He should have stopped this the day they met, before he knew her laugh, before he felt the swell of her hip beneath those ridiculous dresses she wore. Before he went to bed every night wanting a woman he could never—should never—have. The words were right there, on the tip of his tongue. A million reasons to see her home, to return her to her world, to keep her safe.

He couldn't bring himself to turn off the car.

Inside, a light switched on, flooding the transom window over the front door.

"Please," she said.

Gilbert put the car into gear.

They climbed the steps to his small, rented room, the silence stretching between them like a living, breathing thing. Gilbert was glad of it, because he didn't trust himself to speak. Not when Edie's hips swayed a few steps ahead of him. The thin seam of her stockings ran up her calves and disappeared beneath the swirling navy fabric of her skirts, and his trembling fingers ached to follow that seam up and up and up . . .

She stepped aside on the landing, and he unlocked the door. He flipped on the light and held the door for her. She slipped inside, her high heels clicking on the wooden floorboards.

"Do you want something to drink?" His voice rumbled out of his chest, sounding too loud in the quiet room. He shut the door and slipped his hands in his pockets. "Nellie is sleeping, but I could make us a pot of tea."

"I don't want anything to drink," she said. "I just . . . I just don't want to be alone." Her jaw snapped shut with a click. "You might not believe it, but I'm having a hard time with all of this."

She looked so brave, standing there, chin raised, shoulders strong. Defiant, even. Warmth furled through his chest. "I'd be worried if you weren't."

"I think I should buy a gun."

"That's the worst idea I've heard all day," he said. He stepped closer to her. "And I let Marco talk me into the boxing ring."

"I'm scared," she whispered, and some deep part of him wanted to take her in his arms. To make her feel safe and sheltered, to promise her he'd keep her safe. Whole. To grant her the protection of his body, until his dying breath.

"Buying a gun won't help that. It'll only make you dangerous." He reached up and tucked her hair behind her ear. "I've seen what happens when scared people get guns, Edie. They end up on my table, or maybe in a cell at Eastern State, because they let their fear turn them into a killer. I won't let that happen to you."

"Then make me feel safe."

Her words were a challenge, thrown in the air between them. Gilbert took a half step backward, his heart thudding against his chest. "I can't do that."

"You won't, you mean." Edie's eyes never left his. "You're afraid."

Anger surged through him, quick and hot. "I'm not afraid of you," he practically spat.

She tilted her head. "No," she said, "You're right. You're not afraid of me, Gilbert. I'm just a silly, flighty thing. A butterfly. Pretty and powerless. Not something someone like you would ever want anything to do with."

"That's the stupidest thing I've ever heard." The words left his mouth before he could stop them. "Christ, Edie, is that what you think of yourself?"

"I don't know."

He reached out, trembling hand cupping her chin. He brushed the pad of his thumb over the swell of her bottom lip and she closed her eyes, swaying into his touch. "Do you want to know what I think?" he asked. "I look at you, Edie, and I see you charging into the rain without a second thought because a stranger asked for your help. I see you, bleeding in a bright blue coat, because you tried to fight off the thug stealing your purse."

"You don't have to say—"

"I'm not done." He didn't mean for his voice to sound so gruff, but the words grumbled from his chest. "I see *you,* Edie. Brave and bold. Beautiful. And brilliant. So no. I'm not afraid of you. I'm afraid of myself."

"Why?" The question was a gauntlet, thrown on the ground between them. And it cut him straight to the core, that this gorgeous, impossible girl could stand here in his rented room, in a dress that probably cost more than his car and believe for a second that he didn't desire her. Desire wasn't even a strong enough word—he wanted nothing more than to strip off each and every one of those expensive layers and to etch his longing on every inch of her body. Not to own her, or to possess her, but to show her just how much she was worth.

Which was exactly why he didn't move. Couldn't move. Not when she was here, in his arms, and he was so afraid that she would realize, at any instant, that she didn't belong here. Not in this room, not with him. Not when he *should* give her every reason to leave, but he couldn't think of a single one, not when every fiber of his being wanted to drop to his knees and beg her to stay, to leave every comfort of her world behind. To promise her happiness. He'd done that once already. He wouldn't do it again. Couldn't do it again. Because he'd make sure that she would go back to her world, and leave him in his, the way Sarah should have all those years ago.

"Edie," he said, resting his forehead against hers and breathing in her soft vanilla scent. He reached up and cupped her face. He couldn't tell her the things he held deepest in his heart—his fits. His fears. The fact that his mind was still fighting a war three years past, a war he often wished had killed him. A war that had left holes in his memories and torn his soul to shreds. He was a coward, and because of that, he couldn't bear to see the look on her face when she learned the truth about him.

Her tongue darted out and brushed the edge of his thumb, still on her lip. A shudder worked through him, then, not from the shell shock but from a deep, primal need. He stood against the onslaught, even as his other hand snaked around her waist and pulled her flush against him. "I can't be the man you deserve." He paused, making sure she understood him, clearly. That he had nothing to offer, nothing to give beyond the shelter of his arms. "But I could be your scandal. If you let me."

A heartbeat passed between them. Then two. Her dark eyes never left his face.

"I don't want a scandal, Gil," she said, finally. "I just want to stop being afraid. I want to feel safe. I want . . ." her voice trailed off, and a blush rose along her cheekbones, as her gaze swept down his face. "I want . . ."

"What do you want?" He shouldn't have said it. But he had. He leaned forward.

Her mouth fell open, like she was surprised, and he wondered, then, if anyone had ever asked her that question before. *Really* asked her. She swallowed, hard, and desire and hope and something else, something he refused to name, warred within his chest. He leaned forward.

Her lips lifted in a sweet smile he'd remember until his dying breath. "You," she said simply. "I just want you."

CHAPTER 33

Edie's mother had warned her of ruination, back when Edie was young and scared and cared what people thought of her. Warned her away from dark corners and boys with too-familiar hands, of the prying eyes and loose lips and scandal sheets. Edie had watched, with a mix of horror and jealousy, as Sarah Pepper's reputation was torn to shreds by the very people who claimed to love her, who now proclaimed her unworthy of respect, all because she was brave enough to fall in love.

Edie had worried, the first time she and Theo were together, that everyone would find out. That she would be branded with a scarlet letter and tossed out, without ceremony, the way that Sarah had been, just months prior. She didn't worry for long, though, because Theo had promised her everything: a ring, a family. His name.

Gilbert, though, was offering her none of those things. He had nothing to give beyond the way his hand fit against the curve of her waist, and the way his voice rumbled as he asked for her wants. He promised her . . . nothing.

She knew that Gilbert could ruin her.

She didn't care.

"Can I kiss you?" He still hadn't moved, but the question cut through the air between them like a knife.

Lightning zapped through Edie's blood. No one had ever asked her—they'd just gone ahead and done it, like they knew her feelings better than she did. But not Gilbert.

"Yes," she whispered, and finally, finally, he stepped close, looking at her like he really believed all those things he had said—that she was brave, and bold.

Beautiful.

Brilliant.

Slowly, his hands circled her waist, slid up her back. He touched her reverently, gently. Like she was made from spun glass, liable to shatter under his touch. But Edie wasn't crystal. She was diamond, tried and unbreakable. Their noses brushed, once. Twice. And then she rose up on her tiptoes and pressed her mouth to his.

Gilbert froze. His back stiffened and his arms went rigid and Edie's heart plummeted to her toes. She pulled back, just enough to ask, "What's wrong? Was it terrible? Are you all right? Are you—?"

"Stop. Talking." His voice was a low growl, feral and wild and a thrill shot through Edie, from her hair to her toes. And then his mouth was on hers, warm and insistent. And his hands cupped her jaw, his gentle touch at odds with the devastating sweep of his tongue and the heat of his lips.

Edie made a little noise and pressed close, her fingers sliding up into his hair. His right hand left her face and returned to her hip, the fabric of her skirt twisting in his palm, and she knew how it felt, to crumple beneath a simple touch. Her knees hit the bed and they tumbled together, pressed tightly from knee to hip to chest. His name left her like a prayer as his mouth found the soft, sensitive skin below her jaw, trailing kisses down one side of her neck and back up the other.

Slowly, they came back to earth. They parted, foreheads meeting and breaths mingling. Edie opened her eyes. Gil's were still closed, his lashes dark against his pale skin. She wanted to memorize every detail of his face—the slight pout of his lips. The line of his jaw, the slope of his nose. His lips, swollen and smiling. Gil rolled slightly, propping himself up on one elbow. With his free hand, he tugged her dress down into place. Smoothed down her hair.

"You said you didn't want to be alone," he said gently, despite the gravel in his voice. "Does that mean you want to stay here?"

Edie, suddenly bashful, nodded once. "I'd like that."

His cheeks tinged pink, and for a moment, she thought he'd insist on driving her home. But he just pressed a kiss to her temple and stood. She sat on the bed while he readied the room for bed—fetching water for her to wash her face, turning his back while she slipped into a pair of his cotton pajamas, which she rolled at the sleeve and waist. He turned off the lamp and they climbed into his narrow bed together. He held out his arm, and she snuggled close, burying her face in the warm place between neck and shoulder.

"Good night, Gil," she said.

"Good night, Edie," Gilbert whispered back. His heart thumped steadily against her chest, constant and reassuring. She didn't worry about being discovered, as she had the few nights she had spent with Theo. She could even forget, just for a moment, about her grief and her pain, about the killer who seemed closer to her than ever. As she drifted off to sleep, Edie knew for the first time what her mother had meant by ruination.

Because she could live a hundred, thousand times, and never feel like this again.

Edie woke to an empty bed, sometime in the dark hours just before dawn. She stretched her arm out, finding only a cold stretch of linen beside her. Gilbert was gone—she vaguely remembered the door opening, low voices. Work. He'd been called into work, and told her Nellie would call her a cab to see her home in the morning. He'd pressed a kiss to her temple, and Edie had fallen back into a deep, dreamless sleep.

She slipped out of bed and dressed quickly in the darkened room. She leaned down to fasten her garters in the thin slant of gray morning light coming through the curtains. Something metallic pinged against the floorboards as her hair flopped forward—a bobby pin. She knelt to pick it up when her gaze snagged on the glint of metal beneath the bed. A battered steel box the length of her arm, the red paint scraped bare in several places. His mementos from the war, most likely. Her curiosity pinged, and she cast a glance backward over her shoulder.

She shouldn't.

And Gilbert should have known better than to leave her alone in his room.

She pulled the box out from under the bed. It was rectangular, with a raised cross on the lid and the words *ambulance box* stamped on the metal just beneath it, and the most disappointing bit: a heavy padlock on the front. But after a few tries, the bobby pin in her fingers did quick work, and the lock clicked open. The contents of the box were neatly organized. A stack of letters, tied with an olive ribbon. A white armband emblazoned with a red cross. A series of military medals—of course, Gilbert would be the type to be a hero and then shove the evidence beneath his bed. A small field medical roll filled with instruments. His olive green uniform, folded precisely. And beneath that, a gun.

"You bastard," she muttered. "All that talk about, *no, Edie, you can't have a gun, it's dangerous,* and here you are, with one tucked beneath your bed, doing no one any good at all!"

It was heavier than she expected. A cartridge, filled with bullets, sat beneath it. She was relieved to see it was unloaded. Of course it was. Gilbert was too careful to keep a loaded gun beneath his bed. Still, she kept the barrel pointed toward the floor as she stood and sat on the edge of the bed, considering her options.

One, put the gun back and pretend she hadn't seen a thing.

Two, take it with her, just in case she needed it. There was a killer on the loose, after all, and Gilbert was gone. A girl couldn't be too prepared.

Decision made, she closed up the box and slid it back under the bed. The cartridge snapped neatly into a rectangular opening at the bottom of the gun's wooden handle, the grip worn smooth. She slipped it into her handbag.

She didn't need to bother his landlady this early; she was a bold, brilliant, modern girl. She had everything under control, she told herself, and started her long walk home with Gilbert's gun and cartridge full of bullets heavy in her purse.

She arrived at the city house just as the rest of the city began to stir. It was a peaceful walk—she reveled in how alive she felt as the cool morning air, heavy with the promise of rain, kissed her skin and her shoes rang out on the sidewalk, as if to announce her presence to the world. *I am here, I am remade. I am not afraid.* She was practically skipping by the time she opened her front door, humming a little song to herself. She shut the door behind her and started up the stairs.

"Oh, thank God." Frances' voice came from the side parlor, startling Edie out of her daydream. Her sister's hair frizzed out from her face and she clutched the doorframe with one hand. "You're all right."

Edie hurried back down the stairs. "Of course I'm all right," she told her twin. "What are you doing here?"

"I've been worried sick about you. O'Meara told us you didn't come home at all last night. Said you'd left with a man." Frances' face turned scarlet. "Is that where you were? With a *man*?"

"Yes, if you must know," Edie said, forcing her tone to a breezy nonchalance. "It was a very busy evening."

"Edie." Her sister gaped at her. "Do you have any idea how worried I was? No one knew where you were!"

"Everything all right, love?" Theo appeared in the doorway behind Frances. He, too, looked disheveled, as if he'd just woken up.

"Good morning, Theo," Edie said. "You're here early."

"I spent the night, actually."

Edie gave her sister a pointed look.

"It's different and you know it," Frances said softly. "Theo and I are *engaged*."

"How could I forget?" Edie turned to Theo. "How did you two spend your evening?"

Theo leaned against the doorframe. "We went to the Flower Observatory with Artie to see if we could cheer him up with that storm that's sweeping across the sun. A geo-magnetic storm, they're calling it. Did you hear about the electrical surges in Sweden?"

"That's beside the point," Frances interrupted. "We were with people, not alone. No one knew where you were. I was here, worried sick, and you were out with a man?"

Theo's eyes snapped to Edie's, and she forced herself to look at her sister, not at him.

"I don't need your permission," Edie said. "I'm a grown woman, and I can spend my time how I please."

"I want to meet him." Theo sounded so serious—as if he had any claim to how Edie spent her time.

Edie was about to tell Theo absolutely not, but then a thought occurred to her: this was the perfect solution. If she introduced Gilbert to Frances and Theo, she could show Theo that she accepted his choice to marry her sister. And Gilbert was bringing Penelope with him to the zoo this afternoon to see Lizzie, in hopes of persuading her home.

Penelope was Theo's niece, too. And he'd never gotten the chance to meet her. It would be a kindness, then, to introduce them. Two birds, one stone, and all that.

Edie gave her sister and her former lover a bright, brilliant smile. "You know him already, Theo. Don't you remember Gilbert Lawless? Your brother-in-law?"

CHAPTER 34

Gilbert struggled all morning. He tried to turn his attention to his work, to lose himself in the peace of the dead, but Edie haunted his every thought. If he had ever been the type of man to think that kissing a woman would be enough to work the desire for her out of his system . . . Edie proved that hypothesis to be false.

He washed his hands, dried them, and dropped his file in the box on Cecelia's desk.

"Look at this," Cecelia said, thrusting her newspaper at him. "Have you heard about this solar storm?"

SUNSPOT AURORA PARALYZES WIRES, the headline read. *Unprecedented disturbances attributed to ongoing solar manifestations. Broadway lights dimmed; theater crowds returning home amazed at the brilliance of the skies.*

"I swear, I got a shock stepping off the trolley this morning. And they're saying we might even see the Northern Lights here tonight; can you believe it?"

It seemed unlikely. "Who says?" he asked.

"They do," Cecelia shrugged. "Those newspaper people." She titled her head at him, her bespectacled eyes sweeping him from head to toe. "Getting lunch? I forgot to pack mine, so maybe I could join you?"

"I'm sorry, Cecelia," he said, and he meant it, as the hope in her eyes dimmed. "I actually have an appointment, so I'll be out for the rest of the afternoon."

She blinked, surprised. She knew as well as anyone else that Gilbert hadn't taken so much as an hour off in the three years he'd worked for the Coroner's Office. But her surprise only lasted a moment, and she tucked the newspaper away. She picked up the file he'd given her and opened it on her desk, ready to type up the official report. "Well then," she said. "You don't want to be late."

"Have a nice afternoon," he said.

She saw him off with a wave.

Lizzie had said she would be at the zoo at one o'clock, in front of the polar bears. He had just enough time to pick up Penny before meeting Edie at the zoo entrance. Lizzie might be able to say no to Gilbert, but she'd never been able to say no to Penelope. All would be well. All *had* to be well. But he couldn't shake the creeping sense of dread that settled over his shoulders as he sped back toward his parents' house and idled the car in the street. He thought Penny's sweet chatter would chase it away. She squealed in delight when the car crossed the bridge at East Falls, and she peered out the window to the river roaring just below the metal girders. All along the West River Drive, the greenery at the banks had stirred to life, buds giving way to thick green leaves as the sun battled with the heavy gray clouds overhead for dominance.

And still, Gilbert worried.

"And I'm going to feed the camel, all right, Da?" Penny phrased her question in a way that was clear it wasn't a question at all, dragging her father back to the present.

"Of course," he said. "What do camels like to eat, anyway? Popcorn? Lemon drops?"

She scrunched up her little face. "Da."

He paid the attendant at the booth and parked the car. Penny scrambled out of her seat, already three steps ahead of him, racing toward the gingerbread house entrance to the park. He jogged to catch up, capturing her little hand in his own before they crossed the street. Edie waited on the sidewalk for them, dressed in a golden skirt that swirled around her calves and a short-sleeved sweater, gloved hands on her hips as she stared at the statue marking the zoo's entrance: a strong male lion standing guard over a dying lioness, pierced by arrows, and surrounded by a gaggle of cubs. He tightened his grip on Penny's hand.

God, he'd always hated that statue.

"It's a bit . . . grim, isn't it?" she said, when Gilbert joined her. "I never understood why they thought that of all of the statues in the world *this* was the one to put in front of the zoo." At his side-long look, she threw up her hands and gave him a big grin. "Rich people, right? That's what you're going to say?"

Actually, the words had gone dry in his mouth—his only thought had been to lean forward and kiss her again. To publicly put his claim on her, to stand over her like the lion, roaring *mine, stay back!* At anyone who dared look their way. But Penny was there, in between them, her eyes wide at Edie's fine clothes and sparkling beret.

"Da," she said, nearly breathless, "Is she a princess?"

He barked out a laugh. Edie, too, smothered a giggle, raising one gloved hand to cover her scarlet-painted mouth. Before he could say anything, Edie dropped to her knees beside his daughter, never mind the dirt or the soft gold fabric of her skirt. "I'm not a princess," she said, "Though my great-great grandmother's cousin married one."

Penny's eyes grew even wider.

"Close enough," Gilbert said, trying to chase away the warmth flooding his heart. "Pen, this is my . . . this is Miss Shippen. Miss Shippen, this is Penelope."

"Pleased to meet you, Penelope. You're pretty as a picture. Just like your mother."

"You knew my mother?" Penny latched on to Edie's hand.

"She was a few years older than me, and I thought she was the bee's knees," Edie said. "She was very kind, and I know she loved you and your father very much."

Gilbert trailed after them, his middle still churning as he checked his watch. Quarter til. Was Lizzie here already? Waiting? Would she show at all? Penny fired a barrage of questions at Edie, even as she paid her zoo admission. When Gilbert approached the window after her, the woman inside gave him a quizzical look.

"Gil, it's paid for," Edie said, waving her hand at him impatiently. "My treat, today. And," she added, bending down to be on Penny's level, "for the rest of the year. That way you won't forget your new chum, right Penny? We'll be best friends from now on?"

"Edie." His protest was half-hearted. It could only be half-hearted, when Penny squealed in delight and raced back to his side, wielding a tiny paper card with her name printed on it, proclaiming her a yearly member of the Philadelphia Zoological Society. His chest tightened as he tucked it into his wallet, along with the matching one Edie handed him, his own name typed on the membership line. For Penny's sake, he wouldn't make a scene about it. Their eyes met, and he tried to pass along a message through sheer force of will. *Later.*

Edie waggled her eyebrows in response, clearly putting her own interpretation on his look. Heat surged through him and he shoved it aside. Now was not the time.

"You're welcome," she said, out loud. "Now. What's this I hear about a polar bear? Is it some sort of jungle creature?"

Penny giggled. "No, Miss Shippen. They live at the North Pole!"

"Ah, with Santa Claus." Edie gave a serious nod. "Shall we see if we can find him?"

Penny looked back at her father, seeking his permission, and Gilbert gave her a nod, his head still spinning from how shockingly *good* Edie was with his daughter. Hope, too delicate and dangerous to name, rooted somewhere deep in his chest. He'd rip it out later—for now, he'd allow himself the small moment of happiness. "Go on then. I'll be right behind you."

The route to the polar bears was winding—and necessitated a stop in the reptile house first. And a peek at the tigers. Gilbert's nerves grew increasingly on edge as they came down the hill, and he checked his watch for the third time in as many minutes.

She'd be there. She promised she would. And then he'd be able to see with his own two eyes that his sister was well and safe. And he'd be able to figure out what was going on.

Edie drifted beside him at some point, her fingers barely tangling with his for the briefest second, sending fire dancing up his arms. "Theo and Frances came with me," she whispered. "She was waiting up for me when I got home, and it seemed a good opportunity for the two of you to make amends. I know his family was awful to you, and you didn't deserve that. But I know him probably better than anyone, Gilbert. And he'd be thrilled to meet her, if you'd allow it."

It felt as if a hole had opened up in the ground beneath his feet. Anger surged, black and all-consuming, and he stopped still, his hands balling into fists. *Stay here*, he told himself. *She's only trying to help.* And he couldn't make a scene in front of Penny. He wouldn't—couldn't—let his daughter see him like that.

"Edie," he said, fighting to keep his voice even. "You didn't."

"It seemed the least I could do. I didn't think . . ."

"You never do." *Deep breaths*, he reminded himself. "Damn it. That family wants nothing to do with us. How *could* you?"

"Gilbert—"

"Aunt Lizzie!" Penny's ecstatic shout cut through whatever excuses Edie was trying to formulate. His daughter raced over the brick path toward his sister, who looked up sharply at her cry. Her face went pale beneath her wide-brimmed black hat as she dove for the girl, and it was then that Gilbert knew, deep in his bones, that something was wrong.

Deadly wrong.

He broke into a run, ignoring Edie's startled cry, just as a gunshot cracked through the air. For a moment, everything went silent. Still. He waited, expecting the swirling browns and reds to appear, but they didn't. Then the polar bear, who had been sleeping against the iron bars of his cage, woke with a surprised roar. Someone screamed. Reality crashed back over him.

And then Lizzie was running.

He grabbed Edie by the shoulders and pushed her back in the direction they'd come from. "Take Penny away from here," he said. "Take her home. I'll get Lizzie. Go!"

"Gil—"

"Go!" he shouted. She scooped up Penny and fled. He was after his sister in a moment, narrowly avoiding a wandering peacock as he crashed through a bed of white flowers. Lizzie was quick, but his legs were longer. He was faster. And someone had shot at them.

He'd felt so helpless when Sarah died, like he should have been able to stop it.

In France, he'd tried and tried to save the wounded, only to have so many succumb. And when he came home, into the storm of a pandemic, he'd stood helpless against the onslaught.

He wasn't going to lose anyone else. Not his daughter, not his sister, not Edie.

Not like this.

CHAPTER 35

Edie clutched a trembling Penelope by the hand as they ran back the way they came. The girl stumbled, crying out, and Edie scooped her up, cradling Penny to her chest as fear propelled her down the path. *Someone had shot at them.*

At who? Lizzie? Gilbert and Edie? Some other person entirely? Edie wasn't sure it mattered—she just knew Gilbert had told her to run. He'd trusted her with his daughter, even as cross as he was with her. She'd made a mess of everything, somehow, without even trying. And someone was shooting at them and . . .

"Don't be scared," she panted as she ran. "I'll keep you safe. Do you trust me?"

The girl nodded mutely. She was a brave little thing. Brave like her mother. Like her father, too.

"It'll all be all right," Edie said, more to herself than to Penelope. How much could a child so small understand? Edie didn't know. But she didn't want to say the wrong thing. She'd already been through so much.

"Da said to go," Penny told Edie. "Where are we going?"

Go. Run. *The shooter is still here.*

He could be anywhere. Watching them. Waiting to make his next shot—and this time, he may not miss.

"We're going to find somewhere to wait," she told the girl. "Hang on. Daddy will find us soon." She hurried, past the elephants and the apes and the tall domed building filled with exotic birds. Her legs burned and Penelope was so heavy in her arms. But she didn't know what to do. Pain lanced through her skull as her vision exploded in stars. A migraine. *Now?* She stopped short, gasping. She set Penny down gently as she pressed her hands to her temples. Not now. She had to get home. She had to get help. She had to—

"Edie?" Frances' soft voice cut through the noise. Soft footsteps hurried to her side. Her hand caught Edie's sleeve, pulling her to a stop. "Edie, darling, there you are. What's wrong?"

Edie looked up into her twin's stricken face, blinking past the stars. Of course, Frances was worried—Frances always knew what emotion was appropriate for a situation. Behind her, Theo loomed, his features pinched with concern. And beside him, inexplicably: Artie Van Pelt, dressed in a smart blue suit with a black mourning band around his upper arm.

"We heard a gunshot," Theo was saying. "Frances was in the lavatory. Are you all right? Who's this?"

"My head," Edie said. She reached up and wiped at her face, surprised to find it wet. She'd been crying?

"Are you hurt?" Artie asked. Edie wondered, for a second, about his concern—and then she remembered.

Artie was a doctor. A doctor, researching electricity. A doctor, with access to all four of the dead girls.

And he was here, when someone had tried to shoot Lizzie.

Edie couldn't breathe.

"She gets migraines," Frances explained to Artie, oblivious to her sister's distress. To Edie, she asked, "Do you have your tincture?"

"Who's this?" he asked. Theo looked at her sharply, his blue eyes seeming to stare right into her soul, bathed in the bright, blinding sunshine that sent daggers straight into her brain

The sun. That would explain it—perhaps the heat had triggered her episode. Or the noise of the gunshot—that wouldn't be a surprise. She'd had a shock, after all. She had to stay calm. If Artie was the killer, she couldn't let him suspect a thing until she made sure Gilbert's daughter was safely out of his reach. She wrapped a protective arm around Penelope. "I'd like you to meet my friend, Miss Penelope Lawless."

Theo rocked back on his heels as if he'd been struck. The color drained from his face, and he stared at the girl, then up at Edie. His mouth moved, but no sound came out.

"My aunt was here. My Da's gone to fetch her," Penelope announced.

"Your Da?" Theo crouched down to look the little girl in the face.

"Gilbert," Edie said, as quickly as she could . "Pen, I'd like you to meet your Uncle Theo. Your mother's brother."

"I'll be damned," Artie said. "That's Sarah's girl."

"Please to meet you, Uncle Theo," Penelope said seriously. "I've never had an uncle before."

Frances looked at her sister. "What's going on?" she asked quietly.

"Someone shot Aunt Lizzie," Penelope said.

Frances gasped. "What?"

"Someone *might* have shot at Lizzie. Our maid. Penelope's aunt. Or maybe they shot at someone else entirely." Edie swallowed hard. She needed quiet, and dark, and her tincture. She needed to know that Gilbert and Lizzie were safe. "It was hard to tell. But Dr. Lawless asked me to look after Miss Penelope until things settle down. He said to take her home."

"Of course." Frances helped Edie up. She straightened her sister's skirt and tugged at her beret until it was perfect, but Edie still felt askew. Like she'd been rearranged, somehow, and pieces were missing.

Or maybe the pieces no longer quite fit.

Franny caught Edie's hand and gave it a squeeze, then looked down at their new charge. "Miss Lawless," Frances said, "Your father asked Edie to keep you safe. So we're going to bring you home with us. He'll find us there, all right?"

The girl nodded. Theo scooped her up. He held the child gently, reverently. He and Sarah had been close, and now as he held her daughter, after all these years, a storm of emotions crossed his face—grief, anger, longing. Bewilderment. "You look—" His voice cracked. "You have your mother's face," he told the child. "Her eyes."

Penny grinned. "Da says that, too!"

Edie knew Sarah's departure had been scandalous. But maybe, thanks to her, the rift between Theo's family and Gilbert's could begin to mend. Penelope deserved as much.

Artie stepped forward and slipped one arm around Edie's waist. Fear sliced through her, and she stumbled, but then Frances was there, steadying her from the other side. Supported, Edie sagged against her sister—Frances was always the strong one. The good one. The one who took care of things, no matter what.

The drive back to Chestnut Hill passed in a blur as the sky overhead opened beneath the waiting storm. Once Artie dropped them off, Frances swept Edie upstairs with the brusqueness of a battlefield general. Their grandmother, thankfully, was at some sort of charity event in New York, and had taken Annette, her maid, along with her. The rest of the staff had been given the weekend off, Frances explained, and within a few moments, Edie and Penelope had been settled onto a sofa in an upstairs sitting room, a tray of hot tea and cookies beside them. "The tea will help, at least until Theo comes back from the drugstore with your medicine," Frances said, as she tucked Penelope's blanket in tight around her. "Try to rest."

She didn't want tea, though, or cookies. Her head hurt too much to eat. But she sipped at it, like a good patient, even if it was cloyingly sweet and strangely bitter, all at the same time. As soon as Frances left, she made a face and replaced the tea to the tray.

Penelope nibbled at a cookie. "Miss Edie," she said. "This is a fancy house."

"It is," Edie answered, raising her voice over the sound of the rain lashing at the windows. "It's very good for playing hide and seek."

The girl's eyes lit up. "Truly?"

"Oh yes." In truth, all Edie wanted to do was to lie down and close her eyes until her skull stopped feeling like it was trying to pull itself apart, but a game of hide-and-seek with a four-year-old would be fine. She could close her eyes and count. Penny couldn't be *that* good at hiding. She'd manage. "Your mother used to play it with us here all the time. Would you like to try?"

"I'll hide first!" Penny declared, the pitch of her voice shooting straight through to Edie's tender brain.

"Wonderful, dear. Stay on this floor—and stay away from the dumbwaiter, all right? It's dangerous. I'll count to twenty and come find you."

Edie's eyes were already closed when Penelope giggled and fled, her little footsteps hurrying down the corridor to the right.

Edie dutifully counted in time to the strobing flashes in her temples. Storms triggered her migraines like almost nothing else—something about the barometric pressure disagreed with her brain. At fifteen, she stood, her legs shaking like a newborn foal's. Penny had headed down the hall, toward the telephone. She'd start looking there. But first, she'd call Marco at the morgue, and make sure that he knew that she'd taken Penelope back to Shippen House. Marco would know how to get ahold of Gilbert—she had no idea if *home* meant her home, Gilbert's boarding house, or the house in Manayunk where Penelope lived with her grandparents. She didn't want Gilbert to worry.

The corridor was deserted in both directions. On her left, toward the bedrooms, she heard a faint giggle, and smiled. "Oh, where can that little girl be?" She called out, as she lifted the handset. "Here behind the telephone?"

"How may I connect your call?" The operator's voice was shrill in her ear. Edie gritted her teeth against the pain.

"Municipal Five, please. City morgue." The shadows around her seemed to stretch and move, crowding close. Edie closed her eyes and opened them again. Her heart raced so fast she feared it would beat right out of her chest, and desperate *thumpthumpthump* beneath her collarbone. She pressed at her chest. Something was wrong. What was wrong?

"One moment please."

"City morgue," the woman on the other side of the line said, once it clicked through. "How may I help you?"

"Marco Salvatore, please." Footsteps sounded on the stairs, and an irrational panic gripped her middle. She forced herself to calm.

She and Penelope were safe here.

Why wouldn't her heart stop pounding?

"This is Dr. Salvatore."

"Marco," Edie said, the words slurring from her lips. "It's Edie Shippen."

"What's wrong? Are you ill?"

The pounding in her head and her chest was almost too much to bear. She clutched the phone. "Find Gilbert. I'm at Shippen House in Chestnut Hill." She sucked in deep, gasping breaths.

"Edie?" Marco's voice pitched high. "What's going on?"

"Something—I can't breathe. Something's wrong," she whispered. "Please. Marco."

Marco said something on the other side of the line, but Edie couldn't hear him.

"Edie." The shadows in the foyer parted to reveal Theo, his face pinched with worry. He pressed his hand down on the receiver, hanging up the call. "Are you all right?"

"I had to make a phone call," she said.

"I heard," he said. He plucked the phone from her hand and set it on the tabletop. He crowded close, backing her up against the wall. Once, she would have welcomed this advance, met it with a flutter of her lashes and maybe even a kiss. But now, there was but an oil-sick sheen of unease. "Who's Marco? Another boyfriend?"

"What?" Edie shook her head, trying to clear her vision. Her heart still thrummed. She couldn't catch her breath. "No. He's . . . a friend. I wanted him to tell Gilbert we have Penny here. So he doesn't worry."

Theo stepped closer. He was so much bigger than she was; that used to thrill her. Not now. He pitched his voice low. "You shouldn't have brought the girl here. You should have stayed away from him, Edie."

"He loved your sister," Edie answered, her brain spinning to keep up. She felt so strange, so heavy. "He kept his promises to her."

He was pressed against her now, pinning her in place. Her own limbs were weak, sluggish, and sharp pain creased her chest as the shadows crowded closer, the darkness threatening to pull her under. But she wouldn't—couldn't let that happen.

"You don't know him like I do." Theo's breath was hot against her ear. One hand pressed against the wall above her head. The other snaked up her body to rest at her throat. She could feel her pulse drumming under his thumb. "You don't know who he really is."

"I know him."

Theo stilled. His hand tightened, just a fraction. "Edie."

"I know him," Edie said. The words were harder to form now, and she sagged against him as they slurred from her lips.

"Edie." Theo's lips were so close, hovering over hers. "You're going to help me."

Edie pushed at his chest. "Help you with what?"

Anger flashed over his face. "Don't be a dumb bunny, Edie. It isn't cute." His fingers dug into the flesh of her arm, hard enough to bruise. She whimpered in pain, but that didn't seem to concern him. Instead, his grip tightened.

"Stop," Edie said again. This time, she couldn't keep the panic from her voice, and she shoved at him harder as the shadows swam around them. "This isn't right, Theo. If Frances sees us like this, it'll destroy her."

"I'll tell her you seduced me," Theo said. "Who do you think she'll believe, Edie? You? Or me?"

CHAPTER 36

"I'm sorry sir, I'm unable to connect your call." The operator's voice in his ear was pleasant but detached. "Is there another number you'd like me to try?"

Gilbert cursed and hung up the handset hard enough that Lizzie, on the sofa across the room, jumped. He'd caught her quickly, and practically dragged her back to his car. Silent sobs had wracked her during the drive back to his boarding house. Even now, she clutched a handkerchief to her face, muffling her cries.

"Why was someone shooting at you?"

Lizzie flinched. She wouldn't meet his eyes, which troubled him. She'd never been good at lying, not even when they were small children, and she'd broken a toy or stolen the last sweet. "I don't know."

"Don't lie to me. Not now. Do you know who it was? The Slasher?"

"I know who it could have been." She looked at him then, her eyes glassy from the tears. "But I'm worried that if I put it all on the level, you'll panic. Promise me, you won't panic."

"I think I need you to start at the beginning," Gilbert said slowly. He stood, his knees popping through the room. "So figure out where that is. If I go make tea, will you be here when I return?"

She nodded. "I'm done running," she whispered. "I'll be here."

"Good. And then you'll tell me everything. *Everything*, do you hear me?"

He left her there and took the narrow back corridor to the kitchen. Nellie stood at the table, rolling out biscuit dough, while her youngest son worked on his homework. She offered him a kind smile. "Afternoon, Gil. Do you and your sister need anything?"

"Just putting the kettle on," he said, as he filled it up from the tap, like it was a normal afternoon. The water inside the kettle sloshed as he set it on the burner, the metal clanging together. He lit the stove and reached for the tea tin, listening to the chatter happening behind him as he measured out enough of the dried black leaves into the delicate porcelain teapot covered in tiny blue flowers.

"Mom," the boy said, "What's one third of thirty-six?"

Nellie's arms never stopped moving, even as she fixed her son with a beady stare. "Is it your homework, or mine, Dan?"

"Mine."

"Right." She set aside the rolling pin and reached for the biscuit cutter. She didn't say anything else, and Gilbert found himself leaning forward. Dan noticed and turned his bright stare to him. His mother also noticed. "And don't be bothering Dr. Lawless, with that, either. He's got things to do."

"He's just watching water boil."

Gilbert felt Nellie's stare fix on him. "You know what they say about that, Gil," she said, and sighed. "Go on upstairs, honey. I'll send Dan up with the teapot to you when it's fixed."

He really didn't want to leave, but her tone brokered no argument. So he thanked her and took the long way back to the parlor, through the front hall. He checked his mailbox, right near the door, and took longer than necessary to peruse a flier advertising new safety razors. He wanted to give Lizzie enough time to settle her nerves and open up. And she would, eventually. If he gave her the space to do so.

A sharp knock sounded at the door. His heart said, *Edie,* but his mind shoved her name aside as he put the flier back in the box labeled with his name and turned. "I've got it," he called back to Nellie.

"Thank you!" she shouted back.

Marco stood on the front step. His face was pale. He reached forward and pulled Gilbert onto the sidewalk, letting the door slam behind him. "Thank God. I came as fast as I could."

Time slowed down. Gilbert stared down at Marco, uncomprehending. "What's going on?"

"We have to go." He dragged him forward, half a step. "I tried to call you—the whole phone grid is on the fritz. Something to do with spots on the sun, Cecelia said? But Edie called me at the morgue. Slurring her words, not making much sense. I'm worried she's in trouble."

Everything stopped. Somehow, Gilbert made it to the sidewalk, where two men were loading a large truck with furniture. "Marco, Edie has Penny."

Marco's face drained of color.

Bang. One of the men dropped the edge of the sofa he was carrying against the truck bed. Gilbert's world blinked. A strange, high-pitched whistle rose in his ears, and his chest felt strangely tight.

Not now. Not here. *Stay here,* he told himself.

"She said she was at Shippen House. I'll drive," Marco said.

Gilbert tried to take a step, but his legs gave out, sending him sprawling on the sidewalk, his knees sinking into mud from the blast.

Not blast. Not mud. It had been a sofa, not an explosion. Brick. The sidewalk was brick.

He sucked in a breath. Hands grabbed his shoulders, and he climbed back to his feet, his mind warring between reality and memory. Cool metal met his hands. *A gun.* No. Warm flesh. Marco.

"Gil," the man beside him shouted, "Gil you have to—" Sweat beaded along Gilbert's brow. "Please," he said, not caring that he was begging. "I need—I need my medication. It's right in my jacket pocket."

But it wasn't. He was in his shirtsleeves—the medicine and his jacket were inside. Inside with Lizzie. Gilbert gritted his teeth as the world around them shuddered, and he slammed against rocky edge of the trench, his head ringing. All around them, explosions shook the earth, sending mud and blood flying in every direction.

Stay here.

Marco's features shifted, hazel eyes morphing to cold blue, his dark blue suit turning olive. "He's going to get us killed. We have to do something."

Stay here.

Gilbert found himself nodding. He looked over to where Captain Thatcher, their commanding officer, was busy trying to repair a German electrical box. If he could get the wires right, he could have enough power to turn on the radio. Discover enemy troop movements.

Maybe buy enough time for them to scramble back across no-man's land to safety.

"We're not dying in this fucking trench, Lawless. We're going to get back to Philly. Do you hear me?"

Gilbert looked down at himself. His uniform was filthy—streaked brown and red with Lord only knows what. His white armband, the one marking him as a medic, was missing. More machine gun fire rocked over the trench—the one his battalion had recently captured from the Germans, and Gilbert knew, deep in his bones, that if they didn't get out now, they would die. The enemy was angry. And they were returning.

"Do you trust me?"

God, his eyes were so like Sarah's. Grief welled in Gilbert's gut, shocking him. It had been months since he'd felt anything at all, anything but anger, and fear. Maybe death wouldn't be so bad—not when he could see her again. He could see all of her, not just her eyes, staring back out of her brother's face.

She'd be waiting for him. She had promised.

"I trust you," Gilbert told Theo Pepper.

Theo nodded once. And then time slowed as he calmly turned, pulled his service revolver from the leather holster at his waist, and fired point-blank at the back of their commanding officer's head.

Captain Thatcher's body, propelled by the momentum of the surprise and the bullet, wrenched forward in an explosion of blood and bone. He fell into the electrical box he had been attempting to repair, his ruined face hitting the wires and closing the circuit. His body jerked wildly as the electricity sizzled through him, limbs twitching in a strange, electric dance. The smell of scorched meat filled the narrow, concrete lined space, and Gilbert couldn't move. Couldn't breathe. Couldn't blink.

Theo had done that. The man had just told them there was no turning back, and Theo had killed him.

They would both face the firing squad for this.

Theo reached his hand out and clapped Gilbert's shoulder. "Then let's go."

Gilbert nodded. He thought to grab the radio and the blood-spattered notebook beside it—he shoved it down into his pack as he scurried after Theo. Somehow, they made it up the ladder and over the barbed-wire. No-man's land stretched before them. To his left, another barrage of bullets ripped through the dirt. A whistle cut the air.

Grenade.

Gilbert and Theo hit the ground as the world exploded around them. Iron and copper filled Gilbert's mouth and he spit blood as the concussion from the blast rocked them, their bodies knocking together. The air went still. Soundless. Deep inside of Gilbert, the concussions reverberated within him, down to the dark, secret place where his deepest fears resided. His fear of pain. Of death. A strange sort of peace settled over Gilbert as that place cracked, and he picked up his rifle, fixed his bayonet. He gave it a violent thrust at the first man who came at him, the sharp metal scraping against bone as Gilbert stabbed him through his charcoal-gray uniform. The man fell, wrenching the bayonet from Gilbert's grasp.

He scrambled at his belt for his sidearm. The gun was heavy in his hand as he raised it and fired. The man fell.

Gilbert scrambled backward.

He'd never been a fighter. Never been one for violence. That's why he'd volunteered for the medical corps, why he'd gone to medical school. But now, on this thrice-damned stretch of land, he killed, because that was his duty. It was how he could keep himself alive. Keep his friend alive.

Because Theo, for all their tangled history, *had* become a friend to Gilbert in the last long months, since Theo had been assigned to Gilbert's unit in the medical corps. Gilbert, having already spent nearly nine months in France, reached an olive branch out to his younger brother-in-law. They'd bonded over their homesickness, their shared grief over the loss of every friend.

Their shared grief over Sarah.

Theo had asked a million questions about Penelope, the infant daughter Gilbert knew only through his sister's letters. Theo had apologized, over and over again for the way his parents had treated Sarah and Gil. They had talked, long into the night, about Theo's plans for the future: law school, most likely, and marrying the girl he loved, a girl who had grown up next door, with jet-black hair and a wicked sense of humor.

Theo had dragged Gilbert out of the deepest, darkest depths of his personal hell, and given Gilbert a reason to hope.

And then, in the blink of a second, ripped it all away.

Theo turned to him, his blue eyes cold, his face a mask of rage. He said something, but Gilbert's hearing had been blown out by the blast, and all he saw was Theo's lips moving, over and over again, the same two words. And then Theo was in motion, knocking Gilbert flat to his back. All of the air left Gilbert's lungs. He blinked, the gun forgotten in the mud beside him, as Theo's hands gripped his throat. He squeezed, hard, his fingers digging into the soft skin of Gilbert's neck. A tear, hot and angry, splashed from Theo's face and onto Gilbert's own. *I'm sorry,* Gilbert realized Theo was saying. *I'm sorry, I'm sorry, I'm sorry.*

Gilbert understood why Theo was doing this—Gilbert was the lone witness to Theo's crime. The lone voice that could see him court-martialed and sent before a firing squad.

For half a heartbeat, Gilbert thought he would let Theo do it—let him kill him, so he could be with Sarah. But then he thought of Penny—his sweet little girl, robbed of both of her parents. He'd never get to see her grow up. Never get to see how much she looked like her mother.

Black spots danced at the edges of his vision, and Gilbert decided he wasn't going to die. Not here. Not like this.

Gilbert shoved at Theo with his free hands, but his weight was solid, immovable. The gray sky stretched endlessly overhead. He stretched his fingers out, hand brushing cold metal. His sidearm. There, just within reach. With his other hand, Gilbert scratched at Theo's grim face, gasping for breath, but his friend—his brother-in-law—kept squeezing. Determined. His mouth kept moving.

I'm sorry I'm sorry I'm sorry I'm sorry.

Gilbert, somehow, closed his fingers around the butt of the gun. He bashed it into Theo's face, and the other man lurched as something wet and hot splattered over Gilbert's face.

Blood.

God, so much blood.

Theo toppled backward, hand splashing into the puddle beside him.

Gilbert ran.

Not real.

Damp, clammy fabric clung to his chest, even though the room he was in was warm. Nellie's sitting room. He was on the sofa, a pillow tucked beneath his head. He looked down at his hands, scrubbed free of dirt and blood and guilt. His shoulders heaved as he pressed one palm to his heart, forced his breaths to calm.

He was home. In Nellie's sitting room. The war was over. He'd come home with a Bronze Star and a tremor and uncontrollable fits. He'd come home a hero for the plans he'd stolen from that trench, in that blood-spattered notebook, and no memory of how it happened. No proof except for the waking nightmares that haunted him, showing him glimpses but never the truth.

Until now.

He backtracked, trying to remember what had happened before his fit. Lizzie. He'd made tea. And then . . . the door. Marco.

Marco had come to fetch him. Marco had . . .

Marco had said Edie was in trouble. *Christ.* Edie had brought Penny to Theo. Theo, who had a score to settle.

Theo, whom Gilbert had left for dead.

Theo, who had access to morphine. Who had surgical training. Who had been attending a lecture on galvanism. The theory of electric therapy.

Captain Thatcher's body, jolting in that desolate trench, flashed through Gilbert's mind.

A sickening certainty spread through Gilbert's middle, and he pushed himself to standing. Theo had killed their captain and electrocuted his body. Theo had trained as a doctor and conducted research on galvanism. Theo had access to each and every one of the victims.

Theo had been the one they'd been looking for, all along.

And Theo had his daughter.

CHAPTER 37

Edie stared up at the boy she had once loved, the boy who had become a man she didn't know, as the truth bloomed with a slow, cold horror.

Theo had known both Rebecca and Ophelia. Athena worked in his house. And Dottie . . . he was constantly at Shippen House. He could have taken the maid at any point. He was a doctor.

A killer.

"It was you."

Theo. Not Artie, like she had suspected at the zoo. And now Artie was gone, and Frances and Penelope were somewhere in the house. In danger. They were all in danger.

Lightning flashed outside. "You're surprised," he said, with a chuckle. "Oh, Edie. I should have known. You always wind up in over your head, just like that stupid cousin of yours."

She had to think. Had to find a way out of this. But her head was nearly splitting from the barometric pressure, the pain threatening to cleave her in two. How could she help anyone, when she couldn't even help herself?

She had to stall.

"Rebecca was pregnant," she whispered. "But you knew that, didn't you? You were having an affair with her."

"It was one time. And I couldn't have her ruining everything, could I?" he asked. "She should have known better than to let herself get knocked up, but it all worked out, didn't it? I needed specimens for my work, and she was a problem I could no longer let exist. Two birds, one stone."

Specimens. "Theo, what are you talking about?"

Theo grabbed her arms and pulled, dragging her down the hallway after him. She stumbled, and he growled in frustration. "You don't understand," he said. "But you will. Once you see what my research can do—you'll understand."

A deep, bubbling hysteria rose up in her chest. "You're a murderer, Theo."

He turned suddenly, his grip iron, his fingers digging painfully into the soft skin of her upper arms. He brought his face inches from hers, so she could stare into his cold blue eyes—flat and reptilian, so different from the warm, kind eyes she'd known as a child.

"Murderer? I'm a savior, Edie. You'll see. If you want to talk about a killer—you've been awfully cozy with my brother-in-law. Who attacked me and left me to die in no-man's land during the war."

"You're lying." But she thought about the way Gilbert had gone cold at the mention of Theo's name. She'd assumed it was just anger over Sarah, but now . . .

He watched her carefully. "Am I? Have you asked him why he can't sleep at night? About his fits? It's guilt, Edie. He's a coward."

"You're lying," she said again.

"I knew you were easy, but I never thought you'd stoop so low."

She spit in his face.

He reared back with a roar. The back of his hand met her cheek with a crack, and she cried out in pain as she fell, the hot, coppery taste of blood filling her mouth. He grabbed a handful of her hair and yanked, pulling her down the hall. Her feet barely brushed the floor as she scrambled along behind him, hitting at his arm with both hands. He didn't even break his stride as he pushed open the door to her bedroom and shoved her inside.

"I'm giving you a chance to calm yourself," he said. "When I come back, I expect an answer. Either you help me, or Frances and the girl die."

The door slammed shut, key scraping in the lock. She threw herself at it, pounding and screaming until her throat was hoarse, until she could do nothing but sink down to the floor with a moan.

He was going to kill her. Kill her, Frances, and Penelope. *Oh, God, Penelope.* Where had Theo taken her? Was she safe? Scared? Cold terror gripped Edie, and she had to force herself to breathe. She'd delivered the child straight to the devil himself, and by the time Gilbert found them, it would be too late. Theo would make sure of it.

Thunder shook the house, as if the very world outside was raging at her predicament. Another flash of lightning illuminated the room—and Frances's form on her bed. She slammed her hand against the wall plate's black button, turning on the electric light overhead, and hurried over to her. Was she too late? Was she . . .

Frances was on her back, one arm outstretched. She breathed deeply, a small relief, but she was hurt. Blood caked at her temple, the wound already beginning to bruise. He'd struck her. Rage boiled within her, and she pressed her face against her twin's shoulder and sobbed. Frances had to be all right. She had to be.

And then Edie would find Penny. And deal with Theo.

Somehow.

First things first. Edie lurched to her dressing table, yanking open drawers until her fingers closed around a slim glass vial.

The tincture that her previous doctors had given her for her migraines—a mixture of belladonna and laudanum, oddly light in her hand. Nearly empty. She sniffed it. The same earthy, bitter smell that had tainted her tea flooded her nostrils.

The tea had been drugged.

"Oh, Franny," she whispered softly. All of the pieces clicked together in her brain. Of course. Frances must have suspected something nefarious was happening right under her nose and tried in her own way to stop it. Frances had sent Rebecca to Celeste Dupont to end her pregnancy and prevent a scandal. Perhaps Theo had shown an interest in Dottie, too. And Lizzie must have gone to her for help, and Frances sent her into hiding. After all, Frances had lied about Lizzie. She had been the one to encourage Edie to move to the city house. And today, she'd drugged Edie's tea, ostensibly to send her to bed early, so she wouldn't be in Theo's way.

This whole time, Frances hadn't been protecting Theo. She'd been trying to protect everyone else *from* Theo. But Franny had been so worried about Theo's infidelities that she'd overlooked the fact he was a murderer.

"Why didn't you say anything?" she asked, but her sister's still form didn't answer. Edie let her head thunk back against the dressing table, the slim amber vial falling from her hands and rolling across the floor, where it stopped against her handbag with a clink.

◆——————◆◆——————◆

Outside, the rain lashed down, and thunder rumbled overhead. Nearly an hour passed before Theo returned—an hour that felt like it stretched into eternity. A few weeks ago, Edie would have welcomed the sound of his soft footfalls on the carpet outside of her door. She'd have shivered in anticipation at the scrape of the key in the lock.

Now, she just felt sick.

Theo shut the door behind him. He set the key on the small table beside the door, clearly confident in his power over her. His beautiful face was as cold as marble, smooth and white and arranged into hard lines. "Edie," he said.

"Where's Penelope?" She knew she was begging. "Please, Theo. Let me see her."

"She's not here." Theo almost sounded apologetic. "I admit, I wasn't expecting any of this today. I've had to improvise."

"Don't you dare hurt that little girl," Edie said. "She's done nothing wrong. She has to be scared out of her mind."

"Cooperate, and I won't have to hurt her," Theo said, stepping close. He reached out and took Edie's hand, his skin warm against hers. His voice softened. "Now. Enough about her. I want to talk about you. About us. Help me, and I'll help you start a brand-new life, away from all of this. I know you've been unhappy since you came back. I'll find a way to tell your family you've had a breakdown and need some sunshine. I'll put you up in a nice little apartment somewhere. Miami, maybe. Or back to Los Angeles. Wherever you want. I'll come visit you, and we can be together, if that's what you'd want."

She tugged her hand from his grasp. "No thank you, Theo. I'd rather die than ever have you touch me again."

He struck her again. The blow was brutal—a quick crack across her face with the back of his hand. This time, his heavy signet ring hit bone, and she cried out as she fell. Her shoulder knocked against her dressing table, sending two perfume bottles crashing to the floor. He was on her in a minute, picking her up by the front of her dress and pressing her against the wall. Gilbert's gun, hidden beneath her dress, dug painfully in the small of her back, and she prayed it didn't discharge and shoot her in the ass and prove Gilbert right.

"What happened to you, Edie? I don't remember you being such a wet blanket."

Edie somehow got her foot up between them and kicked, pushing him backward. Her cheek throbbed, pain spiderwebbing across her face and down her neck. "I decided I deserve better than to be someone's shameful little secret."

They stared at each other, chests rising and falling. She worried that he would hit her again, that he'd attack her. She'd never been so aware of her physical smallness before—he towered over her, his shoulders dwarfing her frame.

"Gilbert's coming to save us. You'll see."

It was the wrong thing to say. His face twisted, and he surged forward again, closing the gap between them. Edie found herself pressed back against her dressing table, and she scrambled her hands over the surface as he closed his fingers around her throat. "That bastard is going to pay. For everything. Once I bring Sarah back, I'm going to make him pay."

She almost laughed at him, except for the fingers clamped around her throat. She forced her voice to calm. "Bring Sarah back? Theo. Your sister has been dead for years. What are you talking about?"

"I can do it," Theo said. "I'm so close. I just need one . . . more . . . specimen . . ."

He squeezed. Edie's airway constricted, and she gagged, her hand spasming behind her, to where the gun was jammed in the waist of her girdle. The rain lashed down. Lightning flashed outside, chased immediately by a clap of thunder. Spots danced before Edie's eyes. Something outside boomed. Through the window, the sky turned green, an eerie radium glow. A strange electricity rippled through the air, causing the hair on Edie's arms to rise. Theo's grip loosened just a fraction.

"Go to hell," she gasped out.

And then the lights went out.

Edie slammed the butt of the gun down on his head with a scream. Theo reeled backward with a hoarse cry. Edie didn't hesitate. She sprinted for the corridor, leading Theo away from Frances and out into the darkness. She knew this house inside and out.

But so did he.

She darted up the servant's stairs, her low-heeled oxfords silent on the carpet. She prayed no one was upstairs, that everyone had taken advantage of the weekend off. She didn't want anyone else to fall prey to Theo's violent schemes. Heavy footfalls chased her—or was that just her own heart, pounding in her chest? She navigated down the narrow, windowless hall by feel. The storm, or whatever was happening outside, must have cut the power. It gave her an advantage.

But barely.

At the end of the corridor, she pressed herself against the wall. A handle pressed into her back—the dumbwaiter. Just where she remembered it being.

A crash sounded at the other end of the hall. She was running out of time.

"Edie," his voice called out. "I always won this game, remember? You could never hide from me." It echoed down the hall from the top of the stairs, like he was everywhere all at once.

With shaking hands, Edie set the gun on the floor at her feet and opened the door to the dumbwaiter. She pulled at the rope frantically, arm over arm, until the car hit the top of the shaft with a small thud. But the pulley itself had been silent—Mrs. Smith ran a tight ship, so she wasn't surprised the machinery was in perfect working order, operating without so much as a squeak.

It was small. So much smaller than she remembered. As girls, she and Frances had fit in it easily—after all, it was made to carry laundry baskets, bins of coal, and whatever else the staff needed between floors. She took a deep breath, picked up the gun, and climbed into the dumbwaiter.

She fit. But barely, her feet and back pressed against the side, her knees up to her chest, gun balanced atop her knees. There was just enough room for her to swing the door shut, sealing her into the tiny chamber.

She'd never been much for church or praying or God. But as she gripped the pulley ropes across from her, she sent up a silent plea to anyone who was listening.

The dumbwaiter lurched, and her stomach went with it. She squeezed her eyes shut and bit back a scream. *It's just like an elevator,* she told herself. *Just a very, very tiny elevator.*

Slowly, slowly, the dumbwaiter inched downward. Then faster, as she gained confidence. And in a few seconds, she passed the door for the third floor, then the second, and the first, the strange luminous light from the windows pouring through the grates on the dumbwaiter's door.

She kept going. She was so close. The basement door was further down, but she was almost there. And from there, freedom.

And then.

The car jerked to a stop, the ropes burning her palms as they were brutally yanked upward.

"Edie!" Theo's voice rang down the dumbwaiter shaft, raising the hair on her arms. He was close. Too close. Had he made it down to the first floor already? "Come out, come out, wherever you are!"

She inched upward, trapped in the tiny wooden box. He would find her. And she knew, without a doubt, that he would kill her.

No.

No. This wouldn't happen. This couldn't happen. With shaking hands, she raised the gun, pulled back the slide over the barrel. And when Theo threw open the dumbwaiter door, Edie didn't hesitate. She pulled the trigger.

In the tiny space, the gunshot was deafening. Theo lurched backward and fell, releasing the rope.

The dumbwaiter plummeted. Edie plunged downward with a scream she felt more than heard. The box crashed to the floor with a sudden, jarring smash. The wood beneath her splintered as her body slammed against the door. She tumbled out, falling the last few feet to the basement floor. The gun landed beside her, clattering across the floor.

Stunned, she lay there for a moment, gasping for breath, her ears ringing from the blast. Everything hurt, and part of her was relieved for the pain, because it meant she was still alive.

She rolled to her belly. Somehow, she found her feet, and climbed to standing on shaking legs. She picked up the gun.

If Theo was still alive, he'd come for her. Edie knew that. But if he wasn't—if she'd killed him—she was the only person who had a clue where Penny could be.

She knew Theo—maybe even better than anyone else. She knew he had once wanted to be an artist. That he was ticklish beneath his right rib. That as a child, he'd been obsessed with the legend of a colonial mystic who lived along the Wissahickon, the one who had supposedly held the Philosopher's Stone.

Which would allow the person who held it to vanquish death.

As soon as he had said he wanted to bring Sarah back, it all made sense. His medical studies, the séance. His interest in electric shock therapy. The murders.

He wanted to harness the power of electricity to do something that the hermit never could: bring his sister back from the dead.

She had to find Gilbert.

She limped as quickly as she could toward the back door.

Toward the road.

Toward help.

CHAPTER 38

The door to the sitting room opened, and a familiar dark head poked his head in.

Marco. Relief flooded his face when he saw Gilbert was awake and lucid—he rushed to Gil's side. "Steady, man," he said.

"We need to go. Right now."

"I believe you mean to say, 'Thanks, pal, for figuring out how to stop me before I became a danger to myself and everyone around me,' right?" Marco said, parroting Gilbert's soft brogue perfectly.

A small weight eased from Gilbert's heart. "Thank you."

"Sure thing, Lawless."

Gilbert stood. Every inch of him ached. He had to move. "How long have I been out?"

"Maybe half an hour. It took the two of us and Dan to get you in here. Nell sat on you while I gave you the morphine. You were really gone this time." Marco said this as if he was saying, *It's raining* or *you have mustard on your tie.* A simple matter of fact. Not a judgment.

"Where are they?" he asked. His rasped out like sandpaper, and he cleared his throat. "Tell me."

"The call came from Shippen House."

He swore, and ran up the stairs, taking them two at a time. He barreled through the kitchen, the straight up the back stairs, past a startled Lizzie and Nell. He reached his room and pulled his key ring from his pocket, falling to his knees beside his bed. His bed, where he'd been with Edie not even twenty-four hours earlier.

Everything had gone so terribly, horribly wrong. He hauled the battered box out from under his bed. Once, it had been secured behind his seat in the ambulance; now, it contained everything he'd brought home from the war.

The padlock was dangling from the latch, open. Edie.

It had to have been Edie.

"Goddamn her," he snarled, snatching it aside and tossing it on the floor beside him. The scent of vanilla drifted up from inside, and with a sick, sinking feeling, he shoved through the box's contents, all the way down to the bottom. No. *No.*

He picked up the box and turned it over, sending the contents scattering across the floor. His worthless metals hit the wood with a thud. But that was it. His service sidearm was missing. He grabbed the nearest medal and threw it as hard as he could with a vicious roar. It stuck in the wall, ribbon dangling.

Damn her. He should have known better than to leave Edie alone in his room.

She'd gone snooping. And now his gun—his only weapon—was gone.

And so was Edie. With his daughter.

He hoped wherever she was, she was willing to use it.

Marco burst into the room behind him, panting. Gilbert stood up and kicked the box, sending it skidding across the floor. Lizzie was on his heels, her mouth hanging wide at her brother's outburst.

"Gil?"

"She has Penny with her," he told them, by way of explanation. "Edie took Penny back to Shippen House."

The blood drained from Lizzie's face. "He's there, isn't he?" she asked. "He's with them?"

"Who's with them?" Marco asked. He yanked the medal from the wall and tossed it on the bed, before looking quizzically between the siblings.

"Theo Pepper," Gilbert said. "Otherwise known as the Schuylkill Slasher."

◆————————◆◈◆————————◆

The drive to the Shippen House was tense. Quiet. The storm had knocked out electricity everywhere, and the sky . . .

Gilbert had only seen anything like it once before, when he was on the ship to France, right after he'd volunteered with the AEF in the spring of 1917. They'd gone far to the north in order to avoid German U-boats, hewing closely to the Canadian coastline before finding the open sea. He'd stood on deck and watched the Northern Lights dance overhead.

But they shouldn't be able to see them. Not here. Not like this. "Sky's strange," he said, finally. His leg bounced, knocking against the baseball bat he'd nicked from Nell's son. The closest thing to a weapon he could find.

"It's the Aurora Borealis," Marco said. He was driving, his knuckles white on the steering wheel. "Cecelia said there were some sort of electrical currents surging, because of that solar storm. It's been messing with phone wires and electricity all over the northern hemisphere."

The phones were out completely. Nell had sent her son, Dan, to the police headquarters to fetch Finnegan Pyle and his uniformed officers, to tell them their suspicions were wrong. Artie Van Pelt wasn't the killer. Theo was.

Lizzie, sandwiched in the seat between them, crossed herself. She had pulled her rosary beads out from somewhere and clutched them between her knuckles, her fingers working over the beads as she muttered Hail Mary after Hail Mary. Gilbert was half tempted to join in. His breath came in short, staccato bursts as a million images danced through his head, each one more desperate and horrible than the last.

Pray for us sinners. Now and at the hour of our deaths. Amen.

The odd lights shifting over the ground and driving rain made driving slow, treacherous. Marco slowed the car as he took the turn from the wooded lane onto the Shippens' drive, past the darkened gatehouse. No one came out to stop them, and Gilbert gripped the bat harder—twice now, he'd driven through the gate without challenge. What good was a gatehouse if it was never staffed? What was wrong with Ned Shippen? This man had more money than God almighty. He owned a fortress, for Christ's sake. And yet.

They turned the bend and Shippen House jutted out of the darkness, with its towers and gables and huge stone lions, wrapped in a shimmering iridescence. Not a light was lit within. The house was quiet. Still.

Too still.

Gilbert didn't wait for Marco to put the car in park. He pushed open the door and leapt while it was still moving, darting up the stairs, baseball bat raised. He kicked open the front door. "Penny!" His shout echoed through the wide marble hall.

Silence answered.

Lizzie's quick footsteps approached, with Marco close behind her, who carried Nell's big flashlight, throwing a wide beam of yellow light over the black-and-white checked floor. "You search the first floor," she said to Marco as she hurried up the main staircase. "Gil, we can start with Edie's room."

He followed his sister to the second floor. She pushed open the door, which had been left gaping, and lifted flashlight. There'd clearly been a struggle in here—the dressing table was overturned, broken glass glittering in the electric beam of light. He moved carefully, every step of his boots crunching the shattered glass underfoot.

Lizzie's sharp intake of breath had him turning. He raised the bat, expecting an assailant, but his sister was still, one hand over her mouth, as the light illuminated the bed.

And the small, dark haired woman stretched out on it.

Everything stopped. Slowed. *Edie*, his heart screamed, and he froze, unable to look to closely. To confirm what he feared—that the woman on the bed was Edie, and she was dead. Even from here, he could see her pale hand outstretched, the blood on her temple. She'd been hit. Hard. Another blow to the head, so soon after the last—he knew the odds. He could already picture her on his table, could see the way the lesions would stretch across the swirled gray surface of her brain.

Edie. He had no right to mourn her. No claim on her at all. But still, his chest seized and he dropped the bat, which hit the carpet at his feet and rolled.

He'd barely had her, and now she was gone. His head swam, the blood rushing through his ears. He couldn't breathe. Couldn't move.

He forced himself to step closer. He bit down hard, tasting blood. Her hair was dark on the pillow, long and curling.

Long. Her hair was long.

The wave of horror receded, replaced by a tsunami of relief. His whole body sagged, and he clutched the edge of the bed to keep standing.

"That's not Edie," he said.

Lizzie rushed forward with a cry. "Miss Frances," she sobbed. "Oh, no. Oh no." She pressed her head to Frances' chest, and her entire body shuddered in relief. "Oh, merciful Jesus. She's breathing. Let me find the smelling salts."

Gilbert could only stand fast, glued to the floorboards, as Marco appeared. "There's blood on the first floor, but no sign of any bodies."

Lizzie returned from the bathroom and waved a small, pungent bottle beneath Frances' nose. Almost immediately, the woman gasped and lurched forward.

"Shhh," Marco caught her shoulders gently, helping her sit up. "It's all right. We're here to help you."

"Miss Frances," Lizzie said, her voice thick with emotion. "What happened?"

"I—I'm not sure." Frances stared at them all, wide-eyed. She lifted a hand to her temple and winced. "I was in the parlor, looking for Penelope. Theo said my name, and when I turned around . . ." her voice trailed off in horror. She grabbed at Lizzie's hands. "He's the one . . . he's the one killing them. And we're all in danger. Edie. The little girl. He won't stop, not until . . ."

"Where is my daughter?" Gilbert knew he was yelling, but he didn't care. He couldn't care. Not when every second put his daughter into more danger.. "Miss Shippen. You need to tell me. Now."

"I have no proof," Frances closed her eyes. "You have to understand. Theo—people love him. *I* loved him," she added,

her voice cracking. "I thought—I thought he was being inappropriate with the maids. I didn't think he was . . . I didn't know he
was a killer."

Frances sucked in a deep breath. Gilbert was struck by how
different she and Edie were. They were twins, of course. And
there were similarities, physically speaking. But Frances' gaze
didn't carry the same fire as Edie's; her shoulders lacked her twin's
defiance. The woman in front of him looked small. Pale. Afraid.

"I didn't know he was a killer," Frances repeated, "Until
tonight, when he attacked me. I think he's gone mad. His
research . . . It's all something to do with his research."

Theo researched galvanism. The burns. "He's been killing
the girls and electrocuting them? Why?"

Frances shook her head. "I don't know."

Gilbert felt the air leave him at once. He gripped the edge of
Edie's bed. Theo was killing the girls.

Theo had Penelope.

He gripped his hair, willing the tremor in his hands to calm.
He bent down and picked up the baseball bat, flexing his fingers around the smooth wooden grip. Lizzie, Marco, and Frances
were staring at him, but he didn't know what to do. What to say.

Finally, Marco was the one who spoke. "Dan went to get
Detective Pyle. He'll be here, Gil. He'll bring help."

"Where is he, Frances?" Gilbert asked. He stood, drawing
himself to his full height. "Where did Theo take my girl?"

"I don't know," Frances whispered.

"Think, Miss Frances," Lizzie said. "You have to have some
idea."

Gilbert's fingers tightened on the baseball bat. He wanted
to smash it through the window, but that wouldn't help anyone.
Least of all his daughter.

God. Da's coming, sweet girl.

He turned to Frances, his anger a living thing within him. "Where could he be?"

She bit back a sob. "I don't—"

"Think," he growled.

She flinched away from him. "I don't know," she sobbed.

"Wait," Marco said, suddenly. He turned to Gil. "If he's been killing these women—what's the one thing they've all had in common?"

Gilbert stared at his partner. "Besides the precision of the incisions and the scorch marks . . . I don't know. What?"

"The river. They've all been found near the river."

It was a thin connection—barely a thread, let alone a clue. But it was the only thing they had to go on, and Gilbert's heart beat desperately in his chest.

"Then we go to the river."

CHAPTER 39

Edie stumbled and caught herself against a tree, gun clutched in her hand so hard her finger ached, the rough bark scraping against the soft wool of her sweater set. Every inch of her hurt, from her feet pinched in the almond-toed oxfords she'd bought because she found them darling to the wound on her cheek from Theo's ring, throbbing in time with every heartbeat. Her head ached from the migraine and the high-pitched ringing the gunshot had left in her ears. She'd been stumbling over rocks and crashing through brush for nearly a quarter hour. She had no idea if she was close to help, to the road, or if Theo was after her as she ran between trails of a shimmering low-lying fog.

Either she had gone mad, or the entire world had.

The ground dropped off before her, stopping her short. Her arms windmilled as her feet kicked pebbles right over the edge of a small embankment; too short to be considered a cliff, but far enough from the ground below that a fall would have hurt her, badly. Edie squinted, straining her eyes against the ribbons of iridescence swirling lazily through the air. At first, there was nothing but the strange, glittering light, like someone had projected the auras of her migraines onto the night sky, but then—twin beams of yellow, cutting a wide swath over the ground below.

The *road* below.

A car. A car meant people. A car meant . . .

Help.

With a sob, Edie launched herself down the embankment, skidding over mud and rocks and branches. Something sharp snagged on her hose, ripping through the silk to the tender skin below. She stumbled again, throwing herself out into the night, tearing the beret from her head and waving its sequined felt in the air in the middle of the road's smooth asphalt surface, hoping either it or the gun in her opposite hand would catch enough of the light for the car to see her before it ran her over.

"Please," she whispered, and she didn't know if she was asking herself, of the driver, or God himself. Louder, she said again, "Please." She raised her voice to a scream. "Please! Help me!"

The car, by some small miracle, skidded to a stop mere feet from Edie's body. The engine stalled, and from inside the car came a creative swear. Edie's heart thudded. She *knew* that voice.

"Edie!" Marco launched himself out into the rain as Edie stood, chest heaving. Waiting. Because Gilbert hadn't stepped out of the car yet, and Edie didn't know if that meant he hated her.

He should hate her. It was the least he could do. She'd been terrible to him. She'd betrayed his trust, stolen his gun, and delivered his darling daughter into the arms of a monster.

Oh *God*.

Her knees buckled. Strong arms caught her, cradling her against a wide, solid chest. Gentle hands pulled the gun from her hand. Careful fingers skated over her face, her cheeks, her lips.

"I know where he took her," she said, voice calm.

Edie's heart pounded so loudly she wondered if Gilbert could hear it as he stared at her, his gaze steady as the jewel-colored sky danced overhead, blues and greens and purples sliding across his face.

"Tell me."

Laurel Hill Cemetery sat on a bluff overlooking the Schuylkill River, wrapped on three sides by a white stone wall. The fourth side sat open to the cliffs below. The car approached the entrance slowly as the jeweled lights swirled over the Grecian columns at the entrance.

Gilbert checked the gun. He'd taken it back from her without ceremony, only giving her a sharp, questioning look when he checked the number of rounds remaining in the magazine. This was it; they'd sketched out the plan on the drive. She climbed out of the car with shaking legs.

God, she hoped she was right.

"I don't like this," Marco said. "I should go with you."

"No," Gilbert said. "We need help, and Pyle and his men are already on his way to the Shippen House. The faster you get there, the faster we'll have backup."

Marco looked like he wanted to argue, but he bit his tongue, shaking his head. Edie was glad she didn't know how to drive; there wasn't a chance in hell she was sitting this out. Gilbert opened the small trunk at the back of the car. He removed a flashlight and small metal first-aid kit and handed both to Edie.

"You just drive around with these?" she asked, trying for levity, even as she wanted to crawl out of her skin from the nervous energy coursing through her veins.

"I like to be prepared for anything," he said. He hefted a tire iron in one hand, testing its weight. Then he tucked it over his shoulder, leaving the baseball bat in the car.

"Clearly."

He slammed the trunk shut and patted the back of the car. Marco sent one last, panicked look at them from the driver's seat, but the car lurched forward, rumbling off into the darkness.

And Edie and Gil were alone.

"Come on," he said, his voice rough. "Let's go."

They slipped through the gate—left gaping open, which only deepened her unease—and crossed under the tall arched opening to the cemetery. The strange, dancing lights cast a jeweled glow over the gravel path ahead of them, bright enough that they didn't even need the light from the electric torch in her hand.

"What do you think is causing it?" she asked, when she noticed Gilbert frowning up at the sky for the third time in as many minutes. The air felt oddly charged too—a faint *swish-swish* sound curled around the very edges of her damaged hearing, faint enough that Edie wondered if she really had gone screwy, but the hair on her arms stood at attention, proving it was physical.

Somewhere in the distance, a siren wailed, long and shrill.

Edie reached out and grabbed his hand. "I don't know what we're going to find down there, Gil. Just know that if anything is to happen to me—"

"Edie—"

She didn't let him speak. "*If* anything is to happen, I just wanted you to know that I'm sorry. For all of this."

Gilbert shook his hand free. "We can talk after we find Penny. We save her. No matter what."

She nodded, not trusting herself to speak over the thick fingers of dread squeezing at her throat.

"This way." The path split ahead of them—one way led up to the mausoleums where Rebecca was buried, while the other twisted down before flattening out on the bluff overlooking the East River Drive below. They picked their way down the hill, their steps precarious. More than once, Edie thanked her past self for selecting the practical oxfords over her normal pumps—maybe on some subconscious level, she'd anticipated the trip to the zoo would end with her tracking her ex-lover through a cemetery in the middle of the night, under the dancing glow of the northern lights.

The northern lights. In *Philadelphia*.

The whole world had gone topsy-turvy, shimmering and flickering as the blues and greens and purples shifted overhead. The path grew wider. Below them, on the cliff's edge, a lonely, glass-topped crypt waited, ablaze from beneath with the light of a dozen candles.

Theo.

Edie had been right.

Gilbert let out a soft, keening sound, filled with grief and anger that set Edie's teeth on edge. He plunged forward, the tire iron falling to the gravel at his feet as he reached into his waistband. The soft click of the gun cocking was reassuring. Though not as reassuring as if he'd given her one of her own. That was the first thing she'd do, tomorrow morning. Take her gambling winnings and buy herself a damned gun.

But first.

Penny.

Edie bent down and scooped up the tire iron. It was heavy. Heavier than she expected. She rested the end on her shoulder and chased after Gilbert, who had already charged through the open metal door that covered the stairs leading to the crypt and disappeared from sight.

Edie's oxfords carried her soundlessly down the stairs. Not that she should be worried about stealth, not when a huge crash reverberated through the open doorway at the bottom.

Followed by an anguished sound.

Gilbert.

CHAPTER 40

Theo Pepper stood in a blood-stained shirt, wreathed in the blaze of a hundred candles. In one outstretched hand, he held a scalpel. His other arm dangled uselessly by his side—Edie's shot had taken him through the shoulder. And at his feet: Penelope's small, still form.

Jesus, Mary, Joseph and all the saints. Let her be well. Let my baby be all right. The edges of Gilbert's vision tinged red as his finger found the trigger on his gun—the same gun he should have killed Theo with all those years ago.

"Careful with that." Theo raised both hands, the metal glinting in the candlelight. "Kill me, Lawless, and your brat dies too."

Behind him, he'd set up a strange contraption—a black box with a series of dials. Wires ran from the box into patches of dirt on the floor around Penelope, where he'd pulled up the stone floor, exposing the bare earth. Atop the box sat a Tesla coil, already sparking with the same pulsing swishes that filled the air outside.

Underground electric disturbances. The solar storm.

Gilbert's heart slowed, almost in time with the pulsing ribbons of light dancing overhead, visible through the glass.

Penelope's chest rose and fell.

She was breathing.

She was alive.

"What did you give her?"

"It's a slow-acting poison. It won't hurt her—she'll just waste away in her sleep, unless I live to give her the antidote. Which I'll do as soon as you help me."

Gilbert's arm trembled. The trigger was so close—a hairsbreadth of pressure, and Theo would be dead before he hit the ground.

But if he was telling the truth, then so would Penelope.

"Give me my daughter." Gilbert's own voice surprised him, with its steadiness.

"My sister's daughter," Theo said. He looked down at Penelope, and back to her father. "She's the reason Sarah's dead. Doesn't that bother you? To look at her every day and see the life that stole your wife's?"

"I'm going to kill you," Gilbert snarled. "I should have done it then. I would have spared the world a monster."

And yet. His finger didn't move. A bead of sweat dropped onto his nose—those damn candles had the small space blazing with heat.

He couldn't risk her. He wouldn't.

But the moment she was safe, he'd rip Theo limb from limb with his bare hands.

"You won't. You won't risk her." Theo tilted his head. "Put it down."

Slowly, Gilbert lowered the gun to the ground at his feet. Theo, seemingly unthreatened, turned his back to Gilbert, stepping up to the ivory-enameled coffin in the center of the room. The coffin where Gilbert had buried Sarah, four years earlier.

Theo reached for the lid.

Gilbert was going to be sick.

Edie burst into the crypt with a feral scream, tire iron waving. She charged Theo before Gilbert could stop her, bringing the iron down on his wounded shoulder as he turned, a fearsome warrior queen in a sequined cashmere sweater set. Theo fell across the coffin with a cry. It rocked dangerously, sliding close to the candles beside it, and to Penny's still form on the ground below. Gilbert lurched forward, a strangled noise leaving his mouth.

Edie raised the iron again. "You monster!" she cried. "How could you?"

"Wait!" Gilbert caught her arm before she could swing. He needed Theo alive. Needed Theo to reverse whatever he'd given her. He doubted that he would leave this crypt alive, but if he played along, Penny would have a chance. Edie could have a chance.

Edie turned her face up to look at him, the betrayal evident in her wide eyes as Theo drew himself back up to standing, pain turning his mouth into a thin line.

"Edie." Disdain dripped from her name. "You can't leave well enough alone, can you?" He looked at Gil. "Tie her up. Now."

"Gil?" Edie shook her head, backing up quickly. The iron clattered to the ground between them; Penelope didn't even stir.

"He's drugged Penny," Gil said. "If he dies . . ."

Understanding replaced the confusion in her eyes. She held out her hands, wrists up, like an offering.

He yanked off his tie and wrapped the fabric around her wrists, tying her snugly but not too tightly. His gaze didn't leave hers as he checked it, hoping she realized she could easily escape if she tried.

Wait, he tried to tell her silently. *I'll tell you when it's time.*

She closed her eyes.

Theo set the scalpel down on the stone table beside the casket and picked up the gun. He pointed it at Gilbert first, then at Edie. "My bag is on the floor. There's a bottle in the front pocket. Give it to her."

Gilbert didn't move.

Theo gritted his teeth and pulled back the slide. He pointed the gun down at Penelope, and Gilbert's heart lurched. "Now!" he shouted.

Gilbert sprang for the bag. A slim vial waited exactly where Theo had told him it would be. The label was smeared with blood—Theo's blood—obscuring the contents.

Is this what he had given Penelope?

"It's all right," Edie said calmly. Gilbert's fingers trembled as he pulled out the stopper. There wasn't much left—less than a teaspoon.

"Drink it." Theo didn't take the gun from Penelope. Edie tilted her head back and Gilbert poured the liquid into her mouth, and Edie kept her eyes locked on his as she swallowed.

The second Penelope and Edie were safe, he'd make sure Theo would never hurt anyone again.

Whatever it was worked quickly. She blinked slowly up at him, eyes unfocused, mouth closed, and slumped backward. He racked his brain. What could it be? Nothing should metabolize that quickly. But he didn't have time to wonder—not when Theo was moving, the gun still pointed at Penelope.

"Now," Theo said, sounding impatient. "Finally. Step closer."

Theo stood beside Sarah's casket. He'd opened the lid, revealing the tufted white satin lining where Gilbert had last kissed his wife goodbye. Gilbert had closed that lid. It had meant to be closed forever more. A deep, aching chasm opened with Gilbert's chest.

"No." Gilbert couldn't move. He wouldn't. Sarah had been dead four years. Even with embalming, he couldn't bear to look upon her corpse in the state he knew it must be in. "You've gone mad, Theo."

"I'm not mad," Theo said. He stepped over Penelope and raised the gun to point at Gilbert's chest. He motioned Gilbert forward. "No. I've found a way to fix everything, don't you see?"

I'm sorry, Sarah. Gilbert looked down.

Sarah rested on the satin, her hands crossed over her chest, looking as pristine as the day he'd buried her. *Impossible.*

And it was. He leaned closer, barely daring to breathe. Closer, so the tiny seams of skin—the places where Theo had stitched together flesh and hair to rebuild his sister's body—were visible at the place where her neck met her jaw, up the center of her neck, along the edges of her wrist, disappearing beneath her white debutante gown. The same dress he'd married her in. The dress he'd buried her in. Leather straps, studded with metal plates and attached to wires, wrapped around her wrists, ankles, and forehead. Another one crossed her chest.

Gilbert's stomach heaved.

Her hair was wrong, too. The golden curls were cropped short, in the modern style; not long and cascading. Ophelia Van Pelt's parents had described their daughter's blonde bob in desperate detail—he'd seen the photos. He'd know it anywhere.

Holy Mary, Mother of God. Theo hadn't just been murdering the young women in some quest to raise the dead. Dottie Montgomery's missing head; Theo must have taken her brain. Rebecca Shippen's organs. Ophelia Van Pelt's skin and hair. Athena Kostos's eyes and tongue.

He'd been using them to rebuild his sister.

The horror, the wrongness, washed over him and he turned. He forgot about the gun, about the danger. With a roar, Gilbert grabbed Theo by the throat and slammed him against the wall.

Theo's air left him in a gasp. He struggled, both hands on Gilbert's arms, but Gilbert had always been larger than Theo. Stronger. Only Penelope, drugged and unconscious, made Gilbert hesitate. If he killed Theo . . .

Theo fired the gun.

The shot echoed through the crypt. The bullet sliced through Gilbert's abdomen cleanly; so cleanly, that at first, Gilbert barely felt any discomfort, just an odd, wet warmth. He looked down, surprised, at the place where a red stain blossomed on his white shirt.

Pain felled him to his knees, and he gasped, pressing his hand to his middle. He couldn't breathe. Couldn't think.

"Now." Theo squatted beside him, one arm over his shoulder. "It's a shock, I know. But we will bring Sarah back to life, using this machine. Galvanism. Do you remember what happened to Captain Thatcher? The way his body moved? I've figured out the key, Gilbert. I can bring her back, using electricity. I've reassembled her body—doesn't she look beautiful?" Theo looked over at his sister, his face rapt. "All that's left is to fill her with enough fresh blood to get her new heart pumping. The blood has been the tricky part, you see. I tried to collect it as I went, but the blood went rancid—it didn't work. But live blood? From a still beating heart? That should do the trick. At first, I thought I was going to use yours, but now . . ." Theo gave a pointed look down, to where Gilbert's blood spilled out over his fingers. "I think Edie is a better candidate, don't you?"

"It won't work," Gilbert said through gritted teeth. "I won't—"

"You will," Theo hissed. He moved quickly, digging his fingers into Gilbert's bloody wound. Gilbert screamed and fell back.

Theo straightened, wiping his bloodstained hands on his trousers. He turned to a strange metal box beside the casket, flipping switches. The coil sparked to life with a sharp crack and a flash of purple light, as brilliant as the swirling borealis above them. The hum of electricity filled the air, and he smiled as he pulled out a set of tubes attached to needles. Transfusion lines. Gilbert was going to be sick.

"You will," Theo repeated. He tossed the tubes to Gilbert. "Or I'll kill your daughter and make you watch."

CHAPTER 41

Theo had always thought that he was the smartest person in every room. He had always been proud, so sure of his own cleverness. He never thought anyone else could outsmart him.

Edie had spent her entire life believing Theo was smarter than she was. She'd always let him dominate the conversation. She'd made herself small for him, and let him think her weak and flighty and vapid, so he'd never consider her intelligence a threat to their relationship.

Theo had always underestimated her.

And now, he was going to pay for it.

Edie wiggled her wrists out of Gilbert's tie, the slippery fabric falling silently to the floor in front of her. Her movements were sluggish, thanks to the drugs in her system, but Theo had improvised.

That never went well for Theo.

She'd known what he'd given her the second the bitter liquid had hit her tongue, and she'd held it in her mouth long enough for Theo to turn his attention back to Gilbert, and then spat it out on the ground.

Chloral. The same drug that Theo had prescribed for her headaches, the tincture she'd been taking daily for weeks now.

Jenny Adams

And not much of a dose at all; he'd already used some. On Penny. Relief flooded Edie—the girl had been sedated, not poisoned. She'd be all right as soon as they could wake her up.

We'll all be all right, Edie told herself. And she believed it.

Until the moment Theo shot Gilbert.

She watched in horror as Gilbert dropped to his knees, his hands pressed to his middle.

Edie couldn't wait any longer. She climbed to her feet and picked up the forgotten scalpel from the table beside the casket. She lunged for Theo, a fierce cry scraping free from her throat. She landed on Theo's back with a thud, knocking them both into Sarah's coffin. Edie arced her hand down, down, down, into the soft skin of Theo's throat.

The scalpel met bone.

Hot blood spurted between her fingers and Theo staggered forward, knocking the casket from its base and into the table beside it, covered in candles. Edie was thrown to the ground beside Penelope as the candles cascaded into the coffin's interior.

The silk caught with a roar.

Theo let out a wet, gurgling noise, his hands at his throat as he slammed backward into the Tesla coil atop his strange metal box. A loud crackle snapped through the air as Theo's body jerked from the current, his mouth open in a wide, soundless scream.

Edie screamed, too.

"Penny." Gilbert collapsed beside Edie, gathering his daughter into his arms. She looked so small. So still.

And the red stain on Gil's middle kept growing. Edie didn't know where to look. Every direction was a new horror—the burning casket. Theo's madly dancing corpse.

Gilbert's blood, dripping to the floor.

"You. Promised." Gilbert was gasping now, his grip on Edie's calf painful and desperate. "Edie!"

That snapped her to attention. Already, the smoke was grow-ing, thick and oily, burning her nose and throat and eyes. If she didn't move, she would die. They *all* would die. She scooped up the girl and stumbled up the stairs. Somehow, she made it into the cool, wet night. She fell to her knees on the grass outside the crypt as heavy black smoke poured from the open door.

"I'll be right back," she whispered to the girl, even though Penny was still unconscious. "I promise."

And she plunged back into the crypt. In the short time she'd been gone, the coffin and the table beside it were fully engulfed in flame, obscuring Theo and his machine. Something popped in the fire. Edie didn't have time to mourn, time to think—not when Gilbert was so still on the ground.

So still. And so big.

She collapsed to her knees beside him, coughing on the thick black smoke. "Get up," she said.

He was pale, his face streaked with blood and soot. "Can't," he coughed. "Go. Leave."

"Stop telling me what to do," she sobbed. "You always think you know best, you goddamn bastard, and you don't. So shut up and help me."

"Edie." He closed his eyes.

"No!" She wanted to hit him. But instead, she wrapped her arms under his shoulders and tugged, dragging him across the ground. He moaned in pain, but she didn't stop. Slowly, she man-aged to drag him across the floor, falling only twice.

And then they reached the stairs.

He stared up at her, his big brown eyes sad. Exhausted.

Defeated. "I can't go on without her, Edie. Just leave me here. Please. I can't bear it."

"Please," she begged him. "Please. Just a little bit longer. Penny's going to be fine, Gil. He just gave her chloral drops. She's going to wake up, and she'll need her father. Please."

His face creased. "If you're lying . . ."

"I'm not. Please."

Hope lit furiously behind his eyes. She managed to maneuver him to sitting. And then a stand. She slipped her shoulders beneath his good arm and half pulled, half dragged him up the stairs. They stumbled forward a handful of steps collapsed on the cold, wet ground outside, sucking in air. He hissed in pain, dark blood soaking his shirt. A lot of blood. But he crawled, groaning in agony, to the grass where Penelope lay, unconscious.

"We have to go," he ground out. "If the crypt blows . . ."

"I'll carry her." Edie scooped up Penelope. The girl was so small, so still. But she was warm and breathing. And Edie had to hope she would be all right.

They made it almost to the path when a series of sharp pops came from inside the crypt—the fire had found Gilbert's gun—followed by a woosh. And then time stopped, silent, before Edie and Gilbert were thrown forward to their knees from the blast, glass and stone raining down upon them. Gilbert pulled Edie and Penelope to his chest, wrapping his strong frame around them as the air itself seemed to ignite.

As suddenly as the explosion came on, it passed. For a few moments, Edie let Gil hold her, his blood hot and sticky between them. He swayed, and Edie eased him down to the ground, tucking Penelope beside him.

Edie turned back to the crypt. Flames shot up from beneath the glass, as it cracked, steel twisting in the heat. There was no way Theo could have survived it, even if Edie's blow hadn't been fatal. There was no way to know if the fire killed him. Or if Edie had.

But Penelope was safe. And so was she. And Gilbert . . . She turned her back on the flames, on Theo. She pulled off her sweater and pressed it to the still-bleeding wound in Gilbert's side, praying that he'd survive this. "Hang on," she whispered fiercely. "Marco's coming. Marco's going to bring help. It's going to be all right."

CHAPTER 42

Edie's leg bounced up and down as she waited on a hard wooden bench in a third-floor hallway in Hahnemann Hospital. The electricity had returned, bathing the corridor in a hard, yellow light. She was cold and aching, despite the blanket wrapped around her shoulders. Someone had given it to her hours ago, in the ambulance. Detective Pyle, Marco, and a horde of police officers had arrived at the cemetery shortly after the explosion. They'd tried to pull her away from Gilbert and his daughter, but she'd refused to leave their side until they arrived at the hospital, and he was whisked away from her, straight into surgery. Penelope was taken to the children's ward. Edie insisted on staying with the child until Lizzie arrived with Mr. and Mrs. Lawless, driven by none other than Artie Van Pelt. Shortly after that, Penny woke up asking for chocolate. She'd slept through the entire ordeal.

Edie, however, was falling apart.

Theo was dead.

Gilbert could be dying right now.

God. Edie pressed her hands to her mouth and keened, a deep, mournful sound. What a mess.

"Miss Edie." Lizzie appeared in the doorway. She had a rosary clutched between her fingers. "The detective said I could find you up here."

"How is he?" Edie asked.

Lizzie shook her head. "I don't know. He's still in surgery."

"And Penny?"

"No worse for wear, thanks to you." Lizzie reached out and touched Edie's knee.

"Nonsense." Edie's throat was thick, her chest tight. "I brought her straight to him. I nearly got her killed."

"It's not your fault," Lizzie said. "You didn't know. I'm the one who caused this. I—I was wrong about everything."

"What happened, Lizzie? Where did you go?"

Lizzie let out a deep sigh. She slumped her shoulders. "Gilbert seemed to think that Rebecca and Dottie were connected, and so I assumed the killer was in the house. I thought . . . I made an assumption about who it might be. And I knew that no one would believe me without proof."

"So you went to Frances? And she took you to Celeste Dupont?"

Lizzie gave a miserable nod. "I did. I knew Miss Frances had helped your cousin, and I thought, maybe, that Miss Dupont might have known something about who Miss Rebecca's lover had been. I thought Miss Dupont could give me enough evidence to go to the police, and they might believe me."

The pieces clicked together. "You suspected my father?" Edie asked, surprised. Her father's involvement had never even crossed her mind. "Of course. And who would believe you over Councilman Shippen?"

"Dottie worked in his house. Rebecca was close with him." Lizzie swallowed. "I didn't tell your sister that, of course. I was vague when I told her I needed help. I think she assumed it was one of the delivery men—I let her think I'd been mistreated. She seemed to sense I was afraid."

"Celeste pointed us to Ophelia's apartment when we asked after you."

"That was Miss Frances's doing," Lizzie said. "She convinced Ophelia to hire me on, since she knew I had to get out of the house. I was only there one night—Ophelia put me up in her spare room. She had plans that evening, and went out. I fell asleep before she came home, and the next morning, when I went to check on her . . . it was awful." Tears welled up behind Lizzie's eyes. "I don't know how I slept through it."

"So you went to Leo Salvatore."

"I didn't know what else to do," Lizzie said. "I was so afraid."

Edie understood. Lizzie was a poor girl, working in service. Edie's father was a major player in city politics. If Edie had been in Lizzie's shoes, she would have made the same choices.

They'd all been so wrong about everything.

"Miss Shippen?" Detective Pyle stepped into the corridor, softly closing the door behind him. "Can I have a word?"

Lizzie stood. "I'll go check on Penelope. Be nice to her, Finn."

"I'm never nice." He waited until Lizzie's footsteps faded to nothing, then sighed. "Miss Shippen," he said again.

Edie clutched at the blanket around her shoulders. "Yes? Is he all right?"

"He's still in surgery," Pyle said. His hangdog face looked particularly sad, his red-rimmed eyes turned down. "From what I've been told, he's suffered damage to his liver. He's lucky. The bullet passed clean through. Barely missed his diaphragm and lungs. A tiny bit higher, and . . . well." He cut himself off, scrubbing his hand over his face. "He's a tough boy, our Bertie. He'll pull through it."

Edie nodded, not trusting herself to speak. Pyle seemed to take this as an invitation and settled himself on the bench beside her. "I spoke with the superintendent. You're going to have to give an official statement at some point, Miss Shippen, but based on the evidence, he assured me that there will be no inquest. Your name will be kept out of the public paperwork."

"I killed him," Edie said. It was probably a foolish thing to say—admitting murder to a police detective, but she couldn't stop herself. The tears welled up again. "I didn't know what to do, Detective. He killed those girls, and he was going to kill Gilbert and Penny and me and . . ."

"And you were a hero tonight, Miss Shippen. You saved him and his little girl. And yourself too." He patted her knee. The gesture was oddly comforting, if overly familiar, and Edie found that she didn't mind it. He stood. "As far as the law is concerned, you acted in self-defense."

The door opened again. A nurse in a white dress and cap appeared, her smile kind. "Detective," she said. "Doctor Lawless is out of surgery and awake."

"I'll fetch the family," Pyle said. He looked down at Edie. "You coming with me?"

Edie shook her head. That wasn't her place. She doubted Gilbert would want anything to do with her after tonight. She knew that he was all right. That was enough.

That would have to be enough.

No one stopped her as walked down the stairs to the lobby. The hospital, at Fifteenth and Vine, was a handful of blocks from the city house. Edie needed to be home—she wanted a hot bath, and tea, and to fall asleep in her bed beside Aphrodite. She needed to wash the blood from her hands. Scour it from her skin. From her soul.

Edie walked home alone, her tears falling freely beneath an ever-shifting jewel-toned sky.

CHAPTER 43

June 15, 1921
Philadelphia

"Are you finished in there, Edie? We're going to be late."
Frances stood in the doorway to Edie's bedroom at
the city house. She'd put on weight over the last month, and
color had returned to her cheeks. She looked almost radiant now,
dressed in a smart blue frock and gold-trimmed shawl.

"Almost." Edie chose a white hat with a rolled brim and a
pink ribbon, a perfect completement to her own dress—sleeveless
and white, with a drop waist and a large pink bow beneath the
square neckline. Aphrodite, panting on the divan, wore a matching pink bow. The hat looked almost too perfect. Edie pursed her
lips in the mirror. She needed something a little bigger.

"You're going to ruin your hair," Frances said, exasper-
ated. "Why are you so up in arms, anyway? It's just a gallery
opening."

It wasn't *just* a gallery opening. The invitation had arrived
from Colleen the week before—the Twelve had secured their spot
in Isabelle Bateson's boyfriend's gallery after all. And though they
now numbered nine, not twelve, they were honoring the work

of Ophelia, Athena, and Rebecca. "I'll introduce you," Edie said. "They're swell girls."

"Well, hurry up." Frances left, and Edie chose another hat—this one a natural straw with a flat brim and white ribbon—and settled it atop her wavy bob. Aphrodite leapt from the divan and followed her as she followed her twin down the hall. The front door opened, and low voices carried upstairs. Butterflies knotted in Edie's stomach—that must be Lizzie, or maybe Celeste Dupont. Both women had promised to meet Edie and Frances here so they could walk to the gallery together.

Edie had barely spoken to Lizzie since the night Theo died. She'd offered Lizzie a job, but Lizzie had told her she'd needed more time at home. Edie understood, of course. But hopefully, Lizzie would be ready soon. Edie had big plans, and she wanted Lizzie to be a part of them.

Edie hadn't spoken to Gilbert at all. She'd heard, of course, when he was released from the hospital, and Marco had stopped by a few days ago with a bouquet of flowers and the news that Gilbert had returned to work. She was relieved, of course, that he was all right. And she understood his silence. She had put Penelope in danger. He'd probably hate her forever, and she deserved it.

Aphrodite bounded ahead, around the curve in the hall and down the stairs, her tiny body wiggling.

"Miss Shippen," O'Meara's voice came from the bottom of the stairs. "You have a guest."

Lizzie. Edie's steps quickened. She turned the curve and looked down. Frances was nowhere to be seen. Lizzie wasn't there, either. Her breath caught in her chest.

Gilbert stood at the bottom of the stairs, hat in his hands, a new gauntness in the hollows of his cheeks. He'd lost weight during his recovery, which was to be expected, Edie supposed, but he stood steady. Strong. Aphrodite wiggled at his feet, turning in circles, trying to get his attention. But his eyes were fixed on Edie.

"Gil." His name left her in a rush, and she practically flew down the stairs. She wasn't sure what she should do. She wanted to touch him, to run her hands over his chest, to make sure he was real. That he was really here. Instead, she stopped short, her hands fisting at her sides. "I wasn't expecting you."

"Lizzie went ahead to the gallery," he said. "I asked her to. I wanted a chance—I needed to see you."

Warmth prickled deep inside her belly. "You're here," she said. Gosh, she sounded like such a dumb bunny, restating the obvious.

He was holding something in his hand, Edie realized. He held it out, like an offering. "I have something for you."

"What? Why?" She was rooted to the spot. Nothing about this made any sort of sense. "You should hate me, Gil. I'm so sorry. I didn't mean to risk her, I didn't know—"

"Edie." He rubbed his free hand along the back of his neck, and Edie couldn't help but think how beautiful he was, in the soft morning light streaming through the window behind him. He stepped closer and pressed a small white envelope into her hand. "We have a lot to talk about. And we will talk, I promise. But please. Open it first."

Edie opened the envelope and shook the contents into her hand. A creamy white business card slipped into her palm. Elegant black letters, stamped boldly across the front, spelled the path she had chosen to pursue in the last month. Her new life, right there in black and white.

Miss Edith Shippen, Lady Detective.

ACKNOWLEDGMENTS

First and foremost: thank you to my agent, Amy Giuffrida. When I sent you the first few chapters of this book (in an email titled I HAVE NO IDEA WHAT THIS IS), you responded, "Well, it's not YA, and I'm not mad about it!" I'm so grateful for our partnership, your guidance, and your friendship.

A million thank yous to my editor, Melissa Rechter. Your insight and support added so many layers of depth to Edie and Gil's story, and your belief that I was up for the challenge is something I'll be forever grateful for. I also want to extend my deepest gratitude to the rest of the team at Crooked Lane Books who worked so hard to bring Edie and Gil to life: Rebecca Nelson, Thaisheemarie Fantauzzi Pérez, Madeline Rathle, Dulce Botello, Stephanie Manova, and Matt Martz. Thank you, too, to Jessica Khoury for the cover of my dreams!

It's impossible to list every writer friend who has supported me over the years, but know that I am grateful for every single one of you, especially my Hopefully Writing group, the 2024 Debuts, my A-Team siblings, and my DC/NoVa writing friends. I want to especially thank: Alec Marsh, Andrea Rinaldi-Perez, Annie Kopans, Aya McGuire, Caitlin Highland, Carla G. Garcia, Jenny Lane, Jennifer D. Lyle, Kalie Cassidy, Kristen Pipps, LS

Mooney, Lara Ameen, Laya Brusi, Leslie Adame, Maria Tureaud, MK Pagano, Rain Ashton, and Serena Lawless (who graciously let me steal her last name for Gilbert and Lizzie). Teagan Olivia Sturmer, thank you for loving Edie so much, and for always talking me down from ledges, for venting with me, and celebrating all the little wins.

Kyrie McCauley, thank you for texting "I'll watch the baby!" so I could go to that workshop in 2019 that made me start writing again, for reading a gazillion chapters as I dropped them into your inbox, and for doing this whole publishing thing first so I knew what to expect. I am forever grateful we met as teenagers. This book would not exist without you.

Daria Maidenbaum, thank you for taking the most amazing author photos and also for letting me talk your ear off about this book for AGES. Lisa Fall, thank you for telling me to take a chance—I'm so glad I listened to you! Ali Baer, thank you for always knowing what GIF to send. Brooke Garwood and Randi Simon Pillion: thank you for being my Manayunk family. My Maybie Mamas: your generosity and support has been such a blessing. Katie Price, Sarah Kettles, and Tory Morgan: thank you for always, always being the best friends I could have found in elementary school.

I wouldn't have been able to do this without the support of my family, who listened to me talk about the characters in my head for decades at this point, and who served as enthusiastic early readers for (almost) every book I've ever written.

To my daughter, Ellie, who kept asking, "Aren't you done with that book yet?!" Good news, kiddo! I think I'm finally done with this one!

And above all else, to Eric: thank you for letting me follow you around the house reading scenes out loud, for brainstorming and answering my endless historical questions with the patience of a saint, for making sure I don't forget to eat, and for never, ever doubting that this day would come. You have always given me the time and space I need to write, and I can't imagine anyone else I'd rather have by my side as we chase our dreams together. I love you for always.